Denis Oliver Crowley

**Irish Poets and Novelists**

Denis Oliver Crowley

**Irish Poets and Novelists**

ISBN/EAN: 9783744720915

Printed in Europe, USA, Canada, Australia, Japan

Cover: Foto ©Andreas Hilbeck / pixelio.de

More available books at **www.hansebooks.com**

# IRISH POETS and NOVELISTS

PROFUSELY ILLUSTRATED AND EMBRACING

COMPLETE BIOGRAPHICAL SKETCHES OF THOSE WHO AT HOME AND
ABROAD HAVE SUSTAINED THE REPUTATION OF IRELAND
AS THE LAND OF SONG AND STORY

WITH

## COPIOUS SELECTIONS FROM THEIR WRITINGS

BY

### REV. D. O. CROWLEY

President of the Youths' Directory

---

INTRODUCTION BY

### THOMAS R. BANNERMAN

---

" Carmine fit vivax virtus, expersque sepulcri,
Notitiam seræ posteritatis habet."

THE fame of great and noble deeds,
Wing'd with his matchless lore,
The poet's pen sends echoing down
To Time's remotest shore.

---

SAN FRANCISCO, CALIFORNIA
1892

# PREFACE.

IN presenting this volume to the public, the editor claims for his share no other merit than that of accuracy in the biographical data which have been collected from different sources at the cost of considerable time, and not without labor. All other merits belong to the gifted children of the Gael whose life-trials and triumphs he has endeavored to portray.

Irish literature is not wanting in collections of songs and ballads. It is admitted on every side that the songs of Erin stand unrivaled; and both in quantity and quality her ballad-poetry ranks next after that of Scotland. But, up to a very recent date, comparatively little has been done towards preserving biographies of those to whom she is indebted for such priceless treasures. A few books have of late been printed in the United States with a view to remedy this defect; but they are all so bulky and, in many instances, so badly bound as to render them useless, except as works of reference. Besides, the price of those tomes is so high that it places them beyond the reach of the mass of our people.

It is, therefore, to supply a popular want that these sketches and poems have been collected from the pages of the *Celtic Magazine*, in which they first appeared under the title they still retain.

The portrait of Richard D'Alton Williams which appears in this work is the only one ever published of that graceful and gifted writer. The miniature ivory portrait, of which our frontispiece is a faithful copy, was made when "Shamrock" had the honor of being a political prisoner, in Newgate, on account of his participation in the 'Forty-Eight movement. This is the first and only one ever taken of him. As the reader will readily observe, he was sketched in prison garb. His sole surviving son, Mr. Dalton Williams of New Orleans, was good enough to have a copy made specially for IRISH POETS AND NOVELISTS— a favor which is highly appreciated.

The portrait of that sweet charmer of the lyre, James Joseph Callanan, so far as can be learned, has never before appeared in print. The one that accompanies his life-sketch in the present work is supposed to have been taken in his native city before he left forever the land of his love.

Here also the reader will find, for the first time *in extenso*, a memoir of that genuine poet and patriotic Irishman, Bartholomew Dowling, who has done good work in the domain of Irish literature. Like most men of genius he was modest, and wrote seemingly without any intention of leaving his work behind him in a collective form. The *disjecta membra poetae* have, however, been gathered together in this volume. The consciousness of having assisted in rescuing the poems of this excellent author from the brink of oblivion more than compensates for the labor expended on the entire book.

It may be objected that we have omitted many of Ireland's best poetical writers here. Very true; the author of the *Irish Melodies* is not mentioned; nor are many others of greater note than some of those represented, because we seek not so much to increase the fame of well-known poets as to popularize those comparatively unknown, but whose works, nevertheless, entitle them to our gratitude and admiration.

THE EDITOR.

# INTRODUCTION.

THE ruthless efforts of the British Government to degrade and stifle the mental energies of the Irish people are little known to the great mass of their descendants in these later days of intellectual freedom. Occasional mention is made of the atrocious Penal Code, which, even as recently as the beginning of the present century, was enforced by those of whom the immortal Davis wrote:

> ' They bribed the flock, they bribed the son,
> To sell the priest and rob the sire;
> Their dogs were taught alike to run
> Upon the scent of wolf and friar."

But how few, even amongst the friends of the Irish cause, are intimately familiar with the text and the means employed for the execution of those monstrous enactments against the acquirement and dissemination of human knowledge!

The question involves one of the darkest pages of history and possesses a deep import for all who belong either closely or remotely to that widely-scattered but ambitious and hopeful part of the world's population known as the Irish Nation. The Goths and Vandals, sweeping down from the shores of the Baltic and razing to the earth the temples of art and science, were less malignant in their purpose

than the statesmen who framed those statutes for the
suppression of education in Ireland. The former,
rude and barbarous, destroyed the fountain of knowledge but spared the stream that supplied it, whilst
the latter, with ripe experience in the ways of civili-
zation, not only shattered the receptacle but also
penetrated to the depths in order to obstruct the
current upon which a nation depended for intellectual existence. All the furies of a merciless tyranny
were directed against the schoolmasters of Ireland
by a monarchy which boasted of its own wealth of
learning and the liberality of its patronage of art
and literature. It was not the semi-barbarous Goth
but the civilized Anglo-Norman of the seventeenth
and eighteenth centuries that proved the greatest
scourge of knowledge in Ireland. It was not the
wild tribesmen from the mountains of Northern
Europe, but the titled courtiers and mail-clad warriors from the land of Shakespeare, of Bacon, of
Macauley and of Locke, that rifled the archives of
the Irish monasteries and wantonly destroyed the
ancient treasures of a nation of scholars. The
spectacle of a people made helplessly illiterate by
process of law should excite resentment in the mind
of every lover of justice. It should also stand as a
barrier for the protection of their descendants, so
frequently subjected to humiliation and reproach
by those who are either ignorant of or otherwise
blindly prejudiced to the facts of history.

During recent generations the people of Ireland,
both at home and abroad, were but too often com-

pelled to hear the coarsely-insulting designation, "ignorant Irish"—a phrase which found its origin upon the lips of the very enemies who despoiled their country's institutions of learning, and afterwards, by means of the most infamous legislation, sought to obliterate every vestige of their former enlightenment.

This galling insult burned deeply into the hearts of millions who keenly felt its injustice whilst beholding in the ivy-clad ruins of their beloved "Insula Sanctorum" the proofs that they were not ignorant by choice, but because of the Nero-like persecution waged against the teachers who would have instructed them.

The skeleton of the Penal Code should not be permitted to lie undisturbed in the closet of imperial England.

Justice to the Irish people of the present, as well as to the memory of those of the past, demands that the monstrous relic should be exposed. Ours is an age of investigation and progress; and it is due the *educated* Irish of to-day as well as their descendants in this thrice-blessed land of freedom that the reason of the existence of the so-called "ignorant Irish" of years gone by should be fully and effectively explained. The utterance of Burke should be known and remembered by all who would bear testimony to the iniquitous character of the Penal Code and its blighting effects upon the inhabitants of Ireland. "It was," says the eminent statesman, "a machine of wise and elaborate contrivance, and as well fitted

for the oppression, impoverishment and degradation
of a people, and the debasement in them of human
nature itself, as ever proceeded from the perverted
ingenuity of man." With such a machine in opera-
tion it is not at all surprising that the tree of
knowledge ceased to bear fruit amongst the sons and
daughters of Erin. On the contrary, being so per-
fectly equipped for the accomplishment of evil, it is
simply a wonder that the fell purpose of those who
introduced the engine of destruction was not wholly
consummated. The Irish people were oppressed,
impoverished, and degraded; but not all the fiendish
ingenuity of their enemies could produce "the debasement in them of human nature itself." As a
nation, they have never borne the taint of debasement. Even from the remote period of their exalted
paganism down to the days of the present they have
been distinguished as the guardians of social purity,
the patrons of chivalry and the devoted conservators
of song and story. The authors of the Penal Code
succeeded in depriving them of the benefits of education, but struggled in vain to destroy their love and
loyalty for the "Soggarth Aroon" and the ever-
faithful poet, by whose ministry and lays they were
alone preserved from spiritual and national decay.
This love and loyalty, born in the dark days of
oppression and still active and unwavering in the
hearts of millions, is most felicitously commemorated in the pages of the volume herewith given to
the public.

The pen of the reverend author could not have

been more fittingly employed than in spreading the
fame of those who, without the expectation of material reward, devoted their genius and talents to a
poor and helpless motherland in order that she
might perpetuate the existence of her ancient
nationhood. His patient research has brought to
this work much valuable information which has
never before appeared in print, and which, were it
not for his exertions, might have been lost to Irish
biographical literature.

This is notably illustrated in the case of that consummate poet and ardent patriot, Bartholomew
Dowling, whose life and labors are here published
for the first time, and whose career must possess a
special interest for those whose lot like his own was
cast on the golden shores of the Pacific, whence, to
use his own words,

> " That poet's song doth now go forth .
>     To many a distant shore,
>     To fling around his land of birth
>     A glory evermore."

The survivors of the patriotic Boys of '65 to '67
will also read with especial pleasure the pages devoted
to the biography of the gifted Dowling.

It will bring back to their minds the fervent out-
pourings of patriotic sentiment to which they listened, in those hidden gatherings of more than a
quarter of a century ago, by the banks of the Liffey,
the Blackwater or the Shannon.

As in a dream they will listen, once again, to a
deep-toned voice singing the glories of "The Brigade

at Fontenoy," whilst a John Boyle O'Reilly or an
Edmund O'Donovan will give ghostly approval to
the author of the soul-stirring strains:

> " By our camp fires rose a murmur
> At the dawning of the day,
> And the tread of many footsteps,
> Spoke the advent of the fray."

Another particularly interesting and most valuable
feature of the volume is the publication, also for the
first time, of the portrait of the versatile and sub-
limely-endowed Richard D'Alton Williams.   The
reverend biographer has aimed to present as fully as
possible the distinguishing traits of this fondly-re-
membered poet, and that he has succeeded, is amply
shown by the fascinating sketch in which he pictures
the genius and virtue of him who wrote—

> " When I slumber in the gloom
> Of a nameless foreign tomb
> By a distant ocean's boom."

Happily, the anticipations of the exile poet were
not long fulfilled.   His tomb, as we are so beautifully
informed, was not allowed to remain nameless.   All
praise to the noble-hearted soldiers who accomplished
the chivalrous and patriotic duty of honoring the last
resting place of Richard D'Alton Williams.

The most liberal support should be ungrudgingly
given to those who compile and preserve the " materials for a true and complete history of Ireland," and
it is therefore cordially hoped that such support and
patronage may be freely extended to IRISH POETS
AND NOVELISTS.                        T.R.B.

# TABLE OF CONTENTS.

xiv.                        CONTENTS.

CONTENTS.

# ALPHABETICAL INDEX.

# ILLUSTRATIONS.

R.D. WILLIAMS.
"SHAMROCK"

# RICHARD D'ALTON WILLIAMS,

## POET, PHYSICIAN AND PROFESSOR.

WHILE this singer, whose sweet songs have charmed two generations of readers at home and abroad, doth

> Slumber in the gloom
> Of a nameless, foreign tomb,

Innisfail keeps his memory fresh and green.

The life's history of every man who devotes his days to literary pursuits is easily told; and that of Richard D'Alton Williams is no exception to this general rule. Born in the city of Dublin, October 8th, 1822, the future bard was taken at a very early age to Grenanstown, in the County Tipperary, where he spent his boyhood years. He was of a shy, sensitive disposition, fond of poetry, fairy lore, and of solitary rambles by the limpid rills and sombre clefts that abound in the vicinity of the "Devil's Bit." His poetic imagination grew strong and vivid among the gorges of Tipperary mountains, where his youthful footsteps often disturbed the eagles from their lofty perches as his brave little heart bounded with delight to watch them sailing gracefully across the adjacent chasms till they vanished amid the gray rocks of some distant peak. When tired of the wild "Camailte's darkling mountains," he descended to the glens, where his fanciful spirit peopled every gorge and grove with elfin crowds.

About the period that this retiring, timid country lad was bordering on his teens the Irish Nation was nearing a series of memorable events in the history of her people. Three D's—Davis, Dillon and Duffy —representing Mallow, Mayo and Monaghan, met about this time in Phoenix Park, Dublin, and established a newspaper that was destined to become the exponent of Ireland's national hopes and aspirations.

Davis was one of the first poetical contributors to the columns of this national organ, which sent forth its initial number on the 15th of October, 1842, and startled the enemies of Irish freedom.

In January, 1843, D'Alton Williams' first poem appeared in the columns of that journal over the *nom de plume* of "Shamrock." Thenceforth "Shamrock" was a welcome name in the office of the *Nation*, and an assurance to the editor that whatever accompanied it was worthy of insertion. Here is what the *Nation* had to say of "Shamrock's" first effort, some time after Williams had been "borne, an exile on the deep," far from his native land:

"Williams was not among the founders of that memorable school of national poetry which sprang up in '42 and '43, but he was its second recruit.   Early in the first year of the *Nation* a poem reached us from Carlow College which may take its place in literary history with the boyish pastorals of Pope, and the boyish ballads of Chatterton.   It was scrawled in the angular, uncertain hand of a student, and scarcely invited an examination.   But it proved to be a ballad of surpassing vigor, full of new and daring imagery, which broke out like a tide of lava among the faded flowers and tarnished tinsel of minor poetry. And the vigor seems to be held in check by a firm and cultivated judgment; there was not a single flight which Jeffrey would have called extravagant, or a metre to which Pope could object.   This was the 'Munster War Song.'   It was Williams' first poem in the *Nation*.   A couple of months before, Davis had written his first poem, 'The Lament of Owen Roe.'   Memorable beginnings, and beginnings of more than a new race of Irish bards.   At this time, Meagher was a student at Stonyhurst, O'Brien a Parliamentary Liberal, Mitchel a provincial attorney, and McGee an American editor.   McNevin had never been across the threshold of the *Nation* office, either in person or by contribution; nor had MacCarthy, Mr. Walsh, nor De Jean; nor had any two of these young men ever met.   But a new banner had been set up, and here were trumpet-notes sufficient to summon a host about it."

The title of this martial poem is:

## THE MUNSTER WAR SONG.

Can the depths of the ocean afford you no graves,
That you come thus to perish afar o'er the waves—
To redden and swell the wild torrents that flow
Through the valleys of vengeance, the dark Aherlow?

*          *          *          *          *

The sunburst that slumbered, embalmed in our tears,
Tipperary ! shall wave o'er thy tall mountaineers !
And the dark hill shall bristle with sabre and spear,
While one tyrant remains to forge manacles here.

The riderless war-steed careers o'er the plain
With a shaft in his flank and a blood-dripping mane;
His gallant breast labors, and glare his wild eyes!
He plunges in torture, falls, shivers and dies.

Let the trumpets ring triumph! the tyrant is slain!
He reels o'er his charger, deep-pierced thro' the brain;
And his myriads are flying like leaves on the gale;
But who shall escape from our hills with the tale ?

For the arrows of vengeance are showering like rain,
And choke the strong rivers with islands of slain,
Till the waves, " lordly Shannon," all crimsonly flow,
Like the billows of hell, with the blood of the foe.

While this stirring war song was fresh in the
minds of his countrymen, the author went up to
Dublin, and began his career as a medical student
in St. Vincent's Hospital, Stephen's Green. This
institution, under the care of the good Sisters of
Charity, was to the Irish metropolis at that time
what St. Mary's Hospital is at present to our own
City of San Francisco—the best managed hospital in
all the land. Here young Williams gave himself up
to the study of the healing art under Dr. Bellingham,
who had many good things to say afterwards of his
promising pupil when summoned to testify in the

State Trials as to the character of the young medico. It was during his incumbency at St. Vincent's, where he saw with his own eyes the heroic deeds of the Sisters, that he penned the following oft-quoted lines on the

## SISTER OF CHARITY.

Sister of Charity, gentle and dutiful,
   Loving as Seraphim, tender and mild,
In humbleness strong and in purity beautiful,
   In spirit heroic, in manners a child;
Ever thy love, like an angel, reposes
   With hovering wings o'er the sufferer here,
Till the arrows of death are half hidden in roses,
   And hope, speaking prophecy, smiles on the bier.
When life like a vapor is slowly retiring,
   As clouds in the dawning to heaven uprolled,
Thy prayer, like a herald, precedes him, expiring,
   And the cross on thy bosom his last looks behold.
And, oh! as the Spouse to thy words of love listens,
   What hundredfold blessings descend on thee then!
Thus the flower-absorbed dew in the bright iris glistens,
   And returns to the lilies more richly again.

Sister of Charity! child of the Holiest!
   Oh! for thy loving soul, ardent as pure!
Mother of orphans and friend of the lowliest!
   Stay of the wretched, the guilty, the poor!
The embrace of Godhead so plainly enfolds thee,
   Sanctity's halo so shrines thee around,
Daring the eye that unshrinking beholds thee,
   Nor droops in thy presence abashed to the ground.

Dim is the fire of the sunniest blushes,
    Burning the breast of the maidenly rose,
To the exquisite bloom that thy pale beauty flushes
    When the incense ascends and the sanctuary glows;
And the music that seems heaven's language is pealing,
    Adoration has bowed him in silence and sighs,
And man, intermingled with angels, is feeling
    The passionless rapture that comes from the skies.
Oh! that this heart, whose unspeakable treasure
    Of love hath been wasted so vainly on clay,
Like thine, unallured by the phantom of pleasure,
    Could rend every earthly affection away!
And yet, in thy presence, the billows subsiding,
    Obey the strong effort of reason and will;
And my soul, in her pristine tranquility gliding,
    Is calm as when God bade the ocean be still!
Thy soothing, how gentle! thy pity, how tender!
    Choir-music thy voice is, thy step angel-grace,
And thy union with Deity shines in a splendor—
    Subdued, but unearthly, thy spiritual face.
When the frail chains are broken, a captive that bound thee
    Afar from thy home in the prison of clay,
Bride of the Lamb! and Earth's shadow around thee
    Disperse in the blaze of eternity's day;
Still mindful, as now, of the sufferer's story
    Arresting the thunders of wrath ere they roll,
Intervene, as a cloud, between us and His glory,
    And shield from his lightnings the shuddering soul;
And mild as the moonbeams in autumn descending,
    That lightning, extinguished by mercy, shall fall,
While He hears, with the wail of the penitent blending,
    Thy prayer, holy daughter of Vincent de Paul.

In the early part of 1848 Kevin Izod O'Doherty and D'Alton Williams founded and edited the *Irish Tribune*. The first number issued forth on June 10th of that eventful year. Scarcely six weeks had elapsed when the *Tribune's* career was brought to a stop by the British Government, and the editors were locked up under the, pretense that they had intended to levy war against Her Majesty, Victoria, through the columns of a newspaper. The young bard in his new character of traverser was defended by three men who have since become famous in the history of their country—Samuel Ferguson, Colman O'Loghlen and John O'Hagan.

To the charges of infidelity preferred against the patriotic poet, Ferguson answered thus:

" He is not an infidel    With a charity becoming his Christianity he prays that God may forgive his enemies that abominable slander.    Gentlemen, I am not a member of that ancient and venerable Church within whose pale my client seeks for salvation and has found tranquility and contentment in affliction. But I would be unworthy the noble and generous Protestant faith which I profess, if I could withhold my admiration from the services which I am instructed he has rendered to the cause of religion and of charity, not only by his personal exertions in distributing the beneficence of one of the best and most useful charitable institutions existing in our city, but also by his pen in embodying the purest aspirations of religion in sublime and beautiful poetry    When I speak of the services he has rendered religion by his poetry, allow me also to say that he has

also rendered services to the cause of patriotism and of humanity
by it; and permit me to use the privilege of a long apprenticeship in those pursuits by saying that, in my own humble judgment, after our own poet Moore, the first living poet of Ireland
is the gentleman who now stands arraigned at the bar."

Such is the high estimate put on the budding
genius of Richard D'Alton Williams by one who was
a poet himself of very high rank, and whose name
shines to-day among the foremost literary men of
his native land.

During the progress of his trial many kind things
were said of Mr. Williams; and although the jury
were sent back twice to reconsider their decision in
this case, they finally returned with a verdict of
" not guilty." The poet was set at liberty, despite
the efforts of the Crown to convict him.

It was during his apprenticeship in the hospital
conducted by the heroic Sisters of Charity that he
wrote his universally admired little poem on

## THE DYING GIRL.

From a Munster vale they brought her
    From the pure and balmy air,
An Ormond peasant's daughter,
    With blue eyes and golden hair.
They brought her to the city,
    And she faded slowly there—
Consumption has no pity
    For blue eyes and golden hair.

When I saw her first reclining,
　Her lips were moved in pray'r,
And the setting sun was shining
　On her loosened golden hair.
When our kindly glances met her
　Deadly brilliant was her eye
And she said that she was better,
　While we knew that she must die.

She speaks of Munster valleys,
　The pattern, dance and fair,
And her thin hand feebly dallies
　With her scattered golden hair.
When silently we listened
　To her breath with quiet care,
Her eyes with wonder glistened
　And she asked us what was there?

The poor thing smiled to ask it,
　And her pretty mouth laid bare,
Like gems within a basket,
　A string of pearlets rare;
We said that we were trying,
　By the gushing of her blood,
And the time she took in sighing,
　To know if she were good.

Well, she smiled and chatted gaily;
　Though we saw in mute despair
The hectic brighten daily
　And the death-dew on her hair.

And oft, her wasted fingers
  Beating time upon the bed,
O'er some old tune she lingers,
  And she bows her golden head.

At length the harp is broken,
  And the spirit in its strings,
As the last decree is spoken,
  To its source exulting springs.
Descending swiftly from the skies
  Her guardian angel came:
He struck God's lightning from her eyes,
  And bore Him back the flame.

Before the sun had risen
  Through the lark-loved morning air,
Her young soul left its prison,
  Undefiled by sin or care.
I stood beside the couch in tears,
  Where pale and calm she slept,
And though I've gazed on death for years
  I blush not that I wept.
I checked with effort pity's sighs,
  And left the matron there
To close the curtains of her eyes
  And bind her golden hair.

Though gifted like Edgar Allen Poe, Williams had
none of Poe's weaknesses or failings. He was sober,
sedate, benevolent and fervently pious. In fact, it
has been said of him that "he was much more ready
to visit the sick and dying than to join the not

unfrequent *symposia* of his literary and political friends."

He was one of the most active and unselfish members of the Society of St Vincent de Paul. The duties assigned to him in connection with this Society were always faithfully and carefully performed. It is related by personal acquaintances that in making his rounds among the sick and needy the young physician left his overcoat behind him more than once to cover some shivering creature. Reference is made to this Society in the following letter written to the late Denis Florence MacCarthy whose *nom de plume* in those early days was "Desmond" ·

" MY DEAR DESMOND: I send you the standing desk and hope that you may make countless standing jokes and Irish ballads upon it. The bearer is visited by our Society and deals in *Punch* and other periodicals, on which he has some small profit. He supplies me, and I recommend you to get your *Punch* through his hands. If you are here this evening at eight o'clock, you shall have a cup of coffee on our way to Westland Row. With best respects to Mr. MacCarthy and the ladies, I am,

" Sincerely yours,

" R. D. WILLIAMS.

" MARCH 26, 1847."

Though acquitted of the charge preferred against him by the Government, Williams suffered by his imprisonment in Newgate. But he suffered in silence, and like a great man, *never whined.*

The failure of the 'Forty-Eight movement depressed the spirits of young Williams very much, and left him without any occupation for a time. After a while, however, he went over to Scotland, where he stood a successful examination for a medical diploma Returning to his native city, he practiced his profession with considerable success. But the failure of all his schemes for nationhood cast a gloom over his paths, and he soon resolved to try his fortune in a new land.

Early in the summer of 1851 he bade adieu to Erin, and sailed away, never to return. His thoughts on that occasion are feelingly expressed in that pathetic little poem:

### ADIEU, TO INNISFAIL.

Adieu! the snowy sail
Swells her bosom to the gale
And our bark from Innisfail
      Bounds away.
While we gaze upon the shore
That we never shall see more,
And the blinding tears flow o'er,
      We pray:—

*Mavourneen*, be thou long
In peace the queen of song—
In battle proud and strong
      As the sea.

Be saints thine offspring still,
True heroes guard each hill,
And harps by every rill
   Sound free.

Though round her Indian bowers
The hand of nature showers
The brighest, blooming flowers
   Of our sphere;
Yet not the richest rose
In an alien clime that blows
Like the briar at home that grows
   Is dear.

Though glowing hearts may be
In soft vales beyond the sea,
Yet ever, *gramachree!*
   Shall I wail
For the hearts of love I leave,
In the dreary hours of eve,
On thy stormy shores to grieve,
   Innisfail.

But mem'ry o'er the deep
On her dewy wing shall sweep
When in midnight hours I weep
   O'er thy wrongs;
And bring me steeped in tears,
The dead flowers of other years,
And waft unto my ears
   Home's songs.

When I slumber in the gloom
Of a nameless, foreign tomb,
By a distant ocean's boom
        Innisfail!
Around thy em'rald shore
May the clasping sea adore
And each wave in thunder roar,
        " All hail!"

And when the final sigh
Shall bear my soul on high,
And on chainless wings I fly
        Through the blue,
Earth's latest thought shall be,
As I soar above the sea,
"Green Erin, dear, to thee
        Adieu!"

The exiled bard made his home in the New World,

Nearer to the tropic's glow

than most of his countrymen.    Poet-like, he sought
the sunny South, and for a considerable time occupied
the chair of Belles-Lettres in Spring Hill College,
Alabama.    With his old friends, the Jesuits, who
conducted this institution of learning, and in pursuits so congenial to his tastes, he spent a few happy
years.    Marrying Miss Connolly, an estimable and
highly-educated lady of New Orleans, about 1856,
he moved to Thibodeaux, La., where he was to be
found at the outbreak of the late civil war, practicing

medicine and writing for the local press. Here it was that death overtook him, on the 5th day of July, 1862, amid the clash of resounding arms. His grave in the Catholic Cemetery of that town was still red when two companies of the 8th Regiment, New Hampshire Volunteers, came to camp in the vicinity. This regiment was chiefly made up of Irish-Americans, who, on hearing of the death of " Shamrock," sought his final resting place on earth, and resolved to perpetuate his memory by a monument befitting one so gifted and so good.

The Captain of Company G, having collected among the soldiers sufficient money for this purpose, obtained leave of absence for a few days, and repairing to New Orleans, there, in his own language, he

Purchased a stone of pure Carrara marble, weighing one ton, with a pedestal of the same material. This was the best thing of the kind to be procured in the city at that time. Yet, though it has not the loftiness and grandeur of conception of the monument which should rise over the grave of an Irish patriot, it is elegant and chaste in design, and the best that war-worn soldiers could have done who were hourly expecting orders to move further into the State. In the center of the slab is an oak leaf enclosing a sprig of shamrock; and beneath is the following inscription:

SACRED TO THE MEMORY OF

## RICHARD D'ALTON WILLIAMS

THE IRISH PATRIOT AND POET,

Who died July 5th, 1862, aged 40 years,

This stone was erected by his countrymen serving in

Companies G and K, N. H. Volunteers,

As a slight testimonial of their esteem

For his unsullied Patriotism, and his exalted devotion

To the cause of Irish Freedom.

Such is the tribute of his grateful countrymen to the true poet and "unsullied patriot." It was a fitting tribute from the veteran victors of many a hard-fought field to the memory of one who sang such verses as

### THE PATRIOT BRAVE.

I drink to the valiant who combat
 For freedom by mountain or wave;
And may triumph attend like a shadow,
 The sword of the patriot brave!
Oh! never was holier chalice
 Than this at our festivals crowned,
The heroes of Morven, to pledge it,
 And gods of Valhalla float round.
Hurrah for the patriot brave!
 A health to the patriot brave!
And a curse and a blow be to liberty's foe,
 Whether tyrant or coward or knave.

Great spirits, who battled in old time
   For the freedom of Athens, descend!
As low to the shadow of Brian
   In fond hero-worship we bend.
From those that in far Alpine passes
   Saw Dathi struck down in his mail,
To the last of our chief's gallow-glasses,
   The saffron-clad foes of the Pale.
Let us drink to the patriot brave!
   Hurrah for the patriot brave!
But a curse and a blow be to liberty's foe,
   And more chains for the satisfied slave.

O Liberty! hearts that adore thee
   Pour out their best blood at thy shrine,
As freely as gushes before thee
   This purple libation of wine.
For us, whether destined to triumph
   Or bleed as Leonidas bled,
Crushed down by a forest of lances
   On mountains of foreigner dead,
May we sleep with the patriot brave!
   God prosper the patriot brave!
But may battle and woe hurry liberty's foe
   To a bloody and honorless grave.

Having performed their work at the grave of
"Shamrock," the Federal troops moved away to
other quarters; but the graceful act of the Irish-
American Volunteers still remains to point the hal-

lowed spot where all that is mortal of the bard min-
gles with the mold of his adopted land.

So much devotion to the memory of one who had
labored for the cause of Irish freedom naturally
elicited the admiration of many. The life-long friend
of Williams, Thomas D'Arcy McGee, from his home
in the Dominion of Canada, enshrined the touching
incident in a poem of great power and beauty. It
runs thus:

> God bless the brave! the brave alone
>   Were worthy to have done the deed;
> A soldier's hand has raised the stone,
>   Another traced the lines men read,
>       Another set the guardian rail
>       Above thy minstrel—Innisfail!
>
> A thousand years ago, ah! then
>   Had such a harp in Erin ceased,
> His cairn had met the eyes of men
>   By every passing hand increased.
>       God bless the brave! not yet the race
>       Could coldly pass his dwelling place.
>
> Let it be told to old and young,
>   At home, abroad, at fire, at fair,
> Let it be written, spoken, sung,
>   Let it be sculptured, pictured fair,
>       How the young braves stood, weeping, round
>       Their exiled poet's ransomed mound.

How lowly knelt and humbly prayed
The lion-hearted brother band
Around the monument they made
For him who sang the Fatherland!
     A scene of scenes, where glory 's shed
     Both on the living and the dead.

Williams was not only a poet of rare gifts, but also
a scholar of varied acquirements. In Carlow College he won a reputation for learning, and was
excelled by few in his knowledge of the classic
tongues. He read in the originals the Greek and
Latin poets while yet a mere youth, and those
models left by the ancients were not neglected in his
maturer years. Good books were always his delight.

Though sensitive and retiring in his nature, he
made and held hosts of friends wherever he went.
In. college, where manly virtues unfailingly win the
admiration of the students, he was a popular favorite
with professors and pupils alike; and the affectionate
admiration which the many noble traits of his character evoked followed him through every change of
life to his Louisiana grave, where he awaits that
awful scene so vividly described in his translation of
the

### DIES IRAE.

Wo is the day of ire,
Shrouding the earth in fire;
Sybil's and David's lyre
     Dimly foretold it.

Strictly the guilty land,
By the avenger scanned,
Smitten, aghast shall stand
    Still, to behold it.

Start from your trance profound
Through the rent graves around,
Hark! the last trumpet's sound
    Dolorous clangor.
Death sees in mute surprise
Ashes to doom arise
Dust unto God replies—
    God in his anger.

Bring forth the judgment roll—
Blazon aloud the whole
Guilt of each trembling soul—
    Justice hath bidden.
Then shall all hearts be known,
Sin's abyss open thrown,
Vengeance shall have her own,
    Naught shall be hidden.

Oh, on that dreadful day
What shall the sinner say
When scarce the just shall stay
    Judgment securely?
Save me, tremendous King!
Who the saved soul dost bring
Under Thy mercy's wing,
    Through thy grace purely.

Jesus, remember 1
Caused Thee to toil and die—
Sin brought Thee from the sky—
    I am a sinner.
Break my soul's bitter chain—
Thou for her love wert slain—
Gushed Thy heart's blood in vain,
    Saviour ! to win her!

Just Judge and strong, we pray,
Ere the accusing day,
From every stain of clay,
    Grant us remission.
Guilty and sore in fear,
I, clad in shame, appear—
Yet—for Thy mercy hear,
    Lord, my petition:

Who madest Mary pure
And the good thief secure
Gavest me also sure
    Hope of Salvation;
Though to my shrinking gaze
Hell's everlasting blaze
Glare through the judgment day's
    Dire desolation.

Lamb, for the ransom slain!
Then, mid Thy snowy train,
At Thy right hand to reign,
    Place me forever:

While, at Thy dread command,
Those at Thy left who stand,
Far from the chosen band,
    Lightnings shall sever.

Rings the last thunder shock—
Earth's broken pillars rock—
Down the accursed flock
    Numberless falling–
Down to the fiery doom,
Gulfed in hell's hopeless tomb,
Shriek through the ghastly gloom,
    Horrors appalling.

Contrite, in pale dismay,
Lord! hear a sinner pray,
On that tremendous day
    Spread Thy shield o'er him;
Day of great anguish, when
God, from the dust again,
Summons us, guilty men,
    Wailing before Him.

Clement Thou art, as just,
Mercy, O God, on dust—
In Thee alone we trust,
    Shelter and save us!
When, on the day of dole,
Death-bells of nations toll,
Spare the immortal soul
    Thy spirit gave us.

Williams was a man of more than medium height,
with well-knit frame and face strongly marked with

the lines of thought. In youth he possessed a keen sense of humor and a disposition to look always on the " silver lining of the cloud."

In head, heart and soul he was Irish, and his chief aim in life was to serve his native land. His earlier poems were written with that end in view, and not for fame. Having a great deal of serious business on hand, he always wrote in a hurry when the mood took him, and seldom waited to re-read or revise his copy. He did not, like Pope and Edmund Burke, write his compositions over and over several times, but left them as they came gushing from the heart, without a single touch of the *linae labor*.

After the failure of the Young Irelanders his mind and disposition changed from gay to grave. The happy, humorous young rebel to British injustice in Ireland ever after seemed to mourn his blighted hopes. He did not thrive in exile.

His last literary work was the " Song of the Irish-American Regiments," in which his old patriotic fervor seems to burn anew. Two months later and the hand that wrote this was stilled in death.

> Sleep well, O Bard! too early from the field
>   Of labor and of honor call'd away;
> Sleep like a hero, on your own good shield,
>   Beneath the *Shamrock* wreath'd about with bay;
> Not doubtful is thy place among the host,
>   Whom fame and Erin love and mourn the most.

## KATHLEEN.

My Kathleen, dearest! in truth or seeming
  No brighter vision e'er blessed mine eyes
Than she for whom, in Elysian dreaming,
  Thy tranced lover too fondly sighs.
Oh, Kathleen, fairest! if elfin splendor
  Hath ever broken my heart's repose,
'Twas in the darkness, ere purely tender,
  Thy smile, like moonlight o'er ocean, rose.

Since first I met thee thou knowest thine are
  This passion-music, and each pulse's thrill—
The flowers seem brighter, the stars diviner,
  And God and Nature more glorious still.
I see around me new fountains gushing—
  More jewels spangle the robes of night;
Strange harps resounding—fresh roses blushing—
  Young worlds emerging in purer light.

No more thy song-bird in clouds shall hover—
  Oh, give him shelter upon thy breast,
And bid him swiftly, his long flight over,
  From heav'n drop into that love-built nest!
Like fairy flow'rets is Love, thou fearest,
  At once that springeth like mine from earth—
'Tis Friendship's ivy grows slowly, dearest,
  But Love and Lightning have instant birth.

The mirthful fancy and artless gesture—
  Hair black as tempest, and swan-like breast,
More graceful folded in simple vesture
  Than proudest bosoms in diamonds drest.

Nor these, the varied and rare possession
   Love gave to conquer, are thine alone;
But, oh! there crowns thee divine expression,
   As saints a halo, that's all thine own.

Thou art, as poets in olden story
   Have pictured woman before the fall—
Her angel beauty's divinest glory—
   The pure soul shining, like God, through all.
But, vainly, humblest of leaflets springing,
   I sing the queenliest flower of Love:
Thus soars the skylark, presumptuous singing
   The orient morning enthroned above.

Yet hear, propitious, beloved maiden,
   The minstrel's passion is pure as strong,
Though, nature fated, his heart, love-laden
   Must break, or utter its woes in song.
Farewell! If never my soul may cherish
   The dreams that bade me to love aspire,
By mem'ry's altar! thou shalt not perish,
   First Irish pearl of my Irish lyre!

## THE PASS OF PLUMES.

[To the pompous preparations of the Earl of Essex, the results of his government in Ireland formed a most lamentable sequel. Rarely, if ever, indeed, had there been witnessed, in any military expedition, a more wretched contrast between the promises and performances of its leader, or a wider departure in the field from the plans settled in the Council. Provided with an army the largest that Ireland had ever witnessed on her shores, consisting of 20,000 foot and 2,000 horse, his obvious policy, and at first his purpose, was to march directly against Tyrone, and grapple at once with the strength of the Rebellion in its great source and centre, the North. Instead of pursuing this course of policy, at once the boldest and most safe, he squandered both time and reputation on a march of parade into Munster, and the sole result of his mighty enterprise was the reduction of two castles and the feigned submission of three native Chiefs. When passing through Leinster, on his way back to Dublin, he was much harassed by the O'Moores, who made an attack upon his rear-guard, in which many of his men and several of his officers were killed; and, among the few traditional records we have of his visit, it is told that, from the quantity of plumes of feathers of which his soldiers were despoiled, the place of action long continued to be called the Pass of Plumes,—"Thus," says Moryson, in describing the departure of Essex from London, "at the head of so strong an army as did ominate nothing but victory and triumphs, yet with a sunshine thunder happening (as Camden notes for an ominous ill token) this lord took his journey."—*Moore's Ireland*, vol. iv., p. 112.]

"Look out," said O'Moore to his clansmen, "afar
Is yon white cloud, the herald of tempest or war!
Hark! know you the roll of the foreigners' drums?
By Heaven! Lord Essex in panoply comes,
With corselet, and helmet, and gay bannerol,
And the shields of the nobles with blazon and scroll;
And, as snow on the larch in December appears,
What a winter of plumes on that forest of spears!
To the clangor of trumpets and waving of flags,
The clattering cavalry prance o'er the crags;
And their plumes—By St. Kyran! false Saxon, ere night,
You shall wish these fine feathers were wings for your flight.

"Shall we leave all the blood and the gold of the Pale
To be shed at Armagh and won by O'Neill?
Shall we yield to O'Ruark, to McGuire and O'Donnell,
Brave chieftains of Breffny, Fermanagh—Tyrconnell;
Yon helmets, that 'Erick' thrice over would pay
For the Sassenach heads they'll protect not to-day?
No! By red Mullaghmast, fiery clansmen of Leix,
Avenge your sires' blood on their murderers' race!
Now, sept of O'Moore, fearless sons of the heather,
Fling your scabbards away, and strike home and together!"

Then loudly the clang of commingled blows
    Upswell'd from the sounding fields,
And the joy of a hundred trumps arose,
    And the clash of a thousand shields.
And the long plumes danc'd and the falchions rung,
    And flash'd the whirl'd spear,
And the furious barb through the wild war sprung,
    And trembled the earth with fear;
The fatal bolts exulting fled,
    And hissed as they leap'd away;
And the tortur'd steed on the red grass bled,
    Or died with a piercing neigh.

I see their weapons crimson'd; I hear the mingled cries
Of rage and pain and triumph, as they thundered to the skies.
The Coolun'd kern rushes upon armor, knight and mace,
And bone and brass are broken in his terrible embrace!
The coursers roll and struggle; and the riders, girt in steel,
From their saddles, crush'd and cloven, to the purple heather
    reel,
And shatter'd there, and trampled by the charger's iron hoof,
The seething brain is bursting thro' the crashing helmet's roof.
Joy! Heaven strikes for freedom! and Elizabeth's array,
With her paramour to lead 'em, are sore beset to-day.

Their heraldry and plumery, their coronets and mail,
Are trampled on the battle field, or scatter'd on the gale!
As the cavalry of ocean, the living billows bound,
When lightnings leap above them and thunders clang around,
And tempest-crested dazzlingly, caparison'd in spray,
They crush the black and broken rocks, with all their roots
    away

So charged the stormy chivalry of Erin in her ire—
Their shock the roll of ocean, their swords electric fire.
They rose like banded billows that, when wintry tempests blow,
The trembling shore, with stunning roar and dreadful wreck
    o'erflow,
And where they burst tremendously, upon the bloody groun',
Both horse and man, from rear to van, like shiver'd barques
    went down.
Leave your costly Milan hauberks, haughty nobles of the Pale,
And your snowy ostrich feathers as a tribute to the Gael.
Fling away gilt spur and trinket, in your hurry, knight and
    squire,
They will make our virgins ornaments or decorate the lyre.
Ho, Essex! how your vestal Queen will storm when she hears
The "mere Irish" chased her minion and his twenty thousand
    spears.

Go! tell the Royal virgin that O'Moore, McHugh, O'Neill
Will smite the faithless stranger while there's steel in Innisfail.
The blood you shed shall only serve more deep revenge to nurse,
And our hatred be as lasting as the tyranny we curse.
From age to age consuming, it shall blaze a quenchless fire,
And the son shall thirst and burn still more fiercely than his
    sire.
By our sorrows, songs and battles—by our cromleachs, raths
    and tow'rs—
By sword and chain, by all our slain—between your race and
    ours
By naked glaives and yawning graves, and ceaseless tears and
    gore,
Till battle's flood wash out in blood your footsteps from the
    shore!

## THE EXTERMINATION.

*Dominus pupillum et viduam suscipiet.*—Ps. 145.

When tyranny's pampered and purple-clad minions
  Drive forth the lone widow and orphan to die,
Shall no angel of vengeance unfurl his red pinions,
  And, grasping sharp thunderbolts, rush from on high?

"Pity! oh, pity! a little while spare me:
  My baby is sick—I am feeble and poor;
In the cold winter blast, from the hut if you tear me,
  My lord, we must die on the desolate moor!"

'Tis vain—for the despot replies but with laughter,
  While rudely his serfs thrust her forth on the wold;
Her cabin is blazing from threshold to rafter,
  And she crawls o'er the mountain, sick, weeping and cold.

Her thinly-clad child on the stormy hill shivers—
  The thunders are pealing dread anthems around—
Loud roar in their anger the tempest-lashed rivers—
  And the loosened rocks down with the wild torrent bound.

Vainly she tries in her bosom to cherish
  Her sick infant boy, 'mid the horrors around,
Till faint and despairing, she sees her babe perish—
  Then, lifeless she sinks on the snow-covered ground.

Though the children of Ammon, with trumpets and psalters,
  To devils poured torrents of innocents' gore,
Let them blush from deep hell at the far redder altars
  Where the death-dealing tyrants of Ireland adore!

But, for Erin's life-current, thro' long ages flowing,
  Dark demons that pierce her, you yet shall atone;
Even *now* the volcano beneath you is glowing,
  And the Moloch of tyranny reels on the throne.

*B. Wowling*

"The trumpet blast has sounded
  Our footmen to array,
The willing steed has bounded
  Impatient for the fray."—P. 46.

(30)

# BARTHOLOMEW DOWLING

AUTHOR OF "THE BRIGADE AT FONTENOY."

THE subjoined article on Mr. Dowling was written, at our request, by a gentleman who for more than twenty years enjoyed the personal friendship of the deceased poet:

"The author of that beautiful ballad, ' The Brigade at Fontenoy,' was a native of Listowel, County Kerry, Ireland. While Bartholomew Dowling was yet a boy, his parents emigrated to Canada, where they remained for some years, and where the future poet and patriot received a part of his education. Returning to Ireland, after the death of the father, the family settled in Limerick. This circumstance has given, unjustly, to the ' City of the Violated Treaty ' the honor of Mr. Dowling's birth. His parents were, however, from the Kingdom of Kerry, and there he himself was born about the year 1823, as near as I can judge.

"In a review of a recent publication, ' A Chaplet of Verse by California Catholic Writers,' the Boston *Pilot* desired to get information regarding the subject of this sketch. My attention has also been called to a similar inquiry in the *Irish Monthly*, published in Dublin by Rev. Mathew Russell, who takes an active interest in everything that concerns the literature of his native land. In his brief mention the reverend editor gives Mr. Dowling a very high rank in the brilliant galaxy of gifted young Irishmen who threw themselves and their fortunes, heart

(31)

and soul, into the movement inaugurated by the Dublin *Nation*, and which culminated in the disaster of 1848, scattering their hopes and making voluntary exiles of those who escaped penal servitude at the hands of the Government they had labored to overthrow.

" The writer of this brief biography was then a boy, and can now go back in vivid memory to the monster meetings of the Repeal Association, and again almost feel with what eagerness he looked forward to the weekly issue of the Dublin *Nation* and the alacrity with which he read its lessons of Nationality in prose and verse. Standing to-day on this peaceful shore, far from the scenes of so many ardent aspirations and unrealized hopes, after the flight of many years—years that have changed the sand dunes of San Francisco into a beautiful city of wonderful resources and glorious energy—as I turn over the pages of Ireland's ballad poetry, it is with the feelings of one who wanders through a cemetery, reading the names of dead friends.

" Through the kind courtesy of one who is himself a gifted poet as well as a practical patriot, I am afforded this opportunity of supplying the information asked for by Father Russell and the distinguished editor of the *Pilot*, and doing my part towards resuscitating the memory of a good and gifted man who was very dear to me.

" The writer of whom I treat here had the cares and responsibilities of life shifted on to his shoulders, while yet a mere youth, by the death of his father; and well did he sustain the burden, cheering and comforting his mother to the day of her death, and aiding his younger brothers and a sister till time fitted them for the battle of life. The lives of the good are generally devoid of sensation, and he enjoyed an average share of such blessings.

" He did not follow literature as a profession. The best years of his life were devoted to mercantile pursuits, and his contributions to current literature, in prose or verse, were mostly published anonymously, without any effort at preservation; and such as are at our disposal have been gathered from many sources with considerable labor.

" He came to California in the summer of 1852, and, for a time, engaged in mining in the northern counties. Not finding this work congenial, he took to farming in Contra Costa, where he built himself a home and shared the hospitality of his board with John Mitchel, General James Shields and Terence Bellew McManus, while they were sojourning on the ' Golden Slopes.'

" In 1858 he became editor of the San Francisco *Monitor*, at a time when his health was broken down; but yet his writings displayed a vigor and versatility that gave evidence of what he was capable of accomplishing under more favorable circumstances. In this position his gentlemanly and courteous style left no cause of quarrel with those with whom he was compelled to differ.

" Mr. Dowling's death was immediately caused by being thrown from a buggy and having his leg broken. His health previous to this shock being declining, he had no physical strength to bear him up, and his spirit passed from earth to judgment under the kind and holy care of the good Sisters of Mercy, at St. Mary's Hospital, where he was happily removed for surgical treatment.

" This splendid institution was founded by the Sisters of Mercy, and at the time of Mr. Dowling's death, Rev. Mother Russell, sister to Father Russell of the *Irish Monthly*, referred to above, presided over its destiny. I understand that the same noble lady is still Superioress of this hospital, which has been a blessing to San Francisco for more than a quarter of a century.

"Fortified by the Sacraments of the Church, of which he had always been a devoted and faithful member, Bartholomew Dowling died in St. Mary's on the 20th day of November, 1863, in the fortieth year of his age. The Irish-American societies of San Francisco accompanied his mortal remains to their final resting place in Calvary cemetery, where a handsome monument, erected by his brother, Mr. William Dowling, marks his grave and perpetuates his name."

Such is the short story of the author's life from one who knew him intimately and loved him sincerely. Mr. Dowling was a poet of rare gifts and liberal education. Versed in one of the ancient and several of the modern languages, the classic writers were the masters of his youth and the constant companions of his matured years.

Wherever he wandered, whether

> In chapel, church or meeting,
> On prairie, field or strand,
> At home among the hills and streams,
> Or in a foreign land,

He carried along with him a little volume of Beranger's poems, the gift of his friend and compatriot, John Mitchel. From this he made many beautiful translations during his connection with the *Monitor*. At his death this *souvenir* of the indomitable Mitchel became the property of a talented and accomplished young lady of San Francisco, who, judging from her many published translations, knows well how to use and appreciate it. To her we are indebted for "A Memory of Seville," which is here published for the first time from a manuscript in the handwriting of the author.

Though of a retiring disposition and sensitive nature, the talents of Mr. Dowling were recognized and appreciated.

Some prominent business men of San Francisco induced him to quit the seclusion of Crucita Valley, Contra Costa County, and take his place in the heart of the young metropolis, among men of brilliant parts. Mr. P. J. Thomas, the enterprising publisher and patron of every good work, then a young man in full sympathy with the doctrine of the Young Ireland leaders, would not suffer Mr. Dowling to live in the peaceful shade of his own vine. Mr. Thomas was one of the founders of the San Francisco *Monitor*, in March, 1858, and, shortly after, at the earnest solicitation of himself and his partners, Mr. Dowling assumed the editorial management of the paper. Many leading articles and poems written by him at this time show the grasp and fertility of his intellect.

His stories, essays and poems, if collected, would make a portly volume, though, as we are told in this article by his biographer, "he did not make literature a profession," except in the too brief period of

his connection with the pioneer Catholic paper of the
Pacific Coast.

During his labors in the mines of California Mr.
Dowling wrote many interesting sketches and beau-
tiful poems, which may be found in the *California
Pioneer*, under the *nom de plume* of " Hard Knocks."
In a lengthy poem entitled " Reminiscences of the
Mines," he depicts life in the mining camp more
faithfully than and quite as graphically as Bret Harte.
It was published in the *Pioneer* magazine for November, 1855, and thence we refer the old prospector who
packed his pick and pan in the " days of gold."
Sometimes he wrote under the pen-name of *Southern;*
at other times over the initial letter of his surname;
but his favorite signature was *Masque.* In " Hayes'
Ballad Poetry of Ireland," two of Mr. Dowling's
productions are printed anonymously, and only one
bears his name.

We have succeeded in collecting, from different
sources, forty of his best songs and ballads, of a very
high order, deserving, indeed, a better fate than that
to which they have been consigned for a quarter of a
century.

The following introductory remarks to his translation of Körner's " Prayer Before Battle," we give
as a specimen of Mr. Dowling's prose writing. This
short preamble bristles with imaginative power, and

demonstrates how fully his soul sympathized with the subject which evoked his innate love of liberty:

## THEODORE KÖRNER.

"At the commencement of the year 1813 a young man resided in Vienna, whose brilliant talents had won him a most enviable social position. The purity of his principles and the high moral tone of his character fortunately protected him from those fatal allurements that, in Courts and capitals, are so seductive; which first tempt, then tarnish, and finally destroy for all purposes of good the glorious gift of genius.

"Living in a state of society where men had not yet learned to appraise noble aspirations, generous impulses, glowing thoughts or elevated principles of action by the dignified standard, 'How does it pay?' Theodore Körner had given voice to the aspiration of his mind and the feelings of his soul in noble songs that went direct to the hearts of his countrymen and roused the national spirit in an extraordinary degree. It was at this time that Prussia raised her standard to emancipate herself from the humiliating rule of the first Napoleon, and invoked her sons to rise for the Fatherland. Lutznow's celebrated brigade of volunteers was then formed and its ranks filled with the educated youth of the country, amongst whom Körner at once took his place as a private. He was then in the full enjoyment of earthly happiness, fame, social position, fair fortune, high esteem among the good and educated of his country; and, that nothing might be wanted to fill his cup, the first dream of a pure and fortunate love was at this moment illuminating his youth and harmonizing his existence. All these inducements, however, could not win him to rest in the mere enjoyment of life when duty called him to its more active exer-

cise at the post of danger. He thus expressed his motives at
the time, in a letter to his father:

" ' I swear to God the sentiments which animate me are, a
firm belief that no sacrifices are too great for the liberty of our
country. I feel compelled to rush into this tempest. Shall I,
far from the path of my brave brethren, send them hymns and
songs inspired by a safe and cowardly enthusiasm? No!'

"Active, energetic, obedient, disciplined and brave, Körner
became specially distinguished in this great, distinguished corps,
and was soon appointed Adjutant of it. On the 26th of August,
1813, the corps of Lutznow confronted the French at Kitzen.
They halted in the forest to rest for an hour at the grey light
of the morning. During this interval, Körner composed his
celebrated "Prayer during Battle," (of which we give an
attempt at an English version). Körner read it to a friend at
the moment he wrote it; whilst still reciting it the bugle sounded
the advance. In an instant he was in the front of battle, and
as the vanquished French gave way and retreated before the
fiery enthusiasm of Lutznow's corps, Körner exultingly led the
pursuit, and in the act of cheering on his countrymen, he fell,
pierced by a grape shot, and found the glorious death, at the
early age of 22, which he had poetically prophesied. All Ger-
many mourned the fate of the brave and gifted young patriot.
But why should he have been mourned? His was a fortunate
and happy destiny, briefly but nobly accomplished. He passed
from earth with all life's bright illusions undispelled, while fame
and love, and glory, and virtue, were still realities to him, before
a questionable experience had chilled his faith, or worldly wisdom with its plausible expediencies had taken the place of nobler
motives and simpler purpose. He fell on the frontier of his
native land, driving the foe from her soil, giving force and
vitality to heroic sentiment by heroic deeds, and casting over

all the brighter halo of a pure, a virtuous and a devotional spirit."

## PRAYER DURING BATTLE.

[From the German of Theodore Körner.]

FATHER, I call to Thee!
Roaring around me the cannons storm;
Like a shroud their lightnings enwrap my form.
    Guide of the battles, I call to Thee:
    Father! to-day be a guide to me.

Father, oh guide me!
Lord of my life and breath,
Give me to victory or to death;
    Even as thou willest so to me.
    God, I acknowledge Thee!

God, I acknowledge Thee
In the fair woodland's light,
As in the tempest of the fight.
    Fountain of Mercy, I acknowledge Thee!
    Father, give blessing unto me.

Father, oh bless me!
My life into thy hands I give.
'Tis thine to take or bid me live.
    On life or death, oh, let Thy blessing be.
    Father! Thy child gives praise to Thee.

Father, I praise Thee!
This holy strife, bless Thou, O Lord;
Give to me strength and guide my sword.
    Falling or conquering, praise to Thee!
    God, I bow willingly.

God, I bow willingly.
When death comes in the battle glow,
Even as my heart's warm currents flow,
To Thee, my God, I make the offering free.
Father, O Father, hear! I call on Thee!

Since we had the privilege of publishing in the *St. Joseph's Union* the foregoing biographical sketch, Mr. William Dowling, who is himself a writer of ability also, has kindly placed at our disposal a large number of his brother's poems, both in print and manuscript. This collection comprises nearly all of Bartholomew Dowling's reliques, and it affords us much pleasure to think that it is through the medium of IRISH POETS AND NOVELISTS they will be given to the public for the first time in a collected form, and handed down to future generations of Irish-American readers.

Most of the historical verses were written for and published in the *Nation*, at a time when the editors of that journal had determined to write a ballad history of Ireland. This was a pet scheme of Davis, and to the task he addressed himself with an earnestness which was equalled only by his success. Dowling, then residing in Limerick, was commissioned to chronicle in stirring verse all the historic events of national interest that had occurred in recent days or old within the confines of Thomond. As a result we have a number of splendid ballads such as "Sarsfield's Sortie," "The Vision of King Brian," "The Assault on Limerick," "The Brigade at Fontenoy," and many others equally calculated to kindle the enthusiasm of the masses and nerve the arms of struggling patriots.

Though Mr. Dowling wrote not a few sweet lyrics, which go to prove that he possessed in a marked degree both the sentiment and inspiration so essential to success in that species of composition, yet it is quite evident that ballad-writing, or narrative poetry, was his forte; and, had not his plans and those of his associates been frustrated by the brute force that stood behind English bayonets, he undoubtedly would have left us many more ballads as intensely national in tone and spirit as those to be found in this collection.

That awe-inspiring poem entitled "Hurrah for the Next that Dies," conclusively proves that our author possessed a mine of dramatic genius which was no more than *prospected*. He seems to have been unconscious of possessing this power, and it went undeveloped to the grave. In his brief, busy life, perhaps, he never had within reach the opportunity necessary for such development.

His claim to the authorship of this poem has been brought into question of late, and it has been ascribed to one Capt. Walter Dobenay, serving in India at the time of the epidemic to which the verses allude.

But the name of Mr. Dowling has nearly always been attached to this strange poem. It appears over his name on page 787 in Henry Coates' *Encyclopedia of Poetry*, published at Philadelphia, when the poem was yet fresh in the public mind. We have seen it ascribed to Dowling in other publications also, but never more than once heard of its being the composition of "that officer in India," Capt. Dobenay.

About the strongest reason put forward for connecting it with the name of this British captain is the assertion of a pedantic writer in a late issue of a local paper. He gives neither proofs nor authorities, however, to substantiate his assertion.

Mr. Dowling "was never in India," it is true; neither was he ever at Fontenoy. Yet he wrote that inimitable martial ballad called "The Brigade at Fontenoy."

He had an uncle, however, who died in India when the poet was a mere boy, and ever after, both at home and in exile, the genial bard took a deep interest in the happenings of that plundered land.

He has written another poem of much merit, which has for its subject an incident in India, and for title, "The Relief of Lucknow." This poem is now before us, and so far as we are aware, nobody doubts that he is the author of it. It was not necessary, therefore, for him to go to India in order to write such a poem.

Now comes one of our strongest proofs. The poem in dispute was first printed in this city in 1858. Mr. Dowling was then editor of the San Francisco *Monitor*. Mr. P. J. Thomas, 505 Clay street, one of the founders of that paper, was also the publisher. He has a distinct recollection of putting the poem in type from the manuscript of Bartholomew Dowling. He still clearly remembers the comments passed on it in the office of the paper when it was read in his presence by the author We are glad that there is a living witness to settle this question of disputed authorship.

As a prose writer Dowling was brilliant, copious and convincing. His leading articles in the back files of the *Monitor* attest the truth of this assertion and bear us out in saying that he was no novice in the politics of his time. He took no part in politics, however, more than that of giving his views regarding the issues of the day to the readers of the *Monitor*. Though fond of the society of active and learned men, a fine conversationalist and brilliant public speaker, he was never seen in the political arena of his adopted country. The spoils of office had no charms for him. In Ireland, when the hopes and aspirations of the '48 men were high, the part he took in establishing "physical force" clubs proved that he possessed organizing as well as literary ability.

Possessing but one aim in life—the liberation of Ireland from English thraldom—Mr. Dowling never married. All his energies and intellectual gifts were devoted to the cause of Irish independence. Out of that cause he made no capital. He was honestly and honorably devoted to it, and his character as Irish Patriot comes down to us without stain and without reproach. His early youth and manhood were given to a noble cause. His heart and hopes were set on the regeneration of his native land, and although the work was not accomplished he labored not in vain. Nor is his memory likely to perish. It is insepara-bly connected with the "Brigade at Fontenoy," and that is destined to endure as long as the martial spirit of the Irish Celt.

## THE DEATH-SONG OF THE VIKING.

[There is a Scandinavian legend that Siegfried, the "Viking," feeling that he was at the point of death, caused himself to be placed on the deck of his ship; the sails were hoisted, the vessel set on fire, and in this manner he drifted out to sea, alone, and finished his career.]

MY race is run, my errand done, the pulse of life beats low;
My heart is chill, and the conquering will has lost its fiery glow.
Launch once again on the northern main my battleship of old:
I would die on the deck, 'mid storm and wreck, as befits a
      Viking bold.

I know no fears, but the mist of years that has gathered round
      my track
For a moment clears, and my youth's compeers again to my
      side come back;

And the tall ships reel o'er their iron keel, as we sweep down on
    the foe,
Like a giant's form amid the storm, where the mighty tem-
    pests blow.

Again I gaze on the leaping blaze o'er a conquered city rise,
As in those days, when the Skald's wild lays, sang the fame of
    our high emprise;
When our ships went forth from the stormy North with the
    Scandinavian bands
Who backward bore to the Baltic's shore the spoil of the West-
    ern lands.

But my race is run, my errand done; so bear me to my ship.
Place my battle-brand in this dying hand, and the wine-cup to
    my lip;
Then loose each sail to the rising gale and lash the helm a-lee.
Alone, alone, on my drifting throne, I would view my realm.
    the sea.

My realm and grave the northern wave, where the tempest's
    voice will sing
My death-song loud, where flame shall shroud the ocean's war-
    rior-king.
Whilst heroes wait at Valhalla's gate to proudly welcome me.
For my race is run, my errand done.  Receive thy Chief, O sea!

## THE BRIGADE AT FONTENOY.

By our camp-fires rose a murmur
    At the dawning of the day,
And the sound of many footsteps
    Spoke the advent of the fray;

And as we took our places
  Few and stern were our words,
While some were tightening horse-girths,
  And some were girding swords.

The trumpet blast has sounded
  Our footmen to array,
The willing steed has bounded,
  Impatient for the fray.
The green flag is unfolded,
  While rose the cry of joy:
"Heaven speed dear Ireland's banner
  This day at Fontenoy!"

We looked upon that banner,
  And the memory arose
Of our homes and perished kindred,
  Where the Lee or Shannon flows;
And we looked upon that banner,
  And we swore to God on high,
To smite to-day the Saxon's might—
  To conquer or to die.

Loud swells the charging trumpet—
  'Tis a voice from our own land—
God of battles! God of vengeance!
  Guide to-day the patriot's brand:
There are stains to wash away,
  There are memories to destroy
In the best blood of the Briton,
  To-day, at Fontenoy.

Plunge deep the fiery rowels
  In a thousand reeking flanks.
Down, chivalry of Ireland,
  Down on the British ranks!
Now shall their serried columns
  Beneath our sabres reel.
Through their ranks, then, with the war-horse;
  Through their bosoms with the steel!

With one shout for good King Louis,
  And the fair land of the vine,
Like the wrathful Alpine tempest
  We swept upon their line.
Then rang along the battle-field
  Triumphant our hurrah,
And we smote them down, still cheering,
  " *Erin, slanthagal go bragh.*"

As prized as is the blessing
  From an aged father's lip;
As welcome as the haven
  To the tempest driven ship;
As dear as to the lover
  The smile of gentle maid,
Is this day of long-sought vengeance
  To the swords of the brigade.

See their scattered forces flying,
  A broken, routed line.
See, England, what brave laurels
  For your brow to-day we twine.

O, thrice blessed the hour that witnessed
The Briton turn to flee
From the chivalry of Erin
And France's "*fleur de lis.*"

As we lay beside our camp-fires
When the sun had passed away,
And thought upon our brethren
Who had perished in the fray,
We prayed to God to grant us,
And then we'd die with joy,
One day upon our own dear land
Like this at Fontenoy.

## HYMN OF THE IMPERIAL GUARD.

UP, comrades, up, the bugle peals the note of war's alarms,
And the cry is ringing sternly round, that calls the land to arms;
Adieu, adieu, fair land of France, where the vine of Brennus
        reigns;
We go where the blooming laurels grow, on the bright Italian
        plains.
Advance! advance! brave sons of France, before the startled
        world;
For France, once more, her tricolor in triumph hath unfurled.

Our eagles shall fly 'neath many a sky, with a halo round their
        way,
Where History flings, on their flashing wings, the light of
        Glory's ray;

And we shall bear them proudly on, through many a mighty
  fray,
That shall win old nations back to life, in the glorious coming
  day.
Then advance, advance, ye sons of France, before the startled
  world,
For France, once more, her tricolor in triumph hath unfurled.

The glowing heart of the land of Art, throbbing for Liberty,
Our swords invoke, to erase the yoke from beauteous Italy.
And the Magyar waits, with kindling hope, the aid of the Gallic
  hand,
To drive the hated Austrians forth, from the old Hungarian
  land.
Then advance, advance, ye sons of France, before the startled
  world,
For France, once more, her tricolor in triumph hath unfurled.

See the Briton, pale, as he dons his mail, for the coming conflict
  shock,
And before his eyes, see the phantom rise, of the Chief on
  Helena's rock;
In foreboding fears, already he hears through palace and mart
  anew,
Our avenging shout, o'er the battle rout—remember Waterloo!
Then advance, advance, ye sons of France, before the startled
  world.
For France, once more, her tricolor in triumph hath unfurled.

And, hark, a wail from our kindred Gael, comes floating from
  the West—
That gallant race, whose chosen place was ever our battle's
  crest;                          5

Now is the day we can repay the generous debt we owe
To Irish blood, that freely flowed to conquer France's foe.
Then advance, advance, ye sons of France, before the startled
    world,
For France, once more, her tricolor in triumph hath unfurled.

Old Tricolor, as in days of yore, you shall wave o'er vanquished
    kings,
And your folds shall fly 'neath an English sky, on Victory's
    crimson wings;
And Europe's shout shall in joy ring out, hailing freedom in
    thy track,
When our task is done, and we bear thee on, to France with
    glory back.
Then advance, advance, ye sons of France, before the startled
    world,
For France, once more, her tricolor in triumph hath unfurled.


### .  HURRAH FOR THE NEXT THAT DIES!

[This remarkable poem relates to revelry in India at a time when the
English officers serving in that country were being struck down by pestilence.
It has been correctly styled "the very poetry of military despair."]

WE meet 'neath the sounding rafter,
    And the walls around are bare:
As they shout back our peals of laughter,
    It seems as the dead were there.
Then stand to your glasses!—steady!
    We drink 'fore our comrades' eyes;
One cup to the dead already:
    Hurrah for the next that dies!

Not here are the goblets glowing,
　Not here is the vintage sweet;
'Tis cold as our hearts are growing,
　And dark as the doom we meet.
But stand to your glasses!—steady!
　And soon shall our pulses rise.
One cup to the dead already:
　Hurrah for the next that dies.

There's many a hand that's shaking,
　And many a cheek that's sunk;
But soon, though our hearts are breaking,
　They'll burn with the wine we've drunk.
Then stand to your glasses!—steady!
　'Tis here the revival lies;
Quaff a cup to the dead already:
　Hurrah for the next that dies!

Time was when we laughed at others;
　We thought we were wiser then.
Ha! ha! let them think of their mothers,
　Who hope to see them again.
No!　Stand to your glasses!—steady!
　The thoughtless is here the wise;
One cup to the dead already:
　Hurrah for the next that dies!

Not a sigh for the lot that darkles,
　Not a tear for the friends that sink;
We'll fall 'mid the wine-cup's sparkles,
　As mute as the wine we drink.

Come! Stand to your glasses!—steady!
  'Tis this that the respite buys;
One cup to the dead already:
  Hurrah for the next that dies!

Who dreads to the dust returning?
  Who shrinks from the sable shore,
Where the high and haughty yearning
  Of the soul can sting no more?
No! Stand to your glasses!—steady!
  This world is a world of lies;
One cup to the dead already:
  Hurrah for the next that dies!

Cut off from the land that bore us,
  Betray'd by the land we find,
When the brightest are gone before us,
  And the dullest are left behind.
Stand!—stand to your glasses!—steady!
  'Tis all we have left to prize;
One cup to the dead already:
  Hurrah for the next that dies!

## THE FOREIGN SHAMROCK.

Down in the ocean of the years my ship and freight hath gone,
And the wave of Time o'er the perished wreck is slowly surging
    on.
To-day, on the shore of this Western land, that wave brings
    back to me
A shamrock green, and, in its sheen, my long lost argosy.

I place the leaves above my heart, as a wondrous talisman,
For they bear me back to a better time, ere the exile's lot began;
And again, in the flush of glowing youth, among my own
    I stand,
In the bright mirage of a generous hope, in my own lost native
    land.

What mem'ries throng round this triple leaf, and, phantom-
    like, arise,
O'er sordid cares and lonely toil, to the spirit's longing eyes,
When the will was strong, and the purpose proud, and the fresh
    heart only knew
An earnest faith, and a fiery throb, and a trustful love and true!

Hence—hence, with every mean desire, with selfishness and
    pride!
And be this day, on life's rude way, beloved and sanctified;
And from the Irish exile's heart, with many a fault o'ercast
Let Faith and Hope and Love arise, as incense to the past.

## ODORS.

—"A valley where he sees
Things lost on earth."—*Milton.*

A BREATH of south wind, floating free,
    Wafts odors faint from distant flowers,
    Waking a subtle sense—and hours,
Long vanished, come again to me.

A voice, long silent, strikes my ear,
    Whose gentle whisperings, soft and low,
    Woke all the music long ago
That youth's pure dreaming loved to hear.

A vanished hand, whose touch once gave
   A thrill of heavenly life to mine,
Again the spring-flowers seem to twine
Beside a silvery river's wave.

The joy is dead and a dull pain
   Comes wafted on this soft perfume,
   While the dim past seems to entomb
Phantoms of buried dreams again.

## SARSFIELD'S SORTIE.

KING James' banner floats above
   The city's southern tower,
Defying proudly to the last
   The Dutch usurper's power;
And Hope seeks there a resting place
   For Freedom's shattered wing,
And faithful Limerick stands alone
   For Ireland's rightful King.

The Chiefs are gathered for debate
   Within the civic hall,
While foes are gathering thick around
   Her closely leaguered wall;
And news has come that William sends
   A ponderous battering train
To breach the walls that by assault
   His warriors failed to gain.

Out spoke the Mayor: " 'Tis bootless strife
   For James' ruined throne;
The land is vanquished east and west—
   We struggle now alone.

And famine soon will chill the heart
  That fearlessly would brave
An open field or leaguered wall,
  The soldier's bloody grave."

" Now, by the spirit of my sires!"
  The gallant Sarsfield cried,
" We shall not truckle to the foe
  While swords are by our side.
Give me but fifty daring hearts—
  Nay, never frown or chide—
And, by my faith! King William's train
  Ne'er sees the Shannon's side."

He gazed a moment sternly round;
  They hail his words with cheers,
And quick into their saddles spring
  The fifty volunteers.
Then through the eastern sally-port
  They spin with headlong speed,
And " Sarsfield to the rescue!" rings
  In Limerick's hour of need.

On swept they, like a whirlwind,
  Knockanny's hill to gain;
Where twice two hundred cannoniers
  Are guarding William's train;
On, on they dashed, no word they spoke,
  Nor bridle rein they drew,
Till Ireland's hated foreign foe
  Had met their eager view.

Hark, hark! upon the startled foe
  Now bursts their wild hurrah:
" Down, down upon the foreign slaves!
  Upon them! Smite and slay!
Trample the robbers to the earth!
  Ay, cleave them to the core!
To spare the plunderers of our homes
Were scorn for evermore."

The field is won, the prize is gained
  They sallied forth to gain;
The Dutchman's brave artillery
  And all his battering train
Lie shattered wide and harmless
  By noble Sarsfield's skill,
Whose glory haunts our memories,
  And fires our spirits still.

They durst not try to storm again,
  For few came back to tell
How, 'neath the brave defenders,
  The storming party fell.
Next day, before the sun had gilt
  The banner of our liege,
The foe withdrew their army,
  And Ginkle raised the siege.

No monuments are towering
  To honor Sarsfield's name,
But in faithful Irish bosoms
  There are temples to his fame.

And marble shrines shall perish
And ages roll away
Ere his memory is forgotten,
Or the glory of that day.

## THE VISION OF KING BRIAN.

[Time.— The Night before the Battle of Clontarf.]

THE great old Irish houses, the proud old Irish names,
Like stars upon the midnight, to-day their lustre gleams.
Gone are the great old houses, the proud old names are low
That shed a glory on the land a thousand years ago.

These were the great old houses, o'er whom the spirits held
Mystic watchings at Life's closing, in the distant days of eld;
Oft foretold they of Death's advent, in a slowly chanted wail,
And often in the tones that glad a warrior in his mail.

And wheresoe'er a scion of those great old houses be,
In the country of his fathers, or the lands beyond the sea,
In city, or in hamlet, by the valley, on the hill,
The spirit of his brave old sires is watching o'er him still.

'Twas thus before the battle that freed the Irish land,
That crushed the Dane forever on Clontarf's empurpled strand;
'Twas thus that brave King Brian, at the mid hour of the night
Saw a vision as he slumbered, befitting kingly sight:

A woman pale and beautiful, a woman sad and fair—
Proud and stately was her stature, black and flowing was her
    hair;
White as snow the robe around her, floating shadow-like and
    free,
Whilst with a silver trumpet's tone, to the sleeper, thus spoke
    she:

"King! unto thee 'tis given to triumph o'er the Dane—
To drive his routed army forth unto the Northern Main,
But the palace of thy fathers thou shalt never see again;
Thou, and the son thou lovest, shall sleep amongst the slain

"Yet far into the future thy memory shall live,
And to the souls of men unborn a glorious impulse give;
Thy dynasty shall perish before a factious band,
But thy spirit shall forever dwell upon the Irish land.

"Men yet unborn shall know thee as thy country's sword and
      shield,
Wise and prudent in the council, brave and skillful in the field;
When the factious and the spoilers shall trample on the free,
They will pray to God to raise them a Deliverer like thee. ·

"Thou shalt leave unto thy country, and the nations, a proud
      name;
Thou shalt leave it peace and freedom, and a bright and glori-
      ous fame;
Thou shalt leave it upraised altars, happy homes and smiling
      fields
Where the sower shall be reaper of what Heaven's bounty yields.

"Yet, trampling on thy country, the spoiler's foot shall come,
Woo'd to conquest and to plunder, by factious feuds at home;
Milesian with Milesian shall battle day by day,
Till the glory of the Irish land shall pass from it away.

"The fanatic and the bigot shall come with fire and brand,
With foreign swords and foreign laws, black heart and bloody
      hand;
They will trample on the altar, they will trample on the shrine,
And pollute each holy relic that thy country holds divine.

"But thy country shall stand firm, thro' plunder and thro'
    scathe,
To that which thou shalt die for, her consecrated faith;
Tho' her altars be in ruins, tho' her conquerors slay and rive,
Yet, despite of ban or guerdon, her faith shall still survive.

"Thy country's best and bravest shall struggle long and vain,
And some shall seek in distant lands to 'scape a conqueror's chain;
And some shall fall from princely hall e'en to the peasant's shed,
And many on her hard-fought fields shall slumber with the dead.

"But the God whose hand is stretchèd forth thy country to
    chastise,
In His own good time and fitting will bid the prostrate rise;
For her faith He hath recorded where the mighty seal is set,
And His mercy, aye, it shall gush forth and vivify her yet.

"In her deepest hour of sorrow, in her darkest hour of shame,
Thy country still shall treasure the glory of thy name.
In the greatest hour of triumph, when her history shall bear
To the future all her glory, thine shall still be foremost there."

No more she spake unto him, but passed like mist away,
As it floats up from the valley, beneath the summer's ray—
No more spake she unto him, but ever on the gale,
Until the hour of dawning, came a low and mystic wail.

     *     *     *     *     *

Next day amid the foremost brave Murrough, fighting, fell,
The flower of Irish chivalry—the son he loved so well;
And from our shores for ever was swept that day the Dane;
But the old king and his favorite son were numbered with the
    slain.

## IN VAIN.

In vain, how many a year is spent,—
  Aye, long years worn away,
And oh, how much to hope is lent,
  It never will repay!
For who can tell the years of toil,
  The waste of heart and brain,
And the weary travail of the soul
  That have been borne in vain!

The sleepless sage some star hath sought,
  Till hope and sight grew dim—
It shone for eyes that loved it not;
  But never beamed on him.
Thus fate will snatch the gem away
  Which all was given to 'gain,
Or feebly shed the long-sought ray
  Where it may beam in vain.

The poet's song may yet go forth
  To many a distant shore,
To fling around his land of birth
  A glory evermore;
Yet, o'er the lyre hangs cloud and gloom
  Where dwells a witching strain,
And the minstrel yet will find a tomb
  With bright bays crowned—in vain.

The Chief, who seeks for endless life,
  His country's pride and might;
Who wins his way through days of strife
  And watchings of the night;

Whose voice the powers of earth could shake
　In senate, field or fane—
High hearts like these too oft must break,
　And often fall—in vain.

And love, the pure and true, that clings
　In spite of ill or check—
Oh, many give SOME treasured things,
　But THIS holds nothing back.
Yet woe to well-springs of the heart
　Poured forth like summer rain,
While wealth could fail to purchase part
　Of all that's given in vain.

And some have borne the blast unbowed
　To sink beneath the wave,
E'en when the bow was in the cloud,
　Or life-boat near to save.
Thus upon human toil and care
　Some blight will still remain:
So let us lay our treasures where
　They are not heaped in vain.

## SONG FOR THE '82 CLUB.

AT last we meet, as brothers meet,
　A nation's strength combining;
A giant starting to his feet,
　A long-dimmed weapon shining.
No longer foreign rule shall cast
　Its festering chain, to bind us;
The feuds and follies of the past
　Are forever cast behind us.

We boast a still unconquered land,
  Despite their foreign charters;
For that dear isle we take our stand,
  Her champions, or her martyrs.
The memory of her glorious dead
  And her smiling fields remind us
Of the debt we owe the land we tread,
  While our feuds we cast behind us.

Up, brothers! there is work to do—
  Go take a foremost station,
To build the temple up again,
  To raise a fallen nation.
To spread her glory far and wide—
  None shall divided find us;
But working bravely, side by side,
  While the past is cast behind us.


## THE LAUNCHING OF " LA GLOIRE."

[The magnificent French line-of-battle ship "La Gloire" was launched at
Cherbourg in the year 1861. This was then the largest war ship in the world,
presenting the novel feature of being entirely cased in steel. "La Gloire"
was at that time justly considered the pride of the French Navy.]

COME bare the arm and grasp the sledge, to strike the shores
    away,
For our work is finished, and we launch a royal ship to-day.
All panoplied like knight of old—cuirassed in mail of steel,
From stem to stern, from side to side, from bulwark to the keel.

A flag for our ship, our royal ship, to bear to every shore,
To float and fly o'er every sea where waves and tempests roar—
Up to the peak with France's flag, the glorious tricolor,
Sacred to victory, freedom, fame, now and for evermore!

A name for our ship, our royal ship, to live on History's page,
That shall ring like a nation's rallying cry where the fierce sea-
      battles rage;
Sprinkle our ship with the southern wine, from stern to armed
      prow:
In the name of France, and France's fame, we name thee
      " Glory " now.

Oh, wondrous triumph of man's art, what destiny is thine!
Where Northern tempests madly rave, or tropic glories shine—
Wrestling with whirlwinds in their wrath, like a giant fired
      with wine,
Or bearing ocean warriors on through the sea-fight's battle's line!

No galleon from the Spanish Main—no Eastern argosie—
E'er bore so rich a freight as thine, proud monarch of the sea;
For a thousand conquering, fiery hearts are throbbing now in
      thee,
For France's name, for France's fame, for death or victory.

What shadows from the past shall haunt thy pathway on the
      main!—
The great traditions of the land of mighty Charlemagne!
Illuming with their undimmed light a heritage of fame,
For thee to guard, for thee to keep and mingle with thy name.

Up from Atlantic waves shall come, as through the foam you
      sweep,
The echo of a gurgling cheer that once rose from the deep,
As " La Vengeur " fighting England's fleet, sank in the
      whelming sea,
And *Vive le France!* from her thousand men, rose up defiantly.

Go bear thy flag—go bear thy name—along the mountain wave,
Thou proud, mailed warrior of the deep, to conquer and to save!
In storm or fight thy mission still to grandly do and dare,
Showing the world, where'er thou art, that France in Glory's
    there.

## THE CAPTURE OF PARIS.

### (FROM THE FRENCH OF VICTOR CARMINE.)

[In the following lines the writer illustrates the heroic incidents in the
days of July, 1830, when a body of the students of the Polytechnic School
broke out of that institution, and headed the first attacks that were made in
the streets of Paris, which eventuated in the overthrow of the government of
Charles X, and the establishment of Louis Philippe on the throne.]

A MIGHTY crowd, with accents loud, are swaying to and fro,
Where a nation's arm seems lifted up to strike a nation's blow.
Some shout aloud, "Down with the King!" some counsel calm
    and slow,
Some gaze about with anxious doubt, and some with fiery glow.

Thus was it, as the sun arose, o'er lofty Notre Dame,
When a stripling, but a gallant band, among the people came,
With beardless lips, but manly hearts, made for the battle's van,
With skillful hands, and ready swords, to win the rights of man.

Out stepped young Dumont from their ranks, he waved his
    bonnet high,
Proudly he spoke, in words of fire, whilst fiercely flashed his
    eye:
"A bas les Bourbons! Follow us. We'll show you *how* to die!"
"A bas les Bourbons!" rang around, and Paris caught the cry.

Abas les Bourbons! Frenchmen, on! the Polytechnic leads!
The beardless youth shall win to-day the fame of heroes' deeds.
Down falls the first in glory's lap; from twenty wounds he
    bleeds;
Hurrah! close up. His place is filled; another, fearless, leads.

Hurrah! they come, the hireling swords, Switzer and
    Allemagne.
Ho! Saint Antoine! stout Saint Antoine! upon them once again!
Up, up, Saint Jaques! and smite them down! fear not the fiery
    rain!
Hurrah for freedom for the quick, and vengeance for the slain!

Fear not their swooping cavalry, fear not their cannoniers!
Up, to the deadly muzzles—up, heroic Ecoliers!
Forth gushes flame and leaden hail, but as the death-cloud clears,
The Polytechnics' flag above the captured guns appears.

Look up, look up! How brave it floats upon the summer breeze!
The tricolor is planted o'er the haughty Tuilleries.
Then high the shout of triumph rose, that crushed the Bourbon's
    throne:
" Live France, live France! the day is won; proud Paris is our
    own!"

Time-honored be their memories, who for their fathers' land
Rushed from the students' solitude to grasp the patriot's brand;
Time-honored be their gory graves who hated tyrant laws,
Who loved the people—and who died, to right the people's
    cause!

## THE SONG OF THE COSSACK.

[From the French of Beranger]

HARK, hark, my steed! come rouse thy speed; on the wings of
    death let's forth!
Thou, the Cossack's pride and comrade tried—hark! the
    trumpets of the North;
No enriching gold does thy saddle hold; but rouse thee up, my
    steed—
For the ready spoil of city and soil awaits our daring deed.
Then neigh in thy pride, my courser tried, for thy hoof with
    conquest rings,
And trample down Europe's old renown, and her peoples and
    her kings.

Europe is old, her heart is cold, and her ancient ramparts low;
Peace flies the plain, and, with loosened rein, we rush like a
    torrent's flow;
Come, and fill my hands, in the Western lands, with the
    treasures of the mart;
Come, and make thy stall in the stately hall, and repose in the
    homes of art.
Return to drink at that river's brink, where thou before hast
    been,
And lave thy flanks by the sunny banks of rebellious river
    Seine—
Then neigh in thy pride, my courser tried, for thy hoof with
    conquest rings,
And trample down Europe's old renown, and her peoples and
    her kings.

I have seen at night, by our camp-fire's light, a phantom stern
    and grand,
Fix his ardent gaze o'er the bivouack's blaze and point with his
    armed hand
To the West, with pride, as he fiercely cried: "Once more
    begins my reign."
'Twas the mighty Hun, Attilla's son—I obey thy voice again!
Then neigh in thy pride, my courser tried, for thy hoof with
    conquest rings,
And trample down Europe's old renown, and her peoples and
    her kings.

The glory and fame of Europe's name, that wreathe with pride
    her brow,
The wisdom and lore which was hers of yore, but which cannot
    save her now,
It is time they fall! Engulph them all, in the waves of dust
    that rise
'Round the Cossack's track, from thy hoofs flung back, like an
    eclipse in the skies.
Erase, erase from their ancient place, in the wrath of thy new
    career,
Palace and mart, temples and art, laws and each souvenir.
Then neigh in thy pride, my courser tried, for thy hoof with
    conquest rings,
And trample down Europe's old renown, and her peoples and
    her kings.

## THE MIDNIGHT WATCH.

GROUPED in the sick one's stilly room,
Beneath the waning midnight's gloom,
While passed the night hours, sad and slow,
And lamp and life were burning low;
We watched, where, passing forth from clay,
A loved and dying mother lay.

We watched in silence, for the power
Of memory ruled us in that hour,
And pictured all that she had been
Through life in many a changing scene;
For true and firmly had she trod
That earthly path, which ends with God.

What visions thronged around us then
Of childhood's days, come back again!
When, in her fair and early youth,
We basked beneath her eyes of truth;
And sinless hearts saw from above
The great God's through a mother's love;

How at the matron's tranquil hearth,
Where happy hours had gentle birth.
Kindred and friends oft gathered 'round,
Where welcome, frank and kind, was found,
And, spite of change, and years of care,
She, 'mid the young, was youngest there;

How, in more sad and later years,
With " smiles that might as well be tears,"
Faithful and hopeful evermore,
Her cross of life she meekly bore,
Taking no stain from adverse fate
To dim a spirit pure and great.

Fainter and fainter comes each sigh;
At last, the parting hour is nigh,
Her bark is on the shadowy shore
Where cares and fears and hopes are o'er.
Thus, like the twilight time of May,
Her spirit passed from earth away.

No, not all gone! though Heaven may claim
Back to its fount the eternal flame·
Her spirit with us doth abide,
As on through life's dim paths we glide;
Though all unseen, still present there,
Watching with guardian angel's care.

Alas! all we have left undone,
While yet thy life around us shone,
To cheer thy path or glad thy time,
Comes burning on our hearts as crime;
And our atonement now must be
To act, to live, and die like thee.

## THE ASSAULT ON LIMERICK.

Ho, Limerick! ancient Limerick, arouse thy heart to-day;
Put harness on thy citizens and gird thee for the fray;
Nerve thy arm for thy homesteads, for the altar and the shrine,
And the time-enduring memories, proud city, that are thine

Thy battlements are tottering, thy walls are sapped away,
And yawns at length the breach whereon full fifty cannon play,
And, thundering o'er the space between, with fierce exulting
    cheers,
Carlisle and Drogheda lead on King William's grenadiers.

They've mounted on the ruined wall, two thousand, firm arrayed,
Casting before them, on their path, the deadly hand grenade.
And with a shout of triumph they sweep upon their way,
Nor dream of what a welcome we've prepared for them to-day.

Now shall they feel our Irish steel thro' crest and helmet glide;
For Sarsfield's charging in our van with Galway at his side,
And where e'er his plume is waving, the Brandenbergs lie low,
And the shout is raised the loudest: "No quarter for the foe!"

As break the tempest-driven waves recoiling from the rock,
The chosen band of Brandenberg shrink from the fiery shock,
And o'er the din of battle, and o'er the wild hurrah,
Loud swells the gladsome tidings: "The foreigners give way!"

Yet 'tis only for a moment: fierce Hanmer's on the wall.
He charges with his Danish guards, tho' fast and thick they fall;
And the stout brigades of Camdon rush quickly to his side,
And Bolcastel's good regiment to swell the bloody tide.

But tho' we are out numbered and sore pressed by the foe,
While we have hands to grasp the sword we'll deal them blow
    for blow;
Tho' our brethren fall around us, still our bravest and our best
Gather, like eagles to a feast, 'round Sarsfield's towering crest.

In the thickest of the battle, in the sorest hour of need,
When even hope had left us, and but honor bade us bleed,
A vision came upon us, such as warrior seldom saw,
That filled our hearts with daring, and our foemen's hearts with
    awe.

The matrons of our city, whose teachings hallow home,—
The maidens of the city. in their beauty and their bloom,—
Join their kin amid the carnage, and battle by their side,
The mother and the daughter, the sister and the bride.

We paused but for a moment, while o'er our spirits came
All the fond and gentle memories that feed affection's flame,
Then passed into our bosoms a wild and stern glow,
As we looked back at our city, and then forward at the foe.

We paused but for a moment, then arose our thrilling cheer,
Such as men but seldom hearken and forget not when they hear,
While, beside our bravest warriors, soft lily hands assail
The foe that flies before us, like leaves before the gale.

And then the breach their cannon made, we filled up with their
    dead,
And we chased them to their trenches, by gallant Sarsfield led;
And we looked down from our ramparts, that evening, o'er the
    plain,
While the twilight cast its shadows, and the foe entombed his
    slain.

## A REMINISCENCE OF THE MINES.

UP in a mountain solitude
Beside a pile of clay,
A man with shovel, pick and pan
Stood at the close of day.

His shirt and sash were very red,
His nose was very blue,
And, though the scene around was grand,
" The prospect " would not do.

His hat!—enough—'twas shocking bad,
His sunburnt neck was bare;
One eye looked droll, the other sad,
Beneath his unkempt hair.

His muddy jackboots, of all jet
Were long ago bereft,
And unto them, like unto him,
But little sole was left.

From out his pale, unsmiling lips,
With rank beard overgrown,
Outspoke this lonely mining man
In semi-growling tone.

Whilst restlessly his jackboot kept
The devil's tattoo drumming:
' I had no sense in coming here,
I've gained no cents by coming.

" Fortune, 'tis written, smiles on fools,
     Wherever they may labor;
And, surely, I've been fool enough
     To win her choicest favor.

" But ever she eludes my grasp,
     Despite the proofs I give her
That I'm an ass.   She turns from me
     To wanton with my neighbor.

" I have not sinned; as some folk sin—
     I pick, but do not steal—
And though my ways of life are hard,
   My heart is soft to feel.

" My neighbor's failings I let pass;
     I covet not a shade
Of all his goods, his ox, his ass,
     Nor man, nor servant maid.

" But for this last I claim no grace—
     Though some may not approve it—
Because in this infernal place
     There are no maids to covet.

" Nor sparkling eyes, nor beaming smiles
     That filled my dreams of yore!
Alas, alas! those days are passed—
     My day-dreams are now "ore."

" Oh, for one hour where some one's eyes
     Are bright and purely glancing,
And some one's dainty little feet
     To joyous music dancing.

" Where graceful forms are floating round —
    Most potent heart-dissolvers—
None but " rope dancers " here are found,
    Surrounded by " revolvers."

" Oh, for one hour where early life
    Flowed, passing merrily;
Where youth still hung on low-toned words,
    And not upon a tree.

" Where friends could wrangle and debate
    About each passing trifle;
And meet the flash of wit, instead
    Of bowie-knife or rifle."·

He paused, he sighed, he gazed about;
    Then spoke: " 'Tis cussed fine!
Oh, for a pail of double-stout
    To cool this thirst of mine!

" But never more I'll taste a pot
    Of Thunder's glorious beer!"—
The miner turned from the spot,
    And wiped away a tear.

# THE RELIEF OF LUCKNOW.

MARCH 6, 1858.

To THE EDITOR OF THE MONITOR:

Sir—I could not help versifying this heroic episode in current history; but my admiration is confined to the bravery and endurance of the rescuers and rescued, and has no sympathy whatever with the cause, policy or government whose work they were doing. The relation of the British Government to India is simply the relation of the robber to his victim.

Yours, etc.,

MASQUE.

A TORN flag is flying,
 Torn by shot and shell,
O'er wounded men and dying,
 In Lucknow's citadel,
Where the stern European
 Hath fought so long and well.

The ruthless Asiatic,
 Full fifty thousand strong,
With eager fierceness waits its prey,
 And round the ramparts throng;
" We'll die for duty; hope or fear
 To us no more belong.

" Look forth upon the Cawnpore road;
 Look forth to Allabad—
Strain, strain your gaze to every point,
 Whence succor may be had!
Have our countrymen forgot our need?
 This, this, than death 's more sad."

The sun hath westward passed
  On the eighty-seventh day,
Since round the leaguered city,
  The dusky foeman lay;
On the eighty-seventh weary night
  Falls the young moon's tranquil ray.

An island woman muses
  On her long lost highland home,
Where her worn form and longing heart
  Never again may come;
To the pleasant places of her youth,
  Once more her fancies roam.

Upward she springs, all throbbing,
  Beneath the moonbeam's ray;
A cry of joy bursts from her lips,
  " I *hear* the pibroch's play
' Campbells are coming'—they'll be here
  Before the break of day."

Nought spoke the weary warriors,
  All toil-worn, stern and pale;
But every ear was bent to hear
  The tidings on the gale.
Again the night wind brought the sound
  Of the pibrochs of the Gael.

" To arms!" the chieftain cried,
  " We'll conquer once again;
To arms, and to the Cawnpore gate!"
  A fierce hurrah—and then
The word was passed from rank to rank,
  " 'Tis Campbell and his men."

They come, the Highlandmen,
  Upon the dusky foe,
And an aged warrior leads them on,
  With a youthful hero's glow;
And the pibrochs play the charging step
  Of a thousand years ago.

As the flashing muskets roll
  They raise their battle cry,
And, o'er the din of 'the mingling steel,
  It surges fierce and high:
'Tis the Celtic slogan, triumphing
  Beneath that Orient sky.

Ye warriors, tried and true,
  Rescuers, and rescued brave!
No nobler triumph ever
  Hath war or glory gave
Than yours, ye proud immortals,
  To conquer and to save.


## "MORT SUR CHAMP D'HONNEUR."

OH, think not that there's glory won
  But on the field of bloody strife,
Where flashing blade and crushing gun
  Cut loose the silver chords of life.
Carve deep his name in brass or stone,
  Who for his home and country bled,
Who lies uncoffined and unknown,
  Upon the field of honor dead."

But carve there, too, the names of those
  Who fought the fight of faith and truth,
Bending beneath life's wintry snows,
  Or battling in the pride of youth.
Whoe'er have kindled one bright ray
  In hearts whence hope and joy had fled,
Have not lived vainly: such as they
  Are "on the field of honor, dead."

And those who sink on desert sand,
  Or calmly rest 'neath ocean wave,
Dropping the cross from weary hand,
  Telling no more its power to save;
The true, the pure, the brave, the good,
  Falling at duty's post still shed
A radiant light o'er plain and flood—
  Though "on the field of honor, dead."

Thus may we live, thus may we die,
  In earnest, valiant, faithful fight;
True to man's loftiest destiny—
  True to our God, ourselves, and right.
Then when we sleep, as sleep we must,
  In ocean's cell or earth's dark prison,
Be this memorial o'er our dust,
  Though dead "he is not here, but risen."

# JOHN BANIM

POET AND NOVELIST.

---

I saw him on his couch of pain,
  And when I heard him speak,
It was of Hope, long nursed in vain,
  And tears stole down his cheek.
He spoke of honors early won,
  Which youth could rarely boast,
Of high endeavors well begun
  But prematurely lost.

---

**T**HUS sang Thomas Haynes Bayly, the intimate literary friend of Hood, Rogers and
Moore, and the devoted friend and admirer of Banim.
The historic old town of Kilkenny, on the banks of
the Nore, gave birth to the subject of this sketch on
the 3d of April, 1798. His father, Michael Banim,
was a trader, fond of field sports and possessing more
than an ordinary share of common sense and education. His mother, a woman of excellent qualities
both of head and heart, was named Carroll, and
descended from a family of respectability and marked
refinement. Michael, her eldest son, has left us a
faithful portrait of her in Rose Brady, the heroine of
the "Ghost Hunter," and John inherited many of
her best qualities, as he did also her latent talents.

(79)

Latent, indeed, and undeveloped; for in Ireland during those "dark and evil days,"

> Full many a flower was born to blush unseen
> And waste its sweetness on the desert air.

How could it be otherwise? The wonder is, how that dear old Isle of Sage and Saint could have pro-

*John Banim*

duced such an incomparable array of literary lights, while oppressed by the incubus of coercion—while her noblest sons were being forced by *brutal British barbarity* into exile, or sacrificed to the Moloch of British rule. But produce them she did, in spite of all the discouraging circumstances; and the struggles, trials and tribulations of her Swifts, Moores, Griffins and Goldsmiths were equalled only by their fame.

Speaking of his mother, Banim says: "She possessed a mind of a very superior order, and a store of good sense and womanly, wifely patience; and these, with *trust in Heaven*, were her only marriage portion." These qualities her second son, John, possessed in an eminent degree, and they were the mainspring of his success.

Having entered the English academy of his native town, where Mr. Chas. James Buchanan ruled with all the pomp and authority of the schoolmaster mentioned in the "Deserted Village," the future author of the "O'Hara Family" picked up the rudiments, and was soon promoted to a seminary presided over by the learned Father Magrath, a gentleman of acknowledged ability in teaching young ideas how to shoot. Like many other boys whom we remember well, John was wont to play truant in the cool recesses of a ruined monastery, or in the delightful umbrage of a spreading hawthorn, where he would pore for hours over a volume of fairy lore, or con with avidity such magazines as came into his possession. The literary faculty manifested itself in him at even a more tender age than it did in Pope; and when he reached his tenth year his manuscript

7

poems and romances were very considerable. Like
all young literary aspirants who feel the *divinus
sufflatus* within them, he idolized men who had distinguished themselves in the arena of authorship;
and when his arch idol, Tom Moore, came to Kilkenny, rolling up his bundles of manuscript, young
John Banim went to visit the unrivalled melodist,
showed the productions of his young muse, and had
the satisfaction of being called "brother poet" by
the greatest lyrist that the world saw since the days
of Horace.

Whilst at the Kilkenny College the young poet
manifested and developed quite a talent for drawing
and landscape painting; and, having selected the
artist's profession, was transferred to the Academy
of the Royal Irish Society, Dublin. He obtained
the first prize for drawing at this academy, and was
equally distinguished for his industry and regularity
during the two years of pupilage in the metropolis
of his native land. One of his letters to his mother
during this period shows at the same time his filial
attachment, his abiding trust in Providence, and the
hope, which then buoyed his heart, of one day
" tracing the footsteps " of eminent painters:—

" MY DEAR MOTHER.—Your anxious love could not wish me
better than I am, or with better prospects before me. I have
the countenance of all, and the friendship of many of the first
artists and amateurs in my profession. I meet with warm
encouragement and hope of success from everyone."

In a letter written to his father, Christmas Day, 1813, he says: " There is nothing in the intercourse with strangers to compensate one for the absence of kindred; but I must not murmur against what cannot be avoided. The festival of Christmas reminds me that I am desolate. There is no equivalent for the peace and blessings I have hitherto enjoyed at our Christmas hearth." Poor Banim gave expression then to the feelings of many an exiled Celt, who yearned for the " Christmas hearth," at home.

After two years of separation, the artist of eighteen summers returned to the old hearth-stone, and was fortunate in securing a lucrative situation as teacher·of drawing in one of the boarding-schools of his native city. And now the old drama in which the poet-painter was to take his part was enacted anew. Annie D——, a boarder in the academy where he professed drawing, was, we are told, " fair, bright-eyed, full of the fresh beauty of seventeen, artless, innocent ˏand pure-minded." Her teacher, only one year her senior, forgot the grave moral of the history of the tutor Abelard and the pupil Eloise; and, day after day, a deep ardent passion grew within his breast and ripened into a love strong and abiding, which on the part of Annie was reciprocated. Many a sunny morn and dewy eve saw the young artist and his plighted Annie, as they went their way to the favorite trysting place on the flowery

banks of the Nore, ostensibly for the purpose of
sketching landscape views, but in reality to talk of
love, which is closely connected with, and always
had the greatest influence on, the fine arts of painting and poetry.

Of the many effusions to the idol of his heart,
space will permit us to select only one, and that
must be very short:

> I thank thee, high and holy pow'r,
>   That thus upon my natal hour,
> Thy blessed bounty hath bestowed
>   More than to mortal life is owed.
>
> If thy dispensing hand had given
>   All other joys this side of heaven;
> The monarch's crown, the hero's crest,
>   All honors, riches, powers, the best,
> And Anna's love, away the while,
>   I'd change them all for Anna's smile.

Annie's father, a country squire, hearing of his
daughter's attachment, took means of cutting off all
communication between the lovers; but "love that
laughs at locksmiths" soon found means of evading
the vigilance of the squire, and correspondence was
kept up until Annie was removed from the boarding
school and forced to return the miniature, letters and
poems of her lover. The poor girl brooded over the
passion of her heart until it sapped her vitality,

and, as her father was unrelenting in his determination that she should never see John Banim, she died in despair and of a broken heart.

Being informed of Annie's death and of her fidelity to him during so trying and painful a separation, the noble-hearted painter was inconsolable. Being too poor to hire a vehicle, he started on foot for the home of his affianced, some twenty miles distant. It was a cold, rainy November day, and when he reached the corpse of his beloved that night he felt footsore, weary and wet. Entering the house he gazed silently on the pallid cheek and shrunken form which once seemed so beautiful to him. That warm heart and lively, laughing eye were now stilled in death. The agony which his features betrayed, as he stood there beside the bier, attracted attention, and revealed the lover of the deceased girl. Her sister, recognizing Banim, rudely ordered him from the house. He retired to an outhouse, where he fell into a dreamy stupor, which lasted until the funeral cortege was formed next morning. He had not tasted a morsel since the preceding morning; but grief had banished all cravings of hunger, and he only looked for the privilege of seeing his Annie once more before the coffin-lid closed forever on her cherished form. He followed the hearse to the churchyard, saw the last sod placed over her grave, and then, the mourners having departed, cast himself almost unconscious on the mound that marked the final resting-place of all that was dearest to him on earth. How long he remained in this position no one knows. Next day his brother found him some distance from Kilkenny, in a half conscious state, and prostrate, almost, in body and mind. The stamina of life was buried with his first love, ambition fled, and his taste for literature and painting lay dormant for a long time.

After a year of prostration and pain, Banim's health returned, and with it his love of literature. Like Gerald Griffin, he first became a contributor and then editor of a local newspaper, the Leinster *Gazette.* Finding this position ill suited to his taste and independent spirit, he moved to Dublin in 1820, where he wrote not only for the metropolitan press, but also for several country papers. Here he became acquainted with Charles Philips, the poet and orator, who had then published his poem entitled "The Emerald Isle," also with Shiel, William Curran and Lord Cloncurry. To the latter he dedicated his first long poem, "The Celt's Paradise," for which he obtained £20 from Warren, the publisher, of Bond street, London.

This successful adventure in the region of literature prompted the young artist, like Lover and Hazlitt, to relinquish the brush for a mightier instrument, and to launch into the literary ocean. At his very outset he wrote the tragedy, "Damon and Pythias," which his fellow-countryman, Macready, the "reformer of the stage," produced at Covent Garden Theatre in May, 1821. This being a complete success, like Lord Byron, Banim might have said: "I rose next morning a famous man." In London he conceived the idea of rivalling Scott as a novelist, and for that purpose entered into partnership with his brother Michael, to whom he wrote the following instructive letter, which we give here, hoping it may be of some value to the young readers who aspire to literary distinction:

"LONDON, May 2d, 1824.

"MY DEAR MICHAEL—I have read attentively, and with the greatest pleasure, the portion of the tale you sent me by J. H——. So far as it goes, I pronounce that you have been successful. Two of the personages do not stand out sufficiently from the canvas. Aim at distinctness and at individuality of character. Open Shakespeare, and read a play of his; then turn to the list of *dramatis personae* and see and feel what he has done in this way.

"Of a dozen characters, each is himself alone. Look about you; bring to mind the persons you have known; call them up before you; select and copy them. Never give a person an action to do who is not a legible individual. Make that a rule, and I think it ought to be a primary rule with novel writers.

"Suppose one was to get a sheet of paper, draw up thereon a list of persons, and after their names write down what kind of human beings they shall be, leaving no two alike, and not one generalized or undrawn. After Shakespeare, Scott is the great master-hand of character, and hence, one of his sources of great

power. To show you clearly what I mean, not a creature we
ever met in our father's penetralia resembled the other. There
might be somewhat of a conventional, outward similarity,
arising from their pursuits, habits and amusements being
similar; but each was, notwithstanding, distinct.

" I think that, in writing a tale, every character in it should
be drawn from nature. It is impossible all should be absolute
originals. Human nature being the same in all ages, and in all
climes, it cannot be hoped, now-a-days, that a writer can be the
discoverer of new character. It cannot be no more than the
same dough, somewhat differently shaped. Habits of country,
habits of station, habits of any kind, will diversify; but human
nature is the same now as it ever was. I say one can scarcely
draw an original character; but I say, draw like nature—no
matter what kind of nature you draw from—provided that the
likeness be not that of a disgusting object. After all, there is
nothing commonplace in nature.

" Get fourteen or fifteen of any of the persons you ever knew,
put them into scenes favorable to their peculiarities—their
individualities can be exemplified without straining after the
point; in proper situations set them talking for themselves; by
their own word of mouth they will denote their own characters
better than any description from pen. Thus will you dramatize
your tale, and faithful drama is the life and soul of novel-
writing. Plot is an inferior consideration to drama, though
still it is a main consideration.

" A few words more as to the mode of studying the art of
novel-writing. Read any first-rate production of the kind,
with a note-book. When an author forces you to feel with him,
or whenever he produces a more than ordinary degree of pleasure, or when he startles you, stop and try to find out how he

has done it; see if it be by dialogue or by picture, or by description, or by action. Fully comprehend his method, his means for the effect, and note it down. Write down all such impressions. Enumerate these and see how many go to make the combined interest of one book. Observe, by contrasting characters, how he keeps up the balance of the familiar and the marvelous, humorous, serious and romantic.

"This would not be imitation, it would be study—what, I will venture to say, great men have done with their predecessors; what painters do in the study of their art."

"Tales by the O'Hara Family" appeared in April, 1825, and their success was wonderful. The Press said they were *admirably* written; the critics that they were *well written.* Griffin, a book critic himself, wrote of these tales: "I think them most vigorous and original things; overflowing with the very spirit of poetry, passion and painting. Nothing since Scott's first novels has equalled them." For these tales, the joint production of the Banim brothers, they were well paid, and the inducements were so flattering that John soon after sent to the Press "The Boyne Water," a work of three volumes, the sale of which was exceptionally great. John's trenchant pen, made smooth by the oil of his vigorous imagination and fed from the exhaustless stores of his knowledge, was incessantly at work in the field of fiction. Well has it been said:

Morning saw him at his folios,
Twilight saw his fingers run,
Laboring ever, weary never
Of the work he had begun.

But this application, for which Banim was so
remarkable, eventually sapped his by no means
robust constitution, and he was obliged to seek
relaxation and health in Boulogne where embarrassments of a pecuniary complexion soon stared him
in the face, and his only consolation consisted in the
remembrance of happier times and things. From
these embarassments he was, however, soon relieved
by the generosity of his admiring countrymen.

A laudable movement was set on foot by his
friend Mr. Sterling, who, writing in the London
*Times*, of which paper he was editor, made a brilliant and truthful appeal on behalf of his sick and
suffering friend. The appeal was supported by other
journals, and Banim expressed his gratitude in a
letter to the editor of the *Times*. On this occasion,
as on every other, the Irish people were not appealed
to in vain, and the handsome amount realized was
a pleasing testimonial to the sick man of the appreciation and love in which he was held by them.
Prominent in the subscription list were the names
of Earl Grey, Sir Robert Peel, Richard Lalor Sheil
and Samuel Lover. This pecuniary assistance enabled the invalid author to pay off all the debts he

had unavoidably contracted, and to remain on the
Continent for two years for the benefit of his health.
But, alas, poor Banim! he reaped no advantage whatever from his sojourn in Paris and Boulogne. His
complaint (disease of the spine) was, by eminent
Parisian physicians, pronounced to be incurable;
and thus bereft of all hope he had but one wish, to
pass the remainder of his days in his native land,
where the kind and affectionate sympathy of rela-
tives and friends "might gently slope his pathway to
the grave"; and, accordingly, in answer to the urgent
solicitation of his brother, he prepared to return
home. In a reply he wrote to Michael, previous to
setting out, he enclosed a poem, a few stanzas of
which we cannot refrain from quoting, as they show
the affectionate longing which filled his heart to reach
once more the happy scenes of his childhood. It is
entitled

### THE CALL FROM HOME.

From home and hearth and garden it resounds
From chamber stairs, and all the old house bounds,
And from our boyhood's old playgrounds.

    \*       \*       \*       \*       \*

Brother, I come; you summon and I come;
From love like yours I never more may roam—
Yours is the call from brother and from home.

Reaching London he rested there some days, during
which time he was visited by many old familiar

friends, foremost among whom was his ardent admirer, Thomas Haynes Bayly, who was sorely
afflicted at seeing the gifted Banim thus prostrated
by sickness. The feeling of his heart on this occasion found expression in a poem, a stanza of which
prefaces this article.

Quitting London for ever he arrived in Dublin at
the close of July, 1835; here Michael met him after
a separation of thirteen years. This meeting between
the two brothers was a very affecting one. We will
let Michael tell it in his own words: "I entered his
room unannounced. I found him laid listlessly on
a sofa, his useless limbs at full length, and his sunken
cheeks resting on his pillow. I could not at once
recognize the companion of my boyhood in the rem-
nant I now beheld. I had been prepared to meet a
change, but not such a change as was now apparent,
for I looked down on a meagre, attenuated, almost
white-headed old man. We were not long, however,
recognizing each other and renewing our old love."
In Dublin, as in London, old and new friends gathered around Banim, and among these the Viceroy,
the Earl of Musgrave, was most attentive and thought-
ful in his endeavors to aid the poor, broken sufferer.
As a graceful means of increasing his resources there
was opened for him on July 21st a benefit at the
Theatre Royal, Hawkins street, under the immediate
patronage of the Lord Lieutenant; and we are told

by the *Morning Register* of the following day that persons of high and worthy names occupied the private boxes. The affair was in every sense a complete success. Early in the month of September Banim went back to his longed-for home. On his arrival in Kilkenny his fellow-townsmen received him with open arms, and presented him with an address expressive of the pleasure they experienced in welcoming back to his native town one whose talents and worth reflected such credit upon all Ireland. Accompanying the address was a small silver snuff box containing a subscription of £85.

Banim replied in words brimful of warm affection and ardent patriotism. Thus was Banim received by his admiring countrymen.

Space will not permit us to give a detailed account of the events of the last seven years of his life; suffice it to say that during that time, though suffering the most acute pains, he always displayed a fortitude and cheerfulness of spirits which, in the circumstances, was truly commendable. Before he had been a year at home Queen Victoria bestowed a pension on him of £150 a year.

Never was the royal bounty more needed or more truly deserved; for this boon he was indebted to the Earl of Carlisle, aided by his early friend Richard Lalor Shiel. The nobleman often visited Banim, and was very much attracted by his little daughter, then twelve years of age. Knowing her father's anxiety on her account, he obtained an additional pension of £40 for her benefit. Gerald Griffin, who was Banim's life-long friend, often visited him in his home by the Nore during his illness, and spent many a pleasant hour talking with the novelist on literary topics. These two gifted authors in some respects resembled one another, not so much in their works as in the interior sentiments which permeate as an atmosphere their writings, aims and aspirations. Some writers there are, who, when we read their works, awaken in us a sentiment of admiration, while others elicit our esteem and love. In the latter category we must place John Banim and Gerald Griffin; and the perpetuity of their fame is, and, no doubt will ever be due to this benign and salutary influence which they exercise on the minds of their readers.

Seven years had now passed since Banim's return to his Irish home. The malignant complaint to which he was a victim had much impaired his bodily strength, but the will and intellect remained as indomitable as ever until the month of June, 1842, when even these gave signs of waning; and late in the following month his brother Michael was suddenly summoned to his death-bed. John was barely able to recognize him. Taking his hand, he gave one fond long look into his face, and then with a smile upon his pallid countenance, calmly and quietly passed away. •

He lies buried in the graveyard of the Catholic chapel of St. John, Kilkenny, by the side of his mother, whom he loved with such filial affection. He left, surviving him his widow and an only daughter, Mary, whom we had occasion to allude to above. This child, after her father's death, was placed in a convent school at Waterford, under the special care of the sister of Richard Lalor Shiel— this distinguished Irishman being one of her guardians.

She was then a very lovely girl, full of talent, full of endearing affection, and gave promise of doing credit to her father's name. But, alas! in February, 1844, she showed symptoms of chest disease, which were at first thought lightly of, but which soon took the form of that insidious disease, consumption, which has no pity for " blue eyes and golden hair." In the June following she fell a victim to it in the eighteenth year of her age, and her coffin was placed on the yet sound timber encasing her father's remains.

On the death of John Banim's daughter, Sir Robert Peel performed one of those acts which, whether it proceeded from feelings or policy, was none the less praiseworthy. At the solicitation of a committee of twenty-one gentlemen representing all shades of political opinion, he placed Mrs. Banim on the

pension list. Among the distinguished men who took
up Mrs. Banim's case we notice the names of Daniel
O'Connell, Smith O'Brien, Isaac Butt, Charles Lever,
Thomas Davis, William Carleton, Charles Gavan
Duffy, Thomas MacNevin, and others.

We desire, ere closing, to say a few words about
John Banim's writings. By himself, as well as in
conjunction with his brother, he wrote much. His
principal works were "Tales by the O'Hara Family,"
"The Peep o' Day," "The Denounced; or the Last
Baron of Crana," "The Conformist" and "The Boyne
Water." Especially on those mentioned will his fame
as a novelist rest. In them he has portrayed his
country in the colors of truth; delineated without
concealment or exaggeration its national character;
sketched its peasantry as they really are, blending
the charms of truth with the creations of a powerful
fancy, and directing all to the noble purpose of ele-
vating the national character, and vindicating a too
long neglected and oppressed land. In this Banim
has shown himself a benefactor of his country, and
for this very reason his name and fame shall live in
the memory of his countrymen as long as gratitude
and love are ranked as virtues among men. His
poems, though few, are worthy of his genius.

The following paragraph, which refers in compli-
mentary terms to Duffy's collection of Irish ballads
in general, and to our author's "Soggarth Aroon " in

particular, is taken from Cockburn's "Life of Lord Jeffrey":

"I read a very interesting little volume of 'Irish Ballad Poetry,' published by that poor Duffy of the *Nation*, who died so prematurely the other day. There are some most pathetic, and many most spirited, pieces, and all, with scarcely an exception, so entirely *national*. Do get the book and read it. I am most struck with 'Soggarth Aroon,' after the two first stanzas; and a long, racy, authentic, sounding dirge for the Tyrconnel Princes. But you had better begin with 'The Irish Emigrant' and 'The Girl of Loch Dan,' which immediately follows, which will break you in more gently to the wilder and more impassioned parts. It was published in 1845, and as a part of 'Duffy's Library of Ireland.' You see what a helpless victim I still am to these enchanters of the lyre. I did not mean to say but a word of this book, and here I am furnishing you with extracts. But God bless all poets! and you will not grudge them a share even of your Sunday benedictions."

This is an excerpt from a letter written by the great reviewer to Mrs. Empson.

### SOGGARTH AROON.

AM I the slave they say,
    Soggarth Aroon?
Since you did show the way,
    Soggarth Aroon,
*Their* slave no more to be
While they would work with me
Ould Ireland's slavery,
    Soggarth Aroon?

8

Why not her poorest man,
  Soggarth Aroon,
Try and do all he can,
  Soggarth Aroon,
Her commands to fulfil
Of his own heart and will
Side by side with you still
  Soggarth Aroon?

Loyal and brave to you,
  Soggarth Aroon,
Yet be no slave to you,
  Soggarth Aroon,—
Nor, out of fear to you—
Stand up so near to you—
Och! out of fear to *you!*
  Soggarth Aroon!

Who, in the winter's night,
  Soggarth Aroon,
When the could blast did bite,
  Soggarth Aroon,
Came to my cabin-door,
And, on my earthen-flure,
Knelt by me, sick and poor,
  Soggarth Aroon?

Who, on the marriage-day,
  Soggarth Aroon,
Made the poor cabin gay,
  Soggarth Aroon—

And did both laugh and sing
Making our hearts to ring,
At the poor christening,
   Soggarth Aroon?

Who, as friend only met,
   Soggarth Aroon,
Never did flout me yet,
   Soggarth Aroon?
And when my hearth was dim,
Gave, while his eyes did brim,
What I should give to him,
   Soggarth Aroon?

Och! you, and only you,
   Soggarth Aroon!
And for this I was true to you,
   Soggarth Aroon;
*In* love they'll never shake,
When for ould Ireland's sake
We a true part did take,
   Soggarth Aroon!

## HE SAID THAT HE WAS NOT OUR BROTHER.*

HE said that he was not our brother—
   The mongrel! he said what he knew—
No, Eire! our dear Island-mother,
   He ne'er had his black blood from you!
And what though the milk of your bosom
   Gave vigor and health to his veins—
He *was* but a foul foreign blossom
   Blown hither to poison our plains!

---

* The Duke of Wellington.

He said that the sword had enslaved us—
    That still at its point we must kneel,
The liar!—though often it braved us,
    We cross'd it with hardier steel!
This witness, his Richard—our vassal!
    His Essex—whose plumes we trod down!
His Willy—whose peerless sword-tassel
    We tarnish'd at Limerick town!

No! falsehood and feud were our evils,
 · While force not a fetter could twine—
Come Northmen,—come Normans,—come Devils!
    We gave them our *Sparth* to the chine!
And if once again he would try us,
    To the music of trumpet and drum,
And no traitor among us or nigh us—
    Let him come, the Brigand! let him come!

## AILLEEN.

'Tis not for love of gold I go,
    'Tis not for love of fame;
Though fortune should her smile bestow,
    And I may win a name,
              Ailleen,
    And I may win a name.

And yet it is for gold I go,
    And yet it is for fame,
That they may deck another brow,
    And bless another name,
              Ailleen,
    And bless another name.

For this, but this, I go—for this
  I lose thy love awhile;
And all the soft and quiet bliss
  Of thy young, faithful smile,
           Ailleen,
  Of thy young, faithful smile.

And I go to brave a world I hate,
  And woo it o'er and o'er,
And tempt a wave, and try a fate
  Upon a stranger shore,
           Ailleen,
  Upon a stranger shore.

Oh, when the bays are all my own,
  I know a heart will care!
Oh, when the gold is wooed and won,
  I now a brow shall wear,
           Ailleen,
  I know a brow shall wear!

And when with both returned again,
  My native land to see,
I know a smile will meet me there,
  And a hand will welcome me,
           Ailleen,
  And a hand will welcome me!

## THE IRISH MAIDEN'S SONG.

You know it, now—it is betray'd
This moment, in mine eye—
And in my young cheek's crimson shade,
And in my whisper'd sigh.
You know, now—yet listen, now—
Though ne'er was heart more true,
My plight and troth, and virgin vow,
Still, still I keep from you,
                    Ever—

Ever, until a proof you give
How oft you've heard me say
I would not even his empress live,
Who idles life away,
Without one effort for the land
In which my fathers' graves
Were hollow'd by a despot hand
To darkly close on slaves—
                    Never!

See! round yourself the shackles hang,
Yet come you to love's bowers,
That only he may soothe their pang,
Or hide their sting in flowers.
But try all things to snap them, first,
And should all fail, when tried,
The fated chain you cannot burst
My twining arms shall hide,
                    Ever.

# REV. CHARLES P. MEEHAN,

## PRIEST AND HISTORIAN.

**I**N the columns of the Dublin *Nation* for October 29th, 1842, there appeared a paragraph among answers to correspondents which read thus:

" *Clericus*, who offers us the option of inserting or burning his verses, does himself an injustice. They are most admirable, and will appear in our next number."

The verses alluded to by the editor of the *Nation* were written by the subject of this biographical sketch, and appeared according to promise on November 5th, in the Poet's Corner, under the title of

## BOYHOOD'S YEARS.

Ah! why should I recall them—the gay, the joyous years,
Ere hope was cross'd or pleasure dimm'd by sorrow and by tears?
Or why should mem'ry love to trace youth's glad and sunlit way,
When those who made its charms so sweet are gather'd to decay?
The summer's sun shall come again to brighten hill and tower—
The teeming earth its fragrance bring beneath the balmy
    shower—
But all in vain will mem'ry strive; in vain we shed our tears—
They're gone away and can't return—the friends of boyhood's
    years!

Ah! why then wake my sorrow, and bid me now count o'er
The vanished friends so dearly prized—the days to come no
    more—

The happy days of infancy, when no guile our bosoms knew,
Nor reck'd we of the pleasures that with each moment flew?
'Tis all in vain to weep for them—the past a dream appears;
And where are they—the lov'd, the young, the friends of
    boyhood's years?

Go, seek them in the cold churchyard—they long have stol'n to
    rest;
But do not weep, for their young cheeks by woe were ne'er
    oppress'd;
Life's sun for them in splendor set—no cloud came o'er the ray
That lit them from this gloomy world upon their joyous way,
No tears about their graves be shed—but sweetest flowers be
    flung,
The fittest offering thou canst make to hearts that perish
    young—
To hearts this world has never torn with racking hopes and
    fears;
For bless'd are they who pass away in boyhood's happy years!

These lines need no comment; they speak for themselves. We only regret that he has not written more poetry. For, though he devoted most of his time to prose writing, he was a genuine poet, and would have found the ascent to Parnassus both easy and pleasant. If he has not contributed largely to the poetic literature of his native land, however, he has assisted very materially, and encouraged and inspired many of those whose names are to-day dear to the lovers of Irish ballad-poetry. He was the intimate and dearly-beloved friend of Mangan and McGee, the benefactor of "Leo" and "Caviare." McGee's last letter was written to Father Meehan, the friend and counsellor of his youth. With all the ardor of his Catholic heart he loved the patriotic priest who wrought so zealously to rescue from oblivion the records of Erin's elder days.

Mangan this good priest admired and consoled while living, and defended when dead from the aspersions of his enemies. Poor Mangan, who was, indeed, a veritable poet—one who ranks among the best of his time—dined with Father Meehan whenever he chose to do so; and when the memory of the former was assailed by a Dublin essayist about five years ago, Father Meehan wrote the following letter to a literary friend:

"DEAR FRIEND:—Let me tell you that it would be impossible to find *here* a single being, my unfortunate self excepted, who knew Mangan personally. Poor fellow! he did occasionally take what he ought not to have taken. A spoonful of wine or whisky upset his nervous system.

" Mangan, be his faults what they may have been, was a *pure* man, never lowering himself to ordinary debaucheries or sensuality of any sort. He prayed, heard Mass almost every day, and occasionally knelt at the altar rail. He dined with me when he liked; and I never heard him say a word that was not worth remembering."

This loyalty to the "friend of his early days " is much to be admired. Faithful was he to the memory of the Young Irelanders unto death. During the Fenian epoch, he was the patron of the short-lived but brilliant lyrist, John K. Casey, who has left us among his writings a poem descriptive of the incident which led Father Meehan to write his *magnum opus*, "The Fate and Fortunes of the Earls of Tyrone and Tyrconnell."

While Father Meehan was a student in Rome he happened one day in the vicinity of St. Isidore, and there discovered the final resting place of Hugh O'Neill and Rory O'Donnell. There and then the gifted Irish Levite commenced those researches to which the literature of Ireland owes so very much.

This historical episode is thus woven into verse:

> 'Twas summer time long years ago,
> Where shone the skies of Italy,
> And Tiber's waters calmly flow
> Far westward to the sun-lit sea.

Amid the Roman city's crowd,
  Montorio's arches darkly loom,
And, in their shade, with forehead bowed,
  An Irish boy knelt by a tomb.

He read the names above the clay:
  He asked—"What led their footsteps here
From Irish hills far, far away,
  To find an exile's lonely bier?"

"O Pilgrim! in this cold clay rest
  Two chiefs of distant Innisfail,
O'Donnell, of the peerless crest,
  And Ulster's prince, great Hugh O'Neill.

"They fled their land—then all is dim;
  Their after fate none now may tell:
They faded from the earth's wide rim
  The day they bade their homes farewell."

Up rose the youth, with steady eye
  And heart in resolution strong—
He prayed a prayer to God on high
  To save the just and right the wrong.
  *      *      *      *      *
Leaf after leaf, as years passed on,
  He added to the record frail;
Leaf after leaf, till years were gone
  With Time's swift wing to fill the sail.

Now—now the hope's fulfilled at last,
  The path is traced—the work is done;
The stars shine through the misty past—
  The fight 'gainst darkness fought and won.

"Caviare," (John Francis O'Donnell) also was a steadfast admirer of our gifted author. Among the published poems of that talented young man, who perished all too soon for his fame, we find one entitled " Reminiscences of a day in Wicklow," in which Father Meehan is thus apostrophised:

> O, friend of the radiant, lucent mind
>   And boundless charity of heart,
> As through the hills we climb and wind,
>   See the red deer leap up and start
>   Out in the sun—that we mnst part,
> Flings sadness on this tender morn,
>   A lengthening shadow on the path
> That flows in curious maze between
>   The wildwood and the rath.

The author of these lines cast into verse some of the striking parts of Meehan's "Rise and Fall of the Franciscan Monasteries" also, and furnished the poem which we find at the end of our subject's chief work.

Rev. Charles Patrick Meehan was born in Dublin on July 12th, 1812. His parents, who were from Ballymeehan, in the county of Leitrim, were so circumstanced that they could afford to give the future historian the best education then going. In his boyhood he manifested a vocation for the sacred ministry, and his parents sent him to the Irish College at Rome, then presided over by the learned

Dr. Christopher Boylan. During his eight years' course in the metropolis of the Christian world he had for professors such eminent and renowned scholars as Perroné, Manera and De Vico. The lectures of those astute professors were not lost to the 'young Irish boy who noted with care every salient point that was treated in the course of their delivery. His ever busy and inquiring mind sought every source of knowledge in the City of the Tiber; and even in Rome he was considered a "learned youth."

Ordained in 1835, Father Meehan, young, active and zealous, returned to his native land. His first appointment was to the parish of Rathdrum, in the County of Wicklow, where he devoted his leisure moments to the patriotic work of rescuing the exploits of the O'Tooles and O'Byrnes from the oblivion into which they were fast sinking. At the end of his first year in the ministry he was transferred by Archbishop Murray to SS. Michael and John's, Dublin, where he remained and labored for fifty-four eventful years. The period of his appointment to a curacy in his native city is remarkable in the annals of Irish history. The tithe question was then agitating the whole nation, from Malin to the Dursey Head. O'Connell was at the meridian of his fame, and that brilliant band of poets and orators, who a decade of years later loomed up before the world as the Chiefs of the "Young Ireland" party were cleaving a way to prominence in their respective localities. It was the formative period of a new era.

"In Father Meehan's room," writes the reverend editor of the *Irish Monthly*, "Clarence Mangan, Florence MacCarthy and the rest often gathered to spend' the evenings together, with talk as a chief item in the entertainment—*noctes atticae*—with two derivations, classical and modern, for the last epithet."

The junior curate of SS. Michael and John's had doubtless been among the most eager readers of the "*Nation's* first number," and soon his ambition might be expressed in the line which Goldsmith once so cleverly turned against Johnson:

"Forsitan et nostrum nomen miscebetur istis."

His name was soon classed with "Desmond," "Terrae Filius," "Shamrock," "Slievegullion," and the "Celt;" and, although his poems are few, they are of such high merit as to entitle him to a niche with the best of his contemporaries.

Though closely allied to the editors of the *Nation* and in full sympathy with the doctrines of the "Young Ireland" party, only three of his poems appeared in the columns of the great national organ, "Boyhood's Years," "The Fall of the Leaves," and

## THE PATRIOT'S WIFE.

[There is a tradition amongst the Swiss of the Canton of Uri that the
wife of the tyrant Gesler, disgusted at the atrocities perpetrated by her husband, fled from him; and as she was of Swiss extraction, made a vow never
to return to him. The tyrant, however, succeeded in capturing her; and the
following verses record the dialogue which is often repeated by the Swiss
hearth when the peasant recounts to his children the glories and achievements of William Tell.]

How changed thou art since last we met!
   Thy brow is wan—thy smile is cold;
Stern grief her seal has on thee set—
   Thou art not what thou wert of old!

No joy now flashes from that eye
   Which once around shed charms of light;
That voice once sweet can now but sigh;
   Oh, Heavens! whence came this sudden blight!

Say, wilt thou tell?—Great God! how strange
   That beauty thus could pass away,
And mirth to deepest sorrow change
   More quickly than the tomb's decay!

Yes; tell me if the memory lives
   Of early loves and sun-bright years—
If thought but one faint flickering gives—
   Whence all those woes and burning tears?

Nay, do not ask—to tell were vain—
   My grief, not Heaven itself can 'suage;
Nor seraph's breath can cool my pain,
   Nor quench my bosom's burning rage.

My country, prey to tyrant's bands—
   Her glory gone—her brave ones dead—
Her daughter slain by traitor's hands—
   And ask'st thou why my joy is sped?

'Fore Heaven, I prize this faded form,
E'en in its ghastly features, more
Than when you won it young and warm,
And it alone to worship swore.

For now I make thee, tyrant, tremble
O'er all the ruin thou hast made;
In vain thou seekest to dissemble—
Oh! curse thy bloody heart and blade.

And cursèd may her ashes be
Who basely sold her maiden hand
To him who crushed our liberty,
And drowned in blood my fatherland.

The prose works of the patriotic priest are numerous, and of a character calculated to perpetuate his name and fame to many a future generation. In the order of time "The Confederation of Kilkenny" comes first. It is dedicated to Charles Gavan Duffy. It ranks high among the historical works of Ireland. He collected and edited the literary remains of his friends, Thomas Davis and James Clarence Mangan. "The History of the Rise and Fall of the Franciscan Monasteries in Ireland" and a "History of the Geraldines" are the work of his active brain and busy pen. He contributed a good deal to the periodicals of his day, and for many years was chief editor of Duffy's *Irish Catholic Magazine*. It was in this publication that his longest, though by no means his best, poem first appeared, "The Battle of Benburb."

As a linguist Father Meehan had very few superiors in Ireland or elsewhere. German, French, Spanish and Italian were almost as familiar to him as his vernacular tongue, and he made good use of his linguistic learning. He compelled all these tongues to pay tribute to him during his pilgrimage to the celebrated libraries of Europe, in search of unpublished manuscripts referring to his native land, and the portraits of illustrions Irishmen who, after the Treaty of Limerick, had secured fame and fortune in the service of continental potentates.

As early as 1847 he published a translation of "La Monaco di Monza," from the original by Magoni. In 1852 he rendered the Rev. Father Marchese's "Dominican Sculptors, Architects and Painters" into English. His English version of Archdeacon Lynch's "Life of the Right Rev. Dr. Kirwan, Bishop of Killala," is translated from the Latin. This book has improved in the translation. All these works met with a large sale in Ireland and America; for the profit he cared but little.

From annals compiled by one John O'Toole of Wicklow, he wrote an excellent work on the O'Tooles and O'Byrnes, which is long since out of print. But his *great work*, as we have said before—the one on which his literary reputation principally rests—is familiarly known as the "Flight of the Earls."

For this work the reviewers had much praise. They spoke of it in the very highest terms. One Londoner wrote of it:

" The work is big enough, with its recondite research, its multiplicity of invaluable documents, dug out of the strata of libraries and museums, obtained at no mean inconvenience or cost, to be reckoned worthy of the labor of a man's life.

Sir Bernard Burke declared it to be a " most important contribution to the best historical literature;" and many other critics of high repute have spoken of it in words of like import.

The Hon. Thomas D'Arcy McGee wrote to the author from Montreal, Canada, under date of February 27th, 1867, as follows:

" MY DEAR MEEHAN:—Your book has reached me at last, and, after three days' steady reading, I have gone through it from cover to cover. I cannot tell you the fascination I found in its pages. Although I was sorry to part with Cahir O'Doherty, who turns out to be a poor tool, still one is compensated by the heroic firmness of the main figures, and, above all, by Tyrone himself. Considering the obsequiousness of the age which even Bacon and Raleigh bent to, I was afraid that the altered fortunes of the great Hugh might have broken his spirit and tempted him to some declaration unworthy of his great place in history; but, thank God, there is nothing of the kind, and these closing scenes are really among the fairest and worthiest of his whole life. * * *

" James Duffy has done his part nobly, not only to the typography, but those admirable portraits. How I wish you may be so cheered on as to take up Owen Roe! What an admirable sequel it would make to this volume, which, save and except Prendergast's, I hold to be far and away the most valuable contribution to our historical literature for many a long day. If you never put your pen to paper again, you may rest your renown on this book. It will send your name down to posterity with the heroes whose closing scenes it so piously records. * *

" Yours very truly,

" T. D. McGEE.

" REV. C. P. MEEHAN, M. R. I. A..
Dublin, Ireland."

Such was McGee's estimate of the work on which Father Meehan's renown rests.

The reverend writer did not "take up Owen Roe." The duties of his sacred calling were manifold, onerous and pressing, and the vigor of youth was ebbing fast away; so he deemed it best to leave that work for younger hands.

Towards the close of his years, Father Meehan lived a great deal by himself. His old friends and literary associates having all gone to their eternal home, he seemed lonely, and lived a great deal with God alone. Very few fully appreciated the high-souled, large-hearted, simple-minded priest whose noble life was so usefully spent in the service of God and his country.

" Though an honored member of the Royal Irish Academy," writes one who knew him, " he was full of that modesty and humility which are alike the

attributes of true genius and the·true priest." He
was never of a noisy or demonstrative nature. He
thought and felt more than he ever expressed in
words. Well, indeed, might these lines of the Poet-
Priest of the South be applied to that generous and
heroic priest whose heart, without a murmur, has
bled during many a dreary year for the miseries of
his ill-fated country:

> Hearts that are great beat never loud;
>   They muffle their music when they come,
> They hurry away from the thronging crowd
>   With bended brows and lips half dumb.
>
> And the world looks on and mutters: " Proud."
>   But when great hearts have passed away,
> Men gather in awe and kiss their shroud,
>   And in love they kneel around their clay.
>
>   *     *     *     *     *
>
> Hearts that are great are always lone,
>   They never will manifest their best;
> Their greatest greatness is unknown.
>   Earth knows a little—God the rest.

John Mitchel was Father Meehan's ideal of a true
Irish Nationalist, and between the two a lasting
friendship existed. Devin Reilly, Father John Ken-
yon and John Martin were also·in the circle of his
intimate friends. The portraits of these, with those
of Hugh O'Neill, O'Sullivan Beare, Colgan, and Luke

Wadding adorned his walls and kept him company in his hours of loneliness.

The latest edition of " The Poets and Poetry of Munster" was made by our author, and the preface to that very interesting little work, which is also the work of his fertile pen, seems to us the best, if not the most complete, biographical sketch of Clarence Mangan that has yet gone into print.

In concluding this biographical notice of a learned ecclesiastic whose name is so widely known and respected, it is proper to say a few words about his personal appearance. He was very little short of medium height, slender in form, with a well-knit frame and head well poised. His mouth, while indicating sensibility of the finest cast, at the same time betokened that firmness of purpose which was a distinguishing trait of the great good man. Intellectuality was stamped upon his finely-formed forehead; and his blue eyes, dreamy at times, kindled with a brilliant light whenever he discussed subjects congenial to his exalted mind.

In temperament he was purely Celtic—quick and impetuous. Next to his Breviary, which he conned over very carefully every day for more than fifty years, he loved the national poetry of Erin. His appreciation of a good poem was remarkably keen, and his criticism of a bad one telling.

As a preacher he was eloquent, earnest and impressive. The poor of his flock he relieved to the full extent of his means, and loved them only as a zealous priest can love.

The last four lines of the following melancholy little poem have haunted my memory for many years, and will not be forgotten. There is scarcely a couplet in all this exquisitely-mournful piece that is not worth remembering; and therefore do I give it a place in this brief memorial:

### THE FALL OF THE LEAVES.

THEY are falling, they are failing,
  And soon, alas! they'll fade,
The flowers of the garden,
  The leaves of dell and glade.

Their dirge the winds are singing
  In the lone and fitful blast,
And the leaves and flowers of Summer
  Are strewn and fading fast.

Oh, why, then, have we loved them,
  When their beauties might have told
They could not linger long with us,
  Nor stormy skies behold?

Fair creatures of the sunshine,
  Your day of life is past;
Ye are scattered by the rude winds,
  Fallen and fading fast.

And, oh! how oft, enchanted,
   Have we watched your opening **bloom,**
When you made unto the day-god
   Your offerings of perfume!

How vain are our imaginings
   That joy will always last!
'Tis like to you, ye sweet things,
   All dimmed and faded fast.

The glens where late ye bloomed for us
   Are leafless now, and lorn;
The tempest's breath hath all their pride
   And all their beauty shorn.

'Twas ever so, and so shall be;
   By fate that doom was cast—
The things we love are scarcely seen
   Till they are gone and past.

Ay, ye are gone and faded,
   Ye leaves and lovely flowers,
But when Spring comes you'll come again
   To deck the garden's bowers.

And beauty, too, will cull you,
   And twine ye in her hair—
What meeter, truer emblem
   Can beauty ever wear?

But never here, oh, never,
   Shall we the loved ones meet,
Who shone in youth around us
   And, like you, faded fleet.

Full soon affliction bowed them
    And life's day-dawn o'ercast;
They're blooming now in heaven;
    Their day of fading's past!

Ye withered leaves and flowers,
    Oh, may you long impart
Monition grave and moral stern
    Unto this erring heart!

Oh, teach it that the joys of earth
    Are short-lived, vain and frail,
And transient as the leaves and flowers
    Before the wintry gale!

On the 14th of March, 1890, Rev. Father Meehan died at the rectory, in Exchange street, Dublin, where he had labored so long, and his final resting place on earth is Glasnevin, which enshrines all that is mortal of many of his illustrious countrymen.

Of his ability as a historian he has left us palpable and ample proof.

Had the more serious obligations of his sacred calling permitted him to woo the muses more, he would have been equally successful as a poet. That he was one is amply attested by the poems published with this biography.

## THE BATTLE OF BENBURB.

[About the end of May, 1646, Owen Roe O'Neill, at the head of five thousand foot and five hundred horse, approached Armagh. Monroe, who was then stationed within ten miles of the city, marched thither on the 4th of June, at midnight, with eight hundred horse and six thousand foot. Meanwhile, O'Neill, aware of his advance, had encamped his troops at Benburb, betwixt two small hills. The rear of his army was protected by a wood, and the right by the river Blackwater. Here Monroe determiued to attack him. Monroe himself had passed the river at a ford near Kinard, and marched towards Benburb. And now the two armies met in order of battle. The wary O'Neill amused his enemy, during several hours, with various maneuvres and trifling skirmishes, until the sun, which at first had been favorable to the Scots, began to descend in the rear of the Irish troops, and shed a dazzling glare on their enemies. The Scottish General, when he perceived this prepared to retreat. O'Neill, however, seized the opportunity with the promptitude of an experienced commander, and charged the Scots and the British with the most determined valor, and with the result so graphically described by the poet.]

GIVE praise to the Virgin Mother! O'Neill is at Benburb,
The chieftain of the martial soul, who scorns the Saxon curb;
Between two hills his camp is pitch'd, and in its front upthrown,
The "Red Hand" points to victory from the standard of
    Tyrone;
Behind him rise the ancient woods, while on his flank, anear
    him,
The deep Blackwater calmly glides and seems to greet and
    cheer him.

'Tis a glorious morn in glowing June! against the sapphire sky,
Bright glancing in the golden light the adverse banners fly;
With godly boasts the Scottish host, led on by stout Monroe,
Have crossed the main with venal swords to aid our ruthless
    foe;
And never in sorer need than now, the steel of the hireling
    fenc'd him,
For a dauntless Chief, and mighty host, stand in array against
    him!

By all the Saints, they are welcome, across the crested wave!
For few who left Kinard this morn, ere night shall lack a grave.
The hour—the man—await them now, and retribution dire
Shall sweep their ranks from front to rear, by our avenging fire.
Yet on they marched in pride of heart—the hell-engendered
    gloom
Of the grim, predestin'd Puritan impels them to their doom.

A thrilling charge their trumpets blow, but the shout—" O'Neill'
    aboo!"
Is heard above the clarion call,—ringing the wild woods through!
" On," cries Lord Ardes, " On, Cunninghame! Forward with
    might and main!"
And the flower of Scottish chivalry come swooping down the
    plain.
Fiercely they dash and thunder on,—as the rathful waves come
    leaping
Toward Rathlin gray on a wild March day, when western
    winds are sweeping.

Now, where are thy hardy kerne, O'Neill? oh, whither have
    they fled?
Hurrah! that volley from out the brakes hath covered the
    sward with dead.
The horses rear, and in sudden fear, the Scottish warriors flee,
And the field is dyed with a crimson tide from their bravest
    cavalry!
All praise to the Right-protecting God, who guards his own in
    danger,
None fell save one of the Irish host by the gun of a baffled
    stranger.

"On to the charge!" cries fierce Monroe,—"Fear not the bush
    and scrog—
Nor that the river bound your right, and your left be flanked
    with bog."
And on they come right gallantly; but the Fabius of the West
Receives the shock, unmoved as a rock, and calm as a lion at
    rest;
The red artillery flashes in vain, or standeth spent and idle.
While the war-steeds bound across the plain, and foaming
    champ the bridle.

From the azure height of his realm of light the sun is sinking
    low,
And the blinding gleams of his parting beams dazzle the chafing
    foe;
And Owen's voice, like a trumpet note, rings clear through the
    serried ranks:
"Brave brothers in arms, the hour has come, give God and the
    Virgin thanks!
Strike home to-day, or heavier woes will crush our homes and
    altars;
Then trample the foeman in his blood, and curst be the slave
    who falters!"

A wild shout rends the lurid air, and at once from van to rear,
Of the Irish troops each soldier grasps his matchlock, sword or
    spear;
The chieftains haste their steeds to loose, and spring upon their
    feet,
That every chance be thus cut off, of a coward's base retreat.

And, "Onward! Forward!" swells the cry, in one tumultuous
    chorus,
By God and the Virgin's help, we'll drive these hireling Scots
    before us!"

'Tis body to body with push of pike—'tis foe confronting foe;
'Tis gun to gun and blade to blade—'tis blow returning blow.
Fierce is the conflict,—fell the strife; but Heaven defends the
    right.
The Puritan's sword is broken, and his army put to flight.
They break away in wild dismay, while some, to escape the
    slaughter,
Plunge panting into the purple tide that dyes the dark
    Blackwater.

May Mary, our Mother, be ever praised, for the battle fought
    and won!
By Irish hearts and Irish hands, beneath that evening sun.
Three thousand two hundred and forty foes lay dead upon the
    plain,
And the Scots bewailed of their noble chiefs, Lord Blaney
    among the slain.
And ever against a deadly foe no weaponed hand shall falter,
But strike, as the valiant Owen Roe, for home, and shrine, and
    altar!

# FITZ-JAMES O'BRIEN.

**T**HE subject of this sketch derives his origin from the most illustrious house in the history of his native land. The name alone brings to every mind well versed in the annals of Erin a long list of great deeds, coupled with constant fidelity to the cause of faith and fatherland.

This poet and *litterateur*, Fitz-James O'Brien, was born in the County of Limerick, early in the year of our Lord 1828, of parents who were neither poor nor wealthy. His father, an Irish barrister, took a special interest in the future bard, and devoted much of his leisure time in "teaching the young idea how to shoot," and instilling into the gifted mind of Fitz-James that love of philosophy and poetry which distinguished him afterwards in the world of letters. His mother was a lady of superior talent and refinement, much beloved by rich and poor alike for her piety and benevolence. From her, it is said, he inherited those traits of kindness and uprightness that characterized every act of his checkered career.

Having completed his primary education at home and become proficient in the classics, he entered Trinity College, Dublin, where he evinced great aptitude for literature, and acquired that solid and complete education which stood to him so well in the battle of life, and made him a remarkable man among the literary characters of the day.

While yet attending the College of "Old Trinity," and during his second summer vacation, he visited the places of interest along the sea-coast of the County Cork, and spent some days in the vicinity of *Loch Ine*—Lake of the Ivy—near the town of Baltimore, where he wrote that oft-quoted, much admired and beautiful ballad bearing the title "Loch

Ine." This is a picturesque salt-water lake south of Skibbereen, whose shores are dotted with the ivy-clad walls of many an ancient castle:

## LOCH INE.

I KNOW a lake where the cool waves break,
    And softly fall on the silver sand;
And no steps intrude on that solitude,
    And no voice, save mine, disturbs the strand.

And a mountain bold, like a giant of old,
    Turned to stone by some magic spell,
Uprears in might his misty height,
    And his craggy sides are wooded well.

In the midst doth smile a little isle,
    And its verdure shames the emerald's green;
On its grassy side, in ruined pride,
    A castle of old is darkling seen.

On its lofty crest the wild cranes nest,
    In its halls the sheep good shelter find;
And the ivy shades where a hundred blades
    Were hung, when the owners in sleep reclined.

That chieftain of old, could he how behold
    His lordly tower a shepherd's pen,
His corpse, long dead, from its narrow bed
    Would rise, with anger and shame, again.

'Tis sweet to gaze when the sun's bright rays
    Are cooling themselves in the trembling wave;
But 'tis sweeter far when the evening star
    Shines like a smile at Friendship's grave.

There the hollow shells, through their wreathed cells,
    Make music on the silent shore,'
As the summer breeze, through the distant trees,
    Murmurs in fragrant breathings o'er.

And the sea-weed shines, like the hidden mines,
    Or the fairy cities beneath the sea,
And the wave-washed stones are bright as the thrones
    Of the ancient Kings of Araby. ·

If it were my lot in that fairy spot
    To live forever and dream 'twere mine,
Courts might woo, and kings pursue,
    Ere I would leave thee, loved Loch Ine.

This magnificent poem has been published anonymously in the national school series of his native
land, and is as familiar to his countrymen as their
matin prayer.   It also appears anonymously at page
21, Vol. 1, of the "Ballads of Ireland," collected and
edited by Edward Hayes some thirty-five years ago,
and published by Duffy and Sons, Dublin.

The second volume of the same excellent work
contains another of Mr. O'Brien's early poems
named "Irish Castles," printed under the head of
"Miscellaneous Poems," and without the author's
name.

Having completed his curriculum in the great
university of the Irish metropolis, young O'Brien
received a considerable sum of money left him by
the will of his lately deceased father, and emigrated

to London in the fall of 1850; and there, report has it, disburdened himself of the greater part of his inheritance. Through the influence of Dr. Collins, he obtained from his distinguished countryman, Dr. R. Shelton Mackenzie, letters of introduction to prominent literary men in the United States, and, with these in his pocket as his only capital, Fitz-James O'Brien, young and buoyant with hope, sought the shores of the New World whither so many of his countrymen had gone before.

With the summer of 1852 he arrived in New York, where thenceforth he followed journalism as a profession, and secured for his friends and fellow-workers such men as John Brougham, Thomas B. Aldrich, Frank H. Bellew, Frank Wood, Edward F. Mullen, Stephen Fiske, Arnold, and the gifted, genial Ned Wilkins.

His first engagement in the great American metropolis was on the *Lantern*, published by Brougham. In a very short space of time the products of his fertile pen found a ready market, and the *Whig Review*, *Harper's Magazine*, the *Home Journal* and *New York Times* sought with avidity every article that came from his pen.

He was a regular contributor to *Harper's Magazine*, and one of the most valued members of the staff. His connection with that periodical dates from

February, 1853; and between that issue and the time of his death in 1862, his prolific genius may be traced through the most interesting pages of the monthly. His last contribution appeared in it in 1864, two years after poor O'Brien was laid in his final resting-place.

The greatest and best ode of our century was written by him on the death of the famous Arctic Explorer, Dr. Kane, and first appeared in *Harper's Weekly*, whence it was reproduced in almost every paper of note throughout the whole extent of the Republic. We reprint it here to give the readers a concept of our author's mastery over ideas and language:

### KANE.

### I.

ALOFT, upon an old basaltic crag,
Which, scalped by keen winds that defend the Pole,
Gazes with dead face on the seas that roll
Around the secret of the mystic zone,
A mighty nation's star-bespangled flag
          Flutters alone;
And underneath, upon the lifeless front
Of that drear cliff, a simple name is traced—
Fit type of him, who, famishing and gaunt,
But with a rocky purpose in his soul,
Breasted the gathering snows,
Clung to the different floes,
By want beleaguered, and by winter chased,
Seeking the brother lost amid that frozen waste.

## II.

Not many months ago we greeted him,
Crowned with the icy honors of the North.
Across the land his hard-won fame went forth,
And Maine's deep woods were shaken limb by limb.
His own mild Keystone State, sedate and prim,
Burst from its decorous quiet as he came.
Hot Southern lips, with eloquence aflame,
Sounded his triumph.   Texas, wild and grim,
Proffered it's horny hand.   The large-lunged West
From out it's giant breast
Yelled it's frank welcome.   And from main to main,
Jubilant to the sky,
Thundered the mighty cry,
                    Honor to Kane!

## III.

In vain, in vain, beneath his feet we flung
The reddening roses!   All in vain we poured
The golden wine, and round the shining board
Sent the toast circling, till the rafters rung
With the thrice-tripled honors of the feast!
Scarce the buds had wilted and the voices ceased
Ere the pure light that sparkled in his eyes,
Bright as auroral fires in southern skies,
Faded and faded; and the brave young heart
That the relentless Arctic winds had robbed
Of all its vital heat, in that long quest
For the lost Captain, now within his breast
More and more faintly throbbed.
His was the victory; but as his grasp
Closed on the laurel crown with eager clasp,

Death launched a whistling dart;
And, ere the thunders of applause were done,
His bright eyes closed forever on the sun!
Too late, too late, the splendid prize he won
In the Olympic race of science and of art!

## IV.

Like to some shattered berg that, pale and lone,
Drifts from the white north to a tropic zone,
And in the burning day
Wastes peak by peak away,
Till on some rosy even
It dies with sunlight blessing it; so he
Tranquilly floated to a southern sea,
And melted into heaven!

## V.

He needs no tears, who lived a noble life!
We will not weep for him who did so well;
But we will gather round the hearth and tell
The story of his strife.
Such homage suits him well;
Better than funeral pomp or passing-bell!

## VI.

What tale of peril and self-sacrifice!
Prisoned amid the fastnesses of ice,
With hunger howling o'er the waves of snow!
Night lengthening into months; the ravenous floe
Crunching the massive ships, as the white bear
Crunches his prey; the insufficient share
        Of loathsome food;

The lethargy of famine; the despair
Urging to labor, nervelessly pursued;
Toil done with skinny arms, and faces hued
Like pallid masks, while dolefully behind
Glimmered the fading embers of a mind!
That awful hour, when through the prostrate band
Delirium stalked, laying his burning hand
Upon the ghastly foreheads of the crew—
The whispers of rebellion, faint and few
At first, but deepening ever till they grew
Into black thoughts of murder—such the throng
Of horrors round the Hero. High the song
Should be that hymns the noble part he played!
Sinking himself, yet ministering aid
To all around him, by a mighty will
Living defiant of the wants that kill,
Because his death would seal his comrade's fate;
Cheering with ceaseless and inventive skill,
Those polar winters dark and desolate,
Equal to every trial, every fate,
He stands until spring, tardy with relief,
Unlocks the icy gate,
And the pale prisoners tread the world once more,
To the steep cliffs of Greenland's pastoral shore,
Bearing their dying chief.

## VII.

Time was when he should gain his spurs of gold
From royal hands, who wooed the knightly state;
The knell of old formalities is tolled,
And the world's knights are now self-consecrate.

No grander episode doth chivalry hold
In all its annals back to Charlemagne,
Than that long vigil of unceasing pain,
Faithfully kept, through hunger and through cold,
By the good Christian knight, ELISHA KANE.

He has written entirely about fifty poems, all or nearly all of which bear evidence of superior talent and will afford pleasure and instruction to many readers yet unborn.

A writer in the New York *Citizen* of September 30, 1865, referring to the dead poet, says:

" Fitz-James O'Brien would have passed anywhere for a fine-looking man, as he certainly was.   His complexion was florid; his eyes dark blue, with a marvellously winning expression.   His voice in speaking was the richest, the sweetest, the most persuasive and expressive of all the male voices I can now recall.   It was a power in itself.   I shall never forget the impression he made on a little party, one evening, by the manner in which he read several of Emerson's poems.   He threw so much warmth, so much human tenderness and sympathy into them that we were all astonished.   Then, artfully turning the leaves, as if still reading from the book, he recited his own

BACCHUS.

Pink as the rose was his skin so fair
Round as the rosebud his perfect shape,
And there lay a light in his tawny hair,
Like the sun in the heart of a bursting grape.

" You can fancy how we marveled to hear such luscious tropes from Emerson, and how we laughed over the deception when O'Brien informed us of it."

O'Brien's methods of working were in no wise systematic. He often let days and weeks pass without putting a pen to paper. Then, when the inspiration came, he wrote steadily and easily to the end, often without interruption.

One who admired and appreciated him, Stephen Fiske, fifteen years after the death of the poet, journalist and soldier, speaks of him thus:

"Fitz-James O'Brien now stands before me, and I see his stout, athletic figure; his broad, ruddy Irish face; his characteristic suit of that check pattern supposed to be monopolized by British tourists; and, indeed, in those merry Bohemian days, the checks he wore were the only ones he knew.   *   *   * O'Brien, like most of his comrades of that brilliant coterie we knew and loved, died too soon for his fame.  His writings were exquisite; but they are forgotten, except by the select few who collect and prize such literary gems.  The war interposes between his fame and the present generation, like a new deluge. The clear, strong, sweet voice of poetry was drowned by the clash of resounding arms.  Even as a soldier of the Union he fell too soon; for his memory is obscured by the holocausts of later but not more noble sacrifices."

Among O'Brien's writings are many plays which have met with great favor in New York.  For James W. Wallack he wrote a piece entitled, "A Gentleman from Ireland," which held its own on the stage for many years after the author was consigned to the grave.  He possessed great dramatic power and a consummate knowledge of stage business, and acted for some time in the capacity of stage critic and dramatic reviewer for the New York *Saturday Press.* Numerous articles from his pen are scattered through at least fifteen different periodicals, bearing the stamp of originality and genius upon them. His poems and about thirteen of his short stories have been published by Osgood & Co., Boston, Mass.; but the book is entirely out of print now.

A lover of liberty, equality, and the flag of his adopted country, he espoused the cause of the Union when the Civil War broke out in 1861, and, like thousands of his noble-hearted and enthusiastic countrymen, went proudly to the front. While acting on the staff of General Lander, in Virginia, he received a mortal wound in a skirmish with Colonel Ashley's command, on the 26th day of February, 1862, and died on the 6th of April following.

General Lander having commended Lieutenant O'Brien's behavior on this occasion in his dispatches to headquarters, General McClellan returned the following dispatch on the very next day:

"GENERAL LANDER:—Please say to Lieutenant O'Brien that I am much pleased with his gallantry, and deeply pained to hear of his wound. I trust he will soon be well enough to give the cause the benefit of his services again.

"GEORGE B. McCLELLAN."

He died at the house of a Mr. Thruston, in Cumberland, Maryland, on the day given above, and his remains were brought to New York by his numerous friends and associates, for interment in Greenwood Cemetery, where he sleeps the sleep that knows no waking.

He gave to his adopted land the products of his gifted mind to enrich her literature and exalt her name; with all the fervor and fidelity of his generous and heroic race, he championed her cause and laid down his life on the field of battle to maintain the integrity of her government.

## IRISH CASTLES.

SWEET Norah, come here, and look into the fire;
   Maybe in its embers good luck we might see;
But don't come too near, or your glances so shining,
   Will put it clean out, like the sunbeams, machree!

"Just look 'twixt the sods, where so brightly they're burning,
   There's a sweet little valley, with rivers and trees,
And a house on the bank, quite as big as the squire's—
   Who knows but some day we'll have something like these?

"And now there's a coach and four galloping horses,
   A coachman to drive, and a footman behind;
That betokens some day we will keep a fine carriage,
   And dash through the streets with the speed of the wind."

As Dermot was speaking, the rain down the chimney,
   Soon quenched the turf-fire on the hollowed hearth stone:
While mansion and carriage, in smoke-wreaths evanished,
   And left the poor dreamer dejected and lone.

Then Norah to Dermot. these words softly whisper'd:
   " 'Tis better to strive than to vainly desire:
And our little hut by the roadside is better
   Than palace, and servants, and coach—in the fire!"

'Tis years since poor Dermot his fortune was dreaming—
   Since Norah's sweet counsel effected its cure;
For, ever since then hath he toiled night and morning,
   And now his snug mansion looks down on the Suir.

FRIENDS far away—and late exiled,
  Whene'er these scattered pages met your gaze,
Think of the scenes where early fortune smiled—
  The land that was your home in happier days;
  The sloping lawn, in which the tired rays
Of evening stole o'er Shannon's sheeted flood,
  The hills of Clare that in the softening haze
Looked vapor-like, and dim the lonely wood;
  The cliff-bound *Inch*, the chapel in the glen,
Where oft with bare and reverent locks we stood
  To hear th' eternal truths; the small, dark maze
  Of wild stream that clipped the bosom'd plain,
And, toiling thro' the varied solitude,
  Upraised its hundred silvered tongues and babbled praise.

NEARLY fifty-one weary years have passed away since the author of this touching stanza, robed in the simple habit of a Christian Brother, breathed forth his pure and noble spirit into the hands of Him who gave it; and yet these lines have as much interest for "friends far away"—the Irish exiles of to-day—as they had for the generation to which they were addressed. Still is the mere mention of "that land that was his home in happier days" sufficient to bring a flood of affectionate feeling to the heart of every wanderer from that gifted, though ill-fated isle. As gentle Gerald, with patriotic pride and filial devotion, looked back from the cold

land of the Briton to the "cliff-bound Inch and
chapel in the glen," entwined with his fondest recollections, so does many a brave and loving heart to-
day turn from distant shores to those self-same
scenes, hallowed by a thousand memories. The feelings and affections of Gerald Griffin were in common

with the majority of our race, and hence it is that
we claim for him a foremost place in these pages.

Gerald, ninth son of Patrick Griffin, a Brunswick-
street brewer, was born on the 12th of December,
1803, within the old city wall of Limerick. His
mother, who was a woman of more than ordinary

taste and refinement, placed the future poet and novelist under the instruction of a certain Mr. MacEligot, at that time the most learned and successful "hedge teacher" in Limerick county. When Mrs. Griffin, accompanied by an elder brother, first introduced Gerald to this wondrous pedagogue, she remarked: "You will oblige me very much, Mr. MacEligot, by paying particular attention to the boys' pronunciation, and making them perfect in their reading." The knight of the *birchen-switches* gazed for a while with astonishment at her, and answering said: "You had better take your children home, madam. I can have nothing to do with them! Perhaps, Mrs. Griffin, you are not aware that there are only three persons in Ireland who know how to read." "Three persons!" exclaimed Mrs. Griffin. " Yes' madam, only three—the Bishop of Kildare, the Earl of Clare, and your humble servant. Reading is, indeed, a natural gift, not an acquirement." This was the man who first trained Gerald's "young idea how to shoot." After developing considerable talent at the school of Mr. MacEligot, young Gerald moved to a farm about thirty miles from the "City of the Broken Treaty." This homestead, beautifully situated on the banks of the Shannon, they called Fairy Lawn, and here a tutor was secured, under whose guidance and instruction young Griffin became familiar with the best authors in English literature, and cultivated a

taste and developed his talent for poetry. Even
when a mere boy he was a voracious devourer of
books, reading everything on which he could lay
hands, and even copying out with his ever busy pen
whatever struck him as beautiful or beneficial. He
transcribed almost all "Moore's Melodies" with such
care and exactitude as to omit not even a comma.

It is almost a truism that there were but few remarkable men in the world who did not draw their
best inspirations and most salutary principles of
morality from a good mother. Gerald's mother had
no small influence in forming the noble character of
her ninth son, and to the integrity of that well-
formed character he owed most of his success in after
life. This amiable lady is said to have been passionately fond of literature, and had an original turn of
mind. She was well acquainted with the best works
of English classic literature, and took great delight in
training her children to cultivate tastes similar to
her own in this respect. "But," says her son, "a
sound religious instruction she considered as the
foundation of everything good, and it was her constant aim to instill more strongly into the minds of
her children that nobility of sentiment and princely
feeling, in all transactions with others, which are its
necessary fruits, and which the world itself, in its
greatest faithlessness to religion, is compelled to worship. She would frequently, through the day, or in

the evening, ask us questions in history, and these were generally such as tended to strengthen our remembrance of important passages, or to point out in any historical character those traits of *moral beauty* she admired. 'Gerald,' I have heard her ask, 'what did Camillus say to the school-master of Falarii?' Gerald sat erect, his countenance glowing with the indignation such an act of baseness inspired, and repeated with energy: "'Execrable wretch,' cried the Roman, 'offer thy abominable proposals to some creature like thyself—and not to me. What! though we be enemies of your city, are there not natural ties that bind all mankind which should never be broken?'"

Mr Griffin being unsuccessful in business, was induced by one of his sons, who had been an officer in the British army in Canada, to emigrate to America. About the year 1820 a portion of the family found a new home on the banks of the Susquehanna, Pennsylvania, and this sweet spot they called Fairy Lawn, after the old home in the Green Isle. Gerald remained in Ireland, and resided with his brother, a medical doctor, in Adare. There, among the ruins of Erin's former splendor, he conned over the pages of Ovid and Virgil, or feasted on the lyrics of Horace; and there he felt the first inspiration of the muse which he has left us in a beautiful poem descriptive of the scenes and objects of his love:

## ADARE.

Oh, sweet Adare! oh, lovely vale!
   Oh, soft retreat of sylvan splendor·
Nor summer sun nor morning gale
   E'er hailed a scene more softly tender.
How shall I tell the thousand charms
   Within thy verdant bosom dwelling,
Where, lulled in Nature's fostering arms
   Soft peace abides and joy excelling.

Ye morning airs, how sweet at dawn
   The slumbering boughs your songs awaken,
Or linger o'er the silent lawn
   With odors of the hare-bell taken.
Thou rising sun, how richly gleams
   Thy smile from far Knock Fierna's mountain,
O'er waving woods and bounding streams,
   And many a grove and glancing fountain.

Ye clouds of noon, how freshly there,
   When summer heats the open meadows,
O'er parchèd hill and valley fair,
   All coolly lie your veiling shadows.
Ye rolling shades and vapors grey,
   Slow creeping o'er the golden heaven,
How soft you seal the eye of day,
   And wreath the dusky brow of even.

In sweet Adare, the jocund spring
   His notes of odorous joy is breathing.
The wild birds in the meadows sing;
   The wild flowers in the air are breathing.

There winds the Mague, as silver clear
    Among the elms so sweetly flowing;
There fragrant in the early year,
    Wild roses on the banks are blowing.

The wild duck seeks the sedgy bank,
    Or dives beneath the glistening billow,
Where graceful droop and clustering dank
    The osier bright and rustling willow.
The hawthorn scents the leafy dale,
    In thicket lone the stag is belling;
And sweet along the echoing vale
    The sound of vernal joy is swelling.

His passion for literature became so strong while
in Adare, that Gerald abandoned all idea of the
medical craft for which his parents, even then in
America, had destined him. His occasional contributions to the Limerick *Advertiser* attracted the
notice of Mr. McDonnell, then editor and proprietor
of that journal; and the young novelist, after a short
apprenticeship, was placed in the editorial chair of
the *Advertiser*. But the young patriotic Irishman,
instead of adhering to Mr. McDonnell's political
maxim to " please the Castle," "pulled the Castle
around that place-hunter's ears," and, in consequence,
was obliged to beat a hasty retreat from the *sanctum*
of the indignant politician. This was Gerald's starting point for fields of fame—for London—to " revo-

lutionize the dramatic taste of the time by writing for the stage." But we shall not follow him at present to recount his trials and triumphs in the smoky city. We shall linger to cull a few garlands from his poetry, which ought to be fostered and preserved in the household of every true-hearted Celt. The following lines never fail to awaken a responsive chord in every exile's bosom:

### OLD TIMES.

Old times! old times! the gay old times!
    When I was young and free,
And heard the merry Easter chimes
    Under the sally tree.
My Sunday palm beside me placed,
    My cross upon my hand;
A heart at rest within my breast,
    And sunshine on the land!
            Old times! old times!

It is not that my fortunes flee,
    Nor that my cheek is pale;
I mourn when e'er I think of thee,
    My darling native vale!
A wiser head I have, I know,
    Than when I loitered there;
But in my wisdom there is woe,
    And in my knowledge care.
            Old times! old times!

I've lived to know my share of joy,
  To feel my share of pain;
To learn that friendship's self can cloy,
  To love and love in vain;
To feel a pang and wear a smile,
  To tire of other climes;
To love my own unhappy Isle,
  And sing the gay old times!
              Old times! old times!

And sure the land is nothing changed;
  The birds are singing still,
The flowers are springing where we ranged,
  There's sunshine on the hill.
The sally waving o'er my head
  Still sweetly shades my frame;
But oh! those happy days are fled,
  And I am not the same.
              Old times! old times!

Oh, come again, ye merry times!
  Sweet, sunny, fresh and calm;
And let me hear those Easter chimes,
  And wear my Sunday palm.
If I could cry away mine eyes,
  My tears would flow in vain;
If I could waste my heart in sighs,
  They'll never come again!
              Old times! old times!

This sweet, simple poem which "looks longingly back to the days that are forever faded," surpasses in many respects that of Oliver W. Holmes on the same subject, so much admired and so deservedly popular. Once read, its euphonious measures haunt the memory in every stage of life, and gives expression to that yearning for the past so common to humanity. Gerald Griffin's " Sister of Charity " is well known to most readers of poetry.

This beautiful composition, with " O'Brazil the Isle of the Blest," and another equally moral, were written when Gerald began to see the vanity of human ambition, and to think seriously of embracing a religious state of life.

Griffin's lyrics are the best of his pieces, and his simple love songs are the best of all. It is believed, had he devoted his muse to writing songs for the people, that he would be to the "land of song" what Burns was to Scotland—a poet of and for the people. It is to be regretted that, on deciding to pursue a religious life, he destroyed a number of poems which were never published. They were, according to the opinion of his brother, superior to most of his published pieces; but he has left us enough to establish his reputation as a poet whose name is not soon destined to sink into oblivion.

In the autumn of 1823 this aspirant for literary laurels went to London, where he met John Banim and William Maginn, LL. D., the famous editor of *Frazer's Magazine*. Banim, who was then a great success in the literary world, became quite interested in Gerald, soon recognized his ability, and introduced him to the first literary lights of London. In a letter to his brother, Gerald says of Banim: "Mark me, he is a man—the best I have met since I left Ireland. We walked over Hyde Park on St. Patrick's Day, and renewed our home recollections by gathering shamrocks and placing them in our hats, even under the eye of John Bull." In the English metropolis, he was obliged to write for food instead of fame, and, though his tales and articles were promptly accepted by the best magazines, payment was by no means prompt or liberal. Some of the best pages of the *Literary Gazette* were filled by his pen, and the raciest articles of the *European Review* emanated from his fertile brain. He wrote plays which were admired; he translated Prevot's works at the rate of two guineas a volume, and, withal starved in a dark and dismal garret, where he was sought and saved by a kind friend. When discovered in this gloomy retreat he was working hard on one of his tales, though he had not tasted food for three days.

But this was the dark hour which preceded the dawn. The day of public patronage soon shone on him, and success crowned his persevering toil. In 1832 his play of "Gisippus," a tragedy in five acts, was performed in the Drury Lane Theatre, and received from both press and public a magnificent reception. We can best estimate the rapidity of his

success after this by an extract from one of his own
letters:—

"Since the day I received your letter," he says to his brother,
"I have achieved a multiplicity of engagements with publishers
and periodicals. In the first place, I procured an introduction
from Dr. Maginn to the editor of the *Literary Gazette* and got
an engagement from him to furnish sketches at a very liberal
remuneration— a guinea a page. * * *

"Then I sent articles to the *European Magazine*. Here, also,
I was successful—there was not a word of objection, and they
have already inserted several pieces. Then I made an essay on
one of the lions—the *London Magazine*—and was accepted there.
I know not what the proceeds will be yet, but I am told by an
old contributor that I made 'a palpable hit.' I also got an
engagement from the proprietor of the new Catholic newspaper,
by which I have already made several guineas."

Success was now at his command, but possession
seems to have destroyed the charm; for, though he
worked on still with characteristic determination
and energy he wrote to his brother:—

"I am sick and tired of this gloomy, stupid, lonely, wasting,
dispiriting, caterpillar kind of existence, which I endure, however, in hope of a speedy metamorphosis."

It was about this time that he wrote that sweet
pathetic little lyric, of which the following is a verse.
It is an index to his feelings at this stage:

> Why has my soul been given
> A zeal to soar to higher things
> Than quiet rest—to seek a haven
> And fall with scattered wings?

Have I been blest? the sea wave sings
'Tween me and all that was mine own;
I've found the joy Ambition brings,
And walk alone—and walk alone.

Our author's personal appearance, which was of
the best kind, may be inferred from a description
left by his brother, Dr. Griffin, who visited the
novelist in London in the month of September,
1826. "I had not seen him," says the Doctor, "since
he left Adare, and was struck with the change in his
appearance. All color had left his cheek, he had
grown quite thin, and there was a sedate expression
of countenance so unusual in one so young, and
which afterwards became habitual to him. It was
far from being so, however, at the time I speak of,
and readily gave way to that light and lively glance
of his dark eye, that cheerfulness of manner and
observant humor, which from his very infancy had
enlivened our fireside circle at home. Although so
pale and thin, his tall figure, expressive features and
profusion of dark hair thrown back over his fine
forehead, gave an expression of a person remarkably
handsome and interesting."

Here it may not be out of place to mention a very
interesting episode which gave a tinge of romance to
the last ten or twelve years of Gerald Griffin's life.
In Limerick he became acquainted with a certain
gentleman and his wife, members of the Society of

Friends, and a very strong natural attachment soon
formed between them and the amiable author of the
"Collegians." "The feelings of the poet towards the
lady," says Mr. Giles, "though evidently of reveren-
tial purity, were colored—nay beautified—by the
difference of sex. His letters to her were numerous,
eloquent and very often of an elevated character.
His last letter, presenting her with an old desk on
which all his literary work had been accomplished,
was tender and musical with pathos and affection.
Shortly after he became a monk she called upon him.
When her name was announced he was walking in
the garden. He turned pale, hesitated, but at last,
though with strong emotion, refused to see her." On
hearing of his decision, the affectionate lady burst
into tears, for something seemed to tell her that she
would never more see him on earth

The "Collegians," in which he was destined to live
a long time, was written in his 25th year, and the
tragedy of "Gisippus" five years earlier. The stories
which he wrote consist of three series: "Tales of the
Munster Festivals," "Tales of the Jury Room" and
"Holland Tide Tales." His romances are three—
"The Duke of Monmouth," "The Invasion" and
"The Collegians." These, with his plays and poems,
comprise ten handsome volumes published by Sadlier
& Co., New York. As a poet he was sensitive, sweet,
sympathetic and simple. As a novelist he had a

genius at the same time inventive, plastic and bold. His style manifests fancy in a high degree, and his strong natural passion betrays itself very powerfully in many scenes of the "Collegians." In portraying Irish life, he "holds the mirror up to nature." In his literary career he acted in the capacity of musical and stage critic, was employed as Parliamentary reporter, and considered by many London publishers as a consummate literary *connoisseur*.

As to his moral strength and integrity, the eloquent Henry Giles says: "Perhaps no literary adventurer ever endured more hardships in the same space of time in London than did Gerald Griffin, and endured them with less moral injury to his personal or literary character. He kept himself free from all meanness, from low companionship, from degrading habits, and came out of the trial a young man with home-born purity unsullied, a Christian with faith more confirmed, a gentleman unharmed in his honor and refinement, a writer who won success and the public by his own independent genius, bearing the triumph with true and graceful modesty." While blessed with the self-reliance of Johnson, he was entirely free from the egotism of that literary lion. "It is strange," he was wont to say, "that I've never found success except where I depended solely on my own exertions." His motto was "death before failure." Though he wrote nothing so universally admired as the "Deserted Village" or the "Vicar of Wakefield," he possessed nearly as much ability as Goldsmith, without being burdened by any of his defects; and, according to most writers, he was superior both as an author and a man to Dermody and Crabbe.

For some time previous to 1830 our young novelist entertained an idea that he was called to the priesthood, and actually made preparations to enter the Ecclesiastical Seminary at Maynooth for that end In à letter to his parents, on the banks of the Susquehanna, he alludes to this matter as follows:

" To say nothing of the arguments of faith, I do not know any station in life in which a man can do so much good, both for others and himself, as in that of a Catholic priest, and it gave me great satisfaction to find that my friends in America were of the same mind with me on this point. * * * * To say that Gerald, the novel writer, is by the grace of God really satisfied to lay aside for ever all hope of that fame for which he was once sacrificing health, repose and pleasure, and to offer himself as a laborer in the vineyard of Jesus Christ. That literary reputation has become a worthless trifle to him to whom it was once almost all; and that he feels a happiness in the thought of giving all to God is such a merciful favor that all the fame and riches in the world dwindle into nothing at the thought of it."

The idea of becoming a priest, however, he soon abandoned—partly, perhaps, through motives of humility—and resolved to assume the humble habit of a Christian Brother. His brief career with this exemplary body of monks was very happy, and on many occasions he manifested his delight with his vocation. At the instance of his religious superior, he resumed his long-neglected pen, and was engaged on a religious tale, entitled "The Holy Island" when he was stricken down with typhus fever, of which he died at the North Monastery of the Brothers, in the City of Cork, on Friday, June 12th, 1840. In the little cemetery of this Monastery a simple headstone bearing the inscription "Joseph"—his name in religion—still marks the resting-place of the author of the "Collegians," and invites the passing monk to recite a *De Profundis* for the soul of Ireland's beloved poet, reposing there in silence and solitude.

## O'BRAZIL, THE ISLE OF THE BLEST.

[A spectre island, said to be sometimes visible on the verge of the western horizon in the Atlantic, from the Isles of Arran.]

On the ocean that hollows the rocks where ye dwell,
A shadowy land has appeared, as they tell;
Men thought it a region of sunshine and rest,
And they called it O'Brazil—the Isle of the Blest.
From year unto year, on the ocean's blue rim,
The beautiful spectre showed lovely and dim;
The golden clouds curtained the deep where it lay,
And it looked like an Eden, away, far away!

A peasant who heard of the wonderful tale,
In the breeze of the orient, loosened his sail;

From Ara, the holy, he turned to the west,
For though Ara was holy, O'Brazil was blest.
He heard not the voices that called from the shore,
He heard not the rising winds' menacing roar;
Home, kindred and safety he left on that day,
And he sped to O'Brazil, away, far away!

Morn rose on the deep, and that shadowy Isle,
O'er the faint rim of distance reflected its smile;
Noon burned on the wave, and that shadowy shore,
Seemed lovelily distant, and faint as before:
Lone evening came down on the wanderer's track,
And to Ara again he looked timidly back;
Oh! far on the verge of the ocean it lay,
Yet the Isle of the Blest was away, far away.

Rash dreamer, return! O ye winds of the main,
Bear him back to his own peaceful Ara again;
Rash fool! for a vision of fanciful bliss,
To barter thy calm life of labor and peace.
The warning of Reason was spoken in vain,
He never re-visited Ara again;
Night fell on the deep, amidst tempest and spray,
And he died on the waters, away, far away!

To you, gentle friends, need I pause to reveal
The lessons of prudence my verses conceal?
How the phantom of pleasure, seen distant in youth,
Oft lures a weak heart from the circle of truth,
All lovely it seems like that shadowy Isle,
And the eye of the wisest is caught by its smile; .
But ah! for the heart it has tempted to stray
From the sweet home of duty, away, far away!

Poor friendless adventurer! vainly might he
Look back to green Ara, along the wild sea;
But the wandering heart has a guardian above,
Who, though erring, remembers the child of his love.
Oh! who at the proffer of safety would spurn,
When all that he asks is the will to return?
To follow a phantom from day unto day,
And die in the tempest, away, far away!


## 'T IS, IT IS THE SHANNON'S STREAM.

'T IS, it is the Shannon's stream
    Brightly glancing, brightly glancing!
See, oh see the ruddy beam
    Upon its waters dancing!
Thus returned from travel vain,
Years of exile, years of pain,
To see old Shannon's face again,
    Oh, the bliss entrancing!
Hail! our own majestic stream,
    Flowing ever, flowing ever,
Silent in the morning beam,
    Our own beloved river!

Fling thy rocky portals wide
    Western ocean, western ocean;
Bend ye hills on either side,
    In solemn, deep devotion;
While before the rising gales
On his heaving surface sails,
Half the wealth of Erin's vales
    With undulating motion.

Hail! our own beloved stream,
    Flowing ever, flowing ever,
Silent in the morning beam,
    Our own majestic river!

On thy bosom deep and wide,
    Noble river, lordly river,
Royal navies safe might ride,
    Green Erin's lovely river!
Proud upon thy banks to dwell,
Let me ring Ambition's knell
Lured by Hope's illusive spell
    Again to wander, never.
Hail! our own romantic stream,
    Flowing ever, flowing ever,
Silent in the morning beam,
    Our own majestic river!

Let me, from thy placid course,
    Gentle river, mighty river,
Draw such truth of silent force,
    As sophist uttered never.
Thus, like thee, unchanging still,
With tranquil breast and ordered will,
My heaven-appointed course fulfil,
    Undeviating ever!
Hail! our own majestic stream
    Flowing ever, flowing ever,
Silent in the morning beam,
    Our own delightful river!

## THE BRIDAL OF MALAHIDE.

[Of the monuments most worthy of notice in the chapel of Malahide is an altar tomb surmounted with the effigy, in bold relief, of a female habited in the costume of the 14th century, and representing the Honorable Maude Plunket, wife of Sir Richard Talbot. She had been previously married to Mr. Hussey, son to the Baron of Galtrim, who was slain on the day of her nuptials, leaving her the singular celebrity of having been "A maid, wife and widow, on the same day."—*Dalton's History of Drogheda.*]

THE joy-bells are ringing in gay Malahide;
The fresh wind is singing along the sea-side;
The maids are assembling with garlands of flowers,
And the harpstrings are trembling in all the glad bowers.

Swell, swell the gay measure! roll trumpet and drum!
'Mid greetings of pleasure in splendor they come!
The chancel is ready, the portal stands wide
For the lord and the lady, the bridegroom and bride.

What years, ere the latter, of earthly delight
The future shall scatter o'er them in its flight!
What blissful caresses shall Fortune bestow,
Ere those dark-flowing tresses fall white as the snow!

Before the high altar young Maud stands array'd;
With accents that falter her promise is made—
From father and mother for ever to part,
For him and no other to treasure her heart.

The words are repeated, the bridal is done,
The rite is completed—the two, they are one;
The vow, it is spoken all pure from the heart,
That must not be broken till life shall depart.

Hark! 'mid the gay clangor that compass'd their car,
Loud accents in anger come mingling afar!
The foe's on the border, his weapons resound
Where the lines in disorder unguarded are found.

As wakes the good shepherd, the watchful and bold,
When the ounce or the leopard is seen in the fold,
So rises already the chief in his mail,
While the new-married lady looks fainting and pale.

"Son, husband, and brother, arise to the strife,
For the sister and mother, for children and wife!
O'er hill and o'er hollow, o'er mountain and plain,
Up, true men, and follow! let dastards remain!"

Farrah! to the battle! they form into line—
The shields, how they rattle! the spears, how they shine!
Soon, soon shall the foeman his treachery rue—
On, burgher and yeoman, to die or to do!

The eve is declining in low Malahide,
The maidens are twining gay wreaths for the bride;
She marks them unheeding—her heart is afar,
Where the clansmen are bleeding for her in the war.

Hark! loud from the mountain, 'tis Victory's cry!
O'er woodland and fountain it rings to the sky!
The foe has retreated! he flies to the shore;
The spoiler's defeated—the combat is o'er!

With foreheads unruffled the conquerors come—
But why have they muffled the lance and the drum?
What form do they carry aloft on his shield?
And where does he tarry, the lord of the field?

Ye saw him at morning how gallant and gay!
In bridal adorning the star of the day:
Now weep for the lover—his triumph is sped;
His hope it is over! the chieftain is dead!

But, oh for the maiden who mourns for that chief,
With heart overladen and rending with grief!
She sinks on the meadow—in one morning-tide,
A wife and a widow, a maid and a bride!

Ye maidens attending, forbear to condole!
Your comfort is rending the depths of her soul.
True—true, 'twas a story for ages of pride;
He died in his glory—but, oh, he *has* died!

The war cloak she raises all mournfully now,
And steadfastly gazes upon the cold brow.
That glance may for ever unaltered remain,
But the bridegroom will never return it again.

The dead-bells are tolling in sad Malahide,
The death-wail is rolling along the sea-side;
The crowds, heavy-hearted, withdraw from the green,
For the sun has departed that brighten'd the scene!

Ev'n yet in that valley, though years have roll'd by,
When through the wild sally the sea-breezes sigh,
The peasant, with sorrow, beholds in the shade
The tomb where the morrow saw Hussey convey'd.

How scant was the warning, how briefly reveal'd,
Before on that morning death's chalice was fill'd!
The hero that drunk it there moulders in gloom,
And the form of Maude Plunket weeps over his tomb.

12

The stranger who wanders along the lone vale
Still sighs when he ponders on that heavy tale;
" Thus passes each pleasure that earth can supply—
Thus joy has its measure—we live but to die!"

## WHEN FILLED WITH THOUGHTS OF LIFE'S YOUNG DAY.

WHEN filled with thoughts of life's young day,
   Alone in distant climes I roam,
And year on year has rolled away
   Since last we view'd our own dear home,
Oh, then, at evening's silent hour,
In chamber lone, or moonlit bow'r,
How sad, on memory's listening ear,
Come long lost voices sounding near—
Like the wild chime of village bells
Heard far away in mountain dells.

But, oh! for him let kind hearts grieve,
   His term of youth and exile o'er,
Who sees in life's declining eve,
   With alter'd eyes, his native shore!
With aching heart and weary brain,
Who treads those lonesome scenes again!
When first he knew those ruin'd bow'rs,
And hears in every passing gale
Some best affection's dying wail.

Oh, say, what spell of power serene
   Can cheer that hour of sharpest pain,
And turn to peace the anguish keen
   That deeplier wounds, because in vain?
'T is not the thought of glory won,
Of hoarded gold or pleasures gone,

But one bright course, from earliest youth,
Of changeless faith—unbroken truth,
These turn to gold the vapors dun
That close on life's descending sun.

## FOR I AM DESOLATE.

THE Christmas light is burning bright
  In many a village pane,
And many a cottage rings to-night
  With many a merry strain.
Young boys and girls run laughing by,
  Their hearts and eyes elate—
I can but think on mine, and sigh,
  For I am desolate.

There's none to watch in our old cot,
  Beside the holy light,
No tongue to bless the silent spot
  Against the parting night,
I've closed the door, and hither come
  To mourn my lonely fate;
I cannot bear my own old home,
  It is so desolate!

I saw my father's eye grow dim,
  And clasp'd my mother's knee;
I saw my mother follow him—
  My husband wept with me.
My husband did not long remain—
  His child was left me yet;
But now my heart's last love is slain,
  And I am desolate!

## MY MARY OF THE CURLING HAIR.

My Mary of the curling hair,
The laughing teeth and bashful air,
Our bridal morn is dawning fair,
    With blushes in the skies.
        Come! come! come, my darling—
        Come softly, and come, my love!
          My love! my pearl!
          My own dear girl!
        My mountain maid, arise!

Wake, linnet of the osier grove!
Wake, trembling, stainless, virgin dove!
Wake, nestling of a parent's love!
    Let Moran see thine eyes.
          Come, come, etc.

I am no stranger, proud and gay,
To win thee from thy home away,
And find thee, for a distant day,
    A theme for wasting sighs.
          Come, come, etc.

But we were known from infancy,
Thy father's hearth was home to me,
No selfish love was mine for thee,
    Unholy and unwise.
          Come, come; etc.

And yet, (to see what love can do!)
Though calm my hope has burned, and true,
My cheek is pale and worn for you,
    And sunken are mine eyes!
          Come, come, etc.

But soon my love shall be my bride,
And happy by our own fireside;
My veins shall feel the rosy tide
   That lingering hope denies.
             Come, come, etc.

My Mary of the curling hair,
The laughing teeth and bashful air,
Our bridal morn is dawning fair,
   With blushes in the skies.
     Come! come! come, my darling—
     Come softly! and come, my love!
       My love! my pearl!
       My own dear girl!
     My mountain maid, arise!

## GILLE MA CHREE.

*Gille ma chree,*\*
   Sit down by me;
We now are joined and ne'er shall sever:
    This hearth's our own,
    Our hearts are one,
And peace is ours for ever!

    When I was poor,
    Your father's door
Was closed against your constant **lover**;
    With care and pain,
    I tried in vain
My fortunes to recover.

---

\* Brightener of my heart.

I said, "To other lands I'll roam,
Where Fate may smile on me, love;"
I said, "Farewell, my own old home!"
And I said, "Farewell to thee, love!"
          Sing, *Gille ma chree*, etc.

I might have said,
My mountain maid,
Come live with me, your own true lover:
I know a spot,
A silent cot,
Your friends can ne'er discover,
Where gently flows the waveless tide
By one small garden only;
Where the heron waves his wings so wide,
And the linnet sings so lonely!
          Sing, *Gille ma chree*, etc.

I might have said,
My mountain maid,
A father's right was never given
True hearts to curse
With tyrant force
That have been blest in heaven.
But then I said, "In after years,
When thoughts of home shall find her,
My love may mourn with secret tears
Her friends thus left behind her."
          Sing, *Gille ma chree*, etc.

"Oh no," I said;
"My own dear maid,
For me, though all forlorn for ever,
That heart of thine
Shall ne'er repine
O'er slighted duty—never.
From home and thee, though wandering far,
A dreamy fate be mine, love—
I'd rather live in endless war,
Than buy my peace with thine, love."
                    Sing, *Gille ma chree*, etc.

Far, far away,
By night and day,
I toiled to win a golden treasure;
And golden gains
Repaid my pains
In fair and shining measure.
I sought again my native land,
Thy father welcomed me, love;
I poured my gold into his hand
And my guerdon found in thee, love.

Sing, *Gille ma chree*,
Sit down by me;
We are joined and ne'er shall sever:
This hearth's our own,
Our hearts are one,
And peace is ours for ever.

## A PLACE IN THY MEMORY, DEAREST.

A PLACE in thy memory, dearest,
  Is all that I claim,
To pause and look back when thou hearest
  The sound of my name.
Another may woo thee, nearer,
  Another may win and wear;
I care not though he be dearer,
  If I am remembered there.

Remember me—not as a lover
  Whose hope was cross'd,
Whose bosom can never recover
  The light it hath lost;
As the young bride remembers the mother
  She loves, though she never may see;
As a sister remembers a brother,
  O dearest! remember me.

Could I be thy true lover, dearest,
  Could'st thou smile on me,
I would be the fondest and nearest
  That ever loved thee!
But a cloud on my pathway is glooming,
  That never must burst upon thine;
And Heaven, that made thee all blooming,
  Ne'er made thee to wither on mine.

Remember me, then!—oh, remember,
  My calm, light love;
Though bleak as the blasts of November
  My life may prove,

That life will, though lonely, be sweet,
　If its brightest enjoyment should be
A smile and kind word when we meet,
　And a place in thy memory.

## LINES ADDRESSED TO A SEAGULL,

SEEN OFF THE CLIFFS OF MOHER, IN THE COUNTY OF CLARE.

WHITE bird of the tempest! oh, beautiful thing,
With the bosom of snow, and the motionless wing
Now sweeping the billow, now floating on high,
Now bathing thy plumes in the light of the sky·
Now poising o'er ocean thy delicate form.
Now breasting the surge with thy bosom so warm,
Now darting aloft, with a heavenly scorn,
Now shooting along, like a ray of the morn;
Now lost in the folds of the cloud-curtained dome,
Now floating abroad like a flake of the foam;
Now silently poised o'er the war of the main,
Like the spirit of charity, brooding o'er pain;
Now gliding with pinion, all silently furled,
Like an Angel descending to comfort the world!
Thou seem'st to my spirit, as upward I gaze,
And see thee, now clothed in mellowest rays;
Now lost in the storm-driven vapors that fly,
Like hosts that are routed across the broad sky!
Like a pure spirit, true to its virtue and faith,
'Mid the tempests of nature, of passion, and death!

Rise! beautiful emblem of purity! rise
On the sweet winds of heaven, to thine own brilliant skies
Still higher! still higher! till lost to our sight,
Thou hidest thy wings in a mantle of light;

And I think how a pure spirit gazing on thee,
Must long for the moment—the joyous and free—
When the soul, disembodied from nature, shall spring,
Unfettered, at once to her maker and king;
When, the bright day of service and suffering past,
Shapes fairer than thine shall shine round her at last,
While the standard of battle triumphantly furled,
She smiles like a victor, serene on the world!

## A MONODY ON THE DEATH OF GERALD GRIFFIN,

### BY THOMAS D'ARCY M'GEE.

[Written during the author's visit to Ireland in March, 1855.]

WHEN night surrounds the sun, and the day dies,
Leaving to darkness for its hour the skies,
Nought has the heart of man thence to deplore—
The day lived long, was fruitful, is no more;
But when the hurricane at noon o'erspreads
The orb divine, which life and gladness sheds,
Or some disorder'd planet rolls between
The sun and earth, darkling the verdant green,
Eclipsing ocean, shadowing like a pall
The busy town,—men, discontented all,
By sea and land, anxiously pause and pray
For the returning giver of the day—
So have bright spirits been eclipsed and lost,
Forever dark, if by Death's shadow cross'd.

In Munster's beauteous city died a man
As 'twere but yesterday, whose course began
In clouded and in cheerless morning guise—
Had climb'd the summit of his native skies,

And, as he rose, brighter and fairer grew,
Beneath his influence, every scene he knew.
His country hail'd him as a Saviour, given
To chronicle past times; when 'mid the heaven
Of expectation and achievement, lo!
A monastery's gate—therein the Bard doth go,
And sees the children of the poor around
Feed on the knowledge elsewhere yet unfound.
The Poet, then, his former tasks foreswore,
Vowing himself to charity evermore,—
Folded his wings of light—cast his fresh bays aside—
His friends beloved abjured, abjured his pride,
There lived and labor'd, and there early died

Short was his day of labor, but its morn
Prolific was of beauty; thoughts were born
In his heart's secret spots, which grew, attended
By a fine sense—instinct and reason blended—
Till, like a spring, they spread his haunts with glory,
O'er-arched their streams, upraised their hills in story,
Fixed the broad Shannon in its course forever,
And bade it flow for aye, a genius-haunted river.

Ye men of Munster, guard his sleep serene!
Spirits of such bright order are not seen
But once in generations.   He was an echo, dwelling
Amid your mountains, all their secrets telling,
Their mem'ries, their traditions, and their wrongs,
The story of their sins—the music of their songs,
Their tempests, and their terrors, and the forms
They bring forth, impregnated by the storms.

He knew the voices of your rivers, knew
Every deep chasm they leap or murmur through,—
Blindfold, at midnight, by their sounds could tell
Their names and their descent o'er cliff and dell.
Oh! men of Munster, since the ancient time,
Ye have not met such loss as in this monk sublime!

The second summer's grass was on his grave,
When to his memory Melpomene gave
A laurel wreath wove from the self-same tree
That shades Boccaccio's dust perennially;
Fair were the smiles her mournful glances met
In woman's lovely eyes, with heart's-dew wet,
And many voices loudly cried, "Well done!"
As the sad goddess crown'd her lifeless son.
Oh, ever thus: Death strikes the gifted, then
Come the worms—inquests—and the award of men!

Low in your grave, young Gerald Griffin, sleep;
You never looked on him who now doth weep
Above your resting-place—yon never heard
The voice that oft has echo'd every word
Dropped from your pen of light—sleep on, sleep on—
I would I knew you, yet not—now you are gone!

# REV. CHARLES WOLFE,

AUTHOR OF "THE BURIAL OF SIR JOHN MOORE."

IKE Ingram and Gray the Rev. Charles Wolfe is known to the world as the author of a single song. "The Burial of Sir John Moore" has made his name immortal.

He was born in the city of Dublin in the year 1791. His parents were people of means, and his family not without distinction both in Ireland and America. The brilliant but ill-fated Wolfe Tone and the hero of Quebec were closely allied to his family, and others of the same name and lineage subsequently became distinguished in the annals of Irish history. In 1809 Charles Wolfe entered Trinity College, Dublin, after having spent some years of preparation at school in England.

His poetic genius was first revealed to the faculty of the University by the excellence of a Latin class-poem which he wrote during the early part of his second year. But the composition which brought him prominently into public favor was the ode on the burial of Sir John Moore. Lord Byron, seeing this poem, pronounced it "the very best of its kind which the present prolific age has brought forth."

"Medwin's Conversations of Byron," relating a critical discussion that arose between Byron, Shelley and other literary men of their time, has the following passages:

The conversation, after dinner, turned on the lyrical poetry of the day, and a question arose as to which was the most perfect ode that had been produced in the English language. Shelly contended for Coleridge's on Switzerland, beginning— "Ye Clouds," etc. Others named some of Moore's Irish Melodies and Campbell's "Hohenlinden;" and had Lord Byron not been present, the Invocation in "Manfred" or the Ode to Napoleon might have been cited.

"Like Gray," said Byron, "Campbell smells too much of the oil; he is never satisfied with what he does; his finest things have been spoiled by the 'labor of the file.' Like paintings, poems may be too highly finished. The great art is effect, no matter how produced. I will show you an ode you have never seen, that I consider the very best which the present prolific age has brought forth." With this he left the table, almost before the cloth was removed, and soon returned with a magazine from which he read the lines on Sir John Moore's burial. The feeling with which he recited these admirable stanzas I I shall never forget. After he had come to the end he repeated the third, and said it was perfect, particularly the lines:

"But he lay, like a warrior taking his rest,
With his martial cloak around him.

"I should have taken the whole," said Shelley, "for a rough sketch of Campbell's."

"No," replied Byron; "Campbell would have claimed it if it had been his."

The account of Sir John Moore's burial which inspired our author to write this poem was first printed in a Scotch paper, and runs thus:

Sir John Moore had often said that, if he was killed in battle, he wished to be buried where he fell. The body was removed at midnight to the citadel of Corunna, A grave was dug for him on the rampart there, by a party of the Ninth Regiment, the aides-de-camp attending by turns. No coffin could be procured, and the officers of his staff wrapped the body, dressed as it was, in a military cloak and blankets. The interment was hastened, for about eight in the morning some firing was heard, and the officers feared that if a serious attack were made, they should be ordered away and not suffered to pay him their last duty. The officers of his staff bore him to the grave. The funeral service was read by the chaplain and the corpse was covered with earth.

This is the simple narrative that produced the impression which prompted and enabled Wolfe to write his famous poem. His biographer, Archdeacon Russell of Clogher, informs us that it found its way into print without the knowledge of its author.

"It was," he goes on to say, "recited by a friend in presence of a gentleman traveling toward the North of Ireland, who was so much struck with it that he requested and obtained a copy, and, immediately after, it appeared in the *Newry Telegraph* with the initials of the author's name. From that it was copied into most of the London prints, and thence into the Dublin papers, and subsequently it appeared

with some considerable errors in the *Edinburgh
Annual Register,* which contained the narrative that
first kindled the poet's feelings on the subject, and
supplied the materials to his mind."

Besides these given in this volume Wolfe wrote
many other pieces of lesser note. He was ordained
a minister of the Anglican Church, in 1817, and
appointed to a living in Donoughmore, within the
jurisdiction of Armagh. Here he lived for some
years, devoting a good deal of his time to the study of
Irish authors, and preaching when it came his turn
to do so. Ireland's great lyrist, Tom Moore, was his
favorite poet, and it is said that there were very few
contemporaries who possessed a keener appreciation
of the Irish Melodies than did the Rev. Charles
Wolfe.

After a few short years in the ministry, he became
the victim of consumption, which in a brief space
closed a career that opened with the promise of much
more than was ever realized.

With the fond hope of prolonging his life he left
Donoughmore and went southward to that beautiful
watering-place called, in those days, the Cove of Cork.
Even the balmy air of Munster could not restore his
wasted strength or retard the progress of the fatal
disease. He died at Cove in 1823, and was buried
in the neighboring churchyard of Clonmel Parish,
where his grave is almost entirely neglected. Is the

spirit of utilitarianism creeping into Ireland that his countrymen should neglect the final resting-place of this gentle poet? Alas! such is the common fate of genius!

The following lines are from the pen of an American poetess, Mrs. S. M. B. Piatt, the accomplished wife of our Consul at Cork. She was naturally surprised that a people proverbially so fond of poetry should neglect the grave of one whose name has reflected credit on his native land:

## AT THE GRAVE OF REV. CHARLES WOLFE.

WHERE graves were many, we looked for one—
  Oh, the Irish rose was red—
And the dark stones saddened the setting sun
  With the names of the early dead.
Then a child who, somehow, had heard of him
  In the land we love so well,
Kept lifting the grass till the dew was dim
  In the churchyard of Clonmel.

But the sexton came. "Can you tell us where
  Charles Wolfe is buried?" "I can.
See, that is his grave in the corner there—
  Aye, he was a clever man,
If God had spared him! It's many that come
  To be asking for him," said he;
But the boy kept whispering "Not a drum
  Was heard," in the dusk to me.

Then the gray man tore a vine from the wall
  Of the roofless church where he lay,
And the leaves that the withering year let fall,
  He swept with the 'ivy away.
And, as we read on the rock the words
  That, writ in the moss, we found,
Right over his bosom a shower of birds
  In music fell to the ground.

Young poet, I wonder did you care—
  Did it move you in your rest—
To hear that child in his golden hair,
  From the mighty woods of the West,
Repeating your verse of his own sweet will
  To the sound of the twilight bell,
Years after your beating heart was still
  In the churchyard of Clonmel?

## THE BURIAL OF SIR JOHN MOORE.

NOT a drum was heard, not a funeral note,
  As his corse to the ramparts we hurried;
Not a soldier discharged his farewell shot
  O'er the grave where our hero we buried.

We buried him darkly at dead of night,
  The sods with our bayonets turning;
By the struggling moonbeam's misty light,
  And the lantern dimly burning.

No useless coffin enclosed his breast,
  Nor in sheet or in shroud we wound him;
But he lay, like a warrior taking his rest,
  With his martial cloak around him.

Few and short were the prayers we said,
  And we spoke not a word of sorrow;
But we steadfastly gazed on the face of the dead,
  And we bitterly thought of the morrow.

We thought as we hollow'd his narrow bed,
  And smoothed down his lonely pillow,
That the foe and the stranger would tread o'er his head
  And we far away on the billow.

Lightly they'll talk of the spirit that's gone,
  And o'er his cold ashes upbraid him;
But little he'll reck, if they let him sleep on
  In the grave where a Briton has laid him!

But half of our heavy task was done
  When the clock struck the hour for retiring,
And we heard the distant and random gun
  That the foe was sullenly firing.

Slowly and sadly we laid him down,
  From the field of his fame fresh and gory;
We carved not a line, and we raised not a stone,
  But we left him alone with his glory.


## IF I HAD THOUGHT.

If I had thought thou couldst have died,
  I might not weep for thee;
But I forgot, when by thy side,
  That thou couldst mortal be:

It never through my mind had pass'd
　The time would e'er be o'er,
And I on thee should look my last,
　And thou shouldst smile no more.

And still upon that face I look,
　And think 't will smile again;
And still the thought I will not brook
　That I must look in vain.
But, when I speak, thou dost not say
　What thou ne'er left unsaid;
And now I feel, as well I may,
　Sweet Mary! thou art dead.

If thou would'st stay e'en as thou art,
　All cold and all serene,
I still might press thy silent heart,
　And where thy smiles have been!
While e'en thy chill bleak corse I have,
　Thou seemest still mine own;
But there I lay thee in thy grave
　And I am now alone!

I do not think, where'er thou art,
　Thou hast forgotten me;
And I, perhaps, may soothe this heart
　In thinking, too, of thee.
Yet there was round thee such a dawn
　Of light ne'er seen before,
As fancy never could have drawn,
　And never can restore.

## OH! SAY NOT THAT.

OH! say not that my heart is cold
    To aught that once could warm it,
That nature's form, so dear of old,
    No more has power to charm it;
Or that th' ungenerous world can chill
    One glow of fond emotion
For those who made it dearer still,
    And shared its wild devotion.

Still oft those solemn scenes I view
    In rapt and dreamy sadness—
Oft look on those who loved them, too,
    With fancy's idle gladness.
Again I long to view the light
    In nature's features glowing,
Again to tread the mountain's height,
    And taste the soul's o'erflowing.

Stern Duty rose and frowning flung
    Her leaden chain around me;
With iron look and sullen tongue
    He muttered as he bound me:
" The mountain breeze, the boundless heaven
    Unfit for toil the creature;
These for the free alone are given,
    But what have slaves with Nature?'

## GO! FORGET ME.

Go! forget me, why should sorrow
  O'er that brow a shadow fling?
Go! forget me—and to-morrow
  Brightly smile, and sweetly sing.
Smile—though I shall not be near thee;
Sing—though I shall never hear thee.
May thy soul with pleasure shine,
Lasting as the gloom of mine.

Like the sun, thy presence glowing,
  Clothes the meanest things in light;
And when thou, like him, art going,
  Loveliest objects fade in night.
All things looked so bright about thee,
That they nothing seem without thee.
By that pure and lucid mind
Earthly things were too refined.

Go! thou vision, wildly gleaming,
  Softly on my soul that fell,
Go! for me no longer beaming,
  Hope and beauty, fare ye well!
Go! and all that once delighted
Take—and leave me, all benighted,
Glory's burning gen'rous swell,
Fancy and the poet's shell.

CHARLES GRAHAM HALPINE.

# CHARLES GRAHAM HALPINE

POET, EDITOR AND SOLDIER.

LDCASTLE, in the County Meath, Ireland, is the birth-place of the subject of this memoir. The Halpines originally belonged to County Louth, where the Clan Halpine held an honorable place among the well-to-do farmers for many generations. Nicholas Halpine, the father of the future *litterateur*, was educated at old Trinity College, Dublin, and, after graduation, became a minister of the Established Church. Appointed to a living near Oldcastle, he resided there for many years; and there his oldest son, Charles, first drew vital breath, in the year 1829. When this boy was eleven years old the Rev. Nicholas Halpine, growing weary of country life, moved to Dublin where he became editor-in-chief of the *Evening Mail*, at that time the organ of Protestantism in Ireland. Young Charles accompanied his father to the metropolis, and, having attained the proper age, entered Trinity College, where he became not only very popular with the students but also a distinguished classical scholar and a linguist of no mean parts. Having finished his course at the University he graduated with honor,

(183)

and then turned his mind for some time to the study
of medicine. This he discovered to be very uncongenial to his taste and talent, and, for another short
period, his attention was given to the study of Black-
stone. But law proved as distasteful to him as
medicine. The natural bent of his mind was towards literature, and most of his after years were devoted to writing for the press.

When only nineteen years of age he married an
amiable and accomplished Irish lady, and thought
for a while of leading a quiet life in his native land.
Assiduously devoting himself to journalism he found
a ready market for his work both in London and
Dublin. His poetic contributions were always in
high demand at the offices of the English periodicals,
and the Irish newspapers cheerfully paid for his
prose articles on the issues of the time.

But the Greater Ireland was rising in the West,
young, vigorous and progressive. The priests, physicians and poets of the Gael were following the Star
of Empire in the track of the great Irish exodus;
and Halpine, young and hopeful, was drawn into the
current and swept along by the outgoing tide.

Reaching New York in the summer of 1852, about
the same time as his college-mate Fitz-James O'Brien,
he became connected with the New York *Herald*.
His large literary attainments and prolific genius in
a short time asserted themselves and enabled him to

take a prominent place among the distinguished writers of the country. The leading journals throughout the Union paid him handsomely for articles on various subjects. For some great daily he wrote a leader on the politics of the time; to some leading weekly he contributed a stirring song brimful of Irish wit, and for one or other of the high-standard monthlies he translated some short story that was going the rounds of the French, Italian or German press.

After a few busy and successful years spent in New York, Mr. Halpine went down to the metropolis of New England to occupy the editorial chair of the Boston *Post*. Having infused new blood and vigor into the old journal and given it a long lease of life, he formed a partnership with the poet Shillaber, and started a comic paper called the *Carpet Bag*. This literary venture did not prove a pecuniary success, however, and Halpine returned to New York where he was immediately installed as associate editor of the *Times*.

In 1858 Mr. John Clancy and our author commenced the publication of the *Leader*, which in a short time, under their joint control, became a journal not alone of great influence in politics, but also a high-grade literary paper. In the office of the *Leader* Mr. Halpine labored assiduously until Col. Michael Corcoran began to recruit for the

famous Sixty-ninth, when he joined his fellow-
countrymen and went South to defend the Union.

A lover of freedom and member of the Young
Irelanders at home in his native land, he naturally
hated slavery in his adopted country, and his pen
did effective service in the cause of Abolition.

When Anthony Burns, a fugitive slave, was returned by the authorities to his master in the South,
Halpine wrote his remarkable poem, the "Flaunting
Lie," which was for a long time attributed to Horace
Greeley. He loved to see that freedom which he
himself enjoyed under the flag of his adopted country extended to every member of the human race,
irrespective of caste or color. That flag he desig-
nated a "flaunting lie" so long as it shielded slavery
in the South, and he advised the Government to

> Furl, furl the boasted lie!
>   Till Freedom lives again,
> With stature grand and purpose high
>   'Among untrammeled men!
> Roll up the starry sheen,
>   Conceal its bloody stains;
> For in its folds is seen
>   The stamp of rusting chains.

To extend this freedom to the black man of the
South and maintain the integrity of the Republic,
Halpine fought manfully at the Battle of Bull Run.
Transferred to the command of General David

Hunter, he became a staff-officer with the rank of Major, and accompanied that General when he was ordered to North Carolina. Here it was that Major Halpine assumed the pen-name of "Miles O'Reilly" and wrote his comical letters and witty songs. In one of those songs he assailed Dahlgren for not attacking Charleston according to his promise. The song attracted a liberal share of public attention and it was mooted abroad that the writer, Private Miles O'Reilly, was imprisoned for his breach of military discipline and would be court-martialled in a few days. President Lincoln, on hearing the report and taking it to be true, directed the Secretary of War to issue an order for O'Reilly's release and the postponement of his trial. Here the gifted Celt enthusiastically applied himself to the study of military tactics, and in a comparatively short space of time he was considered one of the best-informed officers in the service on military affairs. It was he that suggested the use of colored troops to General Hunter, by whom the negroes were first turned to good account as soldiers.

Recognizing his worth the authorities promoted Major Halpine to the rank of Colonel and transferred him to the staff of Major-General Halleck, with whom he went into active service in the Shenandoah Valley. On the march towards Staunton he was the very soul and centre of the army, acknowledged by all as the most daring in battle, the best story-teller in camp, and the first to sympathize with and come to the assistance of an afflicted associate in arms. Such was the general verdict given by his comrades of Col. C. G. Halpine before he resigned his commission towards the close of the Civil War.

When his command was ordered to Washington, in consideration of efficient services rendered, he was raised to the rank of Brigadier-General of Volunteers and gazetted Major in the regular army. But here he grew weary of inactive life. The cause of Freedom was triumphant. He could not expect to render much more service to his adopted country in the capacity of soldier, and seeing that the struggle was virtually ended he tendered his resignation to the Government. The War Department conferred upon him the rank of Major-General by brevet, and sheathing his sword he once more assumed the pen in the office of the New York *Citizen*.

After the close of the war he was elected to the important and lucrative position of City Registrar, which office he filled to the morning of his death.

When the wires flashed the Fall of Richmond to New York the people almost went wild with joy. No class rejoiced over the triumph of the Government more heartily than the citizens of Irish birth, and, fired by the inspiration of the glad tidings, General Halpine gave expression and form to their

loyal feelings in a remarkable poem from which the
following verses are quoted:

MUSHA, glory to God! for the news you have sint,
Wid your own purty fist, Mister Presidint Linkin!
And may God be around both the bed and the tint
Where our bully boy Grant does his aitin and thinkin'.

Even Stanton, to-night, we'll confess he was right
Whin he played the ould scratch wid our *have-you-his-carkiss;*
And to gallant '' Phil Sherry '' we'll drink wid delight,
On whose bright plume of fame not a spot o' the dark is!

Let the chapels be opened, the altars illumed,
An' the mad bells ring out from aich turret an shteeple;
Let the chancels wid flowers be adorned an' perfumed
While the *soggarths*—God bless 'em—give thanks for the people.

For the city is ours that '' Mac '' sought from the start,
An' our boys thro' its streets '' Hail Columbia '' are yellin';
An' there's peace in the air, an' there's pride in the heart,
An' our flag has a fame that no tongue can be tellin'.

Who but a genuine Irish poet could give fitting
expression to the patriotic feelings of gladness that
filled every Irish heart on that eventful day! Halpine's heart was Irish to the core and therefore
ardently devoted to the institutions of the Republic.
Ireland was his mother; Columbia his spouse. What
he thought of his mother may be learned from his
splendid poem, '' Stamping Out,'' which was written
in reply to an editorial in the London *Times.* The
editor of the British *Thunderer* said:

" We must stamp out the fires of this Fenian insurrection,
and quench its embers in the blood of the wretches who are its
promoters."

The fire of patriotism which had smoldered in the
breast of his loyal father was fanned to a flame by the
brutal threats of the *Times*, and Halpine exclaimed·

> Aye, stamp away!   Can you stamp it out,
> This quenchless fire of a Nation's Freedom?

Before General Halpine had attained to the age of
forty, death overtook and snatched him from the
scene of his labors and with the laurels fresh upon
his brow.   He died in the Astor House, New York,
on the morning of the 3d of August, 1868, from the
effects of a drug taken for insomnia.   His life went
out under circumstances much similar to those which
attended the closing scene of the late John Boyle
O'Reilly's remarkable career.   There was a great
deal in common between the two men, mentally and
physically.

General Halpine was a splendid type of Celtic
manhood—tall, stout and well proportioned.   His
bearing was soldierly and commanding to such a
degree as to make him a marked man in any
gathering of people.   In manners he was amiable,
courteous and refined, while his disposition to assist
the poor and unfortunate was such that no deserving
person ever appealed to him in vain.   His death was
a great loss to periodical literature, and it has caused

a vacancy in New York which will not soon be filled
by another "Private Miles O'Reilly."

Following are a few of General Halpine's poems:

## ON RAISING A MONUMENT TO THE IRISH LEGION.

To raise a column o'er the dead,
  To strew with flowers the graves of those
Who, long ago, in storms of lead,
And where the bolts of battle sped,
  Beside us faced our Southern foes;
To honor these—th' unshriv'n, unhearsed—
  To-day we sad survivors come,
With colors draped, and arms reversed,
And all our souls in gloom immersed,
  With silent fife and muffled drum.

In mournful guise our banners wave;
  Black clouds above the "sunburst" lower;
We mourn the true, the young, the brave
Who, for this land that shelter gave,
  Drew swords in peril's deadliest hour—
For Irish soldiers fighting here
  As when Lord Clare was bid advance,
And Cumberland beheld with fear
The old green banners swinging clear
  To shield the broken lines of France.

We mourn them; not because they died
  In battle, for our destined race,
In every field of warlike pride,
From Limerick's wall to India's tide
  Have borne our flag to foremost place;

As if each sought the soldier's trade,
  While some dim hope within him glows,
Before he dies, in line arrayed,
To see the old green flag displayed
  For final fight with Ireland's foes.

For such a race the soldier's death
  Seems not a cruel death to die,
Around their names a laurel wreath,
A wild cheer as the parting breath
  On which their spirits mount the sky;
Oh, had their hope been only won,
  On Irish soil their final fight,
And had they seen, ere sinking down,
Our em'rald torn from England's crown,
  Each dead face would have flashed with light.

But vain are words to check the tide
  Of widowed grief and orphaned woe;
Again we see them by our side,
As, full of youth and strength and pride,
  They first went forth to meet the foe!
Their kindling eyes, their steps elate,
  Their grief at parting hid in mirth;
Against our foes no spark of hate,
No wish but to preserve the State
  That welcomes all th' oppressed of earth.

Not a new Ireland to invoke,
  To guard the flag was all they sought;
Not to make others feel the yoke
Of Poland, feel the shot and stroke
  Of those who in the legion fought;

Upon our great flag's azure field
  To hold unharmed each starry gem—
This cause on many a bloody field,
Thinned out by death, they would not yield—
  It was the world's last hope to them.

Oh ye, the small surviving band,
  Oh, Irish race wherever spread,
With wailing voice and wringing hand,
And the wild *kaoine* of the dear old land,
  Think of her Legion's countless dead!
Struck out of life by ball or blade,
  Or torn in fragments by the shell,
With briefest prayer by brother made,
And rudely in their blankets laid,
  Now sleep the brave who fought so well.

Their widows—tell them not of pride,
  No laurel checks the orphan's tear;
They only feel the world is wide,
And dark, and hard—nor help nor guide—
  No husband's arm, no father near;
But at their nod our fields were won,
  And pious pity for their loss
In streams of gen'rous aid should run
To help them say: " Thy will be done,"
  As bent in grief they kiss the Cross.

Then for the soldiers and their chief
  Let all combine a shaft to raise—
The double type of pride and grief,
With many a sculpture and relief
  To tell their tale to after days;

14

And here will shine—our proudest boast
   While one of Irish blood survives:
"Sacred to that unfalt'ring host
Of soldiers from a distant coast,
   Who for the Union gave their lives.

"Welcomed they were with generous hand,
   And to that welcome nobly true,
When war's dread tocsin filled the land,
With sinewy arm and swinging brand,
   These exiles to the rescue flew.
Their fealty to the flag they gave,
   And for the Union, daring death.
Foremost among the foremost brave,
They welcomed vict'ry and the grave,
   In the same sigh of parting breath."

Thus be their modest history penned,
   But not with this our love must cease;
Let prayers from pious hearts ascend,
And o'er their ashes let us blend
   All feuds and factions into peace.
Oh, men of Ireland! here unite
   Around the graves of those we love,
And from their homes of endless light
The Legion's dead will bless the sight,
   And rain down anthems from above!

Here to this shrine by reverence led,
   Let Love her sacred lessons teach;
Shoulder to shoulder rise the dead,
From many a trench with battle red.
   And thus I hear their ghostly speech:

" Oh, for the old earth, and our sake,
　　Renounce all feuds, engend'ring fear,
And Ireland from her trance shall wake,
Striving once more her chains to break
　　When all her sons are brothers here."

I see our Meagher's plume of green,
　　Approving nod to hear the words,
And Corcoran's wraith applauds the scene,
And bold Mat Murphy smiles, I ween—
　　All three with hands on ghastly swords—
Oh, for their sake, whose names of light
　　Flash out like beacons from dark shores—
Men of the old race! in your might,
All factions quelled, again unite—
　　With you the Green Flag sinks or soars!

## JANETTE'S HAIR.

OH! loosen the snood that you wear, Janette,
Let me tangle a hand in your hair, my pet;
　　For the world to me had no daintier sight
　　Than your brown hair veiling your shoulders white,
As I tangled a hand in your hair, my pet.

It was brown, with a golden gloss, Janette,
It was finer than silk of the floss, my pet;
　　'T was a beautiful mist falling down to your wrist;
　　'T was a thing to be braided, and jeweled and kissed;
'T was the loveliest hair in the world, my pet.

My arm was the arm of a clown, Janette,
It was sinewy, bristled, and brown, my pet;
   But warmly and softly it loved to caress
   Your round white neck and your wealth of tress—
Your beautiful plenty of hair, my pet.

Your eyes had a swimming glory, Janette,
Revealing the old, dear story, my pet;
   They were gray with that chastened tinge of the sky,
   When the trout leaps quickest to snap the fly,
And they matched with your golden hair, my pet.

Your lips—but I have no words, Janette—
They were fresh as the twitter of birds, my pet;
   When the spring is young, and the roses are wet
   With the dewdrops in each red bosom set,
And they suited your gold-brown hair, my pet.

Oh, you tangled my life in your hair, Janette,
'T was a silken and golden snare, my pet;
   But, so gentle the bondage, my soul did implore
   The right to continue your slave evermore,
With my fingers enmeshed in your hair, my pet.

     *      *      *      *      *

Thus ever I dream what you were, Janette,
With your lips, and your eyes, and your hair, my pet;
   In the darkness of desolate years I moan,
   And my tears fall bitterly over the stone
That covers your golden hair, my pet.

## NOT A STAR FROM THE FLAG SHALL FADE.

Och! a rare ould flag was the flag we bore—
   'T was a bully ould flag an' nice;
It had stripes in plenty, and stars galore—
   'T was the broth of a purty device.
Faix, we carried it South, an' we carried it far,
   And around it our bivouacs made;
An' we swore by the shamrock that never a shtar
   From its azure field should fade.

Ay, this was the oath, I tell you thrue,
That was sworn in the souls of our boys in blue.

The fight it grows thick, an' our boys they fall,
   An' the shells like a banshee scream;
An' the flag—it is torn by many a ball—
   But yield it we never dhream.
Though pierced by bullets, yet still it bears
   All the stars in its tatthered field,
An' again the brigade, like to one man swears,
   " Not a shtar from the flag we yield!"

'T was the deep, hot oath, I tell you thrue,
That lay close to the hearts of the boys in blue.

Shure the fight it was won, afther many a year,
   But two-thirds of the boys who bore
That flag from their wives and sweethearts dear
   Returned to their homes no more.
They died by the bullet—disease had power,
   An' to death they were rudely tossed;
But the thought came warm in their dying hour,
   " Not a shtar from that flag is lost!"

Then they said their pathers and aves through,
An', like Irishmen, died—did our boys in blue.

But now they tell us some shtars are gone,
    Torn out by the rebel gale;
That the shtars we fought for, the States we won,
    Are still out of the Union's pale.
May their sowls in the dioul's hot kitchen glow
    Who sing such a lying shtrain;
By the dead in their graves it shall not be so—
    They shall have what they died to gain!

All the shtars in our flag shall still shine through
The grass growing soft o'er our dead in blue!


## STAMPING OUT

[We must stamp out the fires of this Fenian insurrection, and quench its embers in the blood of the wretches who are its promoters —London *Times.*]

Aye, stamp away!  Can you stamp it out—
    This quenchless fire of a Nation's Freedom?
Your feet are broad and your legs are stout,
    But stouter far for this you'll need 'em!
You have stamped away for six hundred years,
    But again and again the old cause rallies;
Pikes gleam in the hands of our mountaineers,
    And with scythes come the men from our valleys.

The steel-clad Norman, as he roams,
    Is faced by our naked gallow-glasses;
We lost the plains and our pleasant homes,
    But we held the fields and passes!

And still the beltone fires at night—
  If not a man were left to feed 'em—
By widows' hands piled high and bright,
  Flashed for the flame of Freedom!

Aye, stamp away!  Can you stamp it out,
  Or how have your brutal arts been baffled?
You have wielded the power of rope and knot,
  Fire, dungeon, sword and scaffold
But still, as from each martyr's hand
  The Fiery Cross fell down in fighting,
A thousand sprang to seize the brand,
  Our beltone fires re-lighting!

And once again through Irish nights,
  O'er every dark hill redly streaming,
And numerous as the heavenly lights,
  Our rebel fires were gleaming!
And though again might fall that flame,
  Quenched in the blood of its devoted,
Fresh chieftains rose, fresh clansmen came
  And again the Old Flag floated.

That fire will burn, that flag will float—
  By Virtue nursed, by Valor rended—
Till with one fierce clutch upon your throat
  Your Moloch reign is ended!
It may be now, or it may be then,
  That the hour will come we have hoped for ages—
But, failing and foiling, we try again,
  And again the conflict rages.

Our hate, though hot, is a patient hate—
   Deadly and patient to catch you tripping,
And your eyes are many, your crimes are great,
   And the sceptre is from you slipping.
But, stamp away with your brutal hoof,
   While the fires to scorch you are upward cleaving,
For with bloody shuttles, the warp and woof
   Of your shroud the Fates are weaving!

## THE FLAUNTING LIE.

ALL hail the flaunting Lie!
   The stars grow pale and dim—
The stripes are bloody scars,
   A lie the flaunting hymn!
It shields a pirate's deck,
   It binds a man in chains,
And round the captive's neck
   Its folds are bloody stains.

Tear down the flaunting Lie!
   Half-mast the starry flag!
Insult no sunny sky
   With this polluted rag!
Destroy it, ye who can!
   Deep sink it in the waves!
It bears a fellow-man
   To groan with fellow-slaves.

Awake the burning scorn—
   The vengeance long and deep,
That, till a better morn,
   Shall neither tire nor sleep!

Swear once again the vow,
　　By all we hope or dream,
That what we suffer now
　　The future shall redeem.

Furl, furl the boasted Lie!
　　Till Freedom lives again,
With stature grand and purpose high
　　Among untrammeled men!
Roll up the starry sheen,
　　Conceal its bloody stains;
For in its folds are seen
　　The stamp of rusty chains.

Swear, Freemen—all as one—
　　To spurn the flaunting Lie!
Till peace and Truth and Love
　　Shall fill the brooding sky;
Then floating in the air,
　　O'er hill, and dale, and sea,
'T will stand forever fair,
　　The emblem of the Free!

## SAMBO'S RIGHT TO BE KILT.

SOME say it is a burnin' shame
　　To make the naygurs fight,
An' that the thrade o' bein' kilt
　　Belongs but to the white.
But as for me, upon me sowl,
　　So liberal are we here,
I'll let Sambo be murthered in place o' myself
　　On every day in the year.

On every day in the year, boys,
An' every hour in the day,
The right to be kilt I'll divide with him,
An' divil a word I'll say.

In battle's wild commotion
I shouldn't at all object,
If Sambo's body should stop a ball
That was comin' for me direct;
An' the prod of a Southern bagnet,
So liberal are we here,
I'll resign, and let Sambo take it
On every day in the year.

On every day in the year, boys,
.An' wid none o' your nasty pride,
All my right in Southern bagnet-prod
Wid Sambo I'll divide.

The men who object to Sambo
Should take his place and fight, ·
An' it's betther to have a naygur's hue
Than a liver that's wake an' white;
Though Sambo's as black as the ace o' spades
His finger a thrigger can pull,
An' his eye runs straight on the barrel-sights
From under his thatch o' wool.

So hear me all, boys, darlin's!
Don't think I'm tippin' you chaff,
The right to be kilt I'll divide wid him,
An' give him the largest half!

# JAMES JOSEPH CALLANAN

AUTHOR OF "GOUGANE BARRA."

**T**HERE is a romantic islet in Clonakilty Bay, on the south coast of Ireland, where the subject of this memoir wrote his "Childe Harold"— "The Recluse of Inchidony." He was truly the poet of nature, who found pleasure among the gloomy glens of Desmond and "rapture on the lonely shore" of Inchidony. There he communed with nature for a considerable space of time and wrote that splendid poem entitled "Gougane Barra," which Allibone, the biographical compiler and literary critic, designates as "the most perfect, perhaps, of all minor Irish poems, in the melody of its rhythm, the soft, sweet flow of its language and the weird force of its expression." A tradition connected with the shores of his wild retreat suggested another of his pieces, "The Virgin Mary's Bank."

James Joseph Callanan was born in the city of Cork, in May, 1795. His parents were in good circumstances, and gave the future poet all the educational advantages that could be had at that time in his native city. Mrs. Callanan, a lady of piety and

(203)

culture, directed the thoughts and aspirations of her son towards the sacred ministry, from his boyhood.

Having made his classical studies in one of the many Latin schools for which the city of St. Finn-Barr has always been remarkable, he passed an ex-aminaton for the ecclesiastical seminary of May-

nooth and entered there in 1812, when he was but seventeen years of age.

Two years of student life in Maynooth convinced both his spiritual director and himself that he had no vocation to the sacred priesthood, and he left the Seminary to enter Trinity College as an outpensioner.

Owing to the thorough course of training which he had received in Maynooth, his progress at Trinity was both easy and rapid. In *belles-lettres* he excelled, and during his University course took the Vice-Chancellor's prizes for poetry and rhetoric. One of his prize poems had for its subject the " Restoration of the Spoils of Athens;" another, the "Accession of George the Fourth." The latter theme, doubtless, could have very little inspiration for one who loved his country as tenderly and sincerely as Callanan did. After devoting four years to hard study and winning an enviable distinction in the best educational institutions of his country, young Callanan returned to Cork. During his absence both his parents had died; the friends of boyhood's days were scattered far and wide, and those scenes that were so dear to him in former years seemed to have lost their charms. In the state of mind produced by those changes, he joined a regiment of Irish soldiers which was on the eve of leaving for Malta. Fortunately some patriotic friends interfered in time to buy him out of the service before the troops started from Cove, and the poetic literature of their country profited by the act. Shortly after his release, he was engaged as tutor in the family of Mr. M. F. McCarthy of Mill-street, a little town romantically situated on the Blackwater. While acting in this capacity Callanan found time to study the ancient Irish, and gather

from the peasantry of the neighboring glens those
songs which he afterwards translated with so much
felicity and force into the English tongne.
Growing weary of his tutorship in Millstreet, he
returned once more to Cork, where he obtained a
position in the celebrated school of the learned
Dr. William Maginn who, like himself, was a
graduate of Trinity. The Doctor was a man of
keen discernment, and soon discovered that his
assistant possessed talents of a high order. He
encouraged him to translate the relics of the Munster bards, and introduced him to *Blackwood's Magazine*, to which the Doctor himself had been for
some years a valued contributor. In that year—
1823—six translations from the Gaelic language appeared in *Blackwood's* from the pen of "a new Irish
poet." The poet was Callanan; and subsequently any
literary contribution that bore the mark of his genius
was welcomed to the editor's table. The shy, sensitive tutor had now found a friend in his fellow-
townsman, and a broader sphere for the display of his
talents in Mr. Blackwood's publication, and he was
determined to make good use of his genius and
acquirements. But, unfortunately, the friend and
patron who had already won a wide popularity as the
"Sir Morgan O'Doherty" of *Blackwood's* soon gave up
his school, and emigrated to London for the purpose
of devoting all his time to literature. In London,

Dr. Maginn became one of the most learned and prolific writers of his age. So, in 1823, poor Callanan again found himself without an occupation. Had he followed his friend to London there was ample work for him to do on the countless publications of that monster city. But he loved his native land too dearly to leave it, and he now resolved to struggle at home.

Then it was that he took up his residence in the little island above mentioned. From this strange, wild abode he made frequent excursions along the sea-coast of the County Cork, admiring the savage grandeur of the scenery, and collecting from the simple and generous people of those regions the legends and traditions which had been handed down to them through many generations.

A close student of his country's history, the struggles of the brave but honest Gael against the crafty and faithless invader had for him an absorbing interest, and he devoted much of his time to collecting and preserving any records that were calculated to serve the future historian in meting out justice to a traduced and injured people. He was also an ardent lover of Nature, and the finest imagery we find in his poems is not borrowed from the ancient classics in which he was deeply versed, but taken from those inspiring objects that constitute the glorious scenery of " deep-valley'd Desmond."

Every stream, rock and river, every storied pass, sombre glen and hoary fane, every giant cliff that bares its breast to the tossing billows of the Atlantic, every ruined fort and mountain lake from the Lee around to the Kenmare river was as familiar to him as the morning prayer which he never failed to recite. Among those scenes he wandered day after day, lured on by the spirit of Song and the voice of Nature, as he tells us in one of his long poems:

> Spirit of Song! since first I wooed thy smile,
>     How many a sorrow hath this bosom known
> How many false ones did its truth beguile,
>     From THEE and NATURE!   While around it strown
>     Lay shattered hopes and feelings, THOU alone
> Above my path of darkness brightly rose,
>     Yielding thy light when other light was gone:
> Oh, be thou still the soother of my woes,
> Till the low voice of Death shall call me to repose.

During his wanderings through the picturesque barony of Beara, he succeeded in collecting a great deal of information relative to local chiefs.   Where the village of Castletown nestles, at the western extremity of Bantry Bay, in an angle of the Caha hills, he found the manuscript of a poem which stands unrivaled in the whole range of Gaelic com-position, both for energy of expression and vehe-mence of malediction.   In the translation Callanan has admirably retained its primitive power and vigor while adding to it those graces of euphony and diction which characterize all his verses. This piece is called "The Dirge of O'Sullivan Beare," supposed to have been composed by the old nurse of the murdered Chief, whose cruel fate is a striking illustration of the brutal treatment received by the native gentry at the hands of Anglo-Norman marauders.

Mortimer O'Sullivan, commonly called "Morty Oge," was a descendant of

"Donal of the ships, the Chief whom nothing daunted,"

and a young man whose mettle had been tried in the wars of Maria Teresa. After the battle of Fontenoy, he received a commission in the Irish Brigade serving in France, and was dispatched to Ireland in the interest of his regiment. The gallant young soldier naturally directed his course to that part of the Green Isle over which his ancestors had reigned since the close of the tenth century. As a scion of the House of Beara, he was received with open arms by the native population, and his recruiting expedition became a pronounced success. A fine brigantine, which he named the "Clann-na-Darra," after a sept in his native place, carried the "Wild Geese," from certain inlets of the Kenmare river, and from the little harbor of Beal-a-Cravaun to convenient ports in France. The young Colonel managed to win over

to his standard a company of red-coats—beneath
which pulsated warm Irish hearts—just on the eve of
their departure from the city of Cork. This daring
act aroused the Government authorities and cast
some reflections on Mr. Puxley, the revenue officer
for the district in which the recruiting was chiefly
done. Puxley, who was himself a poltroon and the
son of a poltroon, took care to avoid a conflict with
O'Sullivan, whose reputation for skill and courage
was well known in the south of Ireland. But when
he ascertained that Colonel O'Sullivan was away on
the coast of France, he marched at the head of a
company of yeoman across the narrow neck of land
that divides Castletown harbor from Coulach Bay
with the heroic resolution of proving to the Government that he was an active and efficient officer.
While in the neighborhood of the Irish officer's
former home he received information to the effect
that Denis O'Sullivan, a near kinsman to Morty Oge,
resided there, and always extended the hospitality of
his house to the young chief whenever he came into
the vicinity.

Mr. D. O'Sullivan, who owned a smuggling craft,
was at the time somewhere on the coast of Galway;
but his wife (a fine old lady of three score) with a
serving girl was at home. Directing the footsteps
of his gallant yeomen to this house, Mr. Puxley had

the doors and windows nailed up, and then setting fire to the building, watched with complacency and pleasure the progress of the flames.

Fortunately Mrs. O'Sullivan and her servant descended to the cellar and escaped through a subterranean passage. A cat, driven by the heat on to the burning rafters mewed most piteously while the flames lapped everything within reach. Taking the mewing of the cat for the dying groans of the noble old lady, Puxley exclaimed in the midst of his "loyall companie," "Hearken ye the squeals of the old Papist!"

Subsequently this fiendish fellow being informed that the husband of the old lady, whom he had supposed to be dead, was landing some cases of goods in the little cove of Pouleen, hastened to the spot and from behind a huge rock, still pointed out by tradition, shot down the old man in cold blood. After this the authorities could not complain of his inactivity.

Vengeance, however, was near at hand. On the return of Col. O'Sullivan the appalling news met him on his native shore. Immediately mounting his horse he rode over a spur of the Caha hills which separates Coulach from Dunbuie (then the residence of the revenue officer). At a short distance from that ancient stronghold of the O'Sullivans he met

Puxley, who was also on horseback. A flash! and the latter fell to the ground mortally wounded. His wife, who accompanied him on that morning, seeing her husband fall, rode back terror-stricken to the Castle of Dunbuie.

"Let her not escape to tell the tale," exclaimed O'Sullivan's orderly. "Never," replied the Colonel, "shall it be said that an O'Sullivan shot a woman."

About nine months had passed away and Colonel O'Sullivan was back again in his ancestral home by the Atlantic. A company of soldiers came around from Cork under the command of Capt. Fitzsimons, and proceeded in the darkness of a rainy night to the house where O'Sullivan was stopping. It is said that one of his trusty men, named Scully, wet his master's powder, and betrayed him into the hands of the enemy.

The following translation by our author tells the rest of that blood-stained and barbarous tale:

DIRGE OF O'SULLIVAN BEARE.

THE sun on Ivera
No longer shines brightly;
The voice of her music
No longer is sprightly;
No more to her maidens
The light dance is dear,
Since the death of our darling,
O'Sullivan Beare.

Scully! thou false one,
   You basely betrayed him,
In his strong hour of need,
   When thy right hand should aid him.
He fed thee—he clad thee—
   You had all could delight thee;
You left him—you sold him—
   May Heaven requite thee!

Scully! may all kinds
   Of evil attend thee!
On thy dark road of life
   May no kind one befriend thee!
May fevers long burn thee,
   And agues long freeze thee—
May the strong hand of God
   In his red anger seize thee!

Had he died calmly,
   I would not deplore him;
Or if the wild strife
   Of the sea-war closed o'er him;
But with ropes 'round his white limbs
   Through oceans to trail him,
Like a fish after slaughter,
   'T is therefore I wail him.

Long may the curse
   Of his people pursue them;
Scully, that sold him,
   And soldiers that slew him!

One glimpse of Heaven's light
  May they see never!
May the hearth-stone of hell
  Be their best bed forever!

In the hole which the vile hands
  Of soldiers had made thee,
Unhonored, unshrouded,
  And headless they laid thee.
No sigh to regret thee,
  No eye to rain o'er thee,
No dirge to lament thee,
  No friend to deplore thee!

Dear head of my darling,
  How gory and pale
These aged eyes see thee,
  High spiked on the jail!
That cheek in the summer sun
  Ne'er shall grow warm;
Nor that eye e'er catch light,
  But the flash of the storm!

A curse, blessed ocean,
  Is on thy green water,
From the haven of Cork,
  To Ivera of slaughter;
Since the billows were dyed
  With the red wounds of fear
Of Muiertach Oge,
  Our O'Sullivan Beare!

From 1823 to 1828 Callanan devoted all his time to the congenial task of collecting and translating those Irish manuscripts that escaped the vandalism of the invader. For this work he was highly quali- fied, according to the opinion of J. F. Waller, him- self a poet of rare gifts and varied acquirements.

"Thoroughly acquainted," writes Mr. Waller, "with the romantic legends of his country, he was singu- larly happy in the graces and power of language, and the feeling and beauty of his sentiments. There is in his compositions little of that high classicality which marks the scholar; but they are full of exquis- ite simplicity and tenderness, and in his description of natural scenery he stands unrivaled."

Critics, of course, are not wanting who think our author might have done more, had he applied his well-cultivated mind more closely. About what he might have done we care very little; but for what he *has done* we are grateful, and cherish his memory. For critics and fault-finders there should be little respect. Their strictures and opinions should pass unheeded. Though they do not build, they are nearly always pulling down. They are wreckers, and, like those who lure mariners to destruction, they do their work in the darkness.

It must be remembered that Callanan suffered for many years from consumption, and finally suc-

cumbed to that insidious disease. When its effects
were severely telling on his strength, in 1829 he
went as tutor with the family of a Mr. Hickey of
Cork, to Lisbon, indulging the fond hope that the
balmy air of a southern clime would restore his
shattered health.

After a few months' residence in Lisbon he grew
worse and suffered much mental agony from the fear
of dying in a foreign land. His ardent desire was
to be buried in Ireland. He craved to be taken back
to his own land in order that his ashes might mingle
with the land of his fondest affections. But vain
were his desires. He died in the capital of Portu-
gal, September 19, 1829, and

> " By the strangers' heedless hand
> His lonely grave was made."

At the age of thirty-four he resigned his pure and
gentle spirit into the hands of his Divine Master,
leaving behind him a reputation for scholarly
attainments, fidelity to the cause of Ireland and
devotion to the faith of his fathers. He was buried
not in the churchyard of the Irish Franciscans at
Lisbon, as has been said, but in the church of San
José, which was at that time in possession of the
Jesuits. The highly ornamental facade of that
church still stands, but the grave of James Joseph
Callanan is nameless and unknown.

The last edition of his poems was published by Daniel Mulcahy, Cork, in 1861. The biographical notes of this, as well as of the earlier editions, are very poorly written, and do but little justice to the character of that pious, high-souled and generous man. The poems of this gentle bard are not numerous; but such is the excellence of their quality that they have been widely copied into our public school books here, and are destined to transmit to coming generations the unsullied name of their gifted author.

## GOUGANE BARRA.

THERE is a green island in lone Gougane Barra,
Where Allua of songs rushes forth as an arrow;
In deep-valley'd Desmond—a thousand wild fountains
Come down to that lake, from their home in the mountains,
There grows the wild ash, and a time-stricken willow
Looks chidingly down on the mirth of the billow;
As, like some gay child, that sad monitor scorning,
It lightly laughs back to the laugh of the morning.

And its zone of dark hills—oh, to see them all bright'ning,
When the tempest flings out its red banner of lightning,
And the waters rush down, 'mid the thunder's deep rattle,
Like clans from the hills at the voice of the battle;
And brightly the fire-crested billows are gleaming,
And wildly from Mullagh the eagles are screaming.
Oh! where is the dwelling in valley, or highland,
So meet for a bard as this lone little island?

How oft when the summer sun rested on Clara
And lit the dark heath on the hills of Ivera,
Have I sought thee, sweet spot, from my home by the ocean
And trod all thy wilds with a minstrel's devotion,
And thought of thy bards, when, assembling together,
In the cleft of thy rocks, or the depth of thy heather,
They fled from the Saxon's dark bondage and slaughter,
And waked their last song by the rush of thy water!

High sons of the lyre, oh! how proud was the feeling,
To think while alone through that solitude stealing,
Though loftier minstrels green Erin can number,
I only awoke your wild harp from its slumber,
And mingled once more with the voice of those fountains
The songs even echo forgot on her mountains;
And gleaned each grey legend, that darkly was sleeping
Where the mist and the rain o'er their beauty were creeping!

Least bard of the hills! were it mine to inherit
The fire of thy harp, and the wing of thy spirit,
With the wrongs which like thee to our country have bound me.
Did your mantle of song fling its radiance around me,
Still—still in those wilds may young liberty rally,
And send her strong shout over mountain and valley;
The star of the west may yet rise in its glory,
And the land that was darkest be brightest in story.

I, too, shall be gone;—but my name shall be spoken
When Erin awakes, and her fetters are broken;
Some minstrel will come, in the summer eve's gleaming,
When Freedom's young light on his spirit is beaming,

And bend o'er my grave with a tear of emotion,
Where calm Avon-Buie seeks the kisses of ocean,
Or plant a wild wreath, from the banks of that river,
O'er the heart, and the harp that are sleeping forever.

## THE VIRGIN MARY'S BANK.

THE evening-star rose beauteous above the fading day,
As to the lone and silent beach the Virgin came to pray;
And hill and wave shone brightly in the moonlight's mellow fall;
But the bank of green where Mary knelt was brightest of them
    all.

Slow moving o'er the waters, a gallant bark appeared,
And her joyous crew look'd from the deck as to the land she
    near'd;
To the calm and shelter'd haven she floated like a swan,
And her wings of snow o'er the waves below in pride and
    beauty shone.

The master saw our Lady as he stood upon the prow,
And mark'd the whiteness of her robe and the radiance of her
    brow;
Her arms were folded gracefully upon her stainless breast,
And her eyes looked up among the stars to Him her soul lov'd
    best.

He show'd her to his sailors, and he hail'd her with a cheer;
And on the kneeling Virgin they gazed with laugh and jeer;
And madly swore, a form so fair they never saw before;
And they cursed the faint and lagging breeze that kept them
    from the shore

The ocean from its bosom shook off the moonlight sheen,
And up its wrathful billows rose to vindicate their Queen;
And a cloud came o'er the heavens, and a darkness o'er the land,
And the scoffing crew beheld no more that Lady on the strand.

Out burst the pealing thunder, and the lightning leap'd about,
And rushing with his watery war, the tempest gave a shout,
And that vessel from a mountain wave came down with thun-
        d'ring shock;
And her timbers flew like scatter'd spray on Inchidony's rock.

Then loud from all that guilty crew one shriek rose wild and
        high;
But the angry surge swept over them and hush'd their gurgling
        cry;
And with a hoarse exulting tone the tempest pass'd away,
And down, still chafing from their strife, the indignant waters
        lay.

When the calm and purple morning shone out on high Dunmore,
Full many a mangled corpse was seen on Inchidony's shore;
And to this day the fisherman shows where the scoffers sank;
And still he calls that hillock green the "Virgin Mary's Bank."

## THE STAR OF HEAVEN.

SHINE on, thou bright beacon, unclouded and free
From thy high place of calmness, o'er life's troubled sea:
Its morning of promise, its smooth waves are gone,
And the billows roar wildly; then, bright one, shine on.

The wings of the tempest may rush o'er thy ray;
But tranquil thou smilest, undimmed by its sway;
High, high o'er the worlds where storms are unknown
Thou dwellest all beauteous, all glorious,—alone.

From the deep womb of darkness the lightning-flash leaps,
O'er the bark of my fortunes each mad billow sweeps;
From the port of her safety by warring-winds driven,
And no light o'er her course—but yon lone one of Heaven.

Yet fear not, thou frail one, the hour may be near,
When our own sunny headland far off shall appear;
When the voice of the storm shall be silent and past,
In some Island of Heaven we may anchor at last.

But, bark of eternity, where art thou now?
The wild waters shriek o'er each plunge of thy prow,
On the world's dreary ocean thus shatter'd and tost.
Then, lone one, shine on! "If I lose thee, I'm lost!"


## O SAY, MY BROWN DRIMIN.

### [From the Irish.]

O say, my brown Drimin, thou silk of the kine,
Where, where are thy strong ones, last hope of thy line?
Too deep and too long is the slumber they take;
At the loud call of Freedom why don't they awake?

My strong ones have fallen—from the bright eye of day,
All darkly they sleep in their dwelling of clay;
The cold turf is o'er them;—they hear not my cries,
And, since Louis no aid gives, I cannot arise.

Oh! where art thou, Louis? Our eyes are on thee!
Are thy lofty ships walking in strength o'er the sea?
In Freedom's last strife if you linger or quail,
No morn e'er shall break on the night of the Gael.

But should the king's son, now bereft of his right,
Come, proud in his strength, for his country to fight,
Like leaves on the trees will new people arise,
And deep from their mountains shout back to my cries.

When the Prince, now an exile, shall come for his own,
The isles of his father, his rights and his throne,
My people in battle the Saxon will meet,
And kick them before, like old shoes from their feet.

O'er mountains and valleys they'll press on their rout;
The five ends of Erin shall ring to their shout.
My sons all united shall bless the glad day
When the flint-hearted Saxons they've chased far away.


## LAMENT FOR IRELAND.

### [From the Irish.]

How dimm'd is the glory that circled the Gael,
And fall'n the high people of green Innisfail!
The sword of the Saxon is red with their gore,
And the mighty of nations is mighty no more!

Like a bark on the ocean, long shattered and tost,
On the land of your fathers at length you are lost;
The hand of the spoiler is stretched on your plains,
And you're doom'd from your cradle to bondage and chains.

Oh, where is the beauty that beam'd on thy brow?
Strong hand in the battle, how weak art thou now!
That heart is now broken that never would quail,
And thy high songs are turned into weeping and wail.

Bright shades of our sires! from your home in the skies,
Oh, blast not your sons with the scorn of your eyes!
Proud spirit of Gollam, how red is thy cheek,
For thy freemen are slaves, and thy mighty are weak!

O'Nial of the hostages!  Con, whose high name
On a hundred red battles has floated to fame!
Let the long grasses sigh undisturbed o'er thy sleep;
Arise not to shame us, awake not to weep.

In thy broad wing of darkness enfold us, O night!
Withhold, O bright sun, the reproach of thy light!
For freedom or valour no more can'st thou see
In the home of the brave, in the isles of the free.

Affliction's dark waters your spirits have bow'd,
And oppression hath wrapped all your land in its shroud,
Since first from the Brehon's pure justice you stray'd,
And bent to those laws the proud Saxon has made.

We know not our country, so strange is her face;
Her sons, once her glory, are now her disgrace.
Gone, gone is the beauty of fair Innisfail,
For the stranger now rules in the land of the Gael.

Where, where are the woods that oft rung to your cheer,
Where you waked the wild chase of the wolf and the deer?
Can those dark heights, with ramparts all frowning and riven,
Be the hills where your forests wav'd brightly in heaven?

O bondsmen of Egypt, no Moses appears,
To light your dark steps through this desert of tears!
Degraded and lost ones, no Hector is nigh
To lead you to freedom, or teach you to die!

## ADDRESS TO GREECE.

NURSLING of freedom! from her mountain nest
  She early taught thy eagle wing to soar,
With eye undazzled and with fearless breast,
  To heights of glory never reached before.
  Far on the cliff of time, all grand and hoar,
Proud of her charge, thy lofty deeds she rears
  With her own deathless trophies, blazon'd o'er,
As mind-marks for the gaze of after years—
Vainly they journey on—no match for thee appears.

But be not thine, fair land, the dastard strife
  Of yon degenerate race—along their plains
They heard that call—they started into life;
  They felt their limbs a moment free from chains.
The foe came on:—but shall the minstrel's strains
Be sullied by the story?—hush, my lyre.
  Leave them amidst the desolate waste that reigns
Round Tyranny's dark march of lava fire—
Leave them amid their shame—their bondage to expire.

Oh, be not thine such strife!—there heaves no sod
  Along thy fields, but hides a hero's head;
And when you charge for freedom and for God
  Then—then be mindful of the mighty dead!
Think that your field of battle is the bed
Where slumber hearts that never feared a foe,
  And while you feel, at each electric tread,
Their spirit through your veins indignant glow,
Strong be your sabre's sway for freedom's vengeful blow.

O, sprung from those who by Eurotas dwelt!
  Have ye forgot their deeds on yonder plain,
When, pouring through the pass, the Persian felt
  The band of Sparta was not there in vain?
  Have ye forgot how o'er the glorious slain
Greece bade her bard th' immortal story write?
  Oh! if your bosoms one proud thought retain
Of those who perish'd in that deathless fight,
Awake! like them be free, or sleep with names as bright!

Relics of heroes, from your glorious bed,
  Amid your glorious slumbers do ye feel
The rush of war loud thundering o'er your head?
  Hear ye the sound of Hellas' charging steel?
  Hear ye their victor cry?—the Moslems reel!
On, Greeks! for freedom on,—they fly—they fly'
  Oh, how the aged mountains know that peal,
Through all their echoing tops, while, grand and high,
Thermopylae's deep voice gives back the proud reply!

Oh! for the pen of him whose bursting tear
  Of childhood told his fame in after days.
Oh! for that bard, to Greece and freedom dear,
  The bard of Lesbos, with his kindling lays.
  To hymn, regenerate land, thy lofty praise;
Thy brave unaided strife—to tell the shame
  Of Europe's freest sons, who, 'mid the rays
Through time's far vista blazing from thy name,
Caught no ennobling glow from that immortal flame.

16

Not even the deeds of him, who, late afar,
  Shook the astonished nations with his might;
Not even the deeds of her, whose wings of war
  Wide o'er the ocean stretch their victor flight;—
  Not they shall rise with half th' unbroken light
Above the waves of time, fair Greece, as thine;
  Earth never yet produced in Heaven's high sight,
Through all her climates, offerings so divine,
As thy proud sons have paid at freedom's sacred shrine.

Ye isles of beauty, from your dwelling blue,
  Lift up to Heaven that shout unheard too long;
Ye mountains, steep'd in glory's distant hue,
  If with you lives the memory of that song
  Which freedom taught you, the proud strain prolong;
Echo each name that in her cause hath died,
  Till grateful Greece enrol them with the throng
Of her illustrious sons, who on the tide
Of her immortal verse eternally shall guide.


### THE MOTHER OF THE MACHABEES.

  THAT mother viewed the scene of blood;
    Her six unconquer'd sons were gone.
  Tearless she viewed—beside her stood
    Her last—her youngest—dearest one;
  He looked upon her and he smiled.
  Oh! will she save that only child?

"By all my love—my son," she said,
  "The breast that nursed—the womb that bore,—
Th' unsleeping care that watch'd thee, fed,—
  Till manhood's years required no more;
By all I've wept and pray'd for thee,
Now, now, be firm and pity me.

"Look, I beseech thee, on yon heaven,
  With its high field of azure light;
Look on this earth, to mankind given,
  Array'd in beauty and in might;
And think, nor scorn thy mother's prayer,
On him who said it and they *were!*

"So shalt thou not this tyrant fear,
  Nor recreant shun the glorious strife:
Behold! thy battle-field is near;
  Then go, my son, nor heed thy life:
Go, like thy faithful brothers die,
That I may meet you all on high."

Like arrow from the bended bow,
  He sprang upon the bloody pile—
Like sunrise on the morning's snow
  Was that heroic mother's smile:
He died!—nor fear'd the tyrant's nod—
For Judah's law,—and Judah's God.

## MARY MAGDALEN.

To the hall of that feast came the sinful and fair:
She heard in the city that Jesus was there,
She mark'd not the splendor that blazed on their board,
But silently knelt at the feet of the Lord.

The hair from her forehead, so sad and so meek,
Hung dark o'er the blushes that burn'd on her cheek;
And so still and so lowly she bent in her shame,
It seem'd as her spirit had flown from its frame.

The frown and the murmur went round through them all,
That one so unhallow'd should tread in that hall.
And some said the poor would be objects more meet,
For the wealth of the perfumes she shower'd at His feet.

She mark'd but her Saviour, she spoke but in sighs,
She dared not look up to the heaven of His eyes;
And the hot tears gush'd forth at each heave of her breast.
As her lips to His sandals she throbbingly press'd.

On the cloud after tempests, as shineth the bow,
In the glance of the sunbeam, as melteth the snow,
He looked on that lost one—her sins were forgiven;
And Mary went forth in the beauty of Heaven.

## LINES TO THE BLESSED SACRAMENT.

THOU dear and mystic semblance
　Before whose form I kneel,
I tremble as I think upon
　The glory thou dost veil,

And ask myself, can he, who late
   The ways of darkness trod,
Meet, face to face and heart to heart,
   His sin-avenging God ?

My Judge and my Creator,
   If I presume to stand
Amid Thy pure and holy ones,
   It is at Thy command,
To lay before Thy mercy's seat
   My sorrows and my fears,
To wail my life and kiss Thy feet
   In silence and in tears.

Oh, God, that dreadful moment,
   In sickness and in strife,
When Death and Hell seemed watching
   For the last weak pulse of life.
When on the waves of sin and pain
   My drowning soul was tost,
Thy hand of mercy saved me then,
   When hope itself was lost!

I hear Thy voice, my Saviour,
   It speaks within my breast,
" Oh, come to Me, thou weary one,
   I'll hush thy cares to rest."
Then from the parched and burning waste
   Of sin, where long I trod,
I come to Thee, thou stream of Life,
   My Saviour and my God.

## THE EXILE'S FAREWELL.

ADIEU, my own dear Erin,
   Reeeive my fond, my last adieu;
I go, but with me bearing
   A heart still fondly turned to you.

The charms that nature gave thee
   With lavish hand, shall cease to smile,
And the soul of friendship leave thee,
   Ere I forget my own green isle.

Ye fields where heroes bounded
   To meet the foes of liberty;
Ye hills that oft resounded
   The joyful shouts of victory;

Obscured is all your glory,
   Forgotten all your former fame,
And the minstrel's mournful story
   Now calls a tear at Erin's name.

But still the day may brighten
   When those tears shall cease to flow,
And the shout of freedom lighten
   Spirits now so drooping low.

Then, should the glad breeze blowing
   Convey the echo o'er the sea,
My heart with transport glowing
   Shall bless the hand that made thee free.

# LINES TO ERIN.

WHEN dullness shall chain the wild harp that would praise thee,
When its last sigh of freedom is heard on thy shore,
When its raptures shall bless the false heart that betrays thee,
Oh, then, dearest Erin, I'll love thee no more!

When thy sons are less tame than their own ocean waters,
When their last flash of wit and of genius is o'er,
When virtue and beauty forsake thy young daughters,
Oh, then, dearest Erin, I'll love thee no more!

When the sun that now holds his bright path o'er thy mountains,
Forgets the green fields that he smiled on before,
When no moonlight shall sleep on thy lakes and thy fountains,
Oh, then, dearest Erin, I'll love thee no more!

When the name of the Saxon and tyrant shall sever,
When the freedom you lost you no longer deplore,
When the thoughts of your wrongs shall be sleeping forever,
Oh, then, dearest Erin, I'll love thee no more!

# STANZAS.

STILL green are thy mountains and bright is thy shore,
And the voice of thy fountains is heard as of yore.
The sun o'er thy valleys, dear Erin, shines on,
Though thy bard and thy lover forever is gone.

Nor shall he, an exile, thy glad scenes forget,
The friends fondly loved, ne'er again to be met—
The glens where he mused on the deeds of his nation,
And waked his young harp with a wild inspiration.

Still, still, though between us may roll the broad ocean,
Will I cherish thy name with the same deep devotion;
And though minstrels more brilliant my place may supply,
None loves you more fondly, more truly than I.


## A LAY OF MIZEN HEAD.

IT was the noon of Sabbath, the spring-wind swept the sky,
And o'er the heaven's savannah blue the boding scuds did fly,
And a stir was heard amongst the waves o'er all their fields of
    might,
Like the distant hum of hurrying hosts when they muster for
    the fight.

The fisher marked the changing heaven and high his pinnace
    drew,
And to her wild and rocky home the screaming sea-bird flew;
But safely in Cork haven the sheltered bark may rest
Within the zone of ocean hills that girds its beauteous breast.

Amongst the stately vessels in that calm port was one
Whose streamers waved out joyously to hail the Sabbath sun;
And scattered o'er her ample deck were careless hearts and free,
That laughed to hear the rising wind and mocked the frowning
    sea.

One youth alone bent darkly above the heaving tide—
His heart was with his native hills and with his beauteous bride,
And with the rush of feelings deep his manly bosom strove,
As he thought of her he had left afar in the spring-time of
    their love.

What checks the seaman's jovial mirth and clouds his sunny
    brow?
Why does he look with troubled gaze from port-hole, side and
    prow?
A moment—'t was a death-like pause—that signal! can it be?
That signal quickly orders the "Confiance" to sea.

Then there was springing up aloft and hurrying down below,
And the windlass hoarsely answered to the hoarse and wild
        "heave yo;"
And vows were briefly spoken then that long had silent lain,
And hearts and lips together met that ne'er may meet again.

Now darker lowered the threatening sky and wilder heaved the
        wave,
And through the cordage fearfully the wind began to rave;
The sails are set, the anchor weighed—what recks that gallant
        ship?
Blow on! Upon her course she springs like greyhound from the
        slip.

O, heavens! it was a glorious sight, that stately ship to see,
In the beauty of her gleaming sails and her pennant floating free,
As to the gale with bending tops she made her haughty bow,
And proudly spurned the waves that burned around her flash-
        ing prow!

The sun went down and through the clouds looked out the
        evening star,
And westward, from old Ocean's head, beheld that ship afar.
Still onward fearlessly she flew, in her snowy pinion-sweep,
Like a bright and beauteous spirit o'er the mountains of the deep.

It blows a fearful tempest—'tis the dead watch of the night—
The Mizen's giant brow is streaked with red and angry light,
And by its far illuming glance a struggling bark I see.
Wear, wear! the land, ill-fated one, is close beneath your lee!

Another flash—they still hold out for home and love and life,
And under close-reefed topsails maintain th' unequal strife.
Now out the rallying foresail flies, the last, the desperate
        chance—
Can that be she? Oh, heavens, it is the luckless " Confiance!"

Hark! heard you not that dismal cry? 'T was stifled in the
        gale—
Oh! clasp, young bride, thine orphan child and raise the widow's
        wail!
The morning rose in purple light o'er ocean's tranquil sleep—
But o'er their gallant quarry lay the spoilers of the deep.

ERIN, prolific land of genius, has given birth to the Poet-Priest and *litterateur* whose life and labors we briefly here indite. Like many another gifted Gael, he died far away from the land which birth and boyhood had endeared to him by a thousand sacrifices and hallowed associations.

Loughrea, on the banks of the "lordly Shannon," claims the honor of giving birth to the Rev. Father Mullin in the year 1833, when Ireland was fast recovering from the baneful effects of the odious Penal laws. O'Connell was then the uncrowned king of his native land. Three years before the birth of our poet, Catholic Emancipation, through the matchless statesmanship of the Liberator, became a startling reality, and the middle class of Catholics, who had lost neither the virtues nor the traditions of their race, could now reasonably indulge in the hope of educating their sons for the learned professions. The parents of Michael Mullin dedicated him to the service of the Church at the baptismal font, and carefully shaped his career and studies to the destined goal. His primary education was received at St. Jarlath's College, the great seminary of the West, and the *alma mater* of many a learned

Irishman. Here young Mullin gave unmistakable evidence of the talents he possessed, and proved to his professors that his mind was cast in no ordinary mould. With an enthusiasm which overcomes all obstacles he read whatever national literature had escaped the vandalism of English officials in Ireland,

and stored away this well-digested knowledge in his capacious mind for future use.

During the agitation of 1847 he entered the National Ecclesiastical Seminary at Maynooth, near Dublin, where he was destined to win high honors in scholarship, and where the higher honors and dignity of the Priesthood crowned the labors of his youth and noble manhood.

It has been said with truth that among the six hundred students who thronged the recreation grounds and lecture halls of that noble institution, young Mr. Mullin never made an enemy. His nature was such as to attract and edify all who came in close relationship with him. He was gentle and retiring as a convent girl, simple and unassuming as a child. While yet a mere youth the patriotic genius of the student began to assert itself, and the editors of the *Nation* soon discovered in him one of their most valued contributors of prose and verse. From his initial contribution "Clonfert" was able to take front rank among a staff of writers that had attracted the attention and commanded the admiration of Lord Macaulay and some others of his coterie.

During his connection with the *Nation* he wrote many exquisite lyrics and some ballads of superior style and sentiment. As a specimen of the latter we reproduce here the stirring and widely-popular ballad, which first appeared under one of his assumed names in the columns of the *Nation:*

ARTHUR McCOY.

WHILE the snow-flakes of winter are falling
  On mountain, and house-top and tree,
Come olden, weird voices recalling
  The homes of Hy-Faly to me;

The ramble by river and wild-wood,
   The legends of mountain and glen,
When the bright, magic mirror of childhood
   Made heroes and giants of men.

Then I had my dreamings ideal,
   My prophets and heroes sublime,
Yet I found one, true, living and real,
   Surpass all the fictions of time:
Whose voice thrilled my heart to its centre,
   Whose form tranced my soul and my eye;
A temple no treason could enter:
   My hero was Arthur McCoy.

    *      *      *      *      *

As the strong mountain tower spreads its arms,
   Dark, shadowy, silent and tall,
In our tithe-raids and midnight alarms,
   His bosom gave refuge to all.
If a mind, clear and calm, and expanded,
   A soul ever soaring and high,
'Mid a host—gave a right to command it—
   A hero was Arthur McCoy.

While he knelt with a Christian demeanor,
   To his priest or his Maker, alone,
He scorned the vile slave or retainer
   That crouched round the castle or throne.
The Tudor, the Guelph, the Pretender,
   Were tyrants, alike, branch and stem;
But who'd free our fair land, and defend her,
   A nation, were monarchs to him.

And this faith in good works he attested,
  When Tone linked the true hearts and brave,
Every billow of danger he breasted—
  His sword-flash the crest of its wave.
A standard he captured in Gorey,
  A sword-cut and ball through the thigh
Were among the mementoes of glory
  Recorded of Arthur McCoy.

Long the *quest* of the law and its beagles,
  His covert the cave and the tree;
Though his home was the home of the eagles,
  His soul was the soul of the free.
No toil, no defeat could enslave it,
  Nor franchise nor "Amnesty Bill"—
No Lord, but the Maker who gave it,
  Could curb the high pride of his will.

With the gloom of defeat ever laden—
  Seldom seen at the hurling or dance,
Where, through blushes, the eye of the maiden
  Looks out for her lover's advance;
And whenever he stood to behold it,
  A curl of the lip, or a sigh,
Was the silent reproach that unfolded
  The feelings of Arthur McCoy

For it told him of freedom o'ershaded—
  That the iron had entered their veins—
When beauty bears manhood degraded,
  And manhood 's contented in chains.

But he loved that fair race, as a martyr,
And if his own death could recall
The blessings of liberty's charter,
His bosom had bled for them all.

And he died for his love.   I remember,
On a mound by the Shannon's blue wave,
On a dark, snowy eve in December,
I knelt at the patriot's grave.
The aged were all heavy-hearted—
No cheek in the graveyard was dry,
The Sun of our hills had departed—
God rest you, old Arthur McCoy.

This ballad became extremely popular in Ireland.
It is to be found in almost every collection of Irish
ballad poetry that has appeared during the last forty
years, either in or out of Ireland.

Besides the ordinary course of studies in Maynooth,
which occupies eight years, and embraces Humani-
ties, Natural Philosophy, Logic and Metaphysics,
Ecclesiastical History, Scripture and Theology, young
Mr. Mullin spent a term of three years in the "Dunboyne Establishment." A certificate for this department is the highest literary honor that can be conferred on a young man in Maynooth, and it is
obtained only by men of marked ability.   Here also
he won distinction among the master minds of his
country, and endeared himself to his fellow-students.
Having completed his extra course in Dunboyne, he

was appointed to a Professor's chair. For some time he lectured on English Rhetoric, with honor to himself and the great delight of the students. His health, which was never rugged, gave way about this time, and the brilliant Rev. Professor was obliged to seek the bracing air of his native fields and floods in the hope of wooing back his vanished strength and intellectual vigor.

Appointed to a curacy in his native diocese of Clonfert, he labored with an earnestness and humility that won the admiration of his people. So well, indeed, did he succeed as assistant pastor, that the Bishop made him administrator of his own parish in Loughrea. But the man who could lecture most eloquently on learned subjects, write like an inspired prophet and labor zealously for the salvation of souls, was by no means a success in the administration of an important parish. His tastes and mode of thought were not in that direction, and Father Mullin soon resigned his charge into the hands of his Bishop, with the understanding that he would be permitted to join a religious order in Dublin.

A few months in the close confinement of a monastery convinced him that his health was very much impaired, and that he must seek other pursuits than those of a sedentary life.

In 1864 he reached the shores of the New World, whither the fame of his genius and varied attainments had preceded him, and where Archbishop McCloskey received him kindly and cordially. The Archbishop of New York made Father Mullin Professor of Metaphysics and Moral Philosophy in the Provincial Ecclesiastical Seminary at Troy. The duties of this position were too arduous for his delicate constitution, so he was transferred to parochial work in New York City, where, his labor being light, he devoted considerable of his time to writing for the Metropolitan press. After some time spent here, endeavoring to

"Woo back the withered flowers of health,"

his physicians urged him to go West, with the hope that the change of climate would serve to prolong his precious life. In the University of Notre Dame, Indiana, he taught a class, and wrote sketches for the *Ave Maria*.

In Chicago he became editor of the *Young Catholic Guide*, which in his hands gathered new life and vigor.

Here it was that he learned the sad news of the death of his parents in Ireland. The bereavement broke his tender and affectionate heart, and ere its shadows had cleared away he followed them to his reward.

He died far away from his own "sunny Erin" on the 23d of April, 1869, and all that is mortal of him now lies in Calvary Cemetery, Chicago, Illinois.

His writings, which are scattered through the pages of different magazines and periodicals in two hemispheres, have never been collected.

His best known prose work is "The Two Lovers of Flavia Domitilla," which first appeared in the *Catholic World*, and helped, very materially, that magazine in the days of its youth. This beautiful Catholic story suffers nothing by comparison with the late Cardinal Newman's "Calista." The plot is full of absorbing interest, and the style in which it is written attests the oft-repeated truth that "Father Michael Mullin was a perfect master of English."

A poem which he wrote, entitled "The Immaculate Conception," attracted the attention of the illustrious Cardinal Wiseman, who, in his day, had no superior as a judge of the literary merit of original composition appearing in any of the ancient or modern languages. Among his writings in verse the "Celtic Tongue" is undoubtedly the most widely known and best appreciated. It has the characteristics of true Celtic genius. With the glow and fervor of the Celtic soul, it is pathetic and pithy, and, once read, it haunts the memory like some bewitching spell.

We cannot better end this insufficient memorial of

a man of brilliant parts, of solid acquirements and
unsullied patriotism, than by giving in full his

## LAMENT FOR THE CELTIC TONGUE.

'Tis fading, oh, 'tis fading! like the leaves upon the trees!
In murmuring tone 'tis dying, like the wail upon the breeze!
'Tis swiftly disappearing, as footprints on the shore
Where the Barrow and the Erne, and Loch Swilley's waters
     roar—
Where the parting sunbeam kisses Lough Corrib in the West,
And Ocean, like a mother, clasps the Shannon to her breast!
The language of old Erin, of her history and name—
Of her monarchs and her heroes—her glory and her fame—
The sacred shrine where rested, thro' sunshine and thro' gloom,
The spirit of her martyrs, as their bodies in the tomb;
The time-wrought shell, where murmur'd, 'mid centuries of
     wrong,
The secret voice of Freedom, in annal and in song—
Is slowly, surely sinking into silent death, at last,
To live but in the memories of those who love the Past.

The olden tongue is sinking like a patriarch to rest,
Whose youth beheld the Tyrian on our Irish coasts a guest;
Ere the Roman or the Saxon, the Norman or the Dane,
Had first set foot in Britain, o'er trampled heaps of slain;
Whose manhood saw the Druid rite at forest-tree and rock—
And savage tribes of Britain round the shrines of Zernebock;
And for generations witnessed all the glories of the Gael,
Since our Celtic sires sung war-songs round the sacred fires of
     Baal.

The tongues that saw its infancy are ranked among the dead,
And from their graves have risen those now spoken in their
    stead.
The glories of old Erin with her liberty have gone,
Yet their halo linger'd round her, while the Gaelic speech
    lived on;
For 'mid the desert of her woe, a monument more vast
Than all her pillar-towers, it stood—that old Tongue of the Past!
'T is leaving, and for ever, the soil that gave it birth,
Soon—very soon, its moving tones shall ne'er be heard on earth.

O'er the island dimly fading, as a circle o'er the wave—
Receding, as its people lisp the language of the slave,
And with it, too, seem fading, as sunset into night,
The scattered rays of liberty that lingered in its light.
For ah! tho' long, with filial love, it clung to motherland,
And Irishmen were Irish still, in language, heart and hand;
T' install its Saxon rival, proscribed it soon became,
And Irishmen are Irish now in nothing but in name;
The Saxon chain our rights and tongues alike doth hold in thrall.
Save where amid the Connaught wilds and hills of Donegal—
And by the shores of Munster, like the broad Atlantic blast,
The olden language lingers yet and binds us to the Past.

Thro' cold neglect 't is dying now; a stranger on our shore!
No Tara's hall re-echoes to its music as of yore—
No Lawrence fires our Celtic clans round leaguered Athaclee—
No Shannon wafts from Limerick's towers their war-songs to
    the sea.
Ah! magic Tongue, that round us wove its spells so soft and
    dear!
Ah! pleasant Tongue, whose murmurs were as music to the ear!

Ah! glorious Tongue, whose accents could each Celtic heart
    enthrall!
Ah! rushing Tongue, that sounded like the swollen torrent's
    fall!
The Tongue, that in the Senate was lightning flashing bright—
Whose echo in the battle was the thunder in its might!
That Tongue, which once in chieftain's hall poured loud the
    minstrel lay,
As chieftain, serf, or minstrel old, is silent there to-day!
That Tongue whose shout dismayed the foe at Cong and Mul-
    laghmast,
Like those who nobly perished there, is numbered with the Past!

The Celtic Tongue is passing and we stand so coldly by—
Without a pang within the heart, a tear within the eye—
Without one pulse for Freedom stirred, one effort made to save
The language of our fathers from dark oblivion's grave!
Oh, Erin! vain your efforts—your prayers for Freedom's crown,
Whilst offered in the language of the foe that clove it down;
Be sure that tyrants ever with an art from darkness sprung,
Would make the conquered nation slaves alike in limb and
    tongue.
Russia's great Czar ne'er stood secure o'er Poland's shattered
    frame.
Until he trampled from her heart the tongue that bore her name.
Oh, Irishmen, be Irish still! stand for the dear old tongue
Which, as ivy to a ruin, to your native land has clung!
Oh, snatch this relic from the wreck, the only and the last,
And cherish in your heart of hearts the language of the Past!

DR. ROBERT D. JOYCE was born in the village of Glenisheen, Limerick, Ireland, in the year of our Lord, 1830. He came of an old family well and widely known within the borders of Galway for daring as well as devotion to the cause of native land. The stock also produced many men of letters.

The mother of our author was Elizabeth O'Dwyer, a lineal descendant of the renowned bard and huntsman, John O'Dwyer of the Glens—"Shawn O'Dhear na Gleanna"—who after the fall of Limerick became a distinguished officer in the French army.

In the village school young Joyce evinced great aptitude for learning, and gave promise of a bright future. He was passionately fond of languages, and when at an early age he went to Dublin to complete his education, his familiarity with classic lore astonished those who became his preceptors. His college career was marked with great success; and having secured a medical diploma in the Queen's College, Dr. Joyce was appointed Professor of English Literature in the Preparatory Department of the Catholic University. Soon after he was elected a member of the Royal Irish Academy, Dublin, having

(247)

for sponsors such distinguished men as the Earl
of Dunraven and Professor Ingram, the author of
"Who Fears to Speak of Ninety-eight ?"

Though these honors came thick and fast upon the
talented young medico and *litterateur*, they did not

satisfy him. British rule in Ireland did not suit his
ideas of freedom, and he could not and would not
enjoy such honors while his country smarted under
the tyrant's lash. His sympathy was with the
Fenian movement for Irish Independence, and his
pen contributed much, both in prose and verse to

fan the flame of rebellion. The eyes of English officials were upon him and he knew it. Still greater honors, and positions of emolument awaited him, could he only be prevailed upon to trample under foot his national aspirations and go over to the ranks of his country's oppressors.

Rather than surrender his patriotic principles, he followed the heroic example of his ancestors and went into voluntary exile. In 1866 he commenced the practice of his profession in Boston, where his talents were immediately recognized, and his services soon held in high esteem. Among the literary men of the "Hub" who hailed the advent of the young Irish poet may be mentioned such men as ex-Gov. Long, John C. Abbott, Wendell Phillips and Dr. Oliver Wendel Holmes; and all these remained his firm friends and ardent admirers to the end.

His career in Boston was fraught with success. From the exactions of an extremely busy professional life he snatched time enough to write a great number of books, which became popular even in his own day. During " office hours " his ante-room was always crowded with sufferers, seeking advice and medical treatment. Sick calls came to him not only from every quarter of the great city, but also from the surrounding towns that are now incorporated with and in the city of Boston. He spoke kindly to everybody who approached him, and never sent one

away. in a hurry.  With the intelligent and educated
he conversed freely and leisurely, always choosing
some subject with which he knew his patient was
familiar.  Irish history was his delight.  Every phase
of Erin's long and eventful struggle seemed familiar
to him as the simple rudiments of the healing art.
Every stream, ruin and historic plain from Bantry
Bay to Lough Foyle, and from Kingston to Galway,
he knew, and loved with an undying love.  How he
so familiarized himself with the topography of his
native land—and that, too, during the busy days of
student life—has always seemed little less than a
mystery to the writer, who had the honor of his
acquaintance.  This fact is amply illustrated by his
"Ballads of Irish Chivalry," which not only com-.
memorate great events in the struggles of the Gael,
but also vividly and faithfully describe the scene of
every battle.

It was on Erin's elder days, however, that the
poet-physician gloried to dwell.  The days

> When her Kings, with standard of green unfurl'd,
>   Led the Red Branch Knights to danger,
> Ere the emerald gem of the Western world
>   Was set in the crown of a stranger,

seemed to have for Dr. Joyce a peculiar and fascinating charm.  This period of Irish history it was that
inspired "Deirdre," his longest, best and most enduring poem.  Yet Erin was dear to him in her sorrow,

her sufferings and tears. He himself was a man of sorrow and much grief. In his latter days he carried about with him a bleeding heart, which thereby was rendered all the more sensitive to the pains and woes of others. Silently he suffered the throes of mental agony that shook his well-knit frame; yet betimes would his grief find expression in lines like these:

No kindly counsel of a friend
With soothing balm the hurt can mend;
I walk alone in grief, and make
My bitter moan for her dear sake,
For loss of love is man's worst woe,
*And I am suffering, and I know.*

\*     \*     \*     \*     \*

Earth, air and sun, and moon and star,
Of man's strange soul but mirrors are,
Bright when the soul is bright, and dark
As now, without one saving spark,
While the black tides of sorrow flow;
*And I am suffering, and I know.*

To my sad eyes that sorrow dims
The greenest grass the swallow skims,
The flowers that once were fair to me,
The meadow and the blooming tree
Dark as funeral garments grow;
*And I am suffering, and I know.*

This pathetic little song, found in " The Despair of Cuhullin," is nothing but an outward expression of the grief that drove the strong, sweet singer to an untimely grave.

In the spring of 1883 he sickened, and died in the Fall of the same year. Followed by the esteem of her most distinguished citizens, and bearing with him the deep affection of the poor whom he had served, Dr. Joyce left Boston for Ireland early in September, 1883. The close of the next month witnessed his burial in the cemetery of Glasnevin.

About one month before his departure for Ireland the writer, in company with a mutual friend, visited Dr. Joyce in his rooms, on Chambers street, in Boston, and enjoyed his conversation for a space of two hours. Though but the shadow of his former self, he yet seemed vigorous, and talked eloquently nearly all the time. After some remarks relating to his forthcoming trip to Ireland, he changed the conversation over to Irish history and literature. His ruling passion was still strong.

The gentleman who accompanied the writer said: "Come what may, Doctor, you have left your impress on the literature of our native land, and established a lasting fame."

"Fame, I suppose," the writer remarked, "affords very poor consolation to a man when about to close his eyes to earthly things."

"On that point," rejoined the poet, "I do not agree with you. I think it affords one great consolation. It is a great deal to leave behind a name that is likely to be cherished in the hearts of a grateful people.

"I do not, however," he continued, "draw all my consolation from that source. The priest was with me yesterday, and I am prepared for any kind of a journey now. If the worst comes, I am not without hope of a happy resurrection."

It is more than a quarter of a century since, under the signature of "Feardana," Dr. Joyce's first verses appeared in *The Harp*, a magazine then published in the City of Cork, under the editorial management of M. J. McCann the gifted author of "O'Donnell Aboo." The force and spirit of his verses attracted general attention among the Nationalists, and his pen soon found employment in the columns of the *Hibernian Magazine* also. "The Blacksmith of Limerick," which appeared at this period, gained for him a wide popularity, and established his reputation as a poet on a firm and enduring basis. He became a regular contributor to the Dublin *Nation;* and the London *Universal News*, edited at that time by the late John Francis O'Donnell, eagerly sought the productions of his pen, for which he was well paid in all instances. It was not in the domain of poetry alone that "Feardana" (the song-maker) excelled; he also wrote racy sketches for the press. A very interesting novel "The Squire of Castleton," which appeared as a serial in the Dublin *Irishman*, received high praise from the critics, and the opinion prevails that, had he devoted his time and talents to *fiction* instead of medicine, he would have outrivaled Samuel Lover as a novelist. His "Irish Fireside Tales" and "Legends of the Wars in Ireland," collected and compiled during the busiest period of his professional career, are replete with genuine Irish wit and humor. These works added to the fast-increasing popularity of the author, and from them the publisher reaped a rich harvest.

The writer of this sketch can never forget the impression made upon his mind by the perusal of our author's "Ballads of Irish Chivalry, Songs and Poems," when they first appeared in 1872, from the press of Patrick Donahoe, Boston. This work, which was well received at home and abroad, contained all the poems written by Dr. Joyce up to that date. .

The appearance of this volume it was that evoked the following beautiful tribute from the brilliant Bard of Thomond, Michael O'Hogan:

### TO ROBERT D. JOYCE,

#### ON THE PUBLICATION OF HIS POEMS.

BOLD master of the Irish lyre! sweet mouth of song, all hail!
*Feardana* of the lofty verse! *Ard Filea* of the Gael!
As joys the thirsty traveler when a pure spring trickles near,
So burst thy living numbers on my soul's enraptured ear!

The silent, cloud-robed grandeur of the mountain solitude,
The bowery vale, the flowery plain, the emerald-vested wood;
The gaping breach, the 'leaguered town, the reckless battle-
    throng—
All glow before my spirit, in the pictures of thy song!

The mystic Spirit-world, with its fairy splendor gay,
Thy daring genius has unlocked with Poesy's magic key;
The sun-ray'd jewels of Romance, with all their pristine light,
Burst, flashing from thy wizard pen, upon our charmèd sight!

Sweet *Ollav* of the golden lay! oh, would my simple praise
Add one bright floweret to the crown of thy immortal bays,
And place thy brilliant page—a gem—in every Irish hand—
*Feardana* of romantic song were honored in our land!

Then pour upon thy country's ear thy harp-notes wild and
    strong,
And melt into our burning hearts the jewels of thy song;
And let thy eagle Muse tower up to heaven, on flashing wing,
'Till Erin, with admiring soul, delights to hear thee sing!

Here, by old Shannon's noble flood, I drink thy tuneful lore,
And, as my spirit quaffs thy strain, I thirst and long for more!
Back on the spring-tide of thy verse I float to olden times,
And bathe my fancy in the rays of radiant Fairy climes!

"Deirdre" and "Blanid" are, however, the works
on which the fame of Dr. Joyce securely rests. They
are the crowning glory of his labors. The former
has been pronounced by no less a critic than James
Russell Lowell "the greatest epic of the nineteenth
century."

To the writing of this, Dr. Joyce brought all the information attainable on the subject. He had read and digested everything that could be found pertaining to the story of "Deirdre" and the sons of Usna, before a single line of this gorgeous poem was written. For fifteen years, it is said, he had been endeavoring to "strike the proper strain." At last, he succeeded, and in this wise:

About four o'clock, one fine St. Patrick's morning, he was returning by way of St. Patrick's Bridge from a sick call in South Boston. As usual, holding his inseparable blackthorn in the middle, he strode proudly along whistling "St. Patrick's Day in the Morning." Immediately he struck the long-looked-for keynote to his poem, and before reaching his office that morning, "The Feast at the House of Feilimid" was well under way. He went along the rest of the journey in silence with bowed head and vision introverted, composing:

> It happened in Eman at the joyous time
> When wood-flowers bloomed and roses in their prime
> Laughed round the garden, and the new-fledged bird
> 'Mid the thick leaves his downy winglets stirred.

These are the initial couplets of Deirdre, in which adventure, love and war are described with a force and felicity of language unequalled in any epic we have ever read. It contains many pictures of nature

exquisitely drawn. Eman's palace garden is painted
thus:

> Near Eman's hall, beyond the outward fosse,
> There was a slope all gay with golden moss,
> Green grass and lady ferns and daisies white,
> And fairy-caps, the wandering bee's delight,
> And the wild thyme that scents the upland breeze,
> And clumps of hawthorn and fair ashen trees.
> And at its foot there spread a little plain
> That never seemed to thirst for dew or rain;
> For round about it waved a perfumed wood,
> And through its midst there ran a crystal flood
> With many a murmuring song and elfin shout,
> In whose clear pools the crimson-spotted trout
> Would turn his tawny side to sun and sky,
> Or sparkling upward catch the summer fly;
> On whose green banks the iris in its pride,
> Flaming in blue and gold, grew side by side
> With meadow-sweet and snow-white ladies-gowns,
> And daffodils that shook their yellow crowns
> In wanton dalliance with each breeze that blew;
> And there the birds sang songs for ever new
> To those that loved them as friend loveth friend;
> And there the cuckoo first his way would wend
> From far-off climes and kingdoms year by year,
> And rest himself and shout his message clear
> Round the glad woods, that winter was no more,
> And summer's reign begins from shore to shore.

18

The poet's genius as a portrait painter is strikingly
illustrated in this passage:

> Then rose an aged lord, with haughty air
> And shaggy brows and grizzled beard and hair,
> Whose fierce eye o'er the margin of his shield
> Had gazed from war's first ridge on many a field,
> Unblinking at the foe that on him glared,
> And might be ten to one, for all he cared.

And who that has ever strolled through the lovely
vales of Erin can fail to recall and recognize this
autumn scene, depicted by the poet's pen:

> Upon the spreading thorn
> The fieldfares bickered at the ruddy haw,
> The last fruit of the year; the thievish daw
> Fought on the palace gable with his wife,
> And the fierce magpie, born to ceaseless strife,
> Swung on the larch and told his household woes,
> Or plumed his tail and threatened all his foes
> With vicious screams and angry rhapsodies;
> And loud the finches chirruped in the trees.

And then, as so frequently happens there in the
late autumn:

> Spiralling adown the sky, the first great feathery snowflakes
>         made their way,
> Till all the garden changed from brown to gray.

It is in battle bouts, however, that the author's
skill manifests itself to the best advantage:

> Strong knee to knee, and bloody sword to sword
> And the deep vale the echoing tenors roar'd.

The taking of the Fomorian stronghold by the three brothers, Naisi, Ainli and Ardan is referred to in the following lines:

> Mercy fled,
> The field despairing; Rage, or coward Dread
> Possessed all hearts; while raising her wild shriek
> Slaughter with crimson wings and raven beak,
> Flapped the black sky above exultingly,
> Till, as the sinking moon from o'er the sea
> Cast her last beams ere morn across the isle.
> Weirdly they glimmered on the ghastly pile
> Of pirate dead that cumbered all the strand,
> Whereby strong Naisi stood, in his left hand
> Holding aloft the grim and gory head
> Of the Fomorian King!

There is nothing in the Æneid that surpasses this in dramatic effect. That the reading public immediately recognized the high merit of this work is proved by the fact that ten thousand copies of it were sold in one week after publication.

"Blanid" is an epic which equally abounds in bold metaphor and beautiful simile.

Unlike the author of "Lalla Rookh," Joyce

> " Had no heart nor hand,
> For foreign theme in foreign land."

He himself was Irish to the core, and all his themes were Irish too. This truth he beautifully sets forth in his proem to "Blanid." So far have we outrun

the limits of our space that room can be given to
only one stanza of this preface:

> Though many a field I've searched of foreign lore,
>> And found great themes for song, yet ne'er would I
> Seek Greece, or Araby, or Persia's shore
>> For heroes and the deeds of days gone by;
>> To my own native land my heart would fly,
> Howe'er my fancy wandered, and I gave
>> My thoughts to her and to the heroes high
> She nursed in ages gone and strove to save
> Some memory of their deeds from dark oblivion's wave!

"Deirdre" and "Blanid" were published by Rob-
erts Brothers, Boston, in the "No Name" series; and,
long before the authorship was known, their merit
was recognized.


## THE BLACKSMITH OF LIMERICK.

HE grasped the ponderous hammer, he could not stand it more,
To hear the bomb-shells bursting, and thundering battle's roar;
He said, "The breach they're mounting, the Dutchman's mur-
dering crew—
I'll try my hammer on their heads, and see what *that* can do!

"Now, swarthy Ned and Moran, make up that iron well;
'Tis Sarsfield's horse that wants the shoes, so mind not shot or
shell;"—
"Ah sure," cried both, "the horse can wait, for Sarsfield's on
the wall,
And where you go we'll follow, with you to stand or fall!"

The blacksmith raised his hammer, and rushed into the street,
His 'prentice boys behind him, the ruthless foe to meet;—
High on the breach of Limerick with dauntless hearts they
    stood,
Where bomb-shells burst, and shot fell thick, and redly ran the
    blood.

"Now look you, brown-haired Moran; and mark you, swarthy
    Ned,
This day we'll prove the thickness of many a Dutchman's head!
Hurrah! upon their bloody path, they're mounting gallantly;
And now the first that tops the breach, leave him to this and me."

The first that gained the rampart, he was a captain brave,—
A captain of the grenadiers, with blood-stained dirk and glaive;
He pointed and he parried, but it was all in vain!
For fast through skull and helmet the hammer found his brain!

The next that topped the rampart, he was a Colonel bold;
Bright, through the dust of battle, his helmet flashed with
    gold—
"Gold is no match for iron," the doughty blacksmith said,
And with that ponderous hammer he cracked his foeman's head.

"Hurrah for gallant Limerick!" black Ned and Moran cried,
As on the Dutchman's leaden heads their hammers well they
    plied;
A bomb-shell burst between them—one fell without a groan,
One leaped into the lurid air, and down the breach was thrown.

Brave smith! brave smith! cried Sarsfield, beware the treacher-
    ous mine!
Brave smith! brave smith! fall backward, or surely death is
    thine!"

The smith sprang up the rampart and leaped the blood-stained
     wall,
As high into the shuddering air went foeman, breach and all!

Up, like a red volcano, they thundered wild and high,—
Spear, gun, and shattered standard, and foeman through the
     sky;
And dark and bloody was the shower that round the blacksmith
     fell;—
He thought upon his 'prentice boys,—they were avengèd well.

On foeman and defenders a silence gathered down;
'T was broken by a triumph shout that shook the ancient town,
As out its heroes sallied, and bravely charged and slew,
And taught King William and his men what Irish hearts could do.

Down rushed the swarthy blacksmith unto the river's side,
He hammered on the foe's pontoon, to sink it in the tide;
The timber, it was tough and strong, it took no crack or strain;
"*Mavrone!* 't won't break!" the blacksmith roared; "I'll try
     their heads again!"

He rushed upon the flying ranks; his hammer ne'er was slack,
For in thro' blood and bone it crashed, thro' helmet and thro'
     jack;
He's ta'en a Holland captain beside the red pontoon,
And "Wait you here," he boldly cries; "I'll send you back full
     soon!"

Dost see this gory hammer? It cracked some skulls to-day,
And yours 't will crack, if you don't stand and list to what I
     say;—
Here! take it to your cursed King, and tell him, softly, too,
'T would be acquainted with *his* skull if he were here, not you!"

The blacksmith sought his smithy and blew his bellows strong;
He shod the steed of Sarsfield, but o'er it sang no song;
" *Ochone!* my boys are dead!" he cried; " their loss I'll long
    deplore,
But comfort's in my heart, their graves are red with foreign
    gore."

## SWEET GLENGARIFF'S WATER.

WHERE wildfowl swim upon the lake
    At morning's early shining,
I'm sure, I'm sure my heart will break
    With sadness and repining.

As I went out one morning sweet,
    I met a farmer's daughter,
With gown of blue, and milk-white feet,
    By sweet Glengariff's water.

Her jet-black locks, with wavy shine,
    Fell sweetly on her shoulder,
And, ah! they make my heart repine
    Till I again behold her.

She smiled and passed me strangely by,
    Though fondly I besought her,
And long I'll rue her laughing eye
    By sweet Glengariff's water.

Where wild fowl swim upon the lake
    At early morning splendor,
Each day my lonely path I'll take,
    With thoughts full sad and tender.

I'll meet my love, and, sure, she'll stay
  To hear the tale I've brought her—
To marry me this merry May,
  By sweet Glengariff's water.


## THE GREEN AND THE GOLD.

In the soft, blooming vales of our country,
  Two colors shine brightest of all,
O'er mountain and moorland and meadow,
  On cottage and old castle wall;
They shine in the gay summer garden,
  And glint in the depths of the wold,
And they gleam on the banner of Ireland,
  Our colors, the Green and the Gold!
Then hurrah for the Green and the Gold!
  By the fresh winds of Freedom outrolled,
As they shine on the brave Irish banner,
  Our colors, the Green and the Gold!

In the days of Fomorian and Fenian,
  These colors flashed bright in the ray;
And their gleam kept the fierce Roman Eagles
  In Rome—conquered Britain at bay;
When Conn fought his hundred red battles
  And the lightning struck Dathi of old,
As he bore through Helvetia's wild gorges
  Our colors, the Green and the Gold.
Then hurrah for the Green and the Gold!
  May they flourish for ages untold!
May they blaze in the vanguard of freedom,
  Our colors, the Green and the Gold!

In these dark days of doom and disaster,
  Is it dead, the old love for our land?
Are our bosoms less brave than our fathers?
  Comes the sword-hilt less deft to our hand?
No! we've proved us the wide world over,
  Wherever war's surges have rolled,
And we'll raise once again in Old Ireland
  Our colors, the Green and the Gold!
Then hurrah for the Green and the Gold!
  And hurrah for the valiant and bold,
Who will raise them supreme in Old Ireland,
  Our colors, the Green and the Gold'

## THE RAPPAREE'S HORSE AND SWORD.

My name is MacSheehy, from Feal's swelling flood,
A rapparee rover by mountain and wood;
I've two trusty comrades to serve me at need—
This sword at my side and my gallant gray steed.

Now where did I get them,—my gallant gray steed
And this sword, keen and trusty, to serve me at need?
This sword was my father's—in battle he died—
And I reared bold Isgur by Feal's woody side.

I've said it, and say it, and care not who hear,
Myself and gray Isgur have never known fear;
There's a dint on my helmet, a hole through his ear;
'T was the same bullet made them, at Lim'rick last year!

And the soldier who fired it was still ramming down,
When this long sword came right with a slash on his crown;
Dhar Dhia! but he'll ne'er fire a musket again,
For his skull lies in two at the side of the glen!

When they caught us one day at the castle of Brugh,
Of our black-hearted foemen, the deadliest crew,
Like a bolt from the thunder, gray Isgur went through,
And my sword! long they'll weep at the sore taste of you!

Together we sleep 'neath the wild crag or tree,—
My soul! but there ne'er were such comrades as we!
I, Brian the Rover, my two friends at need,
This sword at my side and my gallant gray steed!

## THE CAILIN RUE.

WHEN first I sought her, by Cashin's water
    Fond love I brought her, fond love I told;
At day's declining I found her twining
    Her bright locks shining like red, red gold.
She raised her eyes then in sweet surprise then—
    Ah! how unwise then such eyes to view!
For free they found me, but fast they bound me,
    Love's chain around me for my Cailin Rue.

Fair flowers were blooming, the meads illuming,
    All fast assuming rich summer's pride,
And we were roving, truth's rapture proving,
    Ah! fondly loving, by Cashin's side;
Oh love may wander, but ne'er could sunder
    Our hearts, that fonder each moment grew,
Till friends delighted such love requited,
    And my hand was plighted to my Cailin Rue.

Ere May's bright weather o'er hill and heather,
    Sweet tuned together rang our bridal bells;
But at May's dying, on fate relying,
    Fate left us sighing by Cashin's dells;

Oh! sadly perished the bliss we cherished!
 But far lands flourished o'er the ocean blue,
So as June came burning, I left Erin mourning,
 No more returning with my Cailin Rue.

Our ship went sailing with course nnfailing,
 But black clouds, trailing, lowered o'er the main,
And its wild dirge singing, came the storm out springing,
 That good ship flinging back, back again!
A sharp rock under tore her planks asunder,
 While the sea in thunder swallowed wreck ana crew;
One dark wave bore me where the coast towered o'er me,
 But dead before me lay my Cailin Rue!


## THE SACK OF DUNBUI.

### A. D. 1602.

THEY who fell in manhood's pride,
They who nobly fighting died,
 Fade their mem'ries never, never;
  Theirs shall be the deathless name
  Shining brighter, grander ever,
   Up the diamond crags of Fame!
Time these glorious names shall lift
Up from sunbright clift to clift—
 Upward! to eternity!
 The godlike men of brave Dunbui!

Glorious men and godlike men,
Well they stemmed the Saxon then,
  When he came, with all his powers,
  Over river, plain and sea,
  'Gainst the tall and bristling towers
  Of the Spartan-manned Dunbui—
Traitor Gael and Saxon churl,
Burning in their wrath to hurl
  Ruin on the bold and free
  Warrior men of brave Dunbui!

Thomond with his traitors came,
Carew breathing blood and flame;
  First he sent his message in
    To the Southern gunsmen three,
  Message black as hell and sin,
    Sin and Satan e'er could be;
Would they, trusting freres, betray,
Would they this, for golden pay?
  Demon, no! foul treachery
  Never dwelt in strong Dunbui!

Onward, then, that sunny June,
On they came in the fiery noon,
  On where frowned the stubborn keep
    O'er the rock-subduing flood;
  First they took Beare's island, steep,
    And drenched its crags in helpless blood.
Nought could save—child's, woman's tears—
Curse upon their cruel spears!
  Oh, that sight was hell to see
  By thy bristling walls, Dunbui!

Nearer yet, they crowd and come,
With taunting and yelling, and thundering drum,
　With taunting and yelling the hold they environ,
　　And swear that its towers and defenders must fall,
　　While the cannon are set, and their death-hail of iron
　　　Crash wildly on bastion and turret and wall;
And the ramparts are torn from their base to their brow—
Ho! will they not yield to the murderers now?
　　No! its huge towers shall float over Cleena's bright sea
　　Ere the Gael prove a craven in lonely Dunbui!

Like the fierce god of battle, MacGeoghegan goes
From rampart to wall, in the face of his foes;
　Now his voice rises high o'er the cannon's fierce din,
　　Whilst the taunt of the Saxon is loud as before,
　But a yell thunders up from his warriors within,
　　And they dash through the gateway, down, down to the
　　　shore.
With their chief rushing on, like a storm in its wrath,
They sweep the cowed Saxon to death in their path;
　Ah! dearly he'll purchase the fall of the free,
　Of the lion-souled warriors of lonely Dunbui!

Leaving terror behind them, and death in their train,
Now they stand on their walls 'mid the dying and slain,
　And the night is around them—the battle is still—
　　That lone summer midnight, ah! short is its reign,
　For the morn springeth upward, and valley and hill
　　Fling back the fierce echoes of conflict again.

And see how the foe rushes up to the breach,
Towards the green waving banner he yet may not reach,
  For look how the Gael flings him back to the sea,
  From the blood-reeking ramparts of lonely Dunbui!

Night cometh again, and the white stars look down
From the hold to the beach, where the batteries frown;
  Night cometh again, but affrighted she flies,
    Like a black Indian queen from the fierce panther's roar,
  And morning leaps up in the wide-spreading skies,
    To his welcome of thunder and flame evermore;
For the guns of the Saxon crash fearfully there,
Till the walls and the towers and the ramparts are bare,
  And the foe make their last mighty swoop on the free
  The brave-hearted warriors of lonely Dunbui!

Within the red breach see MacGeoghegan stand,
With the blood of the foe on his arm and his brand;
  And he turns to his warriors, and " Fight we," says he,
    " For country, for freedom, religion, and all;
  Better sink into death, and for ever be free,
    Than yield to the false Saxon's mercy and thrall!"
And they answer, with brandish of sparth and of glaive:
" Let them come; we will give them a welcome and grave;
  Let them come—from their swords could we flinch, could we
      flee,
  When we fight for our country, our God, and Dunbui!"

They came, and the Gael met their merciless shock—
Flung them backward like spray from the lone Skellig rock;
    But they rally, as wolves springing up to the death
        Of their brother of famine, the bear of the snow—
    He hurls them adown to the ice-fields beneath,    .
        Rushing back to his dark norland cave from the foe;—
So up to the breaches they savagely bound,
Thousands still thronging beneath and around,
    Till the firm Gael is driven—till the brave Gael must flee
    In, into the chambers of lonely Dunbui!

In chamber, in cellar, on stairway and tower,
Evermore they resisted the false Saxon's power;
    Through the noon, through the eve, and the darkness of night
        The clangor of battle rolls fearfully there,
    Till the morning leaps upward in glory and light,
        Then, where are the true-hearted warriors of Beare?
They have found them a refuge from torment and chain;
They have died with their chief, save the few who remain,
    And that few—oh, fair Heaven! on the high gallows tree,
    They swing by the ruins of lonely Dunbui!

Long, in the hearts of the brave and the free
Live the warriors who died in the lonely Dunbui—
    Down Time's silent river their fair names shall go,
        A light to our race towards the long-coming day;
    Till the billows of time shall be checked in their flow
        Can we find names so sweet for remembrance as they?
And we will hold their memories for ever and aye,
A halo, a glory that ne'er shall decay;
    We'll set them as stars o'er Eternity's sea,
    The bright names of the warriors who fell at Dunbui!

# SARSFIELD'S RIDE; OR, THE AMBUSH OF SLIAV BLOOM.

[The generally-received historical account of the exploit related in the following ballad differs in several points from the traditionary version. And yet the latter should not be despised, for the peasantry of Limerick and Tipperary have stories of the incident, all agreeing with regard to the ride of Galloping O'Hogan. The songs also of the time preserve the name of that celebrated horseman and outlaw in connection with the affair. It may be also stated that in every song and story of the time, King William is always nicknamed "Dutch Bill," a cognomen by which he is even to the present day remembered in many parts of Munster.]

## PART THE FIRST.

" Come up to the hill, Johnnie Moran, and the de'il's in the
　　sight you will see:
The men of Dutch Bill in the lowlands are marching o'er valley
　　and lea;
Brave cannon they bring for their warfare, good powder and
　　bullets *galeor*,
To batter the grey walls of Limerick adown by the deep Shan-
　　non shore!"

They girded their corselets and sabers that morning so glorious
　　and still;
They leapt like good men to their saddles, and took the lone
　　path to the hill;
And deftly they handled their bridles as they rode thro' each
　　green, fairy coom,
Each woodland, and broad rocky valley, till they came to the
　　crest of Sliav Bloom!

" Look down to the east, Johnnie Moran, where the wings of
　　the morning are spread,
Each basnet you see in the sunlight it gleams on an enemy's head;

Look down on their long line of baggage, their huge guns of
    iron and brass,
That, as sure as my name is O'Hogan, will ne'er to the William-
    ites pass!

" Spur, then, to the green shores of Brosna—see Ned of the
    hills on your way—
Have all the brave boys at the muster by Brosna at close of the
    day;
I'll ride off for Sarsfield to Lim'rick, and tell what I've seen
    from the hill—
If Sarsfield won't capture their cannon, by the Cross of Kildare,
    but we will!"

Away to the north went young Johnnie, like an arbalist bolt in
    his speed,
Away to the west brave O'Hogan gives bridle and spur to his
    steed;
Through the fierce highland torrent he dashes, through copse
    and down greenwood full fain,
Till he biddeth farewell to the mountains, and sweeps o'er the
    flat lowland plain!

You'd search from the grey Rocks of Cashel each side to the
    blue ocean's rim,
Through green dale, and hamlet, and city, but you'd ne'er find
    a horseman like him;
With his foot, as if grown to the stirrup, his knee, with its
    rooted hold ta'en,
With his seat in the saddle so graceful, and his sure hand so
    light on the rein!

As the cloud-shadow skims o'er the meadows, when the fleet-
    wingèd summer-winds blow,
By war-wasted castle and village, and streamlet and crag doth
    he go;
The foam-flakes drop quick from his charger, yet never a bridle
    draws he,
Till he baits in the hot, blazing noontide by the cool fairy well
    of Lisbui!

He rubbed down his charger full fondly, the dry grass he heaped
    for its food,
He ate of the green cress and shamrock, and drank of the sweet
    crystal flood;
He's up in his saddle and flying o'er wood track and broad
    heath once more,
Till the sand 'neath the hoofs of his charger is crunch'd by the
    wide Shannon's shore!

For never a ford did he linger, but swam his good charger
    across—
It clomb the steep bank like a wolf-dog—then dashed over
    moorland and moss.
The shepherds who looked from the highland, they crossed
    themselves thrice as he passed,
And they said 'twas a sprite from Crag Aeivil went by on the
    wings of the blast.

### PART THE SECOND.

Dutch Bill sent a summons to Limerick—a summons to open
    their gate,
Their fortress and stores to surrender, else the pike and the gun
    were their fate.

Brave Sarsfield he answered the summons: "Though all holy
    Ireland in flames
Blazed up to the skies to consume us, we'll hold the good town
    for King James."

Dutch Bill, when he listed the answer, he stamped, and he
    vowed, and he swore
That he'd bury the town, ere he'd leave it, in grim fiery ruin
    and gore;
From black Ireton's Fort with his cannon he hammered it well
    all the day,
And he wished for his huge guns to back him that were yet
    o'er the hills far away.

The soft curfew bell from Saint Mary's tolled out in the calm
    sunset air,
And Sarsfield stood high on the rampart and looked o'er the
    green fields of Clare;
And anon from the copses of Cratloe a flash to his keen eyes
    there came,
'Twas the spike of O'Hogan's bright basnet glist'ning forth in
    the red sunset flame!

Then down came the galloping horseman with the speed of a
    culverin ball,
And he reined up his foam-fleckèd charger with a gallant gam-
    bade by the wall;
And his keen eye searched tower, fosse and rampart—they lay
    all securely and still—
And then to the bold Lord of Lucan, he told what he'd seen
    from the hill!

The good steed he rests in the stable, the bold rider feasts at the
    board,
But the gay, laughing revel once ended, he'll soon have a feast
    for his sword;
And now he looks out at the window, where the moonbeams
    flash pale on the square,
For Sarsfield, full dight in his harness, with five hundred bold
    troopers, is there!

He's mounted his steed in the moonlight, and away from the
    North Gate they go,
Where the woods cast their black spectral shadows, and the
    streams with their lone voices flow;
The peasants awoke from their slumbers, and prayed, as they
    swept through the glen,
For they thought 't was the great Garodh Earla that thundered
    adown with his men!

The grey, ghastly midnight was 'round them, the banks they
    were rocky and steep;
The hills with one sullen roar echoed, for the huge stream was
    angry and deep;
But the bold Lord of Lucan he cared not, he asked for no light
    save the moon's,
And he's forded the broad, lordly Shannon with his galloping
    guide and dragoons.

The star of the morning out glimmered, as fast by Lisearly they
    rode;
As they swept round the base of Comailta the sun on their
    bright helmets glowed.

Now the steeds in the valley are grazing, and the horsemen
    crouch down in the broom,
And Sarsfield peers out like an eagle on the low-lying plains
    from Sliav Bloom.

### PART THE THIRD.

O'Hogan is down in the valleys, a watch on the track of the
    foe,
Johnnie Moran from Brosna is marching, that his men be in
    time for a blow.
All day from the bright blooming heather the tall Lord of Lucan
    looks down
On the roads, where the train of Dutch Billy on its slow march
    of danger is bowne.

The red sunset died in the heavens; night fell over mountain
    and shore;
The moon shed her light on the valleys, and the stars glimmered
    brightly once more;
Then Sarsfield sprang up from the heather, for a horse tramp
    he heard on the waste,
'Twas O'Hogan, the black mountain sweeping, like a specter of
    night, in his haste!

" Lord Lucan, they've camped in the forest that skirts Bally-
    neety's grey tower;
I've found out the path to fall on them and slay in the dread
    midnight hour;
They have powder, pontoons, and great cannons—Dhar Dhia!
    but their long tubes are bright!
They have treasure *galeor* for the taking, and their watchword
    is ' Sarsfield!' to-night."

The star of the midnight was shining when the gallant dragoons
    got the word,
Each sprang with one bound to his saddle, and looked to his
    pistols amd sword;
And away down Comailta's deep valleys the guide and bold
    Sarsfield are gone,
While the long stream of helmets behind them in the cold moon-
    light glimmered and shone.

They stayed not for loud brawling river, they looked not for
    togher or path,
They tore up the long street of Cullen with the speed of the
    storm in its wrath;
When on old Ballyneety they thundered, the sentinel's chal-
    lenge rang clear—
" Ho! Sarsfield's the word," cried Lord Lucan, "and you'll soon
    find that Sarsfield is here!"

He clove through the sentinel's basnet, he rushed by the side of
    the glen,
And down on the enemy's convoy, where they stood to their
    cannons like men;
His troopers with pistol and saber, through the camp like a
    whirlwind tore,
With a crash and a loud-ringing war-cry, and a plashing and
    stamping in gore!

The red-coated convoy they've sabered, Dutch Billy's mighty
    guns they have ta'en,
And they laugh as they look on their capture, for they'll ne'er
    see such wonders again;

Those guns, with one loud roaring volley, might batter a strong
    mountain down,
*Wirristhru* for its gallant defenders, if they e'er came to Limerick
    town!

They filled them and rammed them with powder, they turned
    down their mouths to the clay.
The dry casks they piled all around them, the baggage above
    did they lay;
A mine train they laid to the powder, afar to the greenwood
    out thrown—
" Now, give us the match!" cried Lord Lucan, " and an earth-
    quake we'll have of our own!"

O'Hogan the quick fuse he lighted—it whizzed—then a flash
    and a glare
Of broad blinding brightness infernal burst out in the calm
    midnight air;
A hoarse crash of thunder volcanic roared up to the bright stars
    on high,
And the splinters of guns and of baggage showered flaming
    around through the sky!

The firm earth it rocked and and it trembled, the camp showed
    its red pools of gore,
And old Ballyneety's grey castle came down with a crash and a
    roar;
The fierce sound o'er highland and lowland rolled on like the
    dread earthquake's tramp,
And it wakened Dutch Bill from his slumbers and gay dreams
    that night in his camp!

Lord Lucan dashed back o'er the Shannon ere the bright star of
    morning arose,
With his men through the North Gate he clattered, unhurt and
    unseen by his foes;
Johnny Moran rushed down from Comailta—not a foe was alive
    for his blade,
But his men searched the black gory ruins, and the deil's in the
    spoil that they made!

JAMES CLARENCE MANGAN.

**B**ERENGER, the Gallican Nightingale, was ushered into life in the humble dwelling of a tailor, and Burns—Nature's "bonnie bard"—first opened his eyes to the reality of existence in a peasant's lowly cot. Like these illustrious favorites of the lyric muse, the subject of our present paper was born in humble, inauspicious circumstances His father, a native of Limerick County, about 1801 settled in Fishamble street, Dublin, where he married a Miss Smith, who became the mother of James Clarence, in the early part of that eventful year (1803) which witnessed the noble Emmet's death upon a scaffold and hailed the birth of gentle Gerald Griffin. Of his school-boy days we know little more than that he received the rudiments of an education in Derby lane. What the direction of his young ideas was the school registers say not. But this *tabella erassa* is not a proof that he was devoid of talent; for it is a fact well attested by experience that those who run most successfully through their college *curriculum* very seldom distinguish themselves in the broad arena of the world.

We do know, however, that the youthful Mangan
had a gentle, loving spirit, and that as attorney's
clerk he supported his mother and two sisters, who
were dependent on him for sustenance; he toiled all
day over mechanical formulas of law, in order to
fulfill his filial and fraternal obligations, and pro-
longed his vigils far into the night in pursuit of
knowledge. A few years of well-directed labor and
almost undivided attention sufficed to make him a
prodigy of linguistic learning. Besides being versed
in most of the modern and two or more of the
ancient languages, he acquired an immese fund of
general knowledge; but at what cost of energy and
application those students alone can calculate who
have laid down the principle that to acquire a great
store of knowledge requires great labor. In the language of Æneas:

> Tantæ molis erat Romanam condere gentem.

Thus passed his youth in acquiring the means to
an end of triumph and literary fame. His triumphs,
in a worldly point of view, were indeed like angels'
visits—few and far between. "His fate," says John
Mitchel, "was the common fate of poets—he loved
and was disappointed." An avalon of beauty and
ineffable bliss dawned upon his vigorous imagination, and his feelings found expression in song. The
maiden on whom he lavished his love was enraptured

for a while by the sweetness and depth of his effusions. She encouraged his advances until every fibre
of his soul was entwined round her, until she became
a part of his very existence; and then, meanly bar-
tering the pure and generous affections of a noble
soul for the luxuries of a rich dwelling, she tore him
from her heart and rudely cast him into "outer
darkness."

One of his translations gives color and form to
his own feelings on this occasion:

### AND THEN NO MORE.

I SAW her once, one little while, and then no more;
'Twas Eden's light on Earth awhile, and then no more.
Amid the throng she pass'd along the meadow-floor;
Spring seem'd to smile on Earth awhile, and then no more.
But whence she came, which way she went, what garb she
      wore,
I noted not. I gazed awhile, and then no more.

I saw her once, one little while, and then no more;
'T was Paradise on earth awhile, and then no more;
Oh! what avail my vigils pale, my magic lore?
She shone before mine eyes awhile, and then no more.
The shallop of my Peace is wrecked on Beauty's shore;
Near Hope's fair isle it rode awhile, and then no more!

I saw her once, one little while, and then no more;
Earth looked like Heaven a little while, and then no more.

Her presence thrill'd and lighted to its inner core
My desert breast a little while, and then no more.
So may, perchance, a meteor glance at midnight o'er
Some ruin'd pile a little while, and then no more!

I saw her once, one little while, and then no more;
The earth was Peri-land awhile, and then no more.
Oh, might I see but once again, as once before,
Through chance or wile, that shape awhile, and then no more.
Death soon would heal my griefs! This heart, now sad and sore,
Would beat anew a little while, and then no more!

False Frances was the first and the last that thrilled
his "desert breast." He soon became callous to the
beauties of the world. Life for him had no more
attractions. With the Latin poet he could sadly but
sincerely say: "Nihil amplius volo." Like Edgar
Allen Poe, he "loved and lost," and like him, too,
he fell into despair.

Among his original compositions there is a grim
and ghastly poem, entitled "The Nameless One,"
which is an epitome of the inner-Mangan. It runs
thus:

## THE NAMELESS ONE.

Roll on, my song, like the rushing river
  That sweeps along to the mighty sea;
God will inspire me while I deliver
               My soul to thee.

Tell thou the world when my bones are whit'ning
   Amid the last homes of youth and eld,
That there was once one whose veins ran lightning
            No eye beheld.

Tell how his manhood was one drear night hour—
   How shone for him 'mid the grief and gloom
No star of all that Heaven sends to light our
            Path to the tomb.

Roll on my soul, and to after ages
   Tell how, disdaining all earth can give,
He would have taught men from Wisdom's pages
            The way to live.

Tell how the nameless, condemned for years long
   To herd with demons from hell beneath,
Saw things that made him with groans and tears long
            For even death.

Go on to tell how, with genius wasted,
   Betrayed in friendship, befooled in love,
With spirits shipwrecked and young hopes blasted,
            He still, still strove.

And tell how now, amid wreck and sorrow,
   And want and sickness, and homeless nights,
He bides in calmness the silent morrow
            That no day lights.

And lives he still ?  Yes, old and hoary
   At forty-nine, from despair and woe,
He lives, enduring what future story
            Will never know.

Such is the picture of Mangan's inner life; such, alas! was the life of a consummate poet, an ardent patriot, a man of splendid talents and liberal acquirements. In his social relations, unlike the majority of literary men, he seldom referred to his trials or triumphs. Since the year 1828 to the time of his death he had been before the public as a regular contributor to the best magazines of the Irish metropolis; and even when O'Connell shook the senate halls of England the influence of Mangan's pen was felt and his genius acknowledged. Yet he seldom had a word to say even to friends about his own projects or achievements. It is not so with the *genus irritabile* of our times.

Honest John Mitchel, the poet's faithful friend, describes him as a man under the middle height, with a finely formed head, clear blue eyes, and features of a peculiar mold and delicacy. His countenance bore traces of sorrow, and his figure, though well shaped, was meagre more from care and ill-usage than by nature. Like most men of true genius, he was shy, sensitive and sympathetic almost to a fault; and though he would enter warmly into conversation with intimate friends, he seldom sought society.

He had no ostensible connection with the "Young Ireland Association;" yet there was not a member of that brilliant constellation of Irish genius more active in disseminating the doctrine of physical force and resistance to tyrants. He held, perhaps, the first rank among the staff of poetical writers whose productions gave a high literary standing to the *Nation* almost from the initial number.

All his poems are pregnant with the fire of that patriotism which bade the genius of Davis to vibrate; and as no species of writing has such influence on the human heart as poetry, and as few men, according to Mitchel, were better acquainted with the manifold sounds and exquisite notes of the Irish harp than James Clarence Mangan, it may be safely asserted that his harmonious songs caused many a Celtic heart to pulsate with patriotic emotion,

> From the shelving shore of Antrim
> To the sunny slopes of Beare.

From the establishment of the *United Irishman* by Mitchel until its suppression in '48, Mangan contributed regularly to its columns, and his splendid translations from Spanish, French and German formed a new feature of newspaper literature in Ireland. His translations from the Gaelic were very considerable, and selected from the most mournful pieces of the Munster Bards. "Patrick Sarsfield" and "Dark Rosaleen" lost nothing of their original vigor and intensity under his master hand. Nor did the "Cathaleen Ni Houlihan" lose any of her warmth and beauty in exchanging her "Bearla fina" for an Anglican robe. "Cathaleen Ni Houlihan" was a poetical name for Erin.

LET none believe this lovely Eve outworn and old;
Fair is her form, her blood is warm, her heart is bold—
Though strangers long have wrought her wrong, she will not
      fawn,
Will not prove mean, our Cathaleen Ni Houlihan.

We will not bear the chains we wear, nor wear them long;
We seem bereaven, but mighty Heaven will make us strong.
The God who led through Ocean Red all Israel on
Will aid our Queen, our Cathaleen Ni Houlihan.

He has, according to competent authority, by which the English version was compared with the original manuscript, given us an excellent translation of St. Patrick's Hymn before Tara. This Irish MS., which Usher believed to be 1260 years old, is still preserved in Trinity College, Dublin. In these translations from the language of the Brehon Law, it is said that, "while retaining all the phraseology of the originals, they have lost nothing of their primitive energy and beauty." His rendition of German into English was equally clever and successful. Most literary connoisseurs prefer his translation of Schiller's beautiful poem, "The Ideal," to that of Bulwer from the same original. This is Mangan's version:

## THE IDEAL.

EXTINGUISHED in the darkness lies the sun
  That lighted up my shrivelled world of wonder;
Those fairy-bands Imagination spun
  Around my heart have long been reft asunder.
Gone forever is the fine belief—
  The all too generous trust in the Ideal;
All my divinities have died of grief,
  And left me wedded to the rude and Real.

This needs no commentary.

There is one of his productions which seems to bespeak alike the prophet and the poet—his

## IRISH NATIONAL HYMN.

O IRELAND, ancient Ireland—
  Ancient yet forever young—
You, our mother-home and sireland,
  You, at length have found a tongue.
The flag of freedom floats unfurled,
  And as the mighty God existeth
  Who giveth victory, when and where he listeth,
Thou yet shalt wake and shake the nations of the world.

For this dull world still slumbers,
  Weetless of its wants and loves;
Though, like Galileo, numbers
  Cry aloud: " It moves, it moves!"

All march, but few decry the goal;
  Oh, Ireland, be it thy high duty ·
To teach the world the might of Moral Beauty,
  And stamp God's image on the struggling soul.

          *       *       *       *       *

Go on, then, all rejoiceful,
  Marching on thy career unbowed;
Ireland, let thy noble voiceful
  Spirit cry to God aloud.
  Man will bid thee speed,
  God will aid thee in thy need.
The time, the hour, the power are near;
  Be sure thou soon shalt form the vanguard
  Of that illustrious band whom heaven and man guard,
And these words come from one whom some have called a *seer*.

One specimen more and we shall draw this brief
and imperfect paper to a close.   Such a specimen as
this will not surely tire any true lover of poetry.   It
is a translation of Rucket's

### DYING FLOWER.

AND woe to me! fond, foolish one,
  To tempt the all-absorbing ray,
To think a flower could love a sun
  Nor feel her soul dissolve away;
But vainly in my bitterness
  I speak the language of despair:
In life, in death, I still must bless
  The sun, the light, the cradling air.

Mine early love to them I gave;
 And now that yon bright orb on high
Illumines but a wider grave,
 For them I breathe my final sigh.

How often soared my soul aloft,
 In balmy bliss too deep to speak;
When zephyrs came and kissed with soft
 Sweet incense-breath my blushing cheek!
When beauteous bees and butterflies
 Flew round me in the summer beam,
Or when some virgin's glorious eyes
 Bent o'er me like a dazzling dream.

This is a poem with a moral, almost perfect in rhyme and rhythm, abounding in alliteration and sparkling with beauty of thought and expression.

Strange to say that an admiring public should neglect a man of Mangan's taste and talent; but such neglect is almost the common inheritance of genius. Spencer, the "sweet, foreign songster of the Mula," ended his days in a public hospital; Tasso could seldom get a good suit of clothes; and Dryden, who lived a life of penury, died in distress. Like those, Mangan was destitute of the comforts of a home, and like them he was driven to drinking to excess. Dr. Petrie obtained a situation for him in the Library of Trinity College, but this succor came too late to stay the ravages of want and despair. Nor could all the efforts of the learned Father Meehan effect more than to "gently slope" his pathway to a premature grave. Even when a mere skeleton he still wrote for the newspapers, to procure him the necessaries of life.

The Rev. C. P. Meehan has left us the best memoir of Mangan which has so far been written. The reverend author of the "Flight of the Earls" frequently assisted Mangan while living, and administered to him the last Sacraments when dying. A poet himself, a nationalist and a scholar, he was well qualified for such a work.

We wish, however, he had given us a more striking picture of the coterie of literary worthies— Meagher, Mangan, Mitchel, Duffy and Williams—who were wont to meet one evening of each week in his own little study, at the rectory on Exchange Street, for the discussion of matters, literary and political. But, unfortunately, the writer's modesty deterred him from bringing out in bold relief a group in which he himself was a prominent and important figure.

From 1832 to 1834 Mangan was associated with Dr. O'Donovan, O'Keeffe, O'Curry and Dr. Petrie in writing and arranging the "Ordinance Survey Memoir of Ireland"; and it was during this period that he made most of his translations from the Irish language. O'Donovan and O'Curry rendered many remains of the Irish bards into English prose, and

Mangan turned the literal translations into verse with a felicity which astonished his literary contemporaries. The distinguished archaeologist, Petrie, was at that time editor of the Dublin *Penny Journal*, for which our author wrote almost regularly over the pseudonym of "Clarence." After completing his engagement on the "Survey" business he became a writer in the Dublin *University Magazine*, and through the pages of that brilliant periodical he first appeared in the character of translator from Continental languages. He had an intimate acquaintance with German and Spanish, and needed no outside assistance to select the choicest garlands from foreign gardens. During his incumbency as Librarian of Trinity College he published in the *University Magazine* a series of translations under the caption of "Literæ Orientales." These, of course, were the pure emanations of Mangan's own muse with a savor of Orientalism given thereunto. The best known of this batch are "The Time of the Barmecides," and "Boating Down the Bosphorus." These possess much merit and seem to grow in popularity with the lapse of time.

When Thomas Davis was struck down in the midst of his labors and the flowering of his intellectual strength, Charles Gavan Duffy attempted to supply his place by inducing Mangan to write more frequently for the *Nation*. But he could not get him to pull in harness for any considerable time at a stretch; and although his poetry, in many—very many—respects, is superior to anything Davis wrote, he could not fill the place made vacant by the death of the latter.

In the Fall of 1848 he was a patient at St. Vincent's Hospital, and while there arranged with the patriotic publisher, John O'Daly, for the issuing of the "Poets and Poetry of Munster."

This little work gained at once a wide popularity, and the profits accruing from large sales relieved the pressing wants of the translator and editor. But early in the next year he was to be found in the hospital again—this time in the Meath Hospital. Finding that the end was approaching, he sent for his faithful friend, Father Meehan, who watched over him day after day.

As the Poet-Priest entered the sick-room on the morning of June 19th, 1849, Mangan said to him: "I feel that my hour is near, and I want to be anointed."

On the evening of the following day he expired with the Saviour's name upon his lips, his hands crossed upon his breast and his eyes firmly fixed upon the symbol of Redemption, which was held up to his waning vision by his true friend and spiritual Father.

Such is the outline of Mangan's career. He lived forty-six years, and in that short span accomplished a great deal. "He might have done more," it is true, and he certainly would under different circumstances. We thank him for all he has done, instead of finding fault because he has not done more.

Many of his original poems and translations have found a permanent place in the best standard works of English literature, and his name occupies a warm corner in the affection of the Irish race, both at home and abroad.

Ireland has raised a monument to his memory in Glasnevin; and when the proud ones, who sneered at his threadbare coat and shunned him for his poverty, shall be remembered only in connection with his fame, his songs shall perpetuate untarnished and unimpaired the brilliant genius and ardent patriotism of James Clarence Mangan.

The following ballad was written under the inspiration of the "physical force" doctrines of the "Young Irelanders," and it is certainly well calculated to rouse an oppressed and plundered people to action. Subsequently it became a favorite among the members of the Fenian Brotherhood:

## HIGHWAY FOR FREEDOM.

" My suffering country SHALL be freed,
    And shine with tenfold glory!"
So spake the gallant Winkelreid,
    Renowned in German story.
" No tyrant, ev'n of kingly grade,
    Shall cross or darken *my* way!"
Out flashed his blade, and so he made
    For Freedom's course a highway!

We want a man like this, with power
    To rouse the world by *one* word;
We want a chief to meet the hour,
    And march the masses onward.
But chief or none, through blood and fire,
    My Fatherland, lies *thy* way!
The men must fight who dare desire
    For Freedom's course a highway!

Alas! I can but idly gaze
    Around in grief and wonder;
The People's will alone can raise
    The People's shout of thunder.
Too long, my friends, you faint for fear,
    In secret crypt and by-way;
At last be Men! Stand forth, and clear
    For Freedom's course a highway!

You intersect wood, lea, and lawn,
    With roads for monster wagons,
Wherein you speed like lightning, drawn
    By fiery iron dragons.

So do!   Such work is good, no doubt;
    But why not seek some nigh way
For MIND, as well?   Path also out
    For Freedom's course a highway!

Yes! up! and let your weapons be
    Sharp steel and self-reliance!
Why waste your burning energy
    In void and vain defiance,
And phrases fierce and fugitive?
    'Tis deeds, not words, that *I* weigh—
Your swords and guns alone caň give
    To Freedom's course a highway.

## THE WOMAN OF THREE COWS.

(Translated from the Irish.)

[This ballad, which is of homely cast, was intended as a rebuke to the
saucy pride of a woman in humble life, who assumed airs of consequence
from being the possessor of three cows. Its author's name is unknown, but
its age can be determined, from the language, as belonging to the early part
of the seventeenth century. That it was formerly very popular in Munster
may be concluded from the fact that the phrase, "Easy, oh, woman of the
three cows!" has become a saying in that Province, on any occasion upon
which it is desirable to lower the pretensions of a boastful or consequential
person.]

O, WOMAN of Three Cows, agra! don't let your tongue thus
        rattle!
O, don't be saucy, don't be stiff, because you may have cattle.
I have seen—and, here's my hand to you, I only say what's
        true—
A many a one with twice your stock not half so proud as you.

Good luck to you, don't scorn the poor, and don't be their
    despiser,
For worldly wealth soon melts away, and cheats the very miser;
And Death soon strips the proudest wreath from haughty
    human brows.
Then don't be stiff, and don't be proud, good Woman of Three
    Cows!

See where Mononia's heroes lie, proud Owen More's descendants:
'Tis they that won the glorious name, and had the grand
    attendants!
If *they* were forced to bow to Fate, as every mortal bows,
Can *you* be proud, can *you* be stiff, my Woman of Three Cows!

The brave sons of the Lord of Clare, they left the land to
    mourning;
*Movrone!* for they were banished, with no hope of their
    returning—
Who knows in what abodes of want those youths were driven
    to house?
Yet *you* give yourself these airs, O, Woman of Three Cows!

O, think of Donnell of the Ships, the Chief whom nothing
    daunted—
See how he fell in distant Spain, unchronicled, unchanted!
He sleeps, the great O'Sullivan, where thunder cannot rouse—
Then ask yourself, should *you* be proud, good Woman of Three
    Cows!

O'Ruark, Maguire, those souls of fire, whose names are shrined
    in story—
Think how their high achievements once made Erin's greatest
    glory—

Yet now their bones lie mouldering under weeds and cypress
    boughs,
And so, for all your pride, will yours, O, Woman of Three
    Cows!

Th' O'Carrolls, also, famed when Fame was only for the boldest,
Rest in forgotten sepulchres with Erin's best and oldest;
Yet who so great as they of yore in battle or carouse?
Just think of that, and hide your head, good Woman of Three
    Cows!

Your neighbor's poor, and you it seems are big with vain ideas,
Because, forsooth, you've got three cows, one more, I see, than
    *she* has.
That tongue of yours wags more at times than Charity allows,
But, if you're strong, be merciful, great Woman of Three Cows!

### THE SUMMING UP.

Now, there you go! You still, of course, keep up your scornful
    bearing,
And I'm too poor to hinder you; but, by the cloak I'm wearing,
If I had but four cows myself, even tho' you were my spouse,
I'd thwack you well to cure your pride, my Woman of Three
    Cows!

## THE FAIR HILLS OF EIRE, O!

TAKE a blessing from my heart to the land of my birth,
    '     And the fair Hills of Eire, O!
And to all that yet survive of Eibhear's tribe on earth,
        On the fair Hills of Eire, O!
In that land so delightful the wild thrush's lay
Seems to pour a lament forth for Eire's decay—
Alas! alas! why pine I a thousand miles away
        From the fair Hills of Eire, O!

The soil is rich and soft, the air is mild and bland,
        Of the fair Hills of Eire, O!
Her barest rock is greener to me than this rude land—
        Oh, the fair Hills of Eire, O!
Her woods are tall and straight, grove rising over grove;
Trees flourish in her glens below, and on her heights above,
Oh, in heart and in soul, I shall ever, ever love
        The fair Hills of Eire, O!

A noble tribe, moreover, are the now hapless Gael,
        On the fair Hills of Eire, O!
A tribe in battle's hour unused to shrink or fail
        On the fair Hills of Eire, O!
For this is my lament in bitterness outpoured,
To see them slain or scattered by the Saxon sword—
Oh, woe of woes, to see a foreign spoiler horde
        On the fair Hills of Eire, O!

Broad and tall rise the *Cruachs* in the golden morning's glow
        On the fair Hills of Eire, O!
O'er her smooth grass for ever sweet cream and honey flow
        On the fair Hills of Eire, O!

Oh, I long, I am pining, again to behold
The land that belongs to the brave Gael of old;
Far dearer to my heart than a gift of gems or gold
    Are the fair Hills of Eire, O!

The dew-drops lie bright 'mid the grass and yellow corn
    On the fair Hills of Eire, O!
The sweet-scented apples blush redly in the morn
    On the fair Hills of Eire, O!
The water-cress and sorrel fill the vales below;
The streamlets are hush'd, till the evening breezes blow,
While the waves of the Suir, noble river! ever flow
    Near the fair Hills of Eire, O!

A fruitful clime is Eire's, through valley, meadow, plain,
    And the fair land of Eire, O!
The very " Bread of Life " is in the yellow grain
    On the fair Hills of Eire, O!
Far dearer unto me than the tones music yields,
Is the lowing of the kine and the calves in her fields,
And the sunlight that shone long ago on the shields
    Of the Gaels, on the fair Hills of Eire, O!


## SOUL AND COUNTRY.

Arise! my slumbering soul, arise!
  And learn what yet remains for thee
    To dree or do!
The signs are flaming in the skies;
  A struggling world would yet be free,
    And live anew.

The earthquake hath not yet been born,
  That soon shall rock the lands around,
    Beneath their base.
Immortal freedom's thunder horn,
  As yet, yields but a doleful sound
    To Europe's race.

Look round, my soul, and see and say
  If those about thee understand
    Their mission here;
The will to smite—the power to slay—
  Abound in every heart and hand,
    Afar, anear.

But, God! must yet the conqueror's sword
  Pierce *mind*, as heart, in this proud year?
    Oh, dream it not!
It sounds a false, blaspheming word,
  Begot and born of moral fear—
    And ill-begot!

To leave the world a name is nought;
  To leave a name for glorious deeds
    And works of love—
A name to waken lightning thought,
  And fire the soul of him who reads,
    *This* tells above.
Napoleon sinks to-day before
  Th' ungilded shrine, the *single* soul
    Of Washington;
Truth's name, alone, shall man adore,
  Long as the waves of time shall roll
    Henceforward on!

My countrymen! my words are weak,
My health is gone, my soul is dark,
My heart is chill—
Yet would I fain and fondly seek
Too see you borne in freedom's bark
O'er ocean still.
Beseech your God, and bide your hour—
He cannot, will not long be dumb;
Even now His tread
Is heard o'er earth with coming power;
And coming, trust me, it will come,
Else were He dead!


## CAHAL MOR OF THE WINE-RED HAND.

### (A vision of Connaught in the Thirteenth Century.)

I WALKED entranced
Through a land of morn;
The sun, with wondrous excess of light,
Shone down and glanced
Over seas of corn,
And lustrous gardens aleft and right.
Even in the clime
Of resplendent Spain
Beams no such sun upon such a land;
But it was the time,
'Twas in the reign
Of Cahal Mor of the Wine-red Hand.

Anon stood nigh
By my side a man
Of princely aspect and port sublime.
Him queried I,

" Oh, my lord and khan,
What clime is this, and what golden time ?"
    When he—'' The clime
        Is a clime to praise,
The clime is Erin's, the green and bland;
    And it is the time,
        These be the days
Of Cahal Mor of the Wine-red Hand!"

        Then I saw thrones
            And circling fires,
And a dome rose near me, as by a spell,
        Whence flowed the tones
            Of silver lyres
And many voices in wreathed swell;
        And their thrilling chime
            Fell on mine ears
As the heavenly hymn of angel-band—
    " It is now the time,
        These be the years
Of Cahal Mor of the Wine-red Hand '"

    I sought the hall,
        And, behold!—a change
From light to darkness, from joy to woe;
    Kings, nobles, all,
        Looked aghast and strange
The minstrel-group sate in dumbest show!

Had some great crime
　　Wrought this dread amaze,
This terror?　None seemed to understand.
　'T was then the time,
　　We were in the days
Of Cahal Mor of the Wine-red Hand.

　I again walked forth;
　　But lo! the sky
Showed fleckt with blood, and an alien sun
　Glared from the north,
　　And there stood on high,
Amid his shorn beams, a Skeleton!
　It was by the stream
　　Of the castled Maine,
One autumn-eve, in the Teuton's land
　That I dreamed this dream
　　Of the time and reign
Of Cahal Mor of the Wine-red hand!


## LAMENT FOR BANBA.

Oh, my land! oh, my love!
　　What a woe, and how deep
Is thy death to my long-mourning soul!
　God alone, God above,
　　Can awake thee from sleep—
Can release thee from bondage and dole!
　　Alas, alas, and alas,
　　　For the once proud people of Banba!

As a tree in its prime,
    Which the axe layeth low,
Didst thou fall, O, unfortunate land!
  Not by Time, nor thy crime,
    Came the shock and the blow.
They were given by a false felon hand!
    Alas, alas, and alas,
        For the once proud people of Banba!
  Oh, my grief of all griefs
    Is to see how thy throne
Is usurped, whilst thyself art in thrall!
  Other lands have their chiefs,
    Have their kings; thou alone
Art a wife—yet a widow withal.
    Alas, alas, and alas,
        For the once proud people of Banba!
  The high house of O'Neill
    Is gone down to the dust,
The O'Brien is clanless and banned;
  And the steel, the red steel,
    May no more be the trust
Of the faithful and brave in the land!
    Alas, alas, and alas,
        For the once proud people of Banba!
  True, alas!   Wrong and wrath
    Were of old all too rife,
Deeds were done which no good man admires;
  And, perchance, Heaven hath
    Chastened us for the strife
And the blood-shedding ways of our sires!
    Alas, alas, and alas,
        For the once proud people of Banba!

But, no more!  This our doom,
　　While our hearts yet are warm,
Let us not over-weakly deplore!
　　For the hour soon may loom
　　When the Lord's mighty hand
Shall be raised for our rescue once more!
　　　And our grief shall be turned into joy
　　　For the still proud people of Banba!

## THE TIME OF THE BARMECIDES.

### (Translated from the Arabic.)

My eyes are film'd, my beard is gray,
　　I am bow'd with the weight of years;
I would I were stretched in my bed of clay,
　　With my long lost youth's compeers!
For back to the Past, tho' the thought brings woe,
　　My memory ever glides
To the old, old time long, long ago,
　　The time of the Barmecides
To the old, old time long, long ago,
　　The time of the Barmecides.

Then Youth was mine, and a fierce wild will,
　　And an iron arm in war,
And a fleet foot high upon Ishkar's hill,
　　When the watch-lights glimmer'd afar;
And a barb as fiery as any I know
　　That Khoord or Beddaween rides,
Ere my friends lay low—long, long ago,
　　In the time of the Barmecides.
Ere my friends lay low—long, long ago,
　　In the time of the Barmecides.

One golden goblet illumed my board,
  One silver dish was there;
At hand my tried Karamanian sword
  Lay always bright and bare.
For those were the days when the angry blow
  Supplanted the word that chides—
When hearts could glow—long, long ago,
  In the time of the Barmecides; ·
When hearts could glow—long, long ago,
  In the time of the Barmecides.

Through city and desert my mates and I
  Were free to rove and roam,
Our diaper'd canopy the deep of the sky,
  Or the roof of the palace dome—
Oh! ours was that vivid life, to and fro,
  Which only sloth derides—
Men spent Life so, long, long ago,
  In the time of the Barmecides.
Men spent Life so, long, long ago,
  In the time of the Barmecides.

I see rich Bagdad once again,
  With its turrets of Moorish mould,
And the Khalif's twice five hundred men
  Whose binishes flamed with gold;
I call up many a gorgeous show
  Which the pall of Oblivion hides—
All pass'd like snow, long, long ago,
  With the time of the Barmecides;
All pass'd like snow, long, long ago,
  With the time of the Barmecides!

But mine eye is dim, and my beard is gray,
    And I bend with the weight of years—
May I soon go down to the house of clay
    Where slumber my Youth's compeers!
For with them and the Past, though the thought wakes woe,
    My memory ever abides;
And I mourn for the times gone long ago,
    For the times of the Barmecides!
I mourn for the times gone long ago,
    For the times of the Barmecides!


## THE POET'S PREACHING.

### (From the German of Salis Seewis.)

SEE how the day beameth brightly before us!
    Blue is the firmament, green is the earth—
Grief hath no voice in the universe-chorus—
    Nature is ringing with music and mirth.
Lift up the looks that are sinking in sadness—
    Gaze! and if Beauty can capture thy soul,
Virtue herself will allure thee to gladness—
    Gladness, Philosophy's guerdon and goal.

Enter the treasuries Pleasure uncloses—
    List! how she thrills in the nightingale's lay!
Breathe! she is wafting thee sweets from the roses;
    Feel! she is cool in the rivulet's play;
Taste! from the grape and the nectarine gushing
    Flows the red rill in the beams of the sun—
Green in the hills, in the flower groves blushing,
    Look! she is always and everywhere one.

Banish, then, mourner, the tears that are trickling
  Over the cheeks that should rosily bloom;
Why should a man, like a girl or a sickling,
  Suffer his lamp to be quenched in the tomb?
Still may we battle for Goodness and Beauty;
  Still hath Philanthropy much to essay:
Glory rewards the fulfillment of Duty;
  Rest will pavilion the end of our way.

What, though corroding and multiplied sorrows,
  Legion-like, darken this planet of ours,
Hope is a balsam the wounded heart borrows
  Ever when Anguish has palsied its powers;
Wherefore, though Fate played the part of a traitor,
  Soar o'er the stars on the pinions of Hope,
Fearlessly certain that sooner or later
  Over the stars thy desires shall have scope.

Look round about on the face of Creation,
  Still is GOD's Earth undistorted and bright;
Comfort the captives to long tribulation,
  Thus shalt thou reap the more perfect delight.
Love!—but if Love be a hallowed emotion,
  Purity only its rapture should share;
Love, then, with willing and deathless emotion
  All that is just and exalted and fair.

Act!—for in Action are Wisdom and Glory.
  Fame, Immortality—these are its crown;
Wouldst thou illumine the tablets of story,
  Build on ACHIEVEMENTS thy Dome of Renown.

Honor and Feeling were giv'n thee to cherish,
  Cherish them, then, though all else should decay,
Landmarks be these that are never to perish,
  Stars that will shine on thy duskiest day.

Courage!—Disaster and Peril once over,
  Freshen the spirit as showers the grove,
O'er the dim graves that the cypresses cover
  Soon the Forget-me-not rises in love.
Courage, then, friends!  Though the universe crumble,
  Innocence, dreadless of danger beneath,
Patient and trustful and joyous and humble,
  Smiles through the ruin on Darkness and Death.

## TO JOSEPH BRENNAN.

### BALLAD.

FRIEND and brother, and yet more than brother,
  Thou, endow'd with all of Shelley's soul!
Thou, whose heart so burneth for thy mother,
That, like *his*, it may defy all other
  Flames, while time shall roll!

Thou, of language bland and manner meekest,
  Gentle bearing, yet unswerving will—
Gladly, gladly list I when thou speakest,
Honor'd highly is the man thou seekest
  To redeem from ill!

Truly show'st thou me the one thing needful!
  Thou art not, nor is the world yet blind.
Truly have I been long years unheedful
Of the thorns and tares that choked the needful
  Garden of my mind!

Thorns and tares, which rose in rank profusion
   Round my scanty fruitage and my flowers,
Till I almost deemed it self-delusion,
Any attempt or glance at their extrusion
   From their midnight bowers.

Dream and waking life have now been blended
   Long time in the caverns of my soul—
Oft in daylight have my steps descended
Down to that dusk realm where all is ended,
   Save remed'less dole!

Oft, with tears, I have groan'd to God for pity—
   Oft gone wandering till my way grew dim—
Oft sung unto Him a prayerful ditty—
Oft, all lonely in this throngful city,
   Raised my soul to Him!

And from path to path His mercy track'd me—
   From many a peril snatched He me;
When false friendship pursued, betray'd, attack'd me,
When gloom overdark'd and sickness rack'd me,
   He was by to save and free!

Friend! thou warnest me in truly noble
   Thoughts and phrases! I will heed thee well—
Well will I obey thy mystic double
Counsel, through all scenes of woe and trouble,
   As a magic spell!

Yes! to live a bard, in thought and feeling!
   Yes! to act my rhyme, by self-restraint—
This is truth's, is reason's deep revealing,
Unto me from thee, as God's to a kneeling
   And entrancèd saint!

Fare thee well! we now know each the other,
  Each has struck the other's inmost chords.
Fare thee well, my friend and more than brother,
And may scorn pursue me if I smother
  In my soul thy words!

## IRELAND UNDER IRISH RULE.

### (From the Irish.)

I FOUND in Innisfail the fair,
In Ireland, while in exile there,
Women of worth, both grave and gay men,
Many clerics and many laymen.

I travelled its fruitful provinces round,
And in every one of the five I found,
Alike in church and in palace hall,
Abundant apparel and food for all.

Gold and silver I found, and money,
Plenty of wheat and plenty of honey;
I found God's people rich in pity,
Found many a feast and many a city.

I also found in Armagh the Splendid,
Meekness, wisdom, and prudence blended,
Fasting, as Christ hath recommended,
And noble councillors untranscended.

    *        *        *        *

I found, besides, from Ara to Glea,
In the broad rich country of Ossorie,
Sweet fruits, good laws for all and each,
Great chess-players, men of truthful speech.

I found in Meath's fair principality,
Virtue, vigor, and hospitality;
Candor, joyfulness, bravery, purity,
Ireland's bulwark and security.

I found strict morals in age and youth,
I found historians recording truth;
The things I sing of in verse unsmooth,
I found them all—I have written sooth.

## O MARIA, REGINA MISERICORDLÆ!

THERE lived a knight long years ago,
    Proud, carnal, vain, devotionless.
Of God above, or Hell below,
  He took no thought, but, undismay'd,
    Pursued his course of wickedness.
  His heart was rock; he never pray'd
    To be forgiven for all his treasons;
    He only said at certain seasons,
      " O Mary, Queen of Mercy!"

Years roll'd, and found him still the same,
   ' Still draining Pleasure's poison-bowl;
Yet felt he now and then some shame;
  The torment of the Undying Worm
    At whiles woke in his trembling soul;
  And then, though powerless to reform,
    Would he, in hope to appease that sternest
    Avenger, cry, and more in earnest,
      " O Mary, Queen of Mercy!"

At last Youth's riotous time was gone,
   And loathing now came after sin;
With locks yet brown he felt as one
   Grown gray at heart; and oft with tears
     He tried, but all in vain, to win
From the dark desert of his years
     One flower of hope; yet, morn and e'ening,
     He still cried, but with deeper meaning,
       " O Mary, Queen of Mercy!"

A happier mind, a holier mood,
   A purer spirit, ruled him now;
No more in thrall to flesh and blood,
   He took a pilgrim-staff in hand,
     And, under a religious vow,
Travel'd his way to Pommerland.
     There enter'd he an humble cloister,
     Exclaiming, while his eyes grew moister,
       " O Mary, Queen of Mercy!"

Here, shorn and cowl'd, he laid his cares
   Aside, and wrought for God alone;
Albeit he sang no choral prayers,
   Nor Matin hymn nor Laud could learn,
     He mortified his flesh to stone.
For him no penance was too stern;
     And often pray'd he on his lonely
     Cell-couch at night, but still said only,
       " O Mary, Queen of Mercy!"

And thus he lived long, long; and, when
   God's angels called him, thus he died.
Confession made he none to men,
  Yet, when they anointed him with oil
   He seem'd already glorified;
  His penances, his tears, his toil
   Were past, and now, with passionate sighing,
   Praise thus broke from his lips while dying,
    " O Mary, Queen of Mercy!"

They buried him with Mass and song
   Aneath a little knoll so green;
But, lo! a wonder sight!  Ere long
  'Rose, blooming, from that verdant mound,
   The fairest lily ever seen;
  And, on its petal-edges round,
   Relieving their translucent whiteness,
   Did shine these words in gold-hued brightness:
    " O Mary, Queen of Mercy!"

And, would God's angels give thee power,
   Thou, dearest reader, might behold
The fairness of this holy flower,
  Up-springing from the dead man's heart
   In tremulous threads of light and gold;
  Then wouldst thou choose the better part!
   And thenceforth flee Sin's foul suggestions;
   Thy sole response to mocking questions,
    " O Mary, Queen of Mercy!"

# REV. FATHER RYAN

**T**HE first collection of Father Ryan's Poems, made under his own supervision, contains a preface, in which the author says:

" These verses (which some friends call by the higher title of Poems—to which appellation the author objects) were written at random—off and on, here, there, everywhere—just when the mood came, with little of study and less of art, and always in a hurry.

" Hence they are incomplete in finish as the author is; though he thinks they are true in tone. His feet know more about the humble steps that lead up to the Altar and its Mysteries than of the steps that lead up to Parnassus and the home of the Muses. And souls were always more to him than songs."

This Southern Celt was as modest in his estimation of self as he was truly gifted. Though he knew right well and loved the " steps that led up to the Altar," and served the Altar faithfully, the ascent to Parnassus was to him no difficult task. Yet would he sign himself the *least* of all the bards. It would seem that in a note to Longfellow he made use of language somewhat similar, as we find reference

made to it in the following extract of a letter written
to Father Ryan by the Cambridge Poet:

*Abram J. Ryan.*

"CAMBRIDGE, Dec. 14, 1880.

"  *  *  *  I have read enough of your poetry to see the
fervor of feeling and expression with which you write, and the
melody of the versification.

" Of course, you will hardly expect me to sympathize with
all the ' verses connected with the war.' Yet, in some of
them, I recognize a profound pathos and the infinite pity of it
all.    *    *    *

" P. S.—When you call yourself ' the last and least of those who rhyme,' you remind me of the graceful lines of Catullus to Cicero:

" ' Gratias tibi maximas Catullus
Agit, pessimus omnium poeta:
Tanto pessimus omnium poeta,
Quanto tu optimus omnium patronus.'*

" ' Last and least ' can no more be applied to you than ' pessimus ' to Catullus."

In this comparison a high compliment is paid to the Poet-Priest; and coming from such a distinguished personage as Longfellow it was certainly appreciated.

Late in the Fall of 1880 Father Ryan gave readings from his own poems in the Academy of Music, Baltimore, Md. The proceeds of these public readings were destined to found a Ryan Medal in the Loyola College of that city, and Rev. E. A. McGurk, S. J., presided on the occasion. The audience was made up of the most fashionable and cultured citizens of Maryland, who were anxious to hear the Poet of their " Lost Cause," and to pay to him the homage of their appreciation.

Before reading " A Land Without Ruins," which formed one of his selections on that evening, he pre-

* Catullus sends his thanks to thee,
With most sincere regards—
Thou *greatest* of all Patrons, as he
Is *least* of all the bards.

faced it with a few words.   The lines were applicable
to Ireland, Poland and the South:

" A land without ruins is a land without memories; a land
without memories is a land without a history.   A land that
wears a laurel crown may be fair to see; but twine a few sad
cypress leaves around the brow of any land, and, be that land
barren, beautiless and bleak, it becomes lovely in its consecrated
coronet of sorrow, and it wins the sympathy of the heart and
of history.   Crowns of roses fade; crowns of thorns endure.
Calvaries and crucifixions take deepest hold of humanity; the
triumphs of might are transient; they pass and are forgotten;
the sufferings of right are graven deepest on the chronicle of
nations."

A touching incident, in which originated the
poem entitled " A Death," was thus related by him
during the course of his readings:

" Some years ago the small-pox came to Mobile and raged as
an epidemic.   A great many people died.   I attended many.
I was sent for one evening late, by an outcast of the city, the
leader of the unfortunate class to which she belonged.   Noted
for her beauty, she had fallen away, drifted away from the
paths of virtue, lured by the wiles of others.   I attended her
for thirteen days, and until she died a beautiful death.   The
very words I use in the poem or rhyme I am about to read are
the words she used to me."

Father Ryan here read his charming lines " A
Death."   The words to which he alluded are thus
expressed in his verses:

I have wandered too far, far away,
Oh! would that my mother were here;
Is God like a mother?  Has he
Any love for a sinner like me?

The recitation deeply affected the audience.  As
an introduction to the beautiful poem which came
next in order the gifted poet said:

" There came a time when the yellow fever swept the South;
the politicians were at that time wrangling.  The sympathy of
the North came down with sandals of mercy on her feet to the
poor fever-stricken South, and met her in the sanctuary of her
deepest woe.  The hands of the North and South were thus
clasped once more."

Under these circumstances it was that Father Ryan
wrote " Reunited," which he then read with fine
effect.  So genuinely hearty was the reception given
Father Ryan on this occasion by the best families of
the South that the writer, who had the privilege of
being one of the audience could not help considering, contrary to the dictum of scripture, that this
man was a " prophet in his own country."

The South may be called " his own country," as he
resided there from the cradle to the grave.

Father Ryan was born in Limerick, Ireland, in
April, 1840, and baptized in the old church where
the Florentine Campanaro discovered his lost bells,
as he sailed up the Shannon on a fine summer

evening long ago. While Abram was yet a child his parents came to the United States and settled at Norfolk, Virginia. By industry and tact they surrounded their new home with all the ordinary comforts of life, and devoted not a little of their attention to the education of the future poet and his two brothers. For more than two centuries the family to which Mr. Ryan belonged had given scholarly and zealous priests to the Irish Church, and his ambition, which harmonized with the fondest wish of his pious wife, was to devote one of his sons, at least, to the service of the grand old Church in his adopted land. With this end in view, after having completed his primary studies at home, Abram was sent to St. Vincent's College, Cape Girardeau, Mo., and placed under the watchful care of the Vincentian Fathers, by whom he was educated and prepared for the sacred ministry. In college he gave promise of a brilliant future, and his Rev. Professors spared no labor in drawing out and cultivating the talents he possessed. It is a doctrine, practiced everywhere among the members of this noble Order, never to use two words where one suffices, nor yet a long word where a short one can be made to answer the purpose. Hence their style is remarkably expressive, terse and energetic. Young Ryan, given to literary composition at an early age, very naturally adopted this principle of his devoted teachers, and, as a consequence, his style is direct, precise and without redundancy.

After his ordination, the Rev. A. J. Ryan was appointed to missionary duty at Knoxville, Tenn., where he endeared himself to all classes of society, but especially to the poor.

During the first year of the Civil War his brother David, who was then attending college, joined the Confederate ranks. He possessed a large share of the priest's poetic genius, and his sympathy with the South was equally ardent and strong.

This brother, who in a short time rose to the command of a company, was killed in one of the early engagements. The event is commemorated in the following tender, tearful lines:

### IN MEMORY OF MY BROTHER.

Young as the youngest who donned the gray,
　　True as the truest that wore it,
Brave as the bravest he marched away
(Hot tears on the cheeks of his mother lay),
Triumphant waved our flag one day—
　　He fell in the front before it.

Firm as the firmest where duty led,
    He hurried without a falter;
Bold as the boldest he fought and bled,
And the day was won—but the field was red—
And the blood of his fresh young heart was shed
    On his country's hallowed altar.

On the trampled breast of the battle plain,
    Where the foremost ranks had wrestled,
On his pale, pure face not a mark of pain
(His mother dreams they will meet again),
The fairest form amid all the slain,
    Like a child asleep he nestled.

In the solemn shades of the wood that swept
    The field where his comrades found him,
They buried him there—and the big tears crept
Into strong men's eyes that had seldom wept.
(His mother—God pity her!—smiled and slept,
    Dreaming her arms were around him).

A grave in the woods with the grass o'ergrown,
    A grave in the heart of his mother—
His clay in the one lies lifeless and lone;
There is not a name, there is not a stone,
And only the voice of the wind maketh moan
O'er the grave where never a flower is strewn,
    But—his memory lives in the other.

The Mobile *Register* published this eulogium of the deceased poet:

" No man of genius ever shrank with greater dread from the glare of renown. From his early manhood he has worn the vestments of a priest, and in the solemn pursuits of his office he has spent the power of his life, and through many years of feebleness and pain—

> To the higher shrine of love divine
> His lowly feet have trod;
> He wants no fame, no other name
> Than this—a priest of God.

" But his fame is not his own, it is his country's; and his name fills a page in her history to be cherished by her people for ever.

" When the camp-fires of the war between the States began to cast their lurid glare upon the passions of a people for the first time they profoundly stirred Abram J. Ryan, then a frail and slender youth, who had just entered the priesthood of the Catholic Church. His brother, Captain David Ryan, was among the first to enter the Army of the Confederates, a hopeful young soldier; and in a little while the young priest was found among the Southern host to administer where he could the consolations of religion to the wounded and dying.

" From the stirring scenes of sacrifice and slaughter which a civil war can alone unfold Father Ryan received his first profound impressions. The cradle of his poetic genius was rocked upon the stormy waves of revolution."

Then it was that the sweet, strong voice of the Poet-Priest was heard throughout the land, cheering on the serried hosts and inspiring the champions of a cause in which he sincerely believed to deeds of greater valor.

What could be more war-inspiring than these lines from the " Sword of Lee!"

Out of its scabbard—never hand
Waved sword from stain as free,
Nor purer sword led braver band,
Nor brighter land had a cause so grand,
Nor cause a chief like Lee.

"The Conquered Banner," which is included in the selections we have made from the poems of our author, has taken its place among the greatest lyrics of our language, and there it will remain as long as English is spoken.

"Their Story Runneth Thus," by far his longest poem, is not without defects, but it has many fine qualities which should have won for it a wider recognition than it has ever received. His description of a nun in this plaintive poem is poetically beautiful:

As silent as a star-gleam came a nun,
In answer to his summons at the gate;
Her face was like the picture of a saint,
Or like an angel's smile—her down-cast eyes
Were like a half-closed tabernacle, where
God's presence glowed; her lips were pale and worn
By ceaseless prayer; and when she spoke
And bade him enter, 't was in such a tone
As only voices own which day and night
Sing hymns to God.

In answer to the question "Who sent you here, my child?" put by the Superioress of the convent

where Ethel sought admission, the young postulant
is made to say:

"A youthful Christ," she said,—
"Who, had he lived in those far days of Christ,
Would have been His beloved Disciple, sure,—
Would have been His own gentle John; and would
Have leaned, on Thursday night, upon his breast,
And stood, on Friday eve, beneath His cross
To take His mother from Him when He died.
He sent me here,—he said the word last night
In my own garden,—this the word he said—
Oh! had you heard him whisper:—'Ethel, dear!
Your heart was born with veil of virgin on—
I hear it rustle every time we meet,
In all your words and smiles;—and when you weep
I hear it rustle more.   Go—wear your veil—
And outward be what inwardly thou art,
And hast been from the first.   And, Ethel, list:
My heart was born with priestly vestments on,
And at Dream-Altars I have ofttimes stood,
And said such sweet Dream-Masses in my sleep—
And when I lifted up a white Dream-Host,
A silver Dream-Bell rang—and angels knelt,
Or seemed to kneel, in worship.   Ethel, say—
Thou wouldst not take the vestments from my heart,
Nor more than I would tear the veil from thine.
My vested and thy veiled heart part to-night
To climb our Calvary and to meet in God—
And this, fair Ethel, is Gethsemane.' "

Unlike most poets, Father Ryan loved the Cross better than the Crown, and his sympathies were always with the weak and the oppressed. After the war he moved to Mobile, where he enjoyed the constant friendship of the Right Rev. Bishop Quinlan, who admired both the talents of the poet and the zeal of the priest.

In 1880, or thereabout, he was induced by a brilliant young lawyer of Mobile named Harris Taylor to collect and publish his poems in book form. This was done at Mr. Taylor's expense, and the book proved popular immediately on issuing from the press. So great a favorite did it become that in five years ten different editions were struck off to supply the public demand.

At this time he went on his lecturing tour through the North, where he was received with remarkable cordiality, and thousands thronged to hear him. Every one was anxious, then, to listen to his brilliant lectures and "touch the hem" of the poet's garment.

Father Ryan led a busy and laborious life, and the constant strain began to tell upon his health before he had reached his forty-fifth year.

One month before his death he went to the Monastery of St. Boniface, Louisville, Kentucky, with the intention of making his annual retreat, after which he proposed to finish in the retirement of that place his " Life of Christ."

But his work was done, and the Master called him home on the 22d of April, 1880, before he had reached the age of fifty. His body lay in state at the Franciscan Monastery for two days. On the 24th the ex-Confederate soldiers of the city attended in a body his Requiem Mass in the Church of St. Boniface, and a funeral escort, consisting of distinguished ex-Confederate officers, Judges of the United States and State Courts, conducted his remains to the depot, whence they were conveyed to Mobile for interment. In the sad funeral procession a floral Cross and Crown were borne, bearing the inscription:

"Love and sympathy of the ex-confederate soldiers of Louisville."

Never was poet more loved and honored in any country than this sweet singer in his own Sunny Southland.

He was forty-six years at the time of his death, and had lived nearly all his years "south of Mason and Dixon's line." As a poet all concede to him an exalted place. Miss Early, in her "Songs of the South," has this to say:

"In my estimation the two finest songs called forth by the war were "The Conquered Banner" and "All Quiet Along the Potomac To-night," the former by Father Ryan and the latter by Lamar Fontaine. Both these evince genuine talent."

As an orator his reputation is also an enviable one. General Gordon, in a speech delivered at New Orleans on the occasion of unveiling Sergeant Jasper's monument, styled Father Ryan "the rainbow of poesy and the thunderbolt of oratory."

Whatever he may have been before, since the close of the civil war the poet of the " Lost Cause" has been socially, nearly at all times, a sad and silent man. He seldom gave expression to his sorrows, except in verse, and lived as much as possible alone. No doubt he thought and felt much more than pen or voice ever made manifest. Gentleness characterized his every act, and he was exceedingly fond of children.

The end has crowned his labors; but his memory shall be as lasting as that of the cause which he immortalized in song.

## THE CONQUERED BANNER.

FURL that Banner, for 'tis weary;
'Round its staff 'tis drooping dreary;
  Furl it, fold it, it is best;
For there's not a man to wave it,
And there's not a sword to save it,
And there's not one left to lave it
In the blood which heroes gave it;
And its foes now scorn and brave it;
  Furl it, hide it—let it rest!

Take that Banner down! 'tis tattered;
Broken is its staff and shattered;
And the valiant hosts are scattered
　　Over whom it floated high.
Oh! 'tis hard for us to fold it;
Hard to think there's none to hold it;
Hard that those who once unrolled it
　　Now must furl it with a sigh.

Furl that Banner! furl it sadly!
Once ten thousands hailed it gladly,
And ten thousands wildly, madly,
　　Swore it should forever wave;
Swore that foeman's sword should never
Hearts like theirs entwined dissever,
Till that flag should float forever
　　O'er their freedom or their grave!

Furl it! for the hands that grasped it,
And the hearts that fondly clasped it,
　　Cold and dead are lying low;
And that Banner—it is trailing!
While around it sounds the wailing
　　Of its people in their woe.

For, though conquered, they adore it!
Love the cold, dead hands that bore it!
Weep for those who fell before it!
Pardon those who trailed and tore it!
But, oh! wildly they deplore it,
　　Now, who fold and furl it so.

Furl that Banner!   True, 'tis gory,
Yet 'tis wreathed around with glory,
And 'twill live in song and story,
   Though its folds are in the dust;
For its fame on brightest pages,
Penned by poets and by sages—
Shall go sounding down the ages,
   Furl its folds though now we must.

Furl that Banner, softly, slowly!
Treat it gently—it is holy—
   For it droops above the dead.
Touch it not—unfold it never,
Let it droop there, furled forever,
   For its people's hopes are dead!


## LINES—1875.

"Why does your poetry sound like a sigh."—*Letter to Father Ryan.*

Go down where the wavelets are kissing the shore,
   And ask of them why do they sigh?
The Poet's have asked them a thousand times o'er,
But they're kissing the shore as they kissed it before,
And they're sighing to-day and they'll sigh evermore.
   Ask them what ails them: they will not reply;
.   But they'll sigh on forever and never tell why!
   " Why does your poetry sound like a sigh?"
   The waves will not answer you; neither shall I.

Go stand on the beach of the blue, boundless deep,
   When the night stars are gleaming on high,
And hear how the billows are moaning in sleep,
On the low lying strand by the surge-beaten steep.
They're moaning forever wherever they sweep.
   Ask them what ails them: they never reply;
   They moan, and so sadly, but will not tell why?
   " Why does your poetry sound like a sigh?"
   The waves will not answer you; neither shall I.

Go list to the breeze at the waning of day,
   When it passes and murmurs " good-bye"—
The dear little breeze, how it wishes to stay
Where the flowers are in bloom, where the singing birds play!
How it sighs when it flies on its wearisome way!
   Ask it what ails it: it will not reply;
   Its voice is a sad one, it never told why.
   " Why does your poetry sound like a sigh?"
   The breeze will not answer you; neither shall I.

Go watch the wild blasts as they spring from their lair,
   When the shout of the storm rends the sky;
They rush o'er the earth and they ride thro' the air
And they blight with their breath all the lovely and fair,
And they groan like the ghosts in the " land of despair."
   Ask them what ails them: they never reply;
   Their voices are mournful, and they will not tell why.
   " Why does your poetry sound like a sigh?"
   The blasts will not answer you; neither shall I.

Go stand on the rivulet's lily-fringed side,
  Or list where the rivers rush by;
The streamlets which forest trees shadow and hide,
And the rivers that roll in their oceanward tide,
Are moaning forever wherever they glide;
  Ask them what ails them: they will not reply;
  On—sad voiced—they flow, but they never tell why.
  " Why does your poetry sound like a sigh ?"
  Earth's streams will not answer you; neither shall I.

Go list to the voices of air, earth and sea,
  And the voices that sound in the sky;
Their songs may be joyful to some, but to me
There's a sigh in each chord and a sigh in each key,
And thousands of sighs swell their grand melody.
  Ask them what ails them: they will not reply.
  They sigh—sigh forever—but never tell why.
  " Why does your poetry sound like a sigh ?"
  Their lips will not answer you; neither will I.


## ERIN'S FLAG.

UNROLL Erin's flag! fling its folds to the breeze!
Let it float o'er the land, let it flash o'er the seas!
Lift it out of the dust—let it wave as of yore,
When its chiefs with their clans stood around it and swore
That never! no, never! while God gave them life,
And they had an arm and a sword for the strife,
That never! no, never! that banner should yield
As long as the heart of a Celt was its shield;
While the hand of a Celt had a weapon to wield,
And his last drop of blood was unshed on the field.

Lift it up! wave it high! 'tis as bright as of old!
Not a stain on its green, not a blot on its gold,
Tho' the woes and the wrongs of three hundred long years
Have drenched Erin's Sunburst with blood and with tears!
Though the clouds of oppression enshrined it in gloom,
And around it the thunders of Tyranny boom.
Look aloft! look aloft! Lo, the clouds drifting by;
There's a gleam through the gloom, there's a light in the sky;
'Tis the Sunburst resplendent—far, flashing on high!
Erin's dark night is waning, her day-dawn is nigh!

Lift it up! lift it up! the old Banner of Green!
The blood of its sons has but brightened its sheen.
What though the tyrant has trampled it down,
Are its folds not emblazoned with deeds of renown?
What though for ages it droops in the dust,
Shall it droop thus forever! No! no! God is just!

Take it up! take it up! from the tyrant's foul tread,
Let him tear the Green Flag—we will snatch its last shred,
And beneath it we'll bleed as our forefathers bled,
And we'll vow by the dust in the graves of our dead,
And we'll swear by the blood which the Briton has shed,
And we'll vow by the wrecks which through Erin he spread,
And we'll swear by the thousands who, famished, unfed,
Died down in the ditches, wild-howling for bread,
And we'll vow by our heroes, whose spirits have fled,
And we'll swear by the bones in each coffinless bed,
That we'll battle the Briton through danger and dread;
That we'll cling to the cause which we glory to wed,
Till the gleam of our steel and the shock of our lead
Shall prove to our foe that we meant what we said—
That we'll lift up the green, and we'll tear down the red!

Lift up the Green Flag' oh' it wants to go home,
Full long has its lot been to wander and roam.
It has followed the fate of its sons o'er the world,
But its folds, like their hopes, are not faded nor furled.
Like a weary-winged bird, to the East and the West,
It has flitted and flitted; but it never shall rest,
Till, pluming its pinions, it sweeps o'er the main,
And speeds to the shores of its old home again,
Where its fetterless folds o'er each mountain and plain
Shall wave with a glory that never shall wane!

Take it up! take it up! bear it back from afar!
That Banner must blaze 'mid the lightnings of war.
Lay your hands on its folds, lift your gaze to the sky,
And swear that you'll bear it triumphant or die,
And shout to the clans scattered far o'er the earth
To join in the march to the land of their birth.
And wherever the exiles, 'neath heaven's broad dome,
Have been fated to suffer, to sorrow and roam,
They'll bound on the sea, and away o'er the foam,
They'll sail to the music of "Home, Sweet Home!"


## SONG OF THE MYSTIC.

I WALK down the Valley of Silence—
    Down the dim, voiceless valley—alone!
And I hear not the fall of a footstep
    Around me, save God's and my own;
And the hush of my heart is as holy
    As hovers where angels have flown!

Long ago was I weary of voices,
  Whose music my heart could not win;
Long ago was I weary of noises
  That fretted my soul with their din;
Long ago was I weary of places
  Where I met but the human—and sin.

I walked in the world with the worldly;
  I craved what the world never gave;
And I said: "In the world each Ideal
  That shines like a star on life's wave,
Is wrecked on the shores of the Real,
  And sleeps like a dream in a grave."

And still I did pine for the Perfect,
  And still found the False with the True;
I sought 'mid the Human for Heaven,
  But caught a mere glimpse of its Blue:
And I wept when the clouds of the Mortal
  Veiled even that glimpse from my view.

And I toiled on, heart-tired of the Human,
  And I moaned 'mid the mazes of men;
Till I knelt, long ago, at an altar
  And I heard a voice call me;—since then
I walk down the Valley of Silence
  That lies far beyond mortal ken.

Do you ask what I found in the Valley?
  'Tis my Trysting Place with the Divine.
And I fell at the feet of the Holy,
  And above me a voice said: "Be mine."
And there arose from the depths of my spirit
  An echo—"My heart shall be thine."

23

Do you ask how I live in the Valley?
  I weep—and I dream—and I pray.
But my tears are as sweet as the dewdrops
  That fall on the roses of May;
And my prayer, like a perfume from censers,
  Ascendeth to God night and day.

In the hush of the Valley of Silence
  I dream all the songs that I sing;
And the music floats down the dim Valley,
  Till each finds a word for a wing,
That to hearts, like the Dove of the Deluge,
  A message of Peace they may bring.

But far on the deep there are billows
  That never shall break on the beach;
And I have heard songs in the silence,
  That never shall float into speech;
And I have heard dreams in the Valley,
  Too lofty for language to reach.

And I have seen Thoughts in the Valley—
  Ah! me, how my spirit was stirred!
And they wear holy veils on their faces,
  Their footsteps can scarcely be heard;
They pass through the Valley like Virgins,
  Too pure for the touch of a word!

Do you ask me the place of the Valley,
  Ye hearts that are harrowed by Care?
It lieth afar between mountains,
  And God and His angels are there;
And one is the dark mount of Sorrow,
  And one the bright mountain of Prayer!

# THOMAS D'ARCY McGEE

POET, HISTORIAN AND STATESMAN.

**T**HE subject of this paper was descended from a family remarkable for devotion to the cause of oppressed Ireland. His maternal grandfather took an active part in the rising of 1798, and suffered for his participation in that movement. On the father's side, also, there were patriots whose devotion to the old land was tested and found true.

Thomas D'Arcy McGee, the second son of James McGee and Dorcas Catherine Morgan, was born on the 13th day of April, 1825, at Carlingford, in the County Louth. His mother was a woman of education and refinement, an enthusiastic lover of her country, its music and its ancient lore. The lullaby she chanted over his cradle thrilled with the spirit of "ninety-eight," and Thomas, from his infancy, breathed an atmosphere of patriotism.

Eight listless years had passed over the future poet's head, by the shores of Carlingford Bay, when his father, James McGee, there serving as a coastguard, was transferred to Wexford, whither the family accompanied him. Here the cultured mother instilled into the youthful mind of the bard those

legends and traditions which years and years afterwards formed the ground-work for many a thrilling
ballad.

That gentle, loving mother died while Thomas was

yet a boy, and the darling of her heart wept over her
grave,

> Near the Selskar's ruin'd wall,

as only poets can weep. Though dead, her lessons
lived in his heart to prompt and guide him through
all the changes of a busy and eventful life.

Years went on, and young McGee was busy with the cultivation of a great mind. He attended a day school in the town of Wexford, where his progress was so rapid that after a few years he became his own master. At the age of sixteen he had read a great many books on the history of his native land. Poetry was his chief delight, and, like Collins, he was willing to walk many a weary mile, provided the hope of procuring some old volume of legendary lays at the end of the journey was held out to him.

In 1842, when he was only seventeen years of age, he resolved to seek fame and fortune on the shores of the New World, where

> There is honor for the men of worth
> And wealth for those who toil.

The parting from the land that contained the ashes of his forefathers and the green grave of his idolized mother was to him a source of keen, heart-rending sorrow. Thus he pours forth his agonizing wail as Ireland receded from his sight, and the good ship *Leo* disappeared in the dim horison.

> Tell me truly, pensive sage,
> Seest thou signs on any page?
> Know'st a volume yet to ope,
> Where I may read of hope—of hope?
>
> Dare I seek it where the wave
> Grieves above Leander's grave?
> Must I follow forth my quest
> In the wider, freer West?

He did "follow forth his quest" in the great and beauteous West where he won fame and fortune.

He was not long in Boston when the rejoicing of the multitude ushered in the ever "glorious 4th of July." The youthful immigrant delivered a speech on the great National anniversary that astonished everyone and secured for himself a position from Mr. Patrick Donohue on the Boston *Pilot*.

This boy from the banks of the Slaney soon gained the editorial management of the *Pilot*, and in this capacity did good service for his religion and race. His mighty genius developed rapidly, and in three years he was offered the editorial chair in the office of the Dublin *Freeman's Journal*. He returned to his native land a man of mark at the age of twenty and assumed the chief place in the office of that enterprising journal. The *Freeman's* views were entirely too tame for one who was accustomed to speak his mind in no uncertain or faltering tones. He would not be permitted to change its character, so he decided to change his place, and went over to the office of the *Nation*, where he worked with Duffy, Davis, Mitchel and Devin Reilly for the propagation of "Young Ireland" doctrines. There was not in any metropolis of Europe at that time a paper so ably edited or one that could boast of such a galaxy of genius as the Dublin *Nation*. Mitchel,

McGee, Duffy, Davis and Devin Reilly were men of great minds, and in their hands the pen was truly "a mighty instrument." That brilliant band of agitators, editors, orators and poets has never since been equalled in Ireland

When shall Erin see their like again? She sadly needs such men to-day

O'Connell, the great Liberator, died in 1847. An attempt at Rebellion was made in 1848. The after tale is easily told. In that short and abortive struggle Thomas D'Arcy McGee did faithfully and well all that was assigned to him. While addressing his countrymen in Wicklow he was arrested and lodged in prison. After obtaining his liberty, he went over to Scotland pursuant to the orders of the "Irish Executive," with the intention of securing the co-operation of the Irish operatives in the contemplated rising. While thus engaged in Scotland the chiefs of the Confederation were arrested at home. McGee managed to return to Derry where he was sheltered by the learned Catholic Bishop of the North, Dr. Maginn. After an interview with his young wife, he made his way to Galway whence he sailed a second time for the United States, the Land of Freedom, dressed in the garb of a clergyman. It was while being borne away from the shores of Hibernia that he penned the following · ballad, entitled:

## PARTING FROM IRELAND.

OH, dread Lord of heaven and earth!
   Hard and sad it is to go
From the land I loved and cherished
   Into outward gloom and woe.
Was it for this, Guardian angel!
   When to manly years I came,
Homeward as a light you led me—
   Light that now is turn'd to flame?

I am as a shipwreck'd sailor,
   By one wave flung on shore,
By the next torn struggling seaward
   Without hope forevermore.
I am as a sinner toiling
   Onward to Redemption's Hill—
By the rising sands environ'd,
   By siroccos baffled still.

How I loved this nation ye know,
   Gentle friends, who share my fate,
And you, too, heroic comrades,
   Loaded with the fetter's weight.
How I coveted all knowledge
   That might raise her name with men,
How I sought her secret beauties
   With an all-insatiate ken.

God! it is a maddening prospect
   To see this storied land,
Like some wretched culprit writhing
   In a strong avenger's hand,—

Kneeling, foaming, weeping, shrieking,
  Woman-weak and woman-loud,—
Better, better, Mother Ireland,
  We had laid you in a shroud!

If an end were made, and nobly,
  Of this old, centennial feud—
If, in arms, outnumbered, beaten,
  Less, O Ireland! had I rued;
For the scattered sparks of valor
  Might relight thy darkness yet,
And thy long chain of Resistance
  To the Future had been set.

Now their *Castle* sits securely
  On the old accursed hill,
And their motley pirate standard
  Taints the air of Ireland still;
And their titled paupers clothe them
  With the labor of our hands,
And their Saxon greed is glutted
  From our plunder'd fathers' lands.

But our faith is all unshaken,
  Though our present hope is gone;
England's lease is *not* forever—
  Ireland's welfare is *not* done.
God in Heaven, He is immortal—
  *Justice* is His sword and sign—
If this world is not our ally,
  We have One who is Divine.

Though my eyes no more may see thee,
Island of my early love!
Other eyes shall see the Green Flag
Flying the tall hills above;
Though my ears no more may listen
To the rivers as they flow,
Other ears shall hear a pæan
Closing thy long *caoine* of woe.

These energetic verses faithfully mirrored the
mind of the defeated patriot as he turned a second
time from his native land, leaving nothing but shattered hopes and disaster behind him

On the 10th of October, 1848, he reached Philadelphia, and fifteen days later he issued the first copy
of the New York *Nation*, which was not destined to
equal the career of its Dublin namesake. The paper
was well received, and for a time promised to bring
wealth and additional fame to its proprietor and
editor. The Young Irelander was a radical, smart-
ing keenly under the sting of an ignominious defeat,
and undertook in the columns of the *Nation* to
attribute the failure of the 'Forty-eight rising to the
interposition of the bishops and priests. He strenu-
ously maintained that the priests used all their
mighty influence in preventing the young men of
Ireland from joining the insurgents. Archbishop
Hughes came quickly to the defence of the Irish

priesthood, and in a series of letters ably refuted the assertions of the young refugee

It could not be expected that Mr. McGee could hold his own against Archbishop Hughes, the victor of a dozen controversial fields. As a result the New York *Nation* went under; and at the solicitation of numerous friends the editor removed with his family to the city of Boston, in 1850, where he commenced the publication of the *American Celt*. A year later he removed the publication to New York City, and continued it there till its suspension in 1858. In January, 1855, McGee again visited Ireland, the political disabilities under which he labored having lapsed. He wrote a series of able papers for the *Celt*, entitled "Ireland Re-visited," which were the beginning of the movement for colonization that developed later on.

It is said that the radical revolutionist of twenty summers becomes a stern conservative at forty. So it was with McGee, and the change in his principles evoked severe criticism from the ranks of the Physical Force party. In a letter to Thomas Francis Meagher, the brilliant orator and patriot, he sets forth his reasons for altering his opinions. Among other reasons he assigns the following:

" Having discovered, by close self-examination, that the reading chiefly of modern books, English and French, gave very superficial and false views of political science, I cheerfully said

to myself, ' My friend, you are on the wrong track.   You think
you know something of human affairs; but you do not.   You
are ignorant—very ignorant—of the primary principles that
govern and must govern the world.   You can put sentences
together; but what does that avail you when, perhaps, these
sentences are but the husks and pods of poisonous seeds?
Beware! look to it! you have a soul!   What will all the fame
of talents avail you if you lose that?'   Thus I reasoned with
myself, and then setting my cherished opinions before me, one
by one, I tried, judged and capitally executed every one save
and except those which I found to be compatible with the following doctrines:

" 1st.   That there is a Christendom.

" 2d.   That this Christendom exists by and for the Catholic
Church.

" 3d.   That there is in our age one of the most dangerous
and general conspiracies against Christendom that the world
has yet seen.

" 4th.   That this conspiracy is aided, abetted and tolerated
by many because of its stolen watchword—Liberty.

" 5th.   That it is the highest duty of a Catholic man to go
over cheerfully, heartily and at once to the side of Christendom
—to the Catholic side—and to resist, with all his might, the
conspirators who, under the stolen name of ' Liberty,' make war
upon all Christian institutions."

These are a few of the cogent reasons given by Mr.
McGee for changing his political doctrines.   It must
be acknowledged that his discoveries were based on
solid truths, and the wonder is that they were not
made sooner.   The watchwords of conspirators—

Liberty, Equality and Fraternity—are filched from Catholic writers, stolen from Catholic Christianity, and used with telling effect by popular demagogues and impious opponents of Christian teachings.

McGee was not only a brilliant orator, but also a deep thinker and a writer of inimitable force and unequalled skill. His lectures on "The Catholic History of America" are the best ever written on the subject. "Irish Settlers in North America" contains an important part of the annals from which the future historian of the Irish race in North America will be obliged to draw.

In 1862, he published his "History of Ireland" in two 12mo volumes; and, although this work is not what the history of Ireland should be, it is undoubtedly one of the best we have. "The Reformation in Ireland," from his ever busy and gifted pen, is a marvel of learning, logic and research, which proves at the same time that he was a true lover of his native land and the faith of his fathers. "O'Connell and his Friends," "The Jesuits" and "Irish Writers" are works that bear the impress of his powerful mind. To Mr. McGee must be given the credit of originating the "Catholic Colonization" idea.

He, it was, who conceived the idea, and formulated the plan of locating the immigrants from Ireland on the broad, fertile prairies of the great West. It was a project worthy of the man, and one which, if effectuated, would have proved exceedingly beneficial to the whole Irish race in the United States. While advocating this colonizing scheme in the columns of the *Celt*, he summoned the Buffalo Convention for the purpose of furthering the movement. This Convention was composed of one hundred Irish Americans. The resolutions and suggestions of the Convention met with considerable opposition in different quarters, and were lost sight of until D'Arcy McGee had been gathered to the grave.

Removing to Canada, he commenced in Montreal the publication of the *New Era*. On the second year of his residence in the Province his friends and countrymen elected him to the Canadian Parliament, and thenceforth his public career was both brilliant and successful, even to that fatal moment when the assassin's hand struck down the noble exile at the very threshold of his lodgings.

This lamentable event took place on the 7th day of April, 1868, in the city of Ottawa, and threw all the land into mourning for the illustrious dead. In him Ireland lost a champion of her rights, the Catholic Church a devoted son, and Canada her best and most brilliant statesman.

The Requiem for his eternal repose was chanted in

the Cathedral of Ottawa. He lies buried in Mount Royal, near Montreal, on a sunny slope which faces the St. Lawrence. "Here," writes a distinguished lawyer of Montreal, "sleeps the greatest poet, orator, statesman, historian—the best, the truest friend, counsellor and guide of the Irish race in America."

He died far away from the land of his love, on which all his fondest and dearest hopes were centred, from the sacred spot that clasps the ashes of his dead, and the home where the golden hours of his youth sped swiftly away.

Often, when the labor of the day was done, would he go back in spirit to those scenes hallowed by a thousand memories. His fondest hopes ever turned eastward to the shores of Erin and found expression in pathetic poems like the

### WISHING CAP.

WISHING cap, wishing cap, let us away
To walk in the cloisters, at close of day,
Once trod by the friars of orders gray,
In Norman Selskar's renown'd abbaye
  And Carmen's ancient town;
For I would kneel at my mother's grave,
Where the plumey churchyard elms wave,
  And the old war-walls look down.

Two nations mourned his untimely death, and innumerable prayers were offered for the repose of

his immortal spirit. May he join the celestial sin-
gers, and rest in everlasting glory!

As a poet McGee ranks high, indeed. The lamented
Henry Giles, a man of national reputation, writing
of McGee, says: "How varied the poems were that
he breathed forth upon the woes and wrongs of Ireland! How noble the strains in which he celebrated
that beautiful land of much calamity and countless
wrongs!"

The Dublin *Nation* of May, 1857, referring to our
author's published poems, speaks thus: "We might
search in vain, even through the numberless volumes
of English poems and lyrics, for any that equal in
their passion, fire and beauty his verses entitled
'The War,' 'Sebastian Cabot to his Lady,' 'The Celt's
Salutation,' and many others."

The London *Athenæum*, which could have very little sympathy with McGee, in an article on Canadian
poetry, wrote: "They have one *true* poet within
their borders—that is Thomas D'Arcy McGee. In
his younger days the principle of rebellion inspired
him with stately verse; let us hope that the conservative principles of his more mature years will
yield many a noble song in his new country."

We might keep on quoting the words of praise
that were bestowed on the poetry of McGee almost
*ad infinitum.* He touched the chords of charity and

friendship, war, peace and patriotism, and each he swept with a master hand.

## THE HOMEWARD BOUND.

PALER and thinner the morning moon grew,
Colder and sterner the rising wind blew;
The pole-star had set in a forest of cloud,
And the icicles crackled on spar and on shroud,
When a voice from below we heard feebly cry:
" Let me see, let me see my own land ere I die."

" Ah, dear sailor, say, have we sighted Cape Clear?
Can you see any sign ?  Is the morning light near?
You are young, my brave boy; thanks, thanks for your hand—
Help me up, till I get a last glimpse of the land.
Thank God, 'tis the sun that now reddens the sky;
I shall see, I shall see my own land ere I die.

" Let me lean on your strength, I am feeble and old,
And one-half of my heart is already stone-cold.
Forty years work a change! when I first crossed the sea
There were few on the deck that could grapple with me;
But my youth and my prime in Ohio went by,
And I'm come back to see the old spot ere I die."

'Twas a feeble old man, and he stood on the deck
His arm round a kindly young mariner's neck,
His ghastly gaze fixed on the tints of the east,
As a starveling might stare at the noise of a feast.
The morn quickly rose and revealed to his eye
The land he had prayed to behold, and then die!

24

Green, green was the shore, though the year was near done;
High and haughty the capes the white surf dashed upon;
A gray ruined convent was down by the strand,
And the sheep fed afar, on the hills of the land!
"God be with you, dear Ireland!" he gasped with a sigh;
"I have lived to behold you—I'm ready to die."

He sunk by the hour, and his pulse 'gan to fail,
As we swept by the headland of storied Kinsale;
Off Ardigna Bay it came slower and slower,
And his corpse was clay-cold as we sighted Tramore.
At Passage we waked him, and now he doth lie
In the lap of the land he beheld but to die.

## THE CELTIC CROSS.

THROUGH storm, and fire, and gloom, I see it stand,
      Firm, broad, and tall—
The Celtic Cross that marks our Fatherland,
      Amid them all!
Druids, and Danes, and Saxons vainly rage
      Around its base;
It standeth shock on shock, and age on age,
      Star of our scattered race.

O, Holy Cross! dear symbol of the dread
      Death of our Lord,
Around thee long have slept our Martyr-dead,
      Sward over sward!
An hundred Bishops I myself can count
      Among the slain—
Chiefs, captains, rank and file, a shining mount
      Of God's ripe grain.

The Recreant's hate, the Puritan's claymore,
    Smote thee not down;
On headland steep, on mountain summit hoar,
    In mart and town;
In Glendalough, in Ara, in Tyrone,
    We find thee still,
Thy open arms still stretching to thine own,
    O'er town, and lough and hill.

And they would tear thee out of Irish soil,
    The guilty fools!
How time must mock their antiquated toil
    And broken tools!
Cranmer and Cromwell from thy grasp retired,
    Baffled and thrown;
William and Anne to sap thy site conspired—
    The rest is known!

Holy Saint Patrick, Father of our Faith,
    Beloved of God!
Shield thy dear church from the impending scathe,
    Or, if the rod
Must scourge it yet again, inspire and raise
    To emprise high,
Men like the heroic race of other days,
    Who joyed to die!

Fear! Wherefore should the Celtic people fear
    Their Church's fate?
The day is not—the day was never near—
    Could desolate

The Destined Island, all whose seedy clay
      Is holy ground—
Its Cross shall stand till that predestined day,
      When Erin's self is drowned!


## SALUTATION TO THE CELTS.

### I.

HAIL to our Celtic brethren wherever they may be,
In the far woods of Oregon, or o'er the Atlantic sea—
Whether they guard the banner of St. George in Indian vales,
Or spread beneath the nightless North experimental sails—
      One in name and in fame
      Are the sea-divided Gaels.

### II.

Though fallen the state of Erin, and changed the Scottish land—
Though small the power of Mona, though unwaked Lewellyn's
      band—
Though Ambrose Merlin's prophecies degenerate to tales,
And the cloisters of Iona are bemoan'd by northern gales—
      One in name and in fame
      Are the sea-divided Gaels.

### III.

In Northern Spain and Brittany our brethren also dwell;
Oh! brave are the traditions of their fathers that they tell;—
The eagle and the crescent in the dawn of history pales
Before their fire, that seldom flags, and never wholly fails:
      One in name and in fame
      Are the sea-divided Gaels.

## IV.

A greeting and a promise unto them all we send;
Their character our charter is, their glory is our end;
Their friend shall be our friend, our foe whoe'er assails
The past or future honors of the far-dispersèd Gaels:
        One in name and in fame
        Are the sea-divided Gaels.

## THE EXILE'S REQUEST.

Oh, Pilgrim, if you bring me from the far-off lands a sign,
Let it be some token still of the green old land, once mine;
A shell from the shores of Ireland would be dearer far to me,
Than all the wines of the Rhine land, or the art of Italie.

For I was born in Ireland—I glory in the name—
I weep for all her sorrows, I remember well her fame!
And still my heart must hope that I may yet repose at rest,
On the Holy Zion of my youth, in the Israel of the West.

Her beauteous face is furrowed with sorrow's streaming rains,
Her lovely limbs are mangled with slavery's ancient chains,
Yet, Pilgrim, pass not over with heedless heart or eye,
The Island of the gifted, and of men who knew to die.

Like the crater of a fire-mount, all without is bleak and bare,
But the vigor of its lips still show what fire and force were there,
Even now in the heaving craters, far from the gazer's ken,
The fiery heel is forging that will crush her foes again.

Then, Pilgrim, if you bring me from the far-off lands a sign,
Let it be some token still of the green old land, once mine;
A shell from the shores of Ireland would be dearer far to me
Than all the wines of the Rhine land, or the art of Italie.

## THE LIVING AND THE DEAD.

BRIGHT is the Spring time, Erin, green and gay to see;
But my heart is heavy, Erin, with thoughts of thy sons and thee;
Thinking of your dead men lying as thick as grass new mown—
Thinking of your myriads dying, unnoted and unknown—
Thinking of your myriads flying beyond the abysmal waves—
Thinking of your magnates sighing, and stifling their thoughts
    like slaves!

Oh! for the time, dear Erin, the fierce time long ago,
When your men felt brave, dear Erin, and their hands could
    strike a blow!
When your Gaelic chiefs were ready to stand in the bloody
    breach—
Danger but made *them* steady; they struck, and saved their
    speech!
But where are the men to head ye, and lead you face to face,
To trample the powers that tread ye, men of the fallen race!

The yellow corn, dear Erin, waves plenteous o'er the plain;
But where are the hands, dear Erin, to gather in the grain?
The sinewy man is sleeping in the crowded churchyard near,
And his young wife is keeping his lonesome company there,
His brother shoreward creeping, has begged his way abroad,
And his sister—tho' for weeping, she scarce could see the road.

No other nation, Erin, but only you would bear
A yoke like yours, oh! Erin, a month, not to say a year;
And will you bear it for ever, writhing and sighing sore,
Now learn—learn now, or never, to dare, not to deplore—
Learn to join in one endeavor your creeds and people all—
'Tis only thus can you sever your tyrant's iron thrall.

Then call your people, Erin, call with a Prophet's cry—
Bid them link in union, Erin, and do like men or die—
Bid the hind from the loamy valley, the miller from the fall—
Bid the craftsman from his alley, the lord from his lordly hall—
Bid the old and the young man rally, and trust to work—not
     words,
And thenceforth ever shall ye be free as the forest birds.

## TO A FRIEND IN AUSTRALIA.*

OLD friend! though distant far,
    Your image nightly shines upon my soul;
I yearn toward it as toward a star
    That points through darkness to the ancient pole.

Out of my heart the longing wishes fly,
    As to some rapt Elias, Enoch, Seth;
Yours is another earth, another sky,
    And I—I feel that distance is like death.

Oh! for one week amid the emerald fields,
    Where the Avoca sings the song of Moore;
Oh! for the odor the brown heather yields,
    To glad the pilgrim's heart on Glenmalure!

Yet is there still what meeting could not give,
    A joy most suited of all joys to last;
For, ever in fair memory there must live
    The bright, unclouded picture of the past.

---

* Charles Gavan Duffy.

Old friend! the years wear on, and many cares
  And many sorrows both of us have known;
Time for us both a quiet couch prepares—
  A couch like Jacob's, pillow'd with a stone.

And oh! when thus we sleep may we behold
  The angelic ladder of the Patriarch's dream;
And may my feet upon its rungs of gold
  Yours follow, as of old, by hill and stream!

## CONSOLATION.

### I.

MEN seek for treasure in the earth;
  Where I have buried mine,
There never mortal eye shall pierce,
  Nor star nor lamp shall shine!
We know, my love, oh! well we know,
  The secret treasure-spot,
Yet must our tears forever fall,
  Because that *they* are not.

### II.

How gladly would we give to light
  The ivory forehead fair—
The eye of heavenly-beaming blue,
  The clust'ring chestnut hair—
Yet look around this mournful scene
  Of daily earthly life,
And could you wish them back to share
  Its sorrow and its strife?

### III.

If blessed angels stray to earth,
  And seek in vain a shrine,
They needs must back return again
  Unto their source divine:
All life obeys the unchanging law
  Of Him who took and gave,
We count a glorious saint in heaven
  For each child in the grave.

### IV.

Look up, my love, look up, afar,
  And dry each bitter tear;
Behold, three white-robed innocents
  At heaven's high gate appear!
For you and me and those we love,
  They smilingly await—
God grant we may be fit to join
  Those Angels at the Gate.

## THE EXILE'S DEVOTION.

I'D rather be the bird that sings
  Above the martyr's grave,
Than fold in fortune's cage my wings
  And feel my soul a slave;
I'd rather turn one simple verse
  True to the Gaelic ear,
Than Sapphic odes I might rehearse
  With senates list'ning near.

O Native Land! dost ever mark,
  When the world's din is drown'd,
Betwixt the daylight and the dark
  A wandering solemn sound,
That on the western wind is borne
  Across thy dewy breast?
It is the voice of those who mourn
  For thee, far in the West!

For them and theirs, I oft essay
  Your ancient art of song,
And often sadly turn away,
  Deeming my rashness wrong;
For well I ween, a loving will
  Is all the art I own.
Ah me, could love suffice for skill,
  What triumphs I had known!

My native land, my native land,
  Live in my memory still!
Break on my brain, ye surges grand!
  Stand up, mist-covered hill!
Still in the mirror of the mind
  The land I love I see;
Would I could fly on the western wind,
  My native land, to thee!

## THE DYING CELT TO HIS AMERICAN SON.

My son, a darkness falleth,
  Not of night, upon my eyes;
And in my ears there calleth
  A voice as from the skies;
I feel that I am dying,
  I feel my day is done,
Bid the women hush their crying
  And hear to me, my son!

When Time my garland gathers,
  Oh! my son, I charge you hold
By the *standard* of your fathers
  In the battle-fields of old!
In blood they wrote their story
  Across the fields, my boy;
On earth it was their glory,
  In heaven it is their joy.

By St. Patrick's hand 'twas planted
  On Erin's sea-beat shore,
And it spread its folds, undaunted,
  Through the drift and the uproar;—
Of all its vain assaulters,—
  Who could ever say he saw
The last of Ireland's altars?
  Or the last of Patrick's law?

Through the western ocean driven,
  By the tyrant's scorpion whips,
Behold! the hand of Heaven
  Bore our standard o'er the ships!

In the forest's far recesses,
   When the moon shines in at **night,**
The Celtic cross now blesses
   The weary wanderer's sight!

My son, my son, there falleth
   Deeper darkness on my eyes;
And the Guardian Angel calleth
   Me by name from out the skies.
Dear, my son, I charge thee cherish
   Christ's holy cross o'er all;
Let whatever else may perish,
   Let whatever else may fall.

## THE VIRGIN MARY'S KNIGHT.

### A BALLAD OF THE CRUSADES.

[In the "Middle Ages," there were Orders of Knights especially devoted to
our Blessed Lady, as well as many illustrious individuals of knightly rank
and renown. Thus the Order called Servites, in France, was known as *les
esclaves de Marie;* and there was also the Order of "Our Lady of Mercy,"
for the redemption of captives; the Templars, too, before their fall, were
devoutly attached to the service of our Blessed Lady.]

BENEATH the stars in Palestine seven knights discoursing stood,
But not of warlike work to come, nor former fields of blood,
Nor of the joy the pilgrims feel prostrated far, who see
The hill where Christ's atoning blood pour'd down the penal
      tree;
Their theme was old, their theme was new, 'twas sweet and
      yet 'twas bitter,--
Of noble ladies left behind spoke cavalier and ritter,
And eyes grew bright, and sighs arose from every iron breast,
For a dear wife, or plighted maid, far in the widow'd West.

Towards the knights came Constantine, thrice noble by his
 birth,
And ten times nobler than his blood his high out-shining worth;
His step was slow, his lips were moved, though not a word he
 spoke,
Till a gallant lord of Lombardy his spell of silence broke.
'' What aileth thee, O Constantine, that solitude you seek?
If counsel or if aid thou need'st, we pray thee do but speak;
Or dost thou mourn, like other freres, thy lady-love afar
Whose image shineth nightly through yon European star?''

Then answer'd courteous Constantine—'' Good sir, in simple
 truth,
I chose a gracious lady in the hey-day of my youth;
I wear her image on my heart, and when that heart is cold,
The secret may be rifled thence, but never must be told.
For her I love and worship well by light of morn or even,
I ne'er shall see my mistress dear, until we meet in heaven;
But this believe, brave cavaliers, there never was but one
Such lady as my Holy Love, beneath the blessed sun.''

He ceased, and pass'd with solemn step on to an olive grove,
And, kneeling there, he pray'd a prayer to the Lady of his love.
And many a cavalier whose lance had still maintain'd his own
Beloved to reign without a peer, all earth's unequalled one,
Look'd tenderly on Constantine in camp and in the fight;
With wonder and with generous pride they mark'd the light'ning
 light
Of his fearless sword careering through the unbelievers' ranks,
As angry Rhone sweeps off the vines that thicken on his banks.

"He fears not death, come when it will; he longeth for his love,
And fain would find some sudden path to where she dwells
      above.
How should he fear for dying, when his mistress dear is dead?"
Thus often of Sir Constantine his watchful comrades said;
Until it chanced from Zion wall the fatal arrow flew,
That pierced the outworn armor of his faithful bosom through;
And never was such mourning made for knight in Palestine,
As thy loyal comrades made for thee, belovèd Constantine.

Beneath the royal tent the bier was guarded night and day,
Where with a halo round his head the Christian champion lay;
That talisman upon his breast—what may that marvel be
Which kept his ardent soul through life from every error free?
Approach! behold! nay, worship there the image of his love,
The heavenly Queen who reigneth all the sacred hosts above,
Nor wonder that around his bier there lingers such a light,
For the spotless one that sleepeth WAS THE BLESSED VIRGIN'S
      KNIGHT!


AMERGIN'S ANTHEM ON DISCOVERING INNISFAIL.

          BEHOLD! behold the prize
      ·   Which westward yonder lies!
          Doth it not blind your eyes
                Like the sun?
          By vigil through the night,
          By valor in the fight,
          By learning to unite
                'T may be won! 't may be won!
          By learning to unite, 't may be won!

Of this, in Scythian vales,
Seers told prophetic tales,
Until our Father's sails
   Quick uprose;
But the gods did him detain
In the gen'rous land of Spain,
Where in peace his bones remain
   With his foes, with his foes—
Where in peace his bones remain with his foes.

Sad Scotia! mother dear!
Cease to shed the mournful tear—
Behold the hour draws near
   He foretold;
And, ye men, **with one accord,**
Drop the oar and draw the sword,
For he only shall be lord
   Who is bold, who is bold—
He only shall be lord who is bold!

They may shroud it up in gloom
Like a spirit in the tomb,
But we hear the voice of doom
   As it cries;
Let the cerements be burst,
And from thy bonds accursed,
Isle of Isles, the fairest, first,
   Arise! arise!
Isle of Isles, the fairest, first, arise!

Couch the oar and strike the sail,
Ye warriors of the Gael!
Draw the sword for Innisfail!
    Dash ashore!
With such a prize to gain,
Who would sail the seas again!
Innisfail shall be our Spain
    Evermore! evermore!
Innisfail shall be our Spain evermore!


## THE CELTS.

LONG, long ago, beyond the misty space
  Of twice a thousand years,
In Erin old there dwelt a mighty race,
  Taller than Roman spears;
Like oaks and towers, they had a giant grace,
  Were fleet as deers,
With winds and wave they made their 'biding-place,
  These Western shepherd-seers.

Their ocean-god was Man-a-nan, M'Lir,
  Whose angry lips,
In their white foam, full often would inter
  Whole fleets of ships;
Cromah, their day-god and their thunderer,
  Made morning and eclipse;
Bride was their queen of song, and unto her
  They pray'd with fire-touch'd lips.

Great were their deeds, their passions, and their sports;
   With clay and stone
They piled on strath and shore those mystic forts
   Not yet o'erthrown;
On cairn-crown'd hills they held their council-courts;
   While youths alone,
With giant dogs, explored the elk resorts,
   And brought them down.

Of these was Finn, the father of the bard
   Whose ancient song
Over the clamor of all change is heard,
   Sweet-voiced and strong.
Finn once o'ertook Granu, the golden-hair'd,
   The fleet and young;
From her the lovely, and from him the fear'd,
   The primal poet sprung.

Ossian! two thousand years of mist and change
   Surround thy name—
Thy Finian heroes now no longer range
   The hills of fame.
The very name of Finn and Gaul sound strange—
   Yet thine the same—
By miscall'd lake and desecrated grange—
   Remains, and shall remain!

The Druid's altar and the Druid's creed
   We scarce can trace,
There is not left an undisputed deed
   Of all your race,

Save your majestic song, which hath their speed,
  And strength and grace;
In that sole song they live, and love, and bleed—
  It bears them on through space.

Oh, inspired giant! shall we e'er behold
  In our own time
One fit to speak your spirit on the wold,
  Or seize your rhyme?
One pupil of the past, as mighty soul'd
  As in the prime,
Were the fond, fair, and beautiful, and bold—
  They of your song sublime!

## THE IRISH WIFE.

I WOULD not give my Irish wife for all the dames of the Saxon
    land—
I would not give my Irish wife for the Queen of France's hand:
For she to me is dearer than castles strong, or land, or life—
An outlaw, but I'm near her!—to love, till death, my Irish wife!

Oh! what would be this home of mine—a ruin'd, hermit-haunted
    place—
But for the light that nightly shines upon its walls from Kath-
    leen's face?
What comfort in a mine of gold—what pleasure in a royal life—
If the heart within lay dead and cold—if I could not wed my
    Irish wife?

I knew the law forbade the banns—I knew my king abhorred
    her race—
*Who* never bent before their clans, must bow before their ladies'
    grace.

Take all my forfeited domain; I cannot wage, with kinsmen,
    strife;
Take knightly gear and noble name,—but I will keep my Irish
    wife!

My Irish wife has clear blue eyes—my heaven by day, my stars
    by night—
And twin-like truth and fondness lie within her swelling bosom
    white.
My Irish wife has golden hair—Apollo's harp had once such
    strings—
Apollo's self might pause to hear her bird-like carol when she
    sings!

I would not give my Irish wife for all the dames of the Saxon
    land—
I would not give my Irish wife for the Queen of France's hand!
For she to me is dearer than castles strong, or lands, or life—
In death I would be near her, and rise—beside my Irish wife!


## IF WILL HAD WINGS, HOW FAST I'D FLEE.

If will had wings, how fast I'd flee
To the home of my heart o'er the seething sea!
If wishes were power—if words were spells,
I'd be this hour where my own love dwells.

My own love dwells in the storied land,
Where the Holy Wells sleep in yellow sand;
And the emerald lustre of Paradise beams
Over homes that cluster round singing streams.

I, sighing, alas! exist alone—
My youth is as grass on an unsunn'd stone,
Bright to the eye, but unfelt below—
As sunbeams that lie over Arctic snow.

My heart is a lamp that love must relight,
Or the world's fire-damp will quench it quite.
In the breast of my dear my life-tide springs—
Oh, I'd tarry none here, if will had wings.

For she never was weary of blessing me,
When morn rose dreary on thatch and tree;
She evermore chanted her song of faith,
When darkness daunted on hill and heath.

If will had wings, how fast I'd flee
To the home of my heart o'er the seething sea!
If wishes were power—if words were spells,
I'd be this hour where my own love dwells.


## A LEGEND OF ST. PATRICK.

SEVEN weary years in bondage the young St. Patrick pass'd,
Till the sudden hope came to him to break his bonds at last;
On the Antrim hills reposing with the North star overhead
As the grey dawn was disclosing "I trust in God," he said—
"My sheep will find a shepherd and my master find a slave,
But my mother has no other hope, but me, this side the grave."

Then girding close his mantle, and grasping fast his wand,
He sought the open ocean through the by-ways of the land.
The berries from the hedges on his solitary way,
And the cresses from the waters were his only food by day.

The cold stone was his pillow, and the hard heath was his bed,
Till looking from Benbulben, he saw the sea outspread.

He saw that ancient ocean, unfathomed and unbound,
That breaks on Erin's beaches with so sorrowful a sound.
There lay a ship at Sligo bound up the Median sea,
" God save you, master mariner, will you give berth to me ?
I have no gold to pay thee, but Christ will pay thee yet."
Loud laughed that foolish mariner, " Nay, nay, He might
        forget!"

" Forget! oh, not a favor done to the humblest one,
Of all His human kindred, can 'scape th' Eternal Son!"
In vain the Christian pleaded, the willing sail was spread,
His voice no more was heeded than the sea-birds overhead—
And as the vision faded, the ship against the sky,
On the briny rocks the Captive prayed to God to let him die.

But God, whose ear is open to catch the sparrow's fall,
At the sobbing of his servant frowned, along the waters all—
The billows rose in wonder and smote the churlish crew,
And around the ship the thunder like battle-arrows flew;
The screaming sea-fowl's clangor, in Kishcorran's inner caves,
Was hushed before the anger of the tempest-trodden waves

Like an eagle-hunted gannet, the ship drove back amain,
To where the Christian captive sat in solitude and pain—
" Come in," they cried, " oh, Christian, we need your company,
For it was sure your angry God that met us out at sea."
Then smiled the gentle heavens, and doffed their sable veil
Then sank to rest the breakers and died away the gale.

So sitting by the Pilot the happy captive kept
On his rosary a-reck'ning, while the seamen sung or slept.

Before the winds propitious past Achill, south by Ara,
The good ship gliding left behind Hiar Connaught like an
    arrow—
From the southern brow of Erin they shoot the shore of Gaul,
And in holy Tours, Saint Patrick findeth freedom, friends,
    and all.

In holy Tours he findeth home and Altars, friends and all;
There matins hail the morning, sweet bells to vespers call;
There's no lord to make him tremble, no magician to endure,
No need he to dissemble in the pious streets of Tours;
But ever, as he rises with the morning's early light,
And still erewhile he sleepeth, when the North star shines at
    night;
When he sees the angry ocean by the tempest trod,
He murmurs in devotion—" Fear nothing! Trust to God!"

# SAMUEL LOVER

POET, PAINTER AND NOVELIST.

"OVERS are given to poetry," wrote Shak-speare, and the subject of our memoir was no exception to the general rule. On the 24th of February, 1797, Samuel Lover was born in the city of Dublin. His parents were people of means and education. His first studies were made at a boys' academy in his native city, where he applied himself with so much ardor that his health gave way, and, acting on a physician's advice, his parents procured him a comfortable lodging with a farmer in the County Wicklow, where he could enjoy fresh air and plenty of exercise. At this plastic period the wild and beautiful scenery of Wicklow made a deep and lasting impression on his mind. Rambling at will among the romantic vales, and conversing with the noble and generous peasantry, he gained not only physical strength but also a large fund of knowledge relative to the habits and customs of the people whose traits he was destined to describe in song and story.

The memory of his sojourn in Wicklow remained

with Lover, and in after years he gave to it a more
tangible form in these verses, entitled:

## MY MOUNTAIN HOME.

My mountain home! my mountain home!
   Dear are thy hills to me!
Where first my childhood loved to roam—
   Wild as the summer bee;
The summer bee may gather sweet
   From flowers in sunny prime;
And memory brings with wing as fleet,
   Sweet thoughts of early time.
Still fancy bears me to the hills
   Where childhood loved to roam—
I hear, I see your sparkling rills,
   My own, my mountain home!

At the age of sixteen Samuel was taken from school and placed in his father's office, there to be initiated into the keeping of accounts—uncongenial business for a poet!—and so it proved in the case of young Lover, who gave more of his time to study and sketching than to his father's accounts. For this his father remonstrated with him, but to no purpose. The young poet-painter *would* follow the strong bent of his nature, despite all the remonstrances of an anxious parent. So, with the firm resolution of cleaving his own way in the world he left the paternal mansion and patiently applied himself to the study of art. For three years he labored with indomitable zeal and perseverance, during all this time supporting himself principally by copying music and sketching portraits, which in those days were in good demand. Like Gerald Griffin, young Lover more than once felt the pangs of want; but his purpose never weakened, even in the darkest hour of adversity.

Having spent three years in study he came before the public as a marine and miniature painter. He was then only twenty years old, and towards the close of 1818 he became the most popular artist in Dublin. In literary circles he was also recognized as a man of considerable poetic genius; and, when Moore visited his native city, the citizens invited him to write a poem for the occasion. On the evening of the banquet in honor of the great Irish melodist, Lover was there with his song brimful of Irish humor.

The song describes a caucus of the gods, who were to elect a poet laureate for Mount Olympus.

Scott, Southey, Lord Byron and Campbell were nominated for the exalted position and received some votes, but Moore was the successful candidate. We have room here for three or four verses only:

> T' other day Jove exclaimed, with a nod most profound,
> While the gods of Olympus in state sat around,
> "I have fully resolved, after weighty reflection,
> To soon set a-going a poet's election."
>     "A good thought, Jupiter boy!"

While the gods were discussing matters appertaining to election, Juno put in a claim for *woman's rights*:

> "I request, though," said Juno, "you'll let it be known
> Why this right of election the gods have alone;
> On this point as on others I differ from you,
> And insist every goddess shall have a vote, too."
>     "Brave Juno! stand up for your rights."

> Then Jupiter said, "Let it be so, my dear,
> Let th' election commence; bid the poets appear;
> The polling concluded, whoever is found
> To have carried most votes shall our poet be crowned."
>     "Fair play, Jupiter boy!"

Here each delegate introduced some favorite:

> But Mercury said he " should now bring in sight
> A bard who was every one's pride and delight—
> Who Melpomene, Venus, Thalia, could lure;
> They all knew who he meant, and so need he say Moore ?"

Some time after the festivities of this evening Moore desired to be introduced to the rising poet, whom he warmly thanked for the high compliment he had received on his return from abroad. Moore's mother requested a copy of the verses; and ever after that, Lover remained an esteemed friend of the Moore family

His repution as a portrait painter being established, and with a fast-increasing fame as a poet, Lover married a cultured young lady named Miss Berrel, the daughter of a Dublin architect, a man of marked ability and liberal means. The Berrels were an old Catholic family, very much devoted to the ancient faith; and Lover, who was born and raised a Protestant, had no difficulty in promising never to interfere with his wife in the full and free exercise of her religion. He kept his promise, and his domestic life was a happy one.

In 1828 he became Secretary of the Royal Hibernian Academy, and faithfully discharged the duties of that office up to the time of his removal to London, where the latter part of his life was spent.

Dividing his time about equally between the brush and pen, paintings, poems and stories issued from his studio in rapid succession, and for each piece of work the compensation received was ample. His many-sided mind developed some new talent almost every month; and not the least profitable was the aptitude he had for caricaturing, in a humorous way, certain politicians of his time. His "Irish Horn Book," published in 1831, illustrates this statement. This book contained many clever etchings by Lover, and most of the satirical articles were from his trenchant pen.

In 1832 appeared his "Legends and Stories of Ireland," chiefly made up of articles which he had written for the magazines. The same year he painted a picture of the celebrated violinist, Paganini, which won a world-wide fame. This portrait, when sent the following year to the Art Exhibition at the Royal Academy, London, attracted general attention and took the prize from the miniatures of Ross and the renowned Thorburn. Having painted very fine portraits of the Duke of Wellington, Lord Cloncurry, Sir John Conroy and others, he was invited by the Duchess of Kent to paint a portrait of Princess Victoria. Circumstances, however, which he could not control prevented his going to England. In failing to go to England for this purpose it was said he lost

a great opportunity, as he might have gained for himself the title of "Portrait-painter to her gracious Majesty." Lover, however, was both too patriotic and sensible to attach much value to such a distinction. When it was noised abroad that such an offer was made, a Dublin punster remarked that in case of the Irishman's acceptance the "Court chronicler would havé to announce a *Lover* instead of a *Hayter**
as the incumbent of the office."

He settled permanently in London in 1837, where he devoted most of his time to hard work. Among his intimate friends at that time were Rev. Dr. Crolly, Father Prout, Mrs. Jamieson, Miss Landon, Lady Blessington and Thomas Campbell, the poet.

Here his pen was kept as busy as his brush, and his brain seldom rested. He wrote songs for operas and stories for half a dozen magazines. For Mme. Vestris, then very popular in England, he wrote and set to music, "Under the Rose," "The Angel's Whisper," "The Four-Leaved Shamrock," "The Land of the West," and many other pieces which became immensely popular and were sung daily in the streets of London. In London he dramatized his first real novel, "Rory O'More," and its representation on the stage was a complete success. For one hundred and eight nights it drew a crowded house. Speaking

* Sir George Hayter then held the office.

of its popularity the *Athenæum* said that "Rory
O'More—a triple glory in song, story and drama—
was the attraction of the day, and that Samuel Lover
seemed to communicate his own sweet temperament
to all around him."

In this story the author endeavored to do justice
to the character of his countrymen, and of his efforts
an English magazine says:

"Hearty, honest, comic, sensible, tender, faithful and coura-
geous Rory is the true ideal of the Irish peasant—the humble
hero who embodies so much of the best of the national character, and lifts simple emotion almost to the height of ripened
judgment."

Lover's principal recreation consisted in giving
informal receptions to his intimate friends and
associates. It is related that on being presented at
one of those social gathering to Madame Malibran,
the brilliant artiste exclaimed in broken English:
"Will you lend me the loan of a gridiron?"

At one of his little entertainments, a young lady
of high social standing who had been for years an
ardent admirer of the Irish people remarked that
she was meant for an Irishwoman.

"Cross the channel, Madam," said Lover, "and
thousands of people well say you were meant for an
Irishman."

A great success as miniature painter, Lover now

turned his attention to song-writing, and in that also he excelled.

The Dublin *University Magazine* has well said that "as poet, painter and novelist, Lover won sufficient celebrity to make the fame of three different men."

In the preface to the fifth edition of his "Poetical Works," he designates a few of the rules that should be observed in order to write a good song.

"A song," he says, "must be constructed for singing rather than for reading; and hence, to accommodate the vocalist, it should be built up of words having as many vowels and as free from guttural and hissing sounds as possible."

Moore and Burns, he considers, masters of the art of song-writing, and points out the many beauties of their songs by reason of the liberal use of open-vowelled words.

Of the three hundred poems written by himself, all but fifty are songs adapted to old airs—generally native Irish airs. It is impossible to attempt anything like a criticism of these within the limits of this brief paper; but, in passing, it may be said that "Rory O'More," "The Angel's Whisper" and "The Fairy Boy" are favorites—and very deservedly so—wherever the English language is spoken. Unlike the hedge poets he seldom indulged in classical allusions. His metaphors and similes are home-

spun, the very soul of simplicity—and all the better
for that.

The late Dr. Shelton Mackenzie, who knew Lover
well and was qualified to pass judgment on his
works, wrote in the Philadelphia Press:

" Samuel Lover was the author of many admirable ballads,
humorous and pathetic, which are likely to last even as long
as Moore's beautiful melodies. I need only mention ' Molly
Carew,' ' Widow Machree,' ' The Low Back Car,' ' The Bowld
Sojer Boy,' and the ' Four-leaved Shamrock.' He also wrote
novels and plays, of which ' Handy Andy ' is the best known,
owing to its being several times dramatized.

" Incredible as it may appear," the same distinguished writer
goes on to say, " ' Handy Andy,' the man and his nickname,
was not a mere creation and creature of the imagination.
Years before Lover wrote anything concerning that singular
character I had heard a good deal about him. My knowledge
arose in this manner:

" One stormy day, traveling in the mail-coach from the
County Cork to that of Limerick, whither I was going to
spend the Christmas at my uncle's, it was my misfortune to
be upset, with the total wreck of the vehicle, within a mile of
Kilmallock. As the snow was three feet deep, and no convey-
ance could be obtained, my only fellow-traveler determined that
we should not encounter the fatigue of walking into Kilmallock,
but spend the evening in the only tavern of the little village
where the accident had happened.

" ' It's a plain place,' he said, ' but they can supply as good a
rasher of bacon and eggs as ever was served up; and their beds
are clean and comfortable to a degree.'

"It required little persuasion to induce me to act on this advice, given on my companion's personal experience, and we made out that Christmas Eve in the little village tavern.

"Ere we parted my friend told me that, in the ancient chivalry of Ireland there were four hereditary knights, all of them Fitzgeralds and each of them having living representatives. These were the White Knight, the Red Knight, the Knight of Kerry, and the Knight of Glin. He himself was the last of these, deriving his title from the Castle of Glin, which stands in the center of a fine estate near the River Shannon, and has been owned by one branch of the Fitzgerald family for more than six hundred years.

"That evening as we sat by the cheerful turf fire in the humble hostelry which had received us, the Knight of Glin told me a great deal about Handy Andy. This was fully thirteen years before Mr. Lover had introduced that worthy to the readers of *Bentley's Miscellany*.

"'His name,' the Knight said, 'is Andrew Sullivan, but he had such a propensity for doing and saying things in a way they ought not to be done or said, that from an early age every one spoke of him and to him as "Handy Andy"—he being the unhandiest fellow in the world. His misfortune was that he took everything said to him in a natural sense. One morning when I was shaving with cold water, Andy, good-natured enough, brought me up a small jug of hot water. 'Where am I to empty this?' he asked, pointing to the mug of cold water I had been using. I told him to throw it out of the window, (of course, meaning the water only); but matter-of-fact Andy raised the window, and pitched not only the water, but also the China mug that held it, into the yard below, and then looked cheerfully at me as if he deserved praise for having carried out my instructions to the letter.

" ' On another occasion when I was high sheriff of the county, I had to give a big dinner at Glin Castle to the Judges of Assize, the Grand Jury and the members of the bar. Several baskets of champagne for consumption on that occasion were obtained from the city of Limerick. There was need of many servants to wait on table, and Andy was put into livery. Unfortunately my caterer was an Englishman, who seeing Andy doing nothing, called out: ' You Hoirish feller there, just put this champagne into that 'ere tub of h'ice, h'and look shard that no feller takes some of it!'

" 'Andy literally carrying out his instructions did put the wine into the tub, uncorking bottle after bottle of it to the extent of two dozen; and when champagne was called for at dinner, dragged in the tub, and told how he really had poured the wine into the ice, as he had been ordered. Fortunately there was more of the generous fluid, so no very great harm was done. It was impossible, no matter how angry one might be, to avoid laughing at the numerous and curious blunders of Handy Andy. He has grown gray in my service, and though I dismiss him every three months or so on some new aggravation, he slips back again and I cannot continue angry with him.'

" Many other illustrations of this original character were told me by the Knight, but my limited space does not permit me to mention them."

These and many other ludicrous incidents in the life of Handy Andy, Mr. Lover strung together on a slender thread, and, in the end, landed his hero up among the peers of the realm—the proper place for a booby to end his days.

Lover's eyesight began to fail in 1844, and he was obliged to abandon painting altogether, though this was his chief means of support. In order to make up for the loss he had sustained in this way, he arranged a literary and musical entertainment which he called "Irish Evenings." This species of amusement was not so common in those days as it is with us, and the "Evenings" took immensely both in England and Ireland. This entertainment consisted of an *olla podrida* of his own most popular songs and stories. He selected two young ladies to assist him with the songs, while he always kept for himself the recital of the stories. The proceeds from this source relieved him for a time from financial embarrassments, and the enthusiastic receptions which awaited him everywhere he appeared in Ireland were extremely gratifying to his genial Irish heart.

He repeated his "Evenings" throughout the large cities of the United States in the fall of 1846. Here he did not meet with that measure of success that attended his efforts at home, owing principally to the fact that entertainments of that character were nothing new in our Eastern cities, even at that early day. His mission to the United States was not a failure, however, and, unlike so many literary snobs who come out from "h'old H'england" in the capacity of tourists, he was able to appreciate the worth and progress of our Republican institutions.

At Niagara Falls he wrote a poem commencing:

> Nymph of Niagara! sprite of the mist!
> With a wild magic, my brow thou hast kiss'd;
> I am thy slave, and my mistress art thou,
> For thy wild kiss of magic is yet on my brow.

During his visit to America, Lover's wife died, and shortly after his return to England the death of his favorite daughter made his life desolate, and unfitted him for a long time for any kind of work.

Subsequently, his publishers induced him to edit a volume of poems containing the best selections from the bards of Erin.  This work he accomplished in a very creditable manner.  His notes and comments on the different epochs of Irish poetry are to the present day models of English composition.

When the Burns' Centenary Festival was held in Glasgow, January, 1859, Lover was invited to represent the poets of Ireland there.  Called on to respond to "the ladies," he remarked that it was proper, meet and natural that a *lover* should be chosen to reply to such a toast.

" Rival Rhymes in Honor of Burns," are the products of his pen, though published under the *nom de plume* of Ben Trovato.  These are imitations of Father Prout, Longfellow, Hood, Thackeray, Campbell and

Lord Macaulay. In one of these imitations he felicitiously enumerates the different names by which poets go in different countries:

> In France they called them Troubadours,
> . Or Menestrels by turns;
> The Scandinavians called them *Scalds*,
> The Scotchmen call their's *Burns*.

A writer of his acquaintance having given his opinion on the relative merits of Moore and the author of Rory O'More, Lover replied·

> " I think there is more of the ' touch of nature' in my writings than in his. I think, also, there is more *feeling*, and beyond all doubt *I am much more Irish.*"

Though writing to a Scotchman, Lover seemed to have felt proud of his Irish blood, birth and feeling. and he has left proof positive that he loved his race and country.

As mentioned heretofore, Lover was fond of entertaining his literary friends at his own residence in London. Very often he gave them not only a good dinner, but a little to pay their craving creditors also. Among his guests one evening was a needy friend whom Lover could not accommodate with " a loan."

After supper was over, and while chatting over their punch, it was agreed upon that each one should write a verse embodying his individual opinion of the host.  Slips of paper were procured, and, in a short time, everybody's brain and pencil went to work.  The nameless verses were all deposited in a satchel, well shaken, then extracted one by one and read in the presence of the whole company.  Among many flattering squibs the following was found:

> What he is I've had cause to discover,
>   And thus doth experience tend—
> He may be sublime as a Lover,
>   But very so-so as a friend.

An American writer describes the poet, painter and novelist in the *Atlas*, published in Boston at the time of Lover's visit to the States:

" But who is that lively little gentleman whom everybody is shaking hands with, and who shakes hands with everybody in turn?  He is here, there and everywhere, chattering away delightfully, it would seem, and dispensing smiles and arch looks in profusion.  How his black eyes twinkle, and what fun there is in his face!  He seems brimful and running over with humor, and looks as if Care never had touched him.  And then listen to that Milesian brogue!  Reader, perhaps you have never heard an educated Irishman talk!  Well, if so, you have lost a treat.  That natty, dear duck of a man, as the ladies say, is a universal favorite everywhere.  He is at once poet, painter, musician and novelist.  He writes songs, sets them to music, illustrates them with his pencil, and then sings them as no one else can.

" Hurrah! we have Rory O'More in our midst.  Sam Lover, I beg to introduce you to the American public."

About the end of 1867 close application to work and old age combined began to tell on our author's health, which, early in the following year rapidly failed. In the seventy-second year of his age he calmly passed away, on the 6th day of July, 1868, at St. Helier's, Jersey, England.

On the 15th of the same month he was buried in Kensal Green, London. The Marquis of Donegal in command of the Irish Volunteers, of which Lover was an old member, attended his funeral.

We cannot close this memorial of one who did so much during his long life to vindicate his country's right to the proud title of " Queen of Song " without quoting the tablet to his memory placed in one of the aisles of St. Patrick's Cathedral, Dublin. The inscription runs thus:

" In memory of Samuel Lover, poet, painter, novelist and composer, who in the exercise of a genius as distinguished in its versatility as in its power, by his pen and pencil illustrated so happily the characteristics of the peasantry of his country, that his name will ever be honorably identified with Ireland."

### THE FOUR-LEAVED SHAMROCK.

I'LL seek a four-leaved shamrock
    In all the fairy dells,
And if I find the charmed leaves,
    Oh, how I'll weave my spells.

I would not waste my magic might
   On diamond, pearl or gold;
For treasures tire the weary sense—
   Such triumph is but cold.
But I would play the enchanter's part
   In casting bliss around;
Oh! not a tear nor aching heart
   Should in the world be found,
   Should in the world be found.

To worth I would give honor,
   I'd dry the mourner's tears;
And to the pallid lip recall
   The smile of happier years.
And hearts that had been long estranged,
   And friends that had grown cold,
Should meet again llike parted streams,
   And mingle as of old.
Oh! thus I'd play the enchanter's part,
   Thus scatter bliss around;
And not a tear nor aching heart
   Should in the world be found,
   Should in the world be found.

The heart that had been mourning
   O'er vanished dreams of love,
Should see them all returning,
   Like Noah's faithful dove.
And Hope should launch her blessed bark
   On Sorrow's dark'ning sea,
And Mis'ry's children have an ark,
   And saved from sinking be.

Oh! thus I'd play the enchanter's part,
　　Thus scatter bliss around,
And not a tear nor aching heart
　　Should in the world be found,
　　Should in the world be found.

## RORY O'MORE.

YOUNG Rory O'More courted Kathleen Bawn,
He was bold as a hawk, she as soft as the dawn;
He wish'd in his heart pretty Kathleen to please,
And he thought the best way to do that was to tease.
" Now, Rory, be aisy," sweet Kathleen would cry,
(Reproof on her lip, but a smile in her eye),
" With your tricks I don't know, in troth, what I'm about;
Faith you've teased till I've put on my cloak inside out."
" Oh! Jewel," says Rory, " that same is the way
You've thrated my heart for this many a day;
And 'tis plazed that I am, and why not, to be sure?
For 'tis all for good luck," says bold Rory O'More.

" Indeed, then," says Kathleen, " don't think of the like,
For I half gave a promise to sootherin' Mike;
The ground that I walk on he loves, I'll be bound—"
" Faith," says Rory, " I'd rather love you than the ground."
" Now, Rory, I'll cry if you don't let me go;
Sure I drame ev'ry night that I'm hatin' you so!"
" Oh," says Rory, " that same I'm delighted to hear,
For drames always go by conthraries, my dear;
Oh! jewel, keep dramin' that same till you die,
And bright mornin' will give dirty night the black lie!
And 'tis plazed that I am, and why not, to be sure?
Since 'tis all for good luck," says bold Rory O'More.

" Arrah, Kathleen, my darlint, you've tazed me enough,
Sure I've thrash'd for your sake Dinny Grimes and Jim Duff;
And I've made myself drinkin' your health quite a baste,
So I think after that, I may talk to the priest."
Then Rory, the rogue, stole his arm 'round her neck,
So soft and so white, without freckle or speck,
And he looked in her eyes that were beaming with light,
And he kissed her sweet lips;—don't you think he was right ?
" Now, Rory, leave off, sir; you'll hug me no more.
That's eight times to-day you have kiss'd me before."
" Then here goes another," says he, " to make sure,
For there's luck in odd numbers," says Rory O'More.

### MOLLY BAWN.

OH, Molly Bawn, why leave me pining,
    Lonely waiting here for you;
The stars above are brightly shining,
    Because they've nothing else to do.
The flowers late were open keeping,
    To try a rival blush with you,
But their mother, Nature, set them sleeping,
    With their rosy faces washed with dew.
        Oh, Molly Bawn—oh, Molly Bawn.

The pretty flowers were made to bloom, dear,
    And the pretty stars were made to shine;
The pretty girls were made for the boys, dear,
    And maybe you were made for mine. ·
The wicked watch-dog here is snarling,
    He takes me for a thief, you see;
He knows I'd steal you, Molly, Darling,
    And then " transported " I would be.
        Oh, Molly Bawn—oh, Molly Bawn.

## THE ANGEL'S WHISPER.

A BABY was sleeping,
Its mother was weeping,
For her husband was far on the wild, raging sea,
And the tempest was swelling,
Round the fisherman's dwelling—
And she cried: "Dermot, darling, oh! come back to me!"

Her beads while she numbered,
The baby still slumber'd
And smiled in her face as she bended her knee;
"Oh! blest be that warning,
My child's sleep adorning,
For I know that the angels are whispering with thee.

"And while they are keeping
Bright watch o'er thy sleeping,
Oh! pray to them softly, my baby, with me—
And say thou wouldst rather
They'd watch o'er thy father,
For I know that the angels are whispering with thee."

The dawn of the morning
Saw Dermot returning,
And the wife wept with joy her babe's father to see;
And closely caressing
Her child with a blessing,
Said: "I knew that the angels were whispering with thee."

## THE FAIRY BOY.

[When a beautiful child pines and dies, the Irish peasant believes the healthy infant has been stolen by the fairies, and a sickly elf left in its place.]

A MOTHER came, when stars were paling,
    Wailing 'round a lonely spring;
Thus she cried while tears were falling,
    Calling on the fairy King:
" Why with spells my child caressing,
    Courting him with fairy joy;
Why destroy a mother's blessing,
    Wherefore steal my baby boy?

" O'er the mountain, through the wild wood,
    Where his childhood loved to play;
Where the flowers are freshly springing,
    There I wander, day by day.
" There I wander, growing fonder
    Of the child that made my joy;
On the echoes wildly calling,
    To restore my fairy boy.

" But in vain my plaintive calling,
    Tears are falling all in vain;
He now sports with fairy pleasure,
    He's the treasure of their train!
" Fare thee well, my child, forever,
    In this world I've lost my joy;
But in the *next* we ne'er shall sever,
    There I'll find my angel boy!"

# REV. FRANCIS MAHONY

## (FATHER PROUT).

THERE are, indeed, few pseudonyms in the broad extent of English literature that have attained greater celebrity than that of "Father Prout," the classic sage of Watergrasshill, near Blarney. Even the renowned names of Sir Morgan O'Dougherty and Barry Cornwall pale before that synonym of wit, waggery, and linguistic lore, so often appended to the spiciest articles that ever adorned the pages of *Frazer's Magazine*.

The city of St. Finbar, on the "banks of the Lee," reckons this literary genius among the number of its illustrious sons. In that delightful old capital of Munster he was born in the year 1804, of parents who were neither rich nor poor, but could boast of a long line of ancestors whose martial renown haloes the vicinity of Dromore Castle, the *cunabulum* of the sept of the O'Mahonys, in the Kingdom of Kerry. "By the pleasant waters of the river Lee" Francis Sylvester Mahony grew to the estate of a *gossoon*, and went to school, where, it is said, "he picked up with equal facility the Munster brogue and the rudiments of an education." At the early age of twelve years,

FRANCIS S. MAHONY.

before Frank had had much time for dreaming among the "Groves of Blarney" or kissing the "Eloquent Stone," being destined by his parents for the holy priesthood, he was shipped off to the Continent and placed under the guidance of those great masters of scholastic learning, the Jesuit Fathers, who were soon compelled to recognize the brilliant talents of the laughing, lively Cork boy. Under these teachers, both in St. Acheul and at their seminary in Paris, Frank was wont to say that he "breathed a very atmosphere of Latinity and imbibed Greek with as much facility and gusto as an Irish beggarman would buttermilk." However disposed we may be to take the latter part of this declaration *cum grano salis*, it is certain that those erudite masters of *belles-lettres* seldom cultivated a young mind more fertile and susceptible than was that of the future author of the "Prout Papers." Even before he entered the Jesuit novitiate in the suburbs of Paris, where he was destined to try his vocation for the Order, he could turn his ideas into Latin hexameters with eloquence and ease, while he spoke that classic tongue with a fluency and accent which would do credit to a Roman of the Augustan age. French and Italian were to him a second vernacular, and of the Germanic language and literature he was by no means ignorant.

Having received deaconship in the Jesuit College at Rome, Rev. Francis Mahony set out for Ireland, from which he had been so long absent; but on his way thither he was told by no less a personage than the Provincial that his superiors thought that the young deacon had no vocation—at least for their Society—and therefore would not be admitted to the priesthood by them.

The Rubicon was already passed, the indelible character was stamped, and, undeterred by this admonition, Frank pursued his course to the shores of his native land and gained admission to the Jesuit College of Clongowes Wood, Kildare, in order to test still further his vocation to labor in the ranks of Loyola's sons; for hitherto he had not the remotest intention of becoming a secular priest. *Apropos* of a secular priest, the learned padre was asked by the wits of *Frazer's Magazine*, soon after he had discontinued his sacerdotal functions, for the definition of a "circular priest," when he immediately answered:

> Ens rotundum
> Per universum mundum,
> Nihil agens, sed omnia rapiens.

There is more of a display of learning than of truth in this answer.

In September, 1830, the Roman deacon entered Clongowes College and was soon promoted to the

Chair of Rhetoric by the Rev. Peter Kenny, then President of that institution, and afterwards known in this country as the "great Jesuit of the West." Among his rhetoricians were two young men destined in the near future to be classed among the contributors of *Frazer's* and *Bentley's*, and to impress the names of John Sheehan, "The Irish Whisky Drinker," and F. S. Murphy on the literary records of the period.

Soon after the Rev. Frank's inauguration at Clongowes, the "boys got a free day," for which a coursing party was gotten up, and the master of rhetoric, at the head of his disciples, started out bright and early, making a bee line for Maynooth, where the party took dinner. On their return, the learned youths were entertained at the house of a country squire, where the head of the family treated them with characteristic Irish generosity, until one of the guests frankly confessed that he had "no remembrance of the number of songs sung, of patriotic toasts and healths proposed, of speeches made, or of decanters emptied." The party broke up late, and, starting for the college, they were overtaken by a terrible thunderstorm which completely unnerved the majority of the youths, who, fortunately, were picked up in the nick of time by some passing draymen, and landed about midnight at the gate of their

27

*alma mater.* This luckless episode put a period to the career of Rev. Frank in his native Isle, and in a few days after he was in a position to exclaim, with the hero of Virgil's epic, " Feror exul in altum;" and he might have added, " Ad litora Hiberniæ nunquam rediturus," for, living, he never more beheld the shores of Ireland. Arriving in the Eternal City, where he formed the acquaintance of his distinguished fellow-townsman, Barry, the painter, he resumed and completed his theological studies, and was ordained a priest, having previously obtained an *exeat* from Dr. Murphy, the bishop of his native diocese. As a priest he returned to London, where he acted as curate to the celebrated Dr. Magee; but after due consideration—consideration which came, alas! too late—he concluded that he had entered the fold without being among those of whom the High Priest said, " Ego elegi vos," and thenceforth refrained from obtruding himself on the sanctuary.

The belief that the Rev. Francis Mahony returned to Ireland after his ordination, and served in the capacity of curate under a veritable Father Prout, P.P. of Watergrasshill, whose name the young scribe assumed in writing for the Cork papers, was very common at one time. But the fact is, after his departure from Clongowes in the autumn of 1830, he never returned until he came to mingle his dust with

the ashes of his sires under the shadow of Shandon
steeple, whose " chimes " he praised in exquisite and
immortal verse.

Though Father Prout, forced by conscientious con-
siderations, retired from sacerdotal duties, he always
wore a dark *infra genua* threadbare coat, for which
he seemed to evince as much attachment as did his
fellow-poet, Mangan, for his weather-worn umbrella;
and from the day he was raised to the sub-deaconate
until a short time before his death, when he obtained
a dispensation from Rome, he was faithful to the
recitation of the divine office, and he never suffered
a scoff or jeer directed against the sacerdotal character to escape unreproved.

But in one of his best and most serious papers,
" Literature and the Jesuits," he indulges in droll-
eries. "The Groves of Blarney," writes he, in this
learned paper, " do not better deserve the honor of a
pilgrimage than this (Clongowes) venerable institution. Lady Morgan wishes to explore the learned
cave of these literary cenobites, but the Sons of
Ignatius ' smelt a rat,' and acted on the principle of
the Irish Saint Senanus, who wrote:

> " ' Quid foeminis
> Commune est cum monachis?
> Nec te, nec ullam aliam
> Admittamus in insulam.' "

However, it is seldom that he considers Lady
Morgan or her sex worthy of his steel, while he
always seems ready and willing to leap astride his
Rosinante and "tilt a spear" with Dr. Denis Lard-
ner, or that mortal whom Shelley styles

> " The sweetest lyric of his saddest song."

" the poet of all circles and the idol of his own."
The learned padre handles Tommy without gloves
in " The Rogueries of Tom Moore," where he bare-
facedly accuses the lyrist of pilfering from the Greeks
and Romans, and even the French, to increase the
volume of his song:

> " The best of all ways
> To lengthen our lays
> Is to steal a few thoughts from the French, my dear."

But the melodist's plagiarisms do not stop here,
nor even in India, whence he returns *spoliis Orientis
onustum*, but he must descend to the petty larceny
of appropriating one of Prout's own juvenile effusions to a " Beautiful Milkmaid," who was accustomed to cross his path when yet a tyro in Greek
and Latin lore.   To use Prout's inimitable language,
" Everything was equally acceptable in the way of
song to Tommy, and provided I brought grist to his
mill, he did not care where the produce came from
—even the wild oats and thistles of native growth

on Watergrasshill, all was good provender for his
Pegasus. He saw my youthful effusion to an Irish
milkmaid, grasped it with avidity, and I find he has
given it word for word, in an English shape, in his
'Irish Melodies.' Let the intelligent reader judge
if he has done common justice to my young muse:

## IN PULCHRAM LACTIFERAM.

### CARMEN, AUCTORE PROUT.

Lesbia semper hinc et inde,
　　Oculorum tela movet;
Captat omnes, sed deinde,
　　Quis ametur nemo novit
Palpebrarum, Nora cara,
　　Lux tuarum non est foris,
Flamma micat ibi rara,
　　Sed sinceri lux amoris.
Nora Creina sit regina,
　　Vultu, gressu tam modesto!
Haec, puellas inter bellas,
　　Jure omnium dux esto.

Lesbia vestes auro graves
　　Fert et gemmis, juxta normam,
Gratiae sed, eheu! suaves
　　Cinctam reliquere formam.
Norae tunicam praeferres
　　Flante zephyro volantem,
Oculis et raptis erres
　　Contemplando ambulantem!

Veste Nora, tam decora,
  Semper indui momento,
Semper purae sic naturae
  Ibis tecta vestimento.

Lesbia mentis praefert lumen,
  Quod coruscat perlibenter,
Sed quis optet hoc acumen
  Quando acupuncta dentur?
Norae sinu cum recliner,
  Dormio luxuriose,
Nil corrugat hoc pulvinar,
  Nisi crispae ruga rosae.
Nora blanda, lux amanda
  Expers usque tenebrarum,
Tu cor mulces per tot dulces
  Dotes, fons illecebrarum!

Compare this with Moore's " Nora Creina," and
you will see that it lacks nothing of the original in
rhyme, rhythm or euphony, and that Prout is as
great a master of the mechanism of verse in the
Latin as Moore in the English tongue. It is in this
paper, also, that "The Bells of Shandon" first
appeared, and gained for the gifted author a place
among the poets of his country. This beautiful
ballad has been printed in innumerable newspapers
and magazines, and consequently must be familiar
to every lover of literature.

## THE SHANDON BELLS.

With deep affection
And recollection
I often think of
    Those Shandon Bells,
Whose sounds so wild would,
In days of childhood,
Fling round my cradle
    Their magic spells.
On this I ponder
Where'er I wander
And thus grow fonder,
    Sweet Cork, of thee;
With thy bells of Shandon
That sound so grand on
The pleasant waters
    Of the river Lee.

I've heard bells chiming
Full many a clime in,
Tolling sublime in
    Cathedral shrine,
While at a glibe rate
Brass tongues would vibrate—
But all their music
    Spoke naught like thine;
For memory dwelling
On each proud swelling
Of the belfry knelling,
    Its bold notes free,

Made the bells of Shandon
Sound far more grand on
The pleasant waters
    Of the river Lee.

I've heard bells tolling
Old " Adrian's Mole " in,
Their thunder rolling
    From the Vatican,
And cymbals glorious
Swinging uproarious
In the gorgeous turrets
    Of Notre Dame;
But thy sounds were sweeter
Than the dome of Peter
Flings o'er the Tiber,
    Pealing solemnly—
O! the bells of Shandon
Sound far more grand on
The pleasant waters
    Of the river Lee.

There's a bell in Moscow,
While on tower and kiosk, O!
In Saint Sophia
    The Turkman gets,
And loud in air
Calls men to prayer
From the tapering summits
    Of tall minarets.

Such empty phantom
I freely grant them,
But there's an anthem
 More dear to me—
'Tis the bells of Shandon
That sound so grand on
The pleasant waters
 Of the river Lee.

The first of the Prout Papers, "An Apology for Lent," appeared in *Frazer's* for April, 1834, and won its author a place among the best and most brilliant of those whose contributions made that magazine one of the raciest and most readable publications in the British Isles. Started by Hugh Frazer in 1830, this magazine was placed under the editorial management of William Maginn, LL.D., a fellow townsman of Prout's, and also of the talented Daniel Maclise, ("Alfred Croquis,") whose etchings illustrated and adorned the pages of that monthly, which reckoned among its staff, Southey, Carlyle, Ainsworth, Thackeray and Coleridge. Yet even among such literary geniuses the editor of the "Reliques" does not hesitate to say that "as a philologist, as a wit, as a lyrist, as a master of persiflage, Frank Mahony stepped conspicuously to the front with his earliest contribution to *Frazer's Magazine*." In many of the dead and most of the modern tongues he was *facile princeps;* and this fact we might illustrate by numerous examples, if the limits of this paper allowed. His polyglot edition of Mr. Milliken's "Groves of Blarney" is serio-comic. The idea of clothing this quaint rhapsody in an Athenian mantle or Gallican surtout is in itself sufficient to test the risible faculties of a Stoic philosopher. Imagine how the following lines appear in Greek, to say nothing of the Latin rendering:

> There is a stone there
> That whoever kisses,
> Oh! he never misses
> To grow eloquent.
> 'Tis he may clamber
> To a lady's chamber
> Or become a member
> Of parliament:
> A clever spouter
> He'll turn out, or
> An out-and-outer
> " To be let alone;"
> Don't hope to hinder him,
> Or to bewilder him;
> Sure he's a pilgrim
> From the Blarney Stone.

"The Athenians," says Father Prout, "thought that the ghosts of departed heroes were transferred to our fortunate island, which they call, in the war songs of Hermodius and Aristogiton, the 'land of

O's and Macs;' and so the 'Groves of Blarney' have been commemorated by the Greek poets many centuries before the Christian era." When our author took a place among the confreres of *Frazer's Magazine*, he was thirty years of age, and before he had completed his thirty-second year, those *twenty-four* papers which constitute the "Reliques of Father Prout" had indelibly stamped his name in brilliant characters on the roll of literary worthies. Speaking of the merits of these papers, a writer in the *Universal Review*, after much praise, winds up in the following energetic language: "They are a mixture of toryism, classicism, sarcasm and punch." Of these papers, "A Plea for Pilgrimages" is perhaps in "larky fun" the richest, as the one on the Jesuits is certainly the most learned. In this latter paper, which he illustrates with apt and ample quotations from the poets, he evinces throughout his undying gratitude to the sons of Loyola who have equally distinguished themselves in the Republic of Letters and the Monarchy of the Church.

Contrasting the neglect with which Barry the painter was treated while living, and the public honors paid him when dead, he aptly quotes Fontaine's "Ode to Chateaubriand," which, like Goldsmith's "Bed by night and chest of drawers by day," will serve here in the double capacity of illus-

trating the policy above referred to, and at the same
time demonstrating our author's ability as a translator from the French:

## ODE TO CHATEAUBRIAND.

### TRANSLATION.

I'VE known a youth with genius cursed—
I've marked his eye hope-lit at first,
Then seen his heart indignant burst,
    To find its efforts scorned.
Soft on his pensive hour I stole,
And saw him draw, with anguish'd soul,
Glory's immortal muster-roll,
    His name should have adorn'd.

His fate had been, with anxious mind,
To chase the phantom Fame—to find
His grasp eluded; calm, resigned,
    He knows his doom—he dies.
Then comes Renown, then Fame appears,
Glory proclaims the coffin hers,
Aye, greenest over sepulchres
    Palm-tree and laurel rise.

After severing his connection with *Frazer's*, Father
Mahony returned to the Continent, where he spent
his remaining years, between Rome and Paris, in
the capacity of special correspondent to the London
*Daily News* and *Globe*, writing under the assumed
name of "Don Jeremy Savonarola." Occasionally,

during these years of absence, he contributed to the *Cornhill Magazine,* edited by his old chum Thackeray, and also to Charles Dickens' publication, *Bentley's Miscellany.* He recited his breviary regularly and though well he knew and loved "Vida" and "Virgil," it is said he knew and loved the *Roman Psalter* still better. On account of failing sight, he received, a short time before his death, a dispensation from the divine office substituting, as is customary in such cases, the Rosary.

At length came warnings of the final summons —that summons which consigns alike to the same common clay the brightest genius and the most stupid dullard—and Father Mahony sent to the parish church of St. Roch for Abbe Rogerson, who attended immediately, and found his penitent well disposed to receive the last rites of the Church. As there is much misunderstanding as to the dispositions and circumstances in which Father Mahony died, we shall quote here the words of his confessor, Abbe Rogerson, referring to this disputed question. Finding Father Mahony sitting in an arm-chair, poorly clad and waiting with anxiety the coming of a fellow-priest, the Abbe now writes:

" Thanking me for patient and persevering attention to him during his sickness, he asked pardon of me and of the whole world for offenses committed against God and to the prejudice

of his neighbor, and then sinking down in front of me with his
face buried in his two hands, and resting them on my knees, he
received from me, with convulsive sobs, the words of absolution.
His genial Irish heart was full to overflowing, * * * and
he was as a child wearied and worn out after a day's wanderings when it had been lost and found again, when it had hun-
gered and was again fed. I raised him up, took him in my
arms, and laid him on his bed as I would have treated such a
little wanderer of a child, and left him without leave-taking on
his part, for his heart was too full for words."

These words are conclusive. Prejudice or incre-
dulity need no further proof on this head. On the
morning following the scene just narrated, Abbe
Rogerson, on entering the room of his penitent, was
greeted with the words, "Holy oils," and knowing
their import, the good priest hastened to anoint the
dying priest and litterateur. "Holy oils" were the
last articulate sounds that passed Father Mahony's
lips. On the 18th of May, 1866, he tranquilly
breathed his last in the presence of his sister and
his confessor, and on the twenty-seventh day following his remains arrived from Paris in his native
city, where his body lay in state at St. Patrick's
church till the morning of the 28th, when, after a
Mass of Requiem, Bishop Delaney pronounced the
final absolutions, and all that was mortal of the Rev.
Francis Mahony, the brilliant wit and inimitable
humorist, was deposited in the family vault at Old

Shandon, there to await the resuscitating summons
—*surge ad judicium.*

## DON IGNACIO LOYOLA'S VIGIL

### IN THE CHAPEL OF OUR LADY OF MONTSERRAT.

WHEN at thy shrine, most Holy Maid!
The Spaniard hung his votive blade.
    And bared his helmèd brow—
Not that he feared war's visage grim,
Or that the battle-field for him
    Had aught to daunt, I trow:

" Glory!" he cried, " with thee I've done!
Fame! thy bright theatres I shun,
    To tread fresh pathways now;
To track THY footsteps, Saviour, God!
With throbbing heart, with feet unshod;
    Hear and record my vow.

' Yes, Thou shalt reign! Chained to Thy throne
The mind of man Thy sway shall own,
    And to it's conqueror bow.
Genius his lyre to Thee shall lift,
And intellect it's choicest gift
    Proudly on Thee bestow."

Straight on the marble floor he knelt.
And in his breast exulting felt
    A vivid furnace glow;
Forth to his task the giant sped,
Earth shook abroad beneath his tread,
    And idols were laid low.

India repaired half Europe's loss;
O'er a new hemisphere the Cross
    Shone in the azure sky;
And, from the isles of far Japan
To the broad Andes, won o'er man
    A bloodless victory!

## THE TRI-COLOR.

### A PROSECUTED SONG.

COMRADES, around this humble board,
    Here's to our banner's by-gone splendor!
There may be treason in that word—
All Europe may the proof afford—
    All France be the offender;
        But drink the toast
        That gladdens most,
Fires the young heart and cheers the old:
May France once more
        Her tri-color
Blessed with new life behold!

List to my secret.   That old flag
    Under my bed of straw is hidden,
Sacred to glory!   War-worn rag!
Thee no *informer* thence shall drag,
    Nor dastard *spy* say 'tis forbidden.
        France, I can vouch,
        Will from its couch,
The dormant symbol yet unfold,
And wave once more
        Her tri-color
Through Europe, uncontrolled!

For every drop of blood we spent,
  Did not that flag give value plenty?
Were not our children as they went
Jocund, to join the warrior's tent,
  Soldiers at ten, heroes at twenty?
      FRANCE! who were then
      Your noblemen?
Not *they* of parchment--must and mould!
But they who bore
      Your tri-color
Through Europe, uncontrolled!

Leipsic hath seen our eagle fall,
  Drunk with renown, worn out with glory;
But, with the emblem of old Gaul
Crowning our standard, we'll recall
  The brighest days of Valmy's story!
      With terror pale
      Shall despots quail,
When in their ear the tale is told,
Of France once more
      Her tricolor
Preparing to unfold!

Trust not the lawless ruffian chiel,
  Worse than the vilest monarch he!
Down with the dungeon and Bastile!
But let our country never kneel
  To that grim idol, *Anarchy!*
      Strength shall appear
      On our frontier—

France shall be Liberty's stronghold!
Then earth once more
  The tri-color
With blessings shall behold!

O my old flag! that liest hid,
 There where my sword and musket lie—
Banner, come forth! for tears unhid
Are filling fast a warrior's lid,
 Which thou alone canst dry.
  A soldier's grief
  Shall find relief,
A veteran's heart shall be consoled—
France shall once more
  Her tri-color
Triumphantly unfold!


## PRAY FOR ME.

### A BALLAD.

[From the French of Milleroye, on his death-bed at the village of Neuilly.]

SILENT, remote, this hamlet seems—
 How hushed the breeze! the eve how calm!
Light through my dying chamber beams,
 But hope comes not, nor healing balm.
Kind villagers! God bless your shed!
 Hark! 'tis for prayer—the evening bell—
Oh, stay! and near my dying bed,
 Maiden, for me your rosary tell!

When leaves shall strew the waterfall
  In the sad close of autumn drear, ·
Say, " The sick youth is freed from all
  The pangs and woe he suffered here."
So may ye speak of him that's gone;
  But when your belfry tolls my knell,
Pray for the soul of that lost one—
  Maiden, for me your rosary tell!

Oh! pity *her* in sable robe,
  Who to my grassy grave will come;
Nor seek a hidden wound to probe—
  She was my love!—point out my tomb;
Tell her my life should have been hers—
  'T was but a day!—God's will!—'t is well;
But weep for her, kind villagers!
  Maiden, for me your rosary tell!

### THE BATTLE OF LEPANTO.

LET us sing how the boast of the Saracen host
  In the gulf of Lepanto was scattered,
When each Knight of St. John's from his cannon of bronze,
  With grape-shot their argosies battered.
Oh! we taught the Turks then that of Europe the men
  Could defy every infidel menace—
And that still o'er the main float the galleys of Spain,
  And the red-lion standard of Venice!

Quick we made the foe skulk, as we blazed at each hulk,
  While they left us a splinter to fire at;
And the rest of them fled o'er the waters, blood red
  With the gore of the Ottoman pirate;

And our navy gave chase to the infidel race,
　Nor allowed them a moment to rally;
And we forced them at length to acknowledge our strength
　In the tent, in the field, in the galley!

Then our men gave a shout and the ocean throughout
　Heard of Christendom's triumph with rapture.
Galleottes eighty-nine of the enemy's line
　To our swift-sailing ships fell a capture;
And I firmly maintain that the number of slain
　To at least sixty thousand amounted:
To be sure, 'twas sad work if the life of a Turk
　For a moment were worth being counted.

We may well feel elate, though I'm sorry to state,
　That albeit by the myriad we've slain 'em,
Still, the sons of the Cross have to weep for the loss
　Of six thousand who fell by the Paynim.
Full atonement was due for each man that they slew,
　And a hecatomb paid for each hero;
But could all that we'd kill give a son to Castile,
　Or to Malta a brave cavalhéro?

St. Mark for the slain intercedes not in vain—
　There's a mass at each altar in Venice;
And the saints we implore for the banner they bore
　Are Our Lady, St. George and St. Denis.
For the brave, while we grieve, in our hearts they shall live,
　In our mouths shall their praise be incessant;
And again and again we will boast of the men
　Who have humbled the pride of the Crescent.

# ODE TO THE WIG OF FATHER BOSCOVICH,

## THE CELEBRATED ASTRONOMER.

[From the Italian of Julius Caesar Cerdara.]

WITH awe I look on that peruke,
    Where learning is a lodger,
And think, whene'er I see that hair
Which now you wear, some ladye fair
    Had worn it once, dear Roger!

On empty skull most beautiful
    Appeared, no doubt, those locks,
Once the bright grace of pretty face;
Now far more proud to be allowed
    To deck thy " knowledge box."

Condemned to pass before the glass
    Whole hours each blessed morning,
'T was desperate long, with curling-tong
And tortoise shell, to have a belle
    Thee frizzing and adorning.

Bright ringlets set as in a net,
    To catch us men like fishes!
Your every lock concealed a stock
Of female wares—love's pensive cares,
    Vain dreams, and futile wishes!

That *chevelure* has caused, I'm sure,
    Full many a lover's quarrel;
Then it was decked with flowers select
And myrtle sprig; but now a WIG,
    'T is circled with a laurel!

Where fresh and new, at first they grew,
   Of whims, and tricks, and fancies,
Those locks at best were but a nest;—
Their being spread on learned head
   Vastly their worth enhances.

From flowers exempt, uncouth, unkempt—
   Matted, entangled, thick!
Mourn not the loss of curl or gloss.
'T is *infra dig.*   THOU ART THE WIG
   OF ROGER BOSCOVICH!

## MICHAEL ANGELO'S FAREWELL TO SCULPTURE.

I FEEL that I am growing old—
My lamp of clay! thy flame, behold,
'Gins to burn low; and I've unrolled
   My life's eventful volume!
The sea has borne my fragile bark
Close to the shore—now rising dark,
O'er the subsiding wave I mark
   This brief world's final column.

'T is time my soul, for pensive mood,
For holy calm and solitude;
Then cease henceforward to delude
   Thyself with fleeting vanity.
The pride of art, the sculptured thought,
Vain idols that my hand hath wrought—
To place my trust in such were naught
   But sheer insanity.

What can the pencil's power achieve?
What can the chisel's triumph give?
A name perhaps on earth may live,
    And travel to posterity.
But can proud Rome's Panthèon tell
If for the soul of Raffaelle
His glorious obsequies could quell
    The JUDGMENT-SEAT'S severity?

Yet why should Christ's believer fear,
While gazing on your image dear?—
Image adored, maugre the sneer
    Of miscreant blasphemer.
Are not those arms for me outspread?
What mean those thorns upon thy head?
And shall I, wreathed with laurels, tread
    Far from thy paths, Redeemer?

## ON THE DEATH OF FATHER PROUT.

### BY DENIS FLORENCE M'CARTHY

IN deep dejection, but with affection,
  I often think of those pleasant times,
In the days of Frazer, ere I touched a razor,
  How I read and revelled in thy racy rhymes;
When in wine and wassail we to thee were vassal,
Of Watergrass Hill, O renowned "F. P."—
    May "The Bells of Shandon"
    Toll blithe and bland on
The pleasant waters of thy memory

Full many a ditty, both wise and witty,
  In this social city have I heard since then—
(With this glass before me, how the dreams come o'er me,
  Of those attic suppers, and those vanished men!)
But no song hath woken, whether sung or spoken,
Or hath left a token of such joy in me,
    As '' The Bells of Shandon
    That sound so grand on
The pleasant waters of the River Lee."

The songs melodious, which—a new Harmodius—
  Young Ireland wreathed round its rebel sword,
With their deep vibrations and aspirations,
  Fling a glorious madness o'er the festive board;
But to me seems sweeter the melodious metre
  Of the simple lyric that we owe to thee—
    Of '' The Bells of Shandon
    That sound so grand on
The pleasant waters of the River Lee."

There's a grave that rises on thy sward, Devises,
  Where Moore lies sleeping from his land afar;
And a white stone flashes o'er Goldsmith's ashes
  In the quiet cloister of Temple Bar;
So, where'er thou sleepest, with a love that's deepest
Shall thy land remember thy sweet song and thee,
    While the '' Bells of Shandon
    Shall sound so grand on
The pleasant waters of the River Lee."

www.ingramcontent.com/pod-product-compliance
Lightning Source LLC
Chambersburg PA
CBHW022027110726
47901CB00006B/1673